"Don't you know how dangerous it is to tempt a man this way?" Alex demanded. "Don't you care that I could have ruined you right here, right now?"

Jenna pressed shaking fingertips to her bruised lips, feeling as if a steely band were wrapping itself about her heart. She thought Alex had liked her kissing him. She had believed that in some small way she had touched him with her love. "Is it necessary that you insult me this way?"

"Apparently, since I cannot make you see reason."

Her lips parted, her eyes rounded. All the signs of her dismay were there for Alex to see, and he felt his stomach grip in near-painful remorse.

Heaving a sigh, he searched the treetops, tamping down his frustration. "Jenna, I don't wish to hurt you this way, but you must cease with these foolish notions you have of us."

"It isn't foolishness, Alex."

He held up a hand before she could continue. "I know, you think you love me."

"No, I *know* I love you. And there is nothing foolish about that." Tears of genuine distress threatened, but she refused to let them fall. She refused to give into the hurt, or to let Alex's skepticism sway her.

Without a backward glance at him, she headed for home, more determined than ever that he would come to the realization that a love did exist between them.

He would see, she vowed, that the magic of Christmas was real.

—from IF YOU BELIEVE, by Elizabeth Ann Michaels

WATCH FOR THESE ZEBRA REGENCIES

DECK THE HALLS

Penelope Neri
Colleen Faulkner
Virginia Brown
Holly Harte
Joyce Adams
Elizabeth Ann Michaels

Zebra Books
Kensington Publishing Corp.

http://www.zebrabooks.com

ZEBRA BOOKS are published by

Kensington Publishing Corp.
850 Third Avenue
New York, NY 10022

First Printing: December, 1996
10 9 8 7 6 5 4 3 2 1

Printed in the United States of America

CONTENTS

A Gift from Above

Joyce Adams

One

How fading are the joys we dote upon!
Like apparitions seen and gone.
But those which soonest take their flight
Are the most exquisite and strong—
Like angels' visits, short and bright;
Mortality's too weak to bear them long.
—John Norris
The Parting (1678)

The gentle peace of heaven was broken by the boom of St. Peter's voice.

"Mark! It's time."

A hush resettled immediately, while all within hearing distance waited in anticipation. A novice angel's first assignment was always met with awe, and even more so when it came at Christmas time.

Mark Evans swallowed down the sudden rush of nervousness that swept over him. He straightened his shoulders; they still felt much too light without the magnificent wings the full-fledged angels wore as badges of honor.

After three years it was finally time. Time for him to be trusted to fulfill one special assignment to earn those wings.

"Here I am, sir," Mark answered, standing straight and tall before the imposing figure of St. Peter.

The sainted man smiled at him, then inclined his head

downward and spread out his hands. The clouds parted and a single scene became crystal clear below them. Snow sparkled in the moonlight like diamonds, and a familiar house appeared.

The small white farmhouse set amid the trees was exactly as Mark remembered it. Inside, it was welcome and warm, with bright splashes of color scattered about. A hand-stitched quilt hung over the back of a chair, while print curtains brightened the frosted windows.

A memory of the small house filled with love and laughter brought a smile. He noted the festive warmth cocooning the house and recognized his wife's work. Some things never change—not in three years—not ever. Green garland and bows and the traditional strings of threaded popcorn decorated the home for the Christmas season. Fragrant greenery and red berries hung over the fireplace mantel, embracing the season's spirit of love.

St. Peter cleared his throat, and the scene shifted to a bedroom. Mark's breath caught in his chest as the figure of a little girl kneeling at a window materialized. She peered out the frosted glass, gazing up at heaven, and for an instant he was certain she could see him.

Blonde curling hair brushed her shoulders, and he knew from memory that her eyes were the color of a summer-blue sky. She was beautiful. All innocence and earnestness rolled together in five-year-old wonder. He smiled in pride as he watched his daughter fold her hands in prayer.

It seemed that all of heaven held its breath waiting, watching the little girl below.

December 1868
Virginia

Christy Evans closed her eyes and pressed her hands more tightly together.

"Thank you, God, for the snow today." She paused, thinking about what to say next. Mama told her to always start her prayers by first being thankful.

"Oh, and thank you for Mama's pie at supper," she added for good measure, wrinkling her nose at the memory of the serving of vegetables she'd had to eat to get her piece of pie.

Sighing, she thought harder. Were two thank-yous enough for what she had to ask? She sure hoped so.

"Please, God," Christy whispered fervently, "bring a daddy for my mama so she doesn't cry this Christmas?"

Unfolding her hands, she opened her eyes and looked out the window glass. Perhaps if she watched her prayer soar to God in heaven, he'd see it and answer faster.

One snowflake slowly fluttered to the ground, illuminated by the shimmering moonlight. High above, the last of the storm clouds drifted away, and a single star shone brightly from the heavens.

Christy pressed her nose against the windowpane, her little hands rubbing away at the condensation. She stared in awe at the bright, twinkling star, and her mouth pursed into a wide ooh.

God *had* sent her an answer.

"Wishes on Christmas stars come true," she whispered her mama's earlier promise with all the reverence a five-year-old could muster.

Throwing a glance back over her shoulder to the half-closed door separating her room from that of her mother, she stepped away from the window and crept on tiptoes across the gleaming wood floor to the side of her bed. At the edge she paused, one hand on the feather mattress. She rubbed her hand back and forth across the quilt, thinking.

The lure of the twinkling star was too much to resist. She knew she wasn't supposed to be up, but she had to do this. Christmas was coming next week, and she had to get Mama the one thing that would make her not cry late at night anymore. She knew God was waiting for her to make her Christmas wish on *that* star.

The moonlit landscape outside drew her back to the window, and she pressed her nose against the pane. Her breath made tiny rings of moisture on the frosted glass, and she squinted hard to keep her eyes on the one special star.

She twirled a strand of hair around her finger, thinking hard on what she should do and what she *had* to do. She was torn between the scolding she knew Mama would give her and the promise of the bright star out the window. Then, in a flash, she decided.

Whirling about, Christy grabbed up the pretty pink robe her mother had made for her. Pausing only as long as it took to slip her arms into the sleeves, she raced on slipper-clad feet out of her bedroom and to the front door.

It took three tries before she could pull open the heavy front door, but at last she succeeded and stepped out into the crisp, cold night.

She wasted no time in running through the newly fallen snow to stand beside the indention of the snow angel she'd made with Mama's help that afternoon. The impression lay in the snow almost exactly as it had earlier today.

Christy stared at the indention in the snow for a full minute, then tilted her head way back and focused her gaze on the distant star with all the attentiveness she could muster.

"I wish," she paused and closed her eyes tight.

Everyone knew wishes had to be made with one's eyes shut.

"I wish," she took a deep breath, squeezed her eyes shut tighter, and blurted, "for a daddy to stop Mama from crying."

Keeping her eyes closed, she waited a full minute, giving the wish time to come true, then slowly peeked out through half-opened eyes.

Before her stood a man dressed all in white, like the snow. The air around him seemed to glow with a special light. She looked up at him in wonder.

"Ooh!"

He looked just like the picture of an angel she'd seen in a book. Here was her very own Christmas angel to answer her prayer.

"Ooh," Christy breathed the word out again.

She stared up at the glorious figure and asked in a hush voice, "Are *you* my new daddy?"

The irony of the situation struck Mark as he met his daughter's pleading eyes. He wanted to answer "yes" so badly that it hurt. But he could never tell this precious little girl who he was.

His throat tightened, and he reminded himself that there were no tears in heaven. A little voice whispered that he wasn't in heaven anymore. He'd been sent here for one reason. His assignment was to find a new daddy for his precious daughter . . . and a new husband for his beloved wife, Bethany.

This time Mark's throat closed so tight that he didn't think he'd be able to utter a single sound. As if by a miracle, he heard St. Peter's reassuring voice deep in his heart.

"I have faith in you. And, more importantly, He does, too."

St. Peter's words filled Mark's heart, clearing away the sudden rush of pain that had almost overtaken his resolve.

"No, sweetheart," Mark answered, "I'm the one who is going to find you a new daddy."

"Ooh," Christy breathed out the single word, her eyes round as blue saucers.

Nibbling on her lower lip, she continued to gaze up at the angel.

"Are you really, really an angel?" she asked him in awe.

"Yes." *Or he would be a full-fledged angel once he found a man for Bethany.*

Two

For he shall give his angels charge over thee: to keep thee in all thy ways.

Prayer Book 1662

A snowball whizzed over Bethany's shoulder, scarcely missing her cheek. She whirled around and yelped in pretended surprise. Her daughter's happy peal of laughter was her reward.

"I'm going to get you," Bethany called out over the laughter.

Christy scampered away through the powdery snow as fast as her plump little legs could take her. Bethany ran after her in exaggerated slowness, giving her plenty of time to escape.

A surge of love welled up inside her as she watched her daughter's antics. Christy, with her shoulder-length blonde hair, small-boned features, and bow-shaped mouth, was a miniature of her own features, except for the startling blue eyes, which were pure Mark.

A twinge of pain accompanied the thought, and Bethany hastily tucked it to the back of her mind, where it belonged. This moment belonged to Christy. Christmas week had always been their special time, and she wasn't about to allow anything to interfere with that.

She'd always loved Christmas—believed it was a special time of year. It seemed that no matter what happened, Christmas remained magical—a time when miracles truly could happen.

Ignoring the work still to be done, Bethany gave herself up to the sheer enjoyment of playing with her daughter. The chores, the new greenery needing to be strung, the baking could all wait. After all, it was Christmas time.

No matter what remained to be done, she always strove to give her daughter an extra game of snowball, read her an additional bedtime story, kiss her two more times at this time of year.

The precious season of Christmas was hard for both of them. It never failed to bring painful memories, along with the joy. The memory of the loss of Mark a scarce two days before Christmas still remained as clear and painful as that day three long years ago when she'd first learned of his death.

Shaking off the sadness, Bethany chased after Christy with renewed vigor. She had almost caught up with her when the little girl stopped dead still in front of their snow angel from yesterday.

"Got you," Bethany called out, her breath turning into wisps of frost in the increasing cold.

She scooped her daughter up in her arms and planted a kiss on her soft, pink cheek. Christy giggled and covered her face with mittened hands.

"Tickles, Mama."

As Bethany sat Christy back on her feet, she noticed the small set of footprints leading away from the snow angel to the front door. Her stomach tightened. The footprints weren't fresh—they were hours old. Snow had blown across the tiny prints, almost obscuring them. But not quite hiding the evidence of a forbidden excursion by five-year-old feet.

A chill of fear far colder than the winter day about them skittered its way down Bethany's back. It settled firmly in the pit of her stomach with a hard knot of dread. Her daughter knew she was never to leave the house alone after dark. And here lay proof that she'd done just that.

Bethany gulped down the rising anger spurred on by sheer fear. Anything could have happened to her daughter out here alone at night. The house was situated on a patch of land several miles from town—far enough to offer the privacy Mark had wanted, but also a haven for numerous four-legged animals roaming at night. She drew in deep breaths in an attempt to calm the fright that threatened to set her limbs to trembling.

When she thought she could finally force the question past her numbed lips, she touched her daughter's shoulder.

"Christy," she paused and moistened her lips, "what were you doing outside last night?"

Christy turned about quickly and tilted her head back to look into her mother's face. Surprise widened her blue eyes.

"Did God tell you? I thought it was a secret." Disappointment edged her small voice.

Bethany blinked at the unexpected answer.

"No, those told me." She pointed to the tiny footprints in the snow.

"Ooh." The little girl nibbled on her lower lip, guilt written across her features.

"Christy, why were you outside last night? You know better—"

"But I had to go. I had to make my wish." Christy's face puckered with fierce determination.

"What wish?"

"It's a secret."

"Christy . . ." Bethany ordered her to answer.

The little girl batted her eyes several times in an attempt to get her way, then gave in to the authority in Bethany's voice.

"I made my wish on the Christmas star." She pointed up to the sky. "Now you don't have to cry anymore, Mama. God sent an angel to find me a daddy."

Bethany felt her own mouth fall open in shock. An angel? To find a daddy? She forced her mouth closed as a rush of cold air brushed her tongue.

"And he promised." A wide smile of joy lit Christy's face. "I'll have a daddy for Christmas."

How on earth was she supposed to answer that one? Bethany wondered.

"Honey, I think maybe you dreamed about the snow angel we made and—"

"Did not." Christy planted her pink-mittened fists on her hips in insulted pride. "He was real. He was dressed all in white. And he knew my name, and—"

"Christy—"

"It's true, Mama. I saw an angel and he told me he's getting me a new daddy."

What in heaven's name did she answer to that?

Bethany watched her daughter bend down and begin repacking the snow around their snow angel. Worry gnawed at her. How was she to explain the truth to Christy without ruining her Christmas?

How ever was she to explain that there wouldn't be a new daddy as a Christmas present?

Loving Mark and losing him had cost too much, taken too much from her. She wasn't ready to chance loving again, even if a new daddy for her daughter were on the horizon. If she lost again, she didn't know if she could recover. Once had devastated her. The risk was too high.

Besides, one couldn't simply wish up a man out of the air.

From several feet away Mark watched Bethany and Christy with a surge of protectiveness and pride. An answering smile tugged at his lips as he listened to his daughter's words. However, Bethany's disbelief and pragmatism tore at his heart. It hurt that she didn't believe in him.

Was this the same joyous young girl who he'd practically grown up with, his best friend? She had changed. He ached to reach out to her and touch her cheek, but he knew it wasn't possible. He was no longer of their world.

However, he could do one thing to help her. He could complete his assignment in the time granted to him before

Christmas. Find her a new husband to share her burdens, her joys, her life.

Mark turned away from the beautiful picture of Bethany and Christy standing together. He needed to find a man for Bethany.

Half an hour later Mark found his candidate. A lone traveler, dressed in Union blue, riding a black horse on the snow-packed road drew his attention.

Mark studied the man intently. A small saber scar on his cheekbone bespoke bravery. Dark curling hair dipped low over a wide forehead, while dark eyes seemed to gleam with intelligence and a square jaw showed definite promise of fairness blended with determination.

He struggled to see into the man's mind, to see what lay beyond the handsome exterior. Unexpectedly, pain jolted him. The uniformed officer had suffered a wound that cut far deeper than the scar on his high cheekbone. Loss, grief, and guilt filled the soldier, blocking out any joy of the season.

Yes, this was the man to fill the void in his Bethany's heart. He had exactly what Bethany needed—a wounded heart to heal and thereby heal her own heart.

Mark observed the man for any sign of bitterness, or of a hatred too deep to mend, but found neither. Only pain and a need for lasting love filled the man's heart. Mark smiled as the officer shrugged his shoulders under the cold. He possessed broad shoulders—plenty wide to carry a little girl to play or a woman's burdens.

Yes, he'd found his man. Now to put his plan into action. Mark offered up a prayer for guidance, and suddenly all around him the wind began to blow, gently at first, then picking up in intensity, bringing a miracle along with it.

Captain Luke Falconer swore that the air was becoming colder by the minute. Turning up the collar of his coat against the now biting wind, he urged his mount onward. The last thing he needed was to be further delayed by a snowstorm. He'd been traveling for the better part of the day to join his friends for the holiday season. He was tired, cold, and quite possibly lost.

Snowflakes that had been falling gently for the last half hour now beat down with increasing speed and fury. They stung his face and the strips of wrist exposed above his gloves. The late afternoon sun no longer glinted off the snowbanks rimming the road. The sun had disappeared in the sudden cloud of swirling white.

A strange feeling of expectancy permeated the air, giving the sensation of lightning striking close at hand. But that was ridiculous, he chided himself. He laid the blame for his foolish flight of fancy to his persistent scratchy throat and the clammy sweat that trickled down his neck.

An icy blast of wind tugged at his coat, and he resisted the urge to pull open the buttons and expose his chest to the cool air. A chill would most assuredly not rid him of the fever that was settling in his body. He needed to reach his friends' home soon.

The wind picked up and began to howl about him, turning the snow into a cloud of white that engulfed him. It virtually shut out the world around him. Everything seemed an unusual combination of gray and white.

Strange; he'd never known a storm to come on so sudden. The sun-filled sky had given no warning of an impending blizzard. If this kept up, he would have to take shelter and postpone his arrival at the James's home. He glanced around the landscape for anything familiar. Whiteness began to cover everything in sight with alarming speed. Uneasiness tickled its way down his spine.

Something was wrong.

A blast of cold air drove him forward, but now he could scarcely make out the roadway ahead in the swirl of unending white. It was as if he'd been plunged into the midst of a roaring blizzard in a matter of moments.

Ahead in the distance he thought he could make out the figure of a man standing in the middle of the road. The man's clothing was as white as the air around him, and there was an almost luminescent glow to him.

Luke blinked his eyes several times to clear his vision and his mind. It was as if he was viewing the world through a heavy fog. The man waved his arms and pointed to the left.

Luke kneed his horse, urging him forward. He had to get to the man—a traveler on foot would perish in this blizzard. However, when he reached the place where the man had been standing there was nothing but snow-covered roadway awaiting him.

Glancing to either side, Luke scanned the path for the other traveler. The storm lessened for a moment or two, giving him a clear view of the road. It forked to the left, and there he spotted the man several feet down the road. The stranger gestured again.

Luke stared in amazement. It was almost as if the man was attempting to lead him somewhere. Curiosity ate at his caution.

The storm gathered strength about him, buffeting his mount in the sharp gusts of wind. Luke reined his horse to the left and rode toward the stranger standing in the middle of the road.

Several minutes passed as Luke's mount plodded through the storm. Ahead of him, the stranger waved, then disappeared into the snowy white. Luke searched for him, disoriented by the blizzard whirling around him. He'd never in all his days encountered a storm like this one. It was the strangest thing, almost as odd as the stranger who suddenly appeared again several feet ahead of him.

Luke called out to the man, but he didn't answer. Instead the man motioned him onward. Snow pelted Luke's face, and he hunkered down into the meager protection of his woolen coat.

Wind swirled around him, whipping the snow into piles in

the road. Luke squinted against the cold. Ahead of him, the roadway was empty. The stranger had disappeared once again.

Surely he hadn't imagined the man? But there was no one in sight.

A chill as cold as the air he breathed coursed through him. He questioned whether what he'd been seeing had been brought on by snow blindness or simple fatigue. During the war many men had beheld visions born of weariness. But he hadn't been one of those men. All of his ghosts lived on in the depths of his soul.

In the next instant his horse stumbled over a snow-covered log, almost going down. Caught off guard, Luke was thrown sideways. He hit the hard-packed ground with a resounding thud, his booted foot wedged in the stirrup. Burning pain wrenched his ankle moments before an even sharper pain seared his head. He cried out; then blessed blackness engulfed him.

Bethany crossed the room to glance out the window for the fifth time in as many minutes. She held back the dainty printed curtain. Outside, whiteness coated the glass pane.

A strange compulsion urged her to the doorway. Unable to resist the impulse, she pulled the door open a crack to peer out. A blast of cold air rushed in, bringing with it a flurry of snow. And the shrill whinny of a frightened horse.

She froze at the unexpected sound. Whatever would someone be doing out in a blizzard like this one? Only a fool . . .

"Mama?" Christy called across the room. "What's wrong?"

"I'm not sure, honey," Bethany answered with honesty. *But something was definitely wrong.*

She cocked her head, listening. Another whinny jolted her into action. Reaching for her cloak, she swung it over her emerald green gown and wrapped a scarf around her neck.

She paused a second to glance toward the far side of the room, where Christy sat playing with her doll.

If someone was outside in this storm, there was no time to waste. The person could freeze to death before the storm cleared.

Calling to Christy to stay inside, Bethany plunged through the door and into the world of white and howling wind. She struggled against the snowdrifts that were already piling up in the yard.

It took her several minutes to reach the edge of the road, and her breath came in short gasps with the exertion. As the figure of a horse came into view through the rapidly falling snow, Bethany's heart lurched for her toes.

"Mark?" she called out, then shook herself mentally.

It couldn't be him. She blinked her eyes to clear away the apparition that had returned insistently every Christmas since she'd received word of her husband's death.

While her mind accepted the finality of her loss, her heart staunchly refused to do so. Especially at Christmas. Every year she dreamed that Mark rode into the yard, alive and well, in time to celebrate Christmas with them. Every year, that failed to happen.

The wind swirled the snow about her, blocking out everything in her path. Tears burned behind her dry eyes, but she only allowed herself to cry in the lonely dark of night, long after Christy had fallen asleep. Mark was dead, she reminded herself harshly. Long dead, and she had a daughter to raise. And ghosts to chase away from her own mind.

Blinking against the stinging wind, she started to turn back to the house when the apparition reappeared. She stared in amazement as the riderless horse drew to a stop. Then she caught sight of the man being dragged behind it.

This was no apparition.

Bethany grabbed the bulk of her cloak and skirts in her hands and ran through the growing snowdrifts toward the fallen man. As she reached his side, a sudden gust of wind swept away the snow on his chest, revealing the dark blue of the jacket covering his wide shoulders.

Yankee blue. The thought filled her mind to overflowing as the past three years fell away before her. Swallowing any trace of bitterness, she reminded herself that the war was long over, and people everywhere were struggling to heal the wounds.

The man laying at her feet under the fluffy blanket of falling snow was in need of help. Her help. And she'd yet to refuse anyone in need in all her life.

Bethany caught the horse's reins and pulled the man's foot free. He didn't make a sound at her actions. She bent down and brushed the snow away from his face. His eyes were closed, and his face was pale from the cold. Harsh features met her gaze. The red slash of the scar on his cheekbone stood out prominently in the stark white of his chilled face. She drew back instinctively. Then the stranger opened his eyes.

His soft, dark gaze met hers. Gentleness and pain reached out to her. It was a sensation Bethany had never experienced in her life.

"Hullo," he murmured in a low voice that did strange things to her breathing.

She couldn't help smiling at the absurd greeting, considering their position. Only a man very sure of himself could react that way while lost and injured in a snowstorm.

He returned her smile, and all the dark memories in her heart melted away temporarily. She had a strange sense of belonging. Of being claimed. Whether she wanted to be or not.

His eyelids fluttered closed, shutting out the view she'd had to his soul. More flakes fell over them. The snow was coming down heavily now, covering the ground about them in a thick blanket of deadly white. She had to get him into the shelter of her house.

Half-dragging, half-carrying his heavy bulk, Bethany made

her laborious way back toward the house. The hem of her skirts and cloak grew crusted with frozen snow. Pausing to rest for a moment, and to draw new strength, she wiggled her numbing fingers.

Heavens, the man was heavy. And tall.

And not about to die on her if she could help it.

She dug her hands under his shoulders again and dragged him the rest of the way to the house. Seconds before she reached the door it swung inward, as if by welcome magic.

"Mama?" Christy poked her head past the open door. "Is that my angel?" Worry hovered over her question, bringing tears to her eyes.

"No, dear," she panted, drawing in several deep breaths. "He's no angel. Just a lost traveler."

Heaving with all her strength, she dragged him through the doorway and into the warmth of the room.

"Ooh." Christy gave a long sigh of relief.

"Now run and pull back the covers to my bed, please, darling."

Christy scampered off to do her mother's bidding. At the door she stopped and bowed her head, then said in a voice that carried across the room, "Now I'll have my new daddy. Thank you, mister angel."

With this done, she turned and ran out of the room.

Bethany cringed at the words. She had to sit her daughter down for a long talk. And soon.

First, there was the stranger to tend to. She pulled him across the room, and after three tries managed to get him up onto her bed.

He practically filled her mattress. She brushed his damp hair back from his forehead, resisting the unexpected impulse to trail her fingers down along his cheek to his jaw. Instead, she reached for the buttons to his coat.

She had to get him out of his wet clothes and warmed. Heaven only knew what wounds he'd sustained or how long he'd been out in the storm.

The man opened his eyes again, and Bethany's breath caught in her throat and held there. She'd never seen such pain in another person's eyes as she beheld in this man's dark depths. It reached out and enveloped her for the space of a heartbeat.

He needs you.

The thought came so strong and so sudden that she glanced around to see if someone else had spoken the words. The room was empty except for herself and the injured man.

The lure of his insistent dark gaze pulled her back in time to see again the familiar flash of pain in his eyes, and Bethany knew this time with certainty that his pain had nothing to do with his ankle. This pain came from within—from the heart.

The strange words arose again in her mind.

He needs you.

Three

But men must know, that in this theatre of man's life it is reserved only for God and angels to be lookers on.

Francis Bacon

Bethany shoved the disturbing thought aside. Of course the man needed her. He needed her to tend to his injuries.

Nothing else.

What foolishness was coming over her?

She knew nothing about the man. Not his name, not his business, not even whether he was married with a family of his own. As soon as he was well and able, he would leave their lives as suddenly as he'd arrived.

A twinge of dismay rushed over her, and Bethany drew up her wandering mind sharply. Whatever was she thinking?

Hastily she busied herself removing his outer coat, while attempting to disturb him as little as possible. She needn't have worried; he slept like the dead. The thought concerned her and she leaned closer, checking his breathing. It was even and deep, albeit a mite congested.

The fact spurred her on. She shook out his coat and draped it over a wooden rocker. Within seconds she'd removed his black boots, sitting them beside the rocker.

"Mama?" Christy asked, tugging on her snow-dampened skirt. "What's wrong with him?"

"He was thrown from his horse." She turned to her daughter. "Can you watch over him while I see to his horse?"

The poor beast couldn't be left saddled in this weather. Bethany felt a pang of sympathy for the animal.

"I'll take good care of him, Mama," Christy announced with importance, nodding her little head.

A smile tugged at Bethany's lips and she brushed a kiss across her daughter's cheek.

"You do that, darling. I'll be right back."

Pulling a patchwork quilt over the stranger, she hurried across the room. She hated to venture back out into the storm, but the man's horse needed tending. Wrapping her scarf more tightly about her neck and chin, she pulled open the door and stepped out into the world of swirling white.

The snow seemed to have abated somewhat, but the drifts were piling high about the buildings. No one would be venturing out on the road for several days. It looked like the stranger would be staying with them.

Bethany pondered the implications of this fact while she found the man's horse, led it to the barn, and removed the saddle. She completed her task as quickly as possible, murmuring reassuring words to the horse, then made her way back to the house.

As soon as Bethany stepped through the doorway, she was greeted by the welcome warmth of the fire and the special smells of Christmas—fresh garlands, newly baked cookies, and a sense of love.

Holding to those pleasant thoughts, she discarded her damp cloak and scarf and hurried through the room to her bedroom.

"Hi, Mama," Christy whispered with a finger to her lips. "He's asleep."

Worry etched Bethany's brow at the words. How severe were his injuries?

"Darling, why don't you go get ready for bed while I tend to our guest—"

"But I want to help."

"I know you do. Why don't you put on your nightgown and pick out a story—"

"Can you read it to him, too?"

Bethany opened and shut her mouth on an instant denial. What would it hurt to read to the man? And it would make her daughter happy, while allowing her to believe she was "helping."

"Sure, darling. Now go choose your story while I tend to him."

By "tend" Bethany meant undress him, but she wasn't about to do that in front of an inquisitive five-year-old. Fact was, she didn't want to do it at all, but someone had to get the man out of his damp clothing.

Christy stepped closer to peer at the man asleep in the bed. "Are you sleeping in my bed with me tonight, Mama?" she asked.

"No, darling."

Christy's eyes widened. "Are you sleeping with him?" She pointed to the bed.

Bethany bit back a tickle of laughter. "No, I'm sleeping right here in the chair. So I can watch over him."

"Ooh." Christy returned her attention to the sleeping stranger. "Will he be afraid when he wakes up all alone in the bed?"

A mental picture of herself curled up close with the stranger on her soft feather mattress suddenly swept over Bethany, and she could have sworn that her heart skipped a beat.

She smiled at her daughter's concern. "No, darling. I don't think he'll be afraid."

But she might be if these peculiar feelings didn't go away. And soon.

"I'll pick him out a nice, happy story," Christy announced, "all about Christmas." She skipped from the room, leaving Bethany to her task of undressing the stranger.

She hadn't undressed a man since . . . She cut off the memory of her husband. This was different, she told herself as she drew back the quilt and set to her task.

First, she ran her hands over his limbs, checking for broken bones. Thankfully she found none. Her fingers fairly skimmed over the buttons of his wool uniform jacket, freeing the gold buttons. Using care, she eased the material down over his shoulders.

Heavens, they were broad, she noticed with a gulp.

Schooling her sudden surge of emotion, she bent to her task. He was too heavy to slide the jacket from under him, so she caught his shoulders with both hands and eased him up from the bed. Leaning him forward against her shoulder, she reached around behind him to tug on his damp jacket.

He sighed deeply, and Bethany froze. His breath warmed her neck with a pleasant tickle. The next instant he snuggled his head against her shoulder, then rested his cheek against her breasts. Heat pooled in her chest and spread downward, startling her even more than his unconscious act.

Oh, dear; she gulped again.

Throwing caution to the wind, she yanked his jacket free and pushed him back onto the bed. Amazingly, he slept on. Concerned, she bent down and ran her fingers through his thick hair. She found exactly what she'd expected—a lump the size of a small snowball was forming at the back of his head. That explained his sound sleep. He had likely suffered a concussion.

The warmth of his forehead worried her more, and she made a mental note to gather cool water for bathing his forehead and bring down his fever. Most assuredly he'd suffered a chill as well.

Satisfied with her examination, she resumed her task of freeing him from his wet, cold clothing. She tossed his jacket to the floor and soon added a pair of socks to the pile.

All went fine until her fingers slid to the fastenings of his trousers. Bethany could feel her cheeks heating in an unfamiliar blush. Gulping, she unfastened the pants and eased them down his legs. Legs, she noted, that were long and firmly muscled. Her fingertips heated of their own accord as they slid along his calves to his ankles.

Hastily she dropped his trousers atop the pile of clothes on the wood floor. She absolutely refused to proceed any further. If the man's drawers were damp, they'd simply have to dry while on his body.

Her cheeks heated again and she knew without looking that they were flushed and pink. The rest of her body felt the same strange way. While undressing the stranger might have been purely for medicinal purposes, the act of undressing such a firmly muscled man stirred up some long-forgotten feelings in Bethany. She fanned herself with the palm of her hand.

Morning couldn't come soon enough for her peace of mind.

A smile tipped Mark's lips as he watched her tend to Luke's injuries. He could sense the attraction between the two from clear across the room.

Dear Bethany. She had no idea that the handsome stranger she'd rescued was fated to rescue her from a loveless life. It'd take heavenly intervention to show her that loving was worth any risk.

Assured of success, Mark could almost feel the pleasant weight of his new wings on his shoulders.

The night passed with agonizing slowness for Bethany. Christy had done as she'd promised and picked out a pleasant story. Bethany sat with her curled up in her lap, reading softly, until her daughter fell asleep, then carried her to her room.

After tucking her in Bethany changed into her own lace-trimmed nightgown of soft white muslin and returned to the man asleep in her own bed. It was a most unusual feeling to see him there. As she watched, he became restless, tossing and turning in spite of the cool compresses she'd applied to his forehead. Rewetting the cloth in the bowl at her feet, she wrung it out and placed it back on his brow.

Bethany sank down into the rocker and drew a quilt close about her shoulders. She'd only rest for a moment. Her eyelids grew heavier and heavier, then closed in spite of her efforts.

"Jenny!" a man cried out into the stillness, jolting Bethany to her feet.

Across from her, the stranger struggled to sit up, but she quickly pushed him back onto the bed, using all her weight to do so. His dark eyes met hers, and she felt a further jolt. He strained against her, his fevered gaze searching her face.

"Got to get to Jenny," he choked out the words.

Pain darkened his eyes, and Bethany's heart went out to him. The thought that this Jenny was a lucky woman shot through her mind.

With a ragged sigh of exhaustion, he suddenly relaxed. His eyelids fluttered closed and he drifted back to sleep.

Bethany stared at him in the dim lamplight. His fevered mutterings reminded her that he probably belonged to someone else. The thought disturbed her far more than she'd admit.

The sooner he was gone the better, she decided abruptly, settling back into the rocking chair.

In the wee hours of the morning, shortly before dawn colored the sky, Bethany drifted off to sleep again. Unknown to her, an angel watched over her and the stranger in her bed.

Two hours later, as sunlight reflected off the white snow outside, Christy tiptoed into her mama's bedroom. She crossed to the bed quietly so as not to awaken her mama, asleep in the chair. She eyed the man in the bed. Cocking her head to one side, she studied him intently.

He looked nice enough. She leaned forward, searching his features. That scar didn't make him look mean in the least. He'd make a good daddy, she decided at last. Maybe the angel had sent him. She drew closer to the bed to look for any special sign about the stranger she might have missed earlier.

Luke Falconer awoke to the sensation of being watched. He turned his head and met the intent blue-eyed gaze of a little girl. She leaned forward at the side of the bed, her chin resting on her palms. She couldn't be more than four or five, he thought. Who on earth was she?

He blinked, squinting his eyes against the sunlight streaming in a curtained window.

Where the hell was he?

He remembered the cold and the sudden storm. Frowning, he searched his mind and recalled his fall from his horse. Someone must have rescued him. The stranger on the road? He brushed the possibility aside; that image had surely been brought on by snow blindness or fever.

A vague memory of a beautiful woman bending over him taunted him. The child reminded him of her. She had the same soft, flowing blonde hair, but the woman's eyes had been different.

He knew without a doubt that these weren't the eyes he remembered from his confusing, restless night. Those eyes had been a startling shade of green.

He smiled at the child.

"Hullo," he spoke softly, not wanting to frighten her.

The little girl jumped back, bumping against the chair and sending the rocker careening back and forth.

"Mama, he's awake," she shouted loud enough to wake the dead.

Luke cringed as the sound echoed and re-echoed in his aching head. It throbbed with pain in time to the thump-thump-thump of the rocking chair on the wooden floor.

As he gingerly rubbed the back of his head, a beautiful woman stood up from the depths of the rocker, and he knew instant recognition. As he gazed at her, the ache at the back of his head receded to a bearable level, then disappeared almost entirely.

She was a vision of shimmering blonde hair, trailing to below her shoulders. It flowed loose about her face in soft curls that made a man wish he could bury his face in them. Her eyes were the color of a precious emerald, and right now they were slumberous. And sexy.

Those were the eyes he remembered from his nighttime hours. Cat's eyes, he thought, but not the usual comparison to a spitting cat. Hers brought to mind a soft, warm, purring tabby curled up in the sun. Just then she stretched like a sensuous cat and delicately stifled a yawn behind her hand. Whoever she was, she was definitely a beauty.

But what on earth was she doing here? With him?

He noted that she clutched a quilt with her left hand, drawing it over a virginal white nightgown, and that her hand was devoid of a wedding band. Without giving a thought as to the reason why, he smiled.

"Morning." He spoke in a low voice, testing his head's reaction to speech. He was pleasantly surprised that it hurt far less than he'd anticipated.

"How are you feeling?" Bethany asked. She ran a hand through her tousled hair, mussing it more in the process, and making it even more appealing. The quilt slipped off one shoulder.

"A little worse for wear, I'm afraid." He forced out the response past a throat that had gone unreasonably dry. Swallowing, he forced his gaze away from the temptation standing before him.

He glanced about the bedroom, taking quick note that the room's soft colors and feminine touches marked it as a woman's room. But who on earth was she? And exactly what was he doing here?

He voiced his queries with military precision. "Where am I? What happened?"

"You fell from your horse." She paused, and he watched as worry knitted her forehead.

That part he remembered only too well. It was what happened afterward that was a blur. He remained silent, waiting for her to fill in the gaps.

"What do you remember?" Her voice quivered. "Do you know who you are?"

"Of course I know who I am," he answered with affronted dignity. "Do you think I'm dim-witted?"

"No, I thought you'd lost your memory from the blow to your head," she shouted back.

As he visibly winced with pain, she became instantly contrite. "I'm sorry. I didn't mean to shout."

"And I should say that I'm thankful to you that I'm still alive. And no thanks to my horse."

"He's safe in my barn."

He sent her a wry smile. "Thanks, I think. How did I get here?" He gestured with a sweeping gesture to take in the feather mattress beneath him as well as the room.

"I found you in the storm."

"And the man with you?" he asked, wondering if that was the explanation to the mystery.

She blushed. "No. I'm a widow."

He closed his mouth on what he'd been about to say. Perhaps he'd be wise to remain silent about the man who had seemingly appeared and disappeared with the wind. No need to have her question his sanity. In the bright light of day it would sound too ridiculous to say that a man had appeared and led him here, then disappeared.

"It seems I owe you my life, ma'am." He paused, giving her the opportunity to supply him with her name.

"Bethany Evans," she answered. "And this is my daughter, Christy," she added.

Christy stepped closer and tugged at her skirt. "Mama?" she asked in a loud voice. "Who is he?"

A low chuckle stirred in his throat.

"Captain Luke Falconer, ladies," he answered in a deep voice.

The sound stroked Bethany's senses, and brought a pleasurable warmth she hadn't felt in a long time *And had no business feeling now,* she chided herself. Captain Luke Falconer would be out of their lives as soon as he was well enough to travel—long before Christmas.

"I'll fix some breakfast." She rushed to fill the uncomfortable silence that was forming between them and slipped out of the bedroom before he could stop her.

Following a mouthwatering breakfast, Luke slept away most of the afternoon while Bethany built a snowman with Christy, then baked fresh bread, to be served slathered with butter with a tempting stew and hot chocolate to warm them.

He awoke to soft giggles of pure happiness coming from the kitchen. Delicious smells wafted in from the room along with the laughter, making his stomach rumble with hunger and causing a strange yearning deep inside. He swung his legs over the side of the bed and sat up. A wave of dizziness swept over him.

It took him a full minute to clear his aching head enough so that he was able to grab his pants from the chair and pull them on over his legs. He didn't believe the beautiful Widow Bethany would appreciate him strolling about the house in his drawers.

Smiling at the thought of her reaction, he got to his feet. A twinge of pain reminded him of his injured ankle. He ignored it and took a step forward, heading in the direction of the kitchen.

Bethany walked into the bedroom just in time to break Luke's fall as his ankle gave out and he pitched forward toward the door. His sudden weight on her slim shoulders almost took them both to the floor before Luke staggered and shifted his weight to his uninjured leg.

Struggling to remain upright, Bethany slipped her arms about him, helping to right him. Once she was certain neither of them was going to land on the floor, she shifted one of his arms over her shoulders to help steady him. She could feel the strength and power of his tightly-coiled muscles pressed close against her body. It did strange things to her normally even breathing.

"What are you doing trying to walk so soon?" she accused.

"Something smelled too good to resist," he answered with a shrug of his broad shoulders. The action jostled Bethany, and he caught her as she stumbled forward. Her hair hung free, and several curls entwined themselves about his arm. He sucked in a breath and inhaled the tempting scent of lilacs.

Suddenly he took note of the rose-colored gown she wore and the way it reminded him of a rose blooming in a garden. It fit her shapely body about as well as the petals framed the flower, too. He struggled to breathe evenly as his mind focused on the curves snuggled so close against him.

"Well, my cooking isn't bad, but it usually doesn't bring men to their knees," she said with a smile.

His weight on her shoulders felt strangely comforting, and she tilted her head back to stare up at him. The expression she saw in his eyes held her spellbound. A sense of wonder mixed with desire reached out to almost stroke her. She gasped in surprise, then hastily attempted to recover her common sense, which had seemed to scatter as if blown by the wind.

"Ah, you must be hungry," she said in a rush, feeling foolish and as nervous as a schoolgirl at her first dance. She looked down at the floor and the toes of her rose-colored slippers.

"Definitely." Luke breathed the single word against her temple.

She had the disturbing feeling that he wasn't talking about her stew.

"Ah, the kitchen is this way," she pointed out, turning them toward the door. "There's hot stew and fresh bread. I was coming to tell you."

Luke let her chatter wash over him and concentrated on trying not to put too much of his weight on her slender shoulders while enjoying the feel of her body moving against his. He wasn't so sure he wanted to recover from his injuries any too soon.

* * *

The next afternoon, while Christy was taking her nap, it seemed only natural that Luke and Bethany would drift into low conversation. Cocooned together in the snowbound house, it was as if they were fated to share confidences in front of the crackling fire.

"What were you doing out in the snowstorm?" Bethany asked curiously. She shifted on the sofa to face Luke, who had his injured ankle propped up on her petit-point footstool.

"I was on my way to visit some friends for the holidays."

Bethany's heart tightened in her chest. "Won't they be worried?"

Luke shook his head and sent her an uneven smile. "No. I won't even be missed."

"But what about your family—"

"There's no one to worry about me," he cut her short. "Except you."

A shadow crossed her face at his response. How sad that he had no one to worry or fuss over him.

"Everyone should have someone to make a fuss over them at Christmas," she told him.

"Who fusses over you, Bethany?" he asked in a low, teasing voice, leaning closer.

She smiled at his tease. "With Christy around, I don't have time to even think about it."

"How long have you been widowed?" Luke asked in a gentle tone that belied his growing interest.

"Three years next week."

It seemed that the words tumbled out before she could stop them. Soon she was telling him about her quiet, peaceful life with Mark, and her loss. Luke was a good listener, and she felt drawn to him in a way she'd never felt with anyone before. Not even with Mark.

As she finished speaking, the silence lengthened between them. Unable to restrain her curiosity, Bethany asked the question that had been nagging her since the first night he had spent in her bed.

"Who's Jenny?" The words slipped out before she could stop them. As soon as she'd spoken she shut her eyes, wishing she could call back the impetuous question.

"I'm sorry." She glanced away at the tight look of his set features. Pain etched each line and angle. "It's just that you kept calling her name when you were ill."

She shut her eyes while she waited for his answer. Was he about to tell her that she was his wife? Her breath caught in her throat.

When he finally answered it was in a voice so low that she almost missed it. "She was my baby sister."

Luke's response caused her eyes to snap open. "Your sister?"

"She died in the war."

"I'm sorry."

He rubbed a hand across his forehead and winced. "It was." He stopped suddenly and a shuttered look came over his face. "It's a long story."

Bethany glanced pointedly toward the window, where snowflakes could be seen fluttering down. "I don't think we have a shortage of time. Perhaps if you talked about it, it would help," she offered. "Sometimes old pain is lessened when it's shared."

Luke raised his brows, then nodded. "She died while I was fighting for the Union."

She nodded, encouraging him to continue without any condemnation.

"I'm from North Carolina," he said, as if that explained everything.

"Then why—" This time she succeeded in stopping her next words before they slipped out, but it was too late to call back their implication.

The question of why he fought for the Union hung between them.

Luke sighed, a ragged breath of sound, and leaned his head back against the sofa. "I was at West Point when the war broke out."

Pain drew his features tight, and Bethany ached for him.

"It had been my father's dream that I graduate there. I foolishly refused to leave before that was accomplished. That meant I fought on the side of the Union."

Bethany nodded in understanding. He wouldn't be the first man she'd known who had been torn between two loyalties within themselves. She'd seen many friends fight that personal battle.

He rubbed a hand over his face and along his jaw, and his eyes clouded with guilt.

"My parents and Jenny died during that fighting. I wasn't there with them. My stubbornness cost them their lives."

"You can't believe that."

He looked at her in disbelief.

"If it was fated to be, then your being there would have changed nothing." She laid her hand on his forearm. "And you did fulfill your father's dream for him, didn't you?"

"Yes, but—"

"We all lost someone or something in that war. It's time to put it behind us. You have to stop blaming yourself for something over which you had no control."

The anguish deep in his dark eyes tore at her, and she forgot all about her own concerns, forgot all about what loving and losing had cost her. She only knew that she wanted to ease his pain.

Bethany only meant to comfort him as she drew her hand up his arm to his cheek. But the next thing she knew she was in his arms.

Their gazes met for a frozen second before Luke lowered his head to take her lips in a sweet kiss. It began as a tentative touching of two souls and blossomed as surely as a flower in spring. Warmth, caring, passion flowed between them. It shook Bethany down to her slipper-clad toes.

As the kiss ended, she drew back, her lips parted and her eyes open as wide as a child's. Slowly, she scooted back and got to her feet.

"I . . . I have to check on Christy." She left the room at a pace just short of a run.

Luke's deep chuckle followed her.

Bethany scolded herself all the way to her daughter's bedside. What had she been thinking? This was certain insanity, wasn't it?

She raised her fingertips to her lips and touched where only moments before Luke's warm lips had been. He wasn't staying, she told herself. He wasn't for her.

Four

Then cherish pity, lest you drive an angel from your door.

William Blake

From his post beside a birch tree, Mark observed the small house. For the first time in nearly three years he experienced worry and uneasiness. Christmas and the deadline for his assignment's completion were drawing nearer, and Luke Falconer was mending too fast. The captain now walked through the rooms with the aid of a stick instead of Bethany's arm.

The last two days had passed uneventfully. While there had been no setbacks, Mark hadn't seen much progress either. Bethany still held herself at a safe distance.

Mark frowned, deep in concentration. What more could he do?

Bethany watched her daughter and Luke with a smile. The two of them were bent over the kitchen table, close together, one blonde head and one dark. Intent on icing the oven-warm cookies, neither of them noticed her in the doorway.

It felt natural somehow for Luke to be seated at the table. A sense of rightness, of belonging, filled the small house. Bethany was caught up in the feeling and attributed it to the special season of Christmas.

She could hear Luke and Christy whispering together about

which cookies were the prettiest and reminded herself to cautiously tamp down the surge of joy that welled up in her. This was only temporary.

Christy's gay giggle tugged at her heart, and she dreaded the moment when this would all end. Soon Luke would leave them to return to his own life. A life that didn't include them.

After all, the handsome Captain Luke Falconer wasn't for them, was he?

As Bethany turned away to retrieve a cookie tin from the shelf, Luke shifted in his chair so that he could watch her graceful movements. Bethany intrigued him. No; *fascinated* was a better word.

In spite of her lonely life, she sought to share whatever joy she could with others. With him. He smiled at the thought.

He was doing that a lot more lately. It seemed that the longer he spent in the company of Bethany Evans, the more often he smiled.

Remembering the kiss they'd shared, his smile widened into a broad grin. Yes, the Widow Evans definitely fascinated him. He had no desire to leave her.

Perhaps you're in love with her.

The thought hit him with a jolt, and he snapped his head up to fire a glance around the room. He could have sworn he'd heard the words spoken aloud and in a man's voice, but the only ones in the room with him were Bethany and Christy.

Then the realization of what those words meant hit him hard, and he had trouble keeping his casual position seated at the table. In love? Him?

He couldn't believe it was possible, but he now knew he was very possibly falling in love with Bethany. He shifted his feet, and a twinge of pain cut across his ankle. The injury was healing nicely and he didn't really need the cane any longer, but he didn't think he'd let Bethany know how nicely it was mending—just yet.

Love was beginning to inch its way into his life to replace the pain that had held him in its power for so long. The welcome warmth of Bethany herself and the lure of belonging tugged at him, tempting him to deceive her into letting him stay a little longer.

Like maybe forever, a voice in the back of his mind suggested.

Luke felt a little hand tug on his shirtsleeve and looked over to find Christy studying him intently, a half-eaten cookie in her other hand. She leaned on her knees and propped her chin in one hand. Cookie crumbs sprinkled down onto her blue gingham dress.

"Luke?" she asked in a voice scarcely above a whisper, then took another bite of her cookie.

He ducked his head until it was level with hers. "What?" he murmured in an equally low voice.

"Do you like my mama?" she spoke around the mouthful of cookie.

"Yes," he answered, biting the inside of his cheek to keep from laughing aloud.

Christy cocked her head and asked, "A lot?"

Luke grinned over at her and nodded. "A lot."

A happy sigh left the little girl's lips and they turned up in a smile as she ate the last bite of her cookie. She began to happily hum a Christmas carol. A minute later she glanced over at Luke again and batted her lashes at him.

"My dolly likes cookies, too," she confided, eyeing the plate of treats placed out of her reach on the table near his elbow.

Seeing the opportunity for a few stolen moments with Bethany, Luke grabbed it. "Why don't you go tell your dolly all about our cookies," he suggested. "And I'll bring her one in a few minutes."

Giggling, Christy jumped down off the chair and ran from the room. Bethany watched her departure with confusion.

"What did you do that for?" She returned her gaze to Luke in time to see him push back his chair.

Grinning widely, he stepped toward her, leaving no doubt as to his intentions. "So that I can do this."

Bethany's heart raced in anticipation. She forced herself to speak calmly. "You do realize that she'll expect you to feed her doll a cookie?"

"It will be worth it." His low voice was as smooth as silk brushing across bare skin.

Bethany raised her chin in a show of defiance. "You're that sure of yourself?"

Luke chuckled and covered the distance between them in two strides.

He gave her a mere instant to protest before he swept her into his arms and lowered his mouth over hers. He hadn't needed the gentlemanly gesture—refusing him was the farthest thing from Bethany's mind.

While the first kiss between them had been tentative, exploratory, this one was pure possession. He pulled her close, molding her to the length of his body.

Luke's lips were warm against hers, like the touch of early spring, and heated rapidly to the full blaze of a July sun. Under the pleasurable heat of his kisses she forgot it was December.

A slight rasp of whisker teased her chin. She slipped her arms around him, and the strong muscles of his back rippled and flexed beneath her fingertips. Following an instinct too strong to resist, she clasped him tighter, surrendering herself to him.

"Dolly's ready for her cookie," Christy called from the next room. "I'll bring her in the kitchen."

Luke and Bethany both stiffened and reluctantly drew apart. She stepped out of his embrace, then took an extra step back to help resist the temptation he offered.

Moments later, Christy skipped into the kitchen, her dolly clutched tightly under her arm. Luke did as he'd said he would, willingly "feeding" a cookie to Christy's dolly. His efforts were met with gurgles of laughter.

Bethany slipped away to tidy her disheveled hair and to mull over what was happening to her. As she pulled the brush through her hair, she questioned the wisdom of her actions.

She wasn't prepared to enter into a brief liaison with any man, and she knew Luke wouldn't be staying. Any day now she expected him to say good-bye. What was she thinking of? she asked herself the too familiar question.

She was only opening herself up to the pain of losing again if she allowed herself to get any closer to him. She had to back away. Although she longed to dream that there was a chance for them, she knew better. One only needed common sense to see the foolishness of her dream.

Besides, there was Christy to consider. She refused to offer her daughter heartache and tears as her Christmas gift.

Bethany knew with certainty that she couldn't love and lose again—not so close to the anniversary of losing Mark. It would be more than she could bear and still present a happy face to her daughter on Christmas Day.

As the afternoon lingered, tension filled the house room by room. When Christy begged Bethany to go outside and play in the pretty snow, she wasn't sure which one of the three of them was the happiest to leave the house.

Once Christy was bundled in her pink coat and mittens, she dashed out the door. Kicking up mounds of snow, she proceeded to gather it into snowballs and throw one first at Bethany, then one at Luke. Laughter filled the air as Luke tossed a snowball high over Christy's head. She scampered through the snow after it, struggling in the high drifts.

Bethany's throat tightened at the picture they all made together. They likely as not looked to all the world like a happy, perfect little family. She swallowed down the shaft of pain that followed the thought and renewed her resolve to distance herself from Luke.

He didn't make it easy on her. He persisted in staying close by her side until she thought she'd scream from the pain of his being so close and yet so out of reach.

Frustrated, she balled up a clump of snow into a ball and threw it at him with all her might. It hit him full on the chin, splattering his face and neck with fluffy white snow.

A dangerous gleam in his eyes, Luke advanced on her. Bethany backed up several steps, then decided to follow her daughter's example when faced with possible retribution for her actions. She spun around and ran in the opposite direction.

The thud of footfalls sounded behind her, spurring her on. She sensed that the game had changed in a subtle way. Before she could think any more about it, Luke tackled her, sending her into a high drift of snow.

The snowbank cushioned her fall, but his body atop hers almost knocked the breath out of her. He braced his weight on his hands and leaned over her, his face mere inches from hers.

She saw him lowering his head and knew what was coming next. Something told her she couldn't have stopped him even if she'd wanted to do so. His lips brushed hers, and he tasted of snow and cold and heat all at the same time.

Once, twice—he kissed her thoroughly, completely, wonderfully.

Suddenly a small figure in pink launched herself into the game. Burrowing her head between their bodies, Christy kicked up snow and giggled.

"Cold, Mama."

Cold was the farthest thing from Bethany's mind at that instant. Her cheeks flamed as she pulled away from Luke. He rolled away, and she peeked up at him from beneath lowered lashes, full of embarrassment, and met the twinkle in his own gaze. A deep rumble of laughter followed.

He stood and shook off the snow covering his shoulders, then helped Bethany to her feet. Christy jumped up and down between them, hopping from one foot to the other.

"Cookies?" she pleaded.

Luke caught the little girl up into his arms and hugged her tight. "How's that, little one? Warmer?"

She clasped her arms around his neck and nodded vigorously. Then she peered up at him and batted her lashes, smiling. "Hot chocolate?" she asked. "Please."

Luke grinned at her practiced ploy. "Hot chocolate it is."

Catching Bethany's hand with one of his, he pulled her close to his side. He bent down and whispered in her ear, "We'll continue this later."

With Christy held in one arm and Bethany's hand in his, Luke led the way back to the house. A flutter of excitement took flight in Bethany's stomach. Today she was looking forward to Christy's nap.

Minutes later, minus her coat and mittens, Christy skipped into the kitchen, where Bethany was preparing the hot chocolate. She stopped in front of her mother and stared up at her.

Bethany glanced down and Christy wiggled her finger for her to bend down. When she did the little girl sidled closer.

"Mama, did the angel send us Luke?" she asked in a whisper.

"What?" Since Christy hadn't mentioned the angel since shortly after Luke's arrival, Bethany had assumed it had been forgotten.

"Mama, remember the angel told me I'd have a new daddy," she explained with exaggerated patience. Then she shocked Bethany with her next words. "Is Luke going to be my new daddy?"

Christy's question caught Bethany off guard, and she nearly choked on her own breath. The innocent question brought an avalanche of concerns and fears in its wake.

Luke had never mentioned love or even caring to her. They'd only known each other a few days. It was impossible to fall in love that fast, she chided herself. What they were feeling for each other was merely desire.

Whatever was she doing? The question sounded again like a litany. She was setting both herself and her young daughter up for heartbreak. She had to end this foolishness. Now. Before it was too late.

It was time Luke left and returned to his own life.

As soon as the cookies and hot chocolate were finished, Bethany tucked Christy into bed for her nap. She remembered how she had been looking forward to this time and felt the sudden sting of tears. Grabbing tightly to her earlier resolve, she walked out the door to face Luke.

He sat waiting for her on the sofa. Bethany forced herself to look away from the smile on his face and concentrate on the fire. Watching the flames lick away at the bark of a log, she thought that was how she felt, as if her heart was being chipped away at.

"Luke." She clenched her hands together and turned to face him.

"Christmas is drawing near and I'm sure you're eager to spend it with your friends," she paused, trying to get the words right.

"What are you talking about?" Luke surged to his feet.

"Maybe it's time you left for your friends' house," she blurted out the words.

"Bethany—"

"Luke, I, ah, I can't allow something to happen between us that we'd regret." She twisted her fingers in the blue ribbon tied at the waist of her gown.

"Can't or won't?"

"All right, I won't."

He shook his head. "Bethany, give it a chance between us."

"I can't."

"Bethany, you're making a mistake. You're throwing away our chance at happiness."

She forced herself to resist the lure in his voice. It was too soon. He couldn't be sure of his feelings for her. And she couldn't—wouldn't—take the risk.

"I love you." His softly spoken words fell like stones onto the wood flooring of the room, threatening to crack her composure.

Standing across from him, Bethany took an instinctive step back, shaking her head. "No, you don't. A few kisses—"

"Bethany, I'm in love with you."

"You can't have fallen in love this quickly. Mark and I knew each other for years before he proposed."

"Different people love in different ways." Luke's voice was sharp, with none of the silky smoothness she'd come to associate with it.

Once again she shook her head. "What you're talking about is only desire. Don't you see, you're confusing love with lust."

Anger sparked in his dark eyes. "I'm a grown man. I know the difference. The question is, do you?"

Bethany drew in her breath sharply, as if she'd been struck.

"I guess you don't. Think about it, Bethany. Think real hard." He turned and walked away from her to stand at the fireplace, with his back to her.

Silence stretched between them, lengthening and wrapping itself about the room. It shut off any further closeness between them.

When she didn't respond and didn't attempt to stop him he turned and strode to the bedroom door. He drew in a ragged breath. "I'll leave at daylight," he announced.

Crossing her arms across her chest to hold the sudden stab of pain at bay, Bethany refused to allow her reaction to his statement to show on the outside. She only nodded her acquiescence. After all, it was what she wanted, wasn't it?

Christy crept on tiptoes across the darkened living room to the front door. After several tries she pulled the door open and slipped outside into the cold night.

Once again she looked up at the sky. Tonight there weren't

any stars to wish upon. And she needed one—Luke was leaving. She'd heard her mama and him talking.

Her bottom lip quivering, she folded her hands and closed her eyes. "God, please send my angel back. I need his help real bad."

A sob tore at her throat and she rubbed her mittened hand across her nose. Holding her breath for a moment, she listened. Nothing.

With a sigh of despair she opened her eyes. And there stood her angel!

"You're back!"

"I'll always be here whenever you need me, sweetheart," Mark promised her.

"Everything's wrong," she blurted out, and her bottom lip quivered again.

"Do you want to tell me about it?" Mark lowered himself onto the snowy ground to be at her height.

Christy nodded vigorously. "You said you were going to find me a daddy. And then Luke came. But now he's leaving."

Mark reached out and wiped a tear away from her cheek. "Don't cry, sweetheart."

Christy's chin quivered along with her lower lip this time.

"Tomorrow's only Christmas Eve," he reminded her. *His last day.*

She bobbed her head up and down in agreement.

"There's still time for Christmas. Don't worry. I will get you a daddy," Mark vowed.

"You promise?"

"Yes."

She smiled through her tears. "Will it be Luke?"

Mark nodded in a solemn promise. "Yes, it will be."

Her smile brightened and she reached out and hugged him. "Thank you, mister angel."

Mark swallowed down the lump in his throat. He would keep his promise. No matter what.

"Hadn't you better go back to bed?" He stood tall above her.

"Will I see you again?" Christy tilted back her head to look up at him.

Mark bent down and winked at her. "Someday."

Sighing with relief, Christy waved good-bye to her angel and slipped back into the house. Everything was going to be all right.

Mark watched his daughter until the door shut behind her. He had a problem.

Things were not going according to plan.

He leaned his back against the broad tree trunk and folded his arms across his chest. Bethany was going to ruin everything if he didn't do something. With the slow pace things were proceeding, coupled with her sending Luke away, he would never get his wings.

Luke Falconer was planning on leaving tomorrow. Much too soon. He and Bethany needed more time together. Time to realize they were falling in love.

The possibility of failure gnawed at Mark with a strange foreboding.

The days were whizzing past. Christmas Day drew near. Too near. His deadline loomed before him like a specter. Only one day left to fulfill his assignment.

It was time to take desperate action.

Intent on keeping his promise to Christy, he forgot to pray for divine guidance.

Morning dawned bright and clear, with sunlight glinting off the white snow and reflecting from the icicles hanging from the tree branches. The crystalline beauty was a mockery of the darkness and emptiness Bethany felt deep within. It was a somber group that gathered to see Luke off. Christy sniffed back tears, and Bethany fought hard not to do the same.

"Mama?" Christy tugged on her skirt. "I don't want Luke to go."

Bethany forced herself to smile reassuringly at her daughter. "He has to join his friends."

Christy's bottom lip quivered. "Can we all go look at the snow angel together before he leaves?"

"I'm afraid the one we made is gone."

"Not that one. The new one."

A puzzled frown knit Bethany's forehead as the little girl pointed to a spot about ten feet away beside a birch tree. Glancing at Luke, she saw him nod in agreement and walk toward the tree. There was nothing for her to do but follow.

At the base of the tree was a perfectly formed impression of a life-size snow angel. Overhead an ominous crack sounded, and Bethany looked up. Icicles covered the branches of the stark tree.

"I think we'd better—"

Another crack followed, directly above Luke. As Bethany stepped forward to push Luke out of the way, the large branch crashed down.

Five

Stone walls do not a prison make
Nor iron bars a cage;
Minds innocent and quiet take
That for an hermitage;
If I have freedom in my love,
And in my soul am free;
Angels alone, that soar above,
Enjoy such liberty.

                                    Richard Lovelace

Bethany crumpled to the ground under the weight of the branch.

As Christy screamed, Luke rushed to Bethany's side. Fear coursed through his veins. Nothing could happen to her. He loved her.

Carefully, he lifted the branch away. Bethany lay quiet and still in the snow. Luke calmed the fear that threatened to incapacitate him. Brushing away the snow from her pale cheek, he bent over her.

Bethany's eyes opened and she stared up at him.

"What happened?" she murmured.

"You saved me."

Luke swept her up into his arms and carried her into the house. This time it was Bethany who was placed on the bed and covered with the quilt. A quick examination showed that she'd suffered nothing but a few bruises.

Luke sighed and his voice caught. "You could have been killed—"

"So could you," she answered in a soft voice.

"Let me stay. My darling, we need each other. Who else is going to take care of our bruises?"

He leaned closer.

"Bethany, I do love you. I love you too much to ever bring you pain. I can't promise not to ever die." He caught her hands in his. "Life gives no promises as to the time we have. What we have to do is make the most of what we are given."

Bethany blinked back the tears that threatened.

"Darling, take what we've been offered. Grab it with both hands." He squeezed her hands between both of his.

Bethany stared deep into his eyes, noticing for the first time the love shining forth. Her heart raced as if it were struggling to be closer to his.

If she gave into her feelings and admitted that she was in love, it would have the power to destroy her. She couldn't do it, could she? Then she realized that it was already too late. She was hopelessly, thoroughly, completely in love with Luke.

What he'd said about time giving no promises was true. Could she risk it?

How could she not risk it?

"Yes," she said in a whisper.

"Yes, you'll marry me?" he asked.

For the first time she heard insecurity in his voice, and the vulnerability tugged at her heart.

"Yes, I'll marry you," she answered.

Luke drew her into his arms and sealed the promise with a kiss. "Can I wish you a Merry Christmas a day early?"

Christmas Day

"Mark?" St. Peter inquired, his arms crossed. "Come look."

Mark joined him. A smile creased his face as St. Peter gestured to the Christmas Day scene below.

Once again the small farmhouse materialized. Fluffy white snow covered the ground, lending the scene an unearthly beauty. Bethany stood in the circle of Luke's arms, her head nestled against his chest. Together they watched as Christy patted the snow around Mark's snow angel.

"Christmas truly is a magical, wonderful time, isn't it?" Mark said.

St. Peter smoothed a feather on the angel's new wings. "That it is."

"Isn't he a pretty angel?" Christy leaned back and asked.

"Yes, darling, it is," Bethany answered from the warm haven of Luke's embrace.

"It looks like my Christmas angel."

Bethany frowned. "What angel are you talking about?" She hadn't given her daughter any toy angel for Christmas, and neither had Luke.

Christy stood and whirled around to face them. "Mama, remember, I told you about the angel who knew my name and was finding me a new daddy?" She proceeded to give a full description of the angel, ending with, "He sent us Luke."

Bethany gasped in disbelief, and her heart skipped a beat. Her daughter had described her dead husband, Mark, perfectly, even down to the dimple in his chin. But it couldn't be? Could it?

Luke hugged Bethany to him. "Yes, someone sent me to you, and I'm glad."

"Me, too," she answered in a soft voice.

"Merry Christmas, my darling," Luke breathed the words against Bethany's ear.

The tendrils of her hair tickled his nose and he inhaled her scent, assuring himself that this moment and this woman were real and not merely a dream.

Bethany tilted her head back and gazed with equal wonder into his eyes. "Merry Christmas."

A smile of pure happiness lit her face. Luke couldn't resist its lure. Lowering his head, he met her lips with a kiss of promise and treasured love.

Christy watched them for a moment, then closed her eyes and folded her hands. "Thank you, God. Thank you, mister angel." She sighed. That was two thank-yous, but she didn't have anything to ask for. She had everything she wanted.

She smiled and whispered, "And merry Christmas."

A Colorado Christmas

Virginia Brown

One

December 6, 1888

"This is stupid. I ought to sling you over my shoulder and take you home right now."

Jake Lassiter glared at Caitlin, his mouth set in a tight line. People milled about them on the train platform, but he didn't attempt to lower his voice. His temper was so obviously frayed that she took a cautious step back.

"Jake, we've already discussed this. . . ."

"Yeah, and I still haven't changed my mind."

Caitlin eyed him with wary trepidation. She nervously shoved her gloved hands into the fur muff dangling from her wrist. It was no warmer on the open platform than it was inside the drafty station house, and she'd just as soon deal with an angry husband outside as in.

It was an effort to keep her voice calm when she said, "I realize that. But neither have I changed my mind."

Jake's eyes narrowed slightly. Despite the frigid air, he was hatless. His long, dark hair curled over the turned-up collar of his heavy sheepskin coat; a brisk wind tumbled strands into his eyes. Caitlin suppressed the urge to reach out and brush them back.

Jake looked away from her. His black eyes focused on distant Colorado peaks wreathed in clouds. The silence between them was colder than an icy mountain stream. After a moment he wrenched his gaze back to her and said in a rough growl, "You should stay here and fight it out. Like we always do."

"That's just it." Caitlin swallowed the huge lump in her throat that threatened to choke her. "Every time we argue you win. Nothing is ever settled."

Jake's eyes narrowed even more. "If I always win, then it's settled now. You're staying here."

"No, not this time, Jake. You only win because you're louder. I'm tired of always being the one to give in." She drew in a deep breath of cold air to steady her nerves and wished she knew the right thing to say. But what could she say? That she loved him? Oh yes, but that would only end with Jake smiling his crooked little smile and cajoling her back into his arms. It would settle nothing. She needed time. Time to think, to rearrange her priorities and try and figure out exactly *what* was making her so unhappy in Colorado— and with Jake. She wished she knew.

Jake took a step closer, and she could feel the tension in him even from a foot away. She clutched her fur muff more tightly, as if it were a barrier between them, and he jerked to a halt only inches from her.

"Damn your red head, Kate—you don't need to do this."

"Yes, Jake. I do." When her eyes met his she felt a familiar jolt. Even after seven years of marriage and four children he still had the power to make her body tingle and her senses reel. There had always been that between them, since the first time they'd met. It was what had kept them together in the beginning, even against incredible odds. And now—now she wasn't certain that attraction was enough anymore. There were other things that mattered, unanswered questions that circled in her mind and destroyed her peace. She had to get away for a while to think things through.

"Mama, Mama," six-year-old Clay said insistently, running out from the station to tug at her skirts, "the train is comin'! I can hear the whistle!"

Caitlin's heart lurched. It was almost time. She knelt to

hold Clay close, her arms going around his sturdy little body as if he would somehow disappear if she didn't hold him tightly. "You should be inside the station with Mrs. Baker," she murmured to her squirming son.

Grunting his displeasure with this maternal display, Clay successfully wriggled loose and ran to his father. He clasped Jake's knees, his eyes shining up at him with that mixture of hero worship and love that always made Caitlin smile.

"Papa," little Clay implored, "won't you go with us to see Uncle Devon and Aunt Maggie? They'd be glad to see you."

Jake looked down and ruffled the boy's dark, shining hair. "Not this time, son. I need to stay here and tend to business." He caught Caitlin's eyes as she straightened and added softly, "But I'll be here when you come home again."

That last bit almost made her change her mind. To hide her confusion and pain, she turned blindly toward the children's nurse as she emerged from the station-house door. "I'll take the baby, Mrs. Baker. You tend the twins, and Clay can help."

Jake stood silently, his hands jammed into his coat pockets while Caitlin took the baby and fussed with the edges of his blanket. She avoided Jake's eyes as long as she could. Grief clogged her throat and filled her eyes, and she felt that overwhelming sense of despair that had pervaded her days since the baby's birth. She had to escape it, but she didn't know how.

The shriek of a train whistle cut into the air and she winced. The locomotive was inching its way up the steep incline to the station. The clack of iron wheels grew louder, accompanied by billowing steam that seemed to quickly blend with snow clouds hovering low. Soon—too soon—she would be on her way to Texas and her brother. It had been almost a year since she'd seen Devon and Maggie. Away from Jake, maybe she could sort out her confusion and recapture the peace and contentment she'd once known.

She buried her nose into the sweet-smelling spot between

the baby's neck and his blanket, squeezing him so tightly he protested with a faint "No!"

Caitlin smiled. Even at fourteen months, little Devon knew his own mind and wasn't shy about voicing his opinions. Like his namesake, she supposed. He even had the same pale blond hair and ice-blue eyes as Devon. What would Devon say when she arrived on his doorstep? Her brother knew she was coming for a visit, but she had not told him she planned to stay.

"Guess it's almost time," Jake said gruffly when the train ground to a halt in front of the station. Caitlin turned blindly toward the huge iron monster belching steam onto the wooden platform. Tears stung her eyes, and she hoped Jake wouldn't see them. This was difficult enough.

With a loud screech of iron wheels, the train shook the wooden platform and released another cloud of steam. Little Clay whooped with delight. He loved trains and was so excited about this journey to Texas. She wished she could feel the same anticipatory pleasure. It should be wonderful to see Devon and Maggie. So why did she feel as if she were leaving her heart behind?

Minutes passed in a blur of excited children and Jake's dark, steady stare, until Caitlin felt as if she would explode with anxiety. Then the conductor was calling the summons to board, and passengers pressed forward to mount the iron steps leading into the train. Caitlin did not board immediately; she stood silently while Jake bade the twins farewell and told them to be good. Melissa and Molly hugged their father tightly, all smiles and red-gold curls.

Straightening at last, Jake turned to look at Caitlin as he said, "If I don't see you, have a happy Christmas."

She felt a twinge of guilt. This would be the first Christmas in over seven years that she would spend without him.

"You, too," she managed to say, and turned blindly toward the train. In the next instant she felt Jake's hand on her arm and he was whirling her around. Jerking her to him, he tan-

gled one hand in the hair on the back of her neck to hold
her tight.

Before she could voice a protest his mouth came down on
hers, warm and hard and demanding. The pressure of his kiss
parted her lips and his tongue darted between them, searing
her despite the cold wind that blew around them. *Damn him.*
This was the Jake she knew best, this fiercely demanding
man who stole away her breath, and Caitlin felt her resolve
go as weak as the muscles in her legs. She sagged into his
embrace in a kind of helpless surrender.

Then he released her as abruptly as he'd grabbed her, and
she swayed slightly at the sudden loss of support. Their eyes
clashed, his dark and angry and imploring all at the same
time, and hers wet with frustrated tears.

"Good-bye, Jake," she managed to say in a husky whisper.
"I'll write. . . ."

Disbelief flashed briefly in his face; then he nodded.
"Yeah. You do that." He stepped back, hands jammed into
his pockets.

Caitlin turned and fumbled for the iron hand guide attached
to the side of the train. The conductor put a hand under her
elbow to assist her aboard, and she stepped up and into the
passenger car. She moved down the narrow aisle without glancing back. It would turn her to stone if she looked at Jake again,
and she didn't think her heart could bear it.

Yet when the train finally puffed away from the station
and down the glistening curve of tracks, she fought the urge
to run back. Her throat ached with suppressed tears. This was
much more difficult than she'd thought it would be. Somehow,
in the safety of her bedchamber, with Jake only a few feet
away, leaving had seemed much easier. But now he was growing more distant by the minute, and all she could think was
to wonder if she was doing the right thing.

"Mama," little Clay said insistently, "when will we get
there?"

Caitlin forced her attention to him with a sigh. Five minutes into the journey and he was already asking when they would arrive. This promised to be the longest train ride of her life.

High rock walls hewn into the mountainsides with dynamite and months of hard labor had gradually given way to more scenic views as the Colorado Central train puffed its way along the tracks. Miles and miles of glistening iron rails had been laid in the past few years. From the windows of the train, passengers could see icy mountain streams winding through rocks and trees. Even in winter men often stood in the icy streams with shallow pans, sluicing the frigid waters in hopes of finding gold. Icicles hung from tree limbs overhead, testimony to the cold on those high, steep trails pocked with mining holes.

Caitlin stared out the window. Her breath frosted the glass pane and it was chilly, but she didn't mind. The stove at the far end of the passenger car wasn't putting out much heat. The children were all bundled into blankets and asleep at last, so she had a few minutes of peace. The swaying motion of the train was soothing, with the wheels constantly clacking a rhythmic melody. Mrs. Baker had already succumbed to slumber.

After a moment of adjusting her position on the hard seat, Caitlin was able to get comfortable. She curled one hand under her chin and leaned her head against the window. Some of the terrain looked vaguely familiar. She'd ridden over so much of it years before with Devon when they had been part of the Lost Canyon Gang, but she'd forgotten all the little hideaways and trails they once used in their train hold-ups. Heavens, it seemed like another lifetime. Even another person's life . . .

Had that really been her? Swaggering down the aisle of a train in men's pants, wearing a gun belt and brandishing a pistol that she knew very well how to use? Oh, yes, it certainly had. Of course, she and Devon had only robbed silver trains belonging to G. K. Durant, who had stolen their parents' silver mine, but they had been infamous throughout Colorado nonetheless. What, Caitlin wondered with a faint sigh, would her daughters say to her one day when they discovered the truth about their mother's past activities? She hoped her explanation would suffice.

After all, if she hadn't been the infamous Colorado Kate, she would never have met her children's father. Jake Lassiter, as feared for his reputation as a fast gun-for-hire as he was a ruthless lawman—it had been Jake who had finally captured the notorious train robbers by first capturing Colorado Kate.

And she had married him a year later, after the devastating gun battle that had almost killed her brother, and did kill Devon's young wife. So much pain and sorrow before the peace and joy she'd found with Jake; and now here she was, leaving Jake behind when she wasn't even certain why.

Caitlin sighed, her breath forming a frost cloud on the blurred glass. Idly, she rubbed the edge of her palm over it. The clear glass provided an excellent view of the wintry slopes. Miles of snow-covered ground stretched monotonously beyond the tracks. Lost in contemplation of the Colorado hills and her own inner turmoil, Caitlin stared out the window and lost track of time.

A flicker of motion flashed at the edge of her vision, then disappeared. She frowned. The glimpse of color against the stark white slopes had seemed—unusual. She leaned forward. The train had begun to round a curve in the track. Ahead on the right lay a stretch of thick pine trees edging a flat plain. On the left rose a sheer rock wall. There was no other movement that she could see, only the tops of the pines shifting in the wind. A trail of smoke from the steam engine rose in thick gray-white clouds that blended into the sky.

After a moment she decided it had been her imagination and sat back. The swaying motion and rhythmic noise was soothing, and she closed her eyes. Suddenly she felt the jerk of the train.

Her eyes snapped open. Something was wrong. She sensed danger and jerked to an upright position.

"Mrs. Baker. *Mrs. Baker.*"

The tone of her voice, soft but urgent, penetrated the nurse's slumber, and she opened her eyes. "Yes, Mrs. Lassiter? Do the children need me?"

"No. Not yet." Caitlin felt suddenly foolish. There had been only that slight hesitation. Nothing else. Perhaps she was wrong. She met Mrs. Baker's curious gaze and smiled faintly. "I thought I heard something out of the ordinary. That's all. It must be nothing. Go back to sleep and—"

A shot rang out, followed by a bang as the back door to the car was opened. A rough voice rang out, "This is a hold-up. Nobody move!"

Caitlin felt a cold chill. The voice was familiar, as was the whole moment. How many times had she done this before? Only then she had been the one wearing a mask and firing a pistol. And she did not have frightened children to comfort.

Even as she was soothing Clay, who had awakened and was sitting up with wide eyes, Caitlin winced in remembered shame. She had done as these men were doing, swaggering down the narrow aisles of a train and demanding money. For the first time Caitlin knew what it was to experience a train robbery from the victim's point of view. It was not at all reassuring.

Two of the masked men came closer. One of them was thrusting a cloth bag into the faces of the passengers and demanding jewelry and money; the other kept a wary eye on the men in the car, his pistol cocked and ready.

Their actions were obviously well planned and swiftly executed. Before she could prepare herself the masked bandit with the cloth bag was in front of her.

"I'll take your jewels and your money, lady," he said gruffly. Caitlin looked up, holding Clay in the crook of her arm as if to shield him. The bandit impatiently jiggled the cloth bag. There was the faint *chink* of coins and jewels. "And gimme that pin at your neck."

"Hush, Clay," Caitlin murmured when her small son began to whimper. "It will be all right." She gave him a reassuring pat, then released him. Mrs. Baker was making odd, choking sounds but had leaned forward protectively over the other children on the seat next to her. With shaking fingers, Caitlin reached up to unclasp the gold cameo pin she wore at the neck of her dress. She fumbled clumsily, apprehension and a stuck clasp slowing her movements.

"I'll take them rings, too," the bandit snapped. "And hurry up." He gave the cloth bag another impatient shake.

Caitlin glared at him, and her voice was tart. "Keep your damn pants on, mister. Can't you see I'm trying?"

"Look, missy, ain't no need for you to go gettin' all uppity with me. You're damn lucky I ain't yanked 'em off you."

The stubborn clasp finally released, pricking her finger, and Caitlin jerked it free. "And you're damn lucky I don't have my pistol, mister, or you'd be whistling Dixie through a hole in your throat," she shot back at him.

The bandit first looked startled, then wary. "Hey. I know you. Look up here."

Caitlin froze. She still held out the cameo pin. The teasing familiarity she'd first felt became a sudden certainty. Slowly, she looked up, and then knew—"Charwell."

The bandanna over the lower half of his face fluttered as he laughed. "Yeah, it's me. Hell, Kate, what are you doin' on this train?"

"Traveling with my children, as any fool with half an eye could see," she snapped. "Here. Take the damn pin."

As she shoved the pin into the bag, Charwell asked, "Where's that fast-draw brother of yours?"

"Wouldn't you be surprised if I said he was right behind you?" Caitlin smiled at Charwell's nervous glance around.

"You always were scared of Devon, Charwell. And you were smart to be."

Charwell laughed and half-turned to his companion. "Zeke, you know who this is? Colorado Kate. Remember me tellin' you about her?"

The man he'd called Zeke came forward, peering at Caitlin over the top of his bandanna mask. "Yeah. So? Get her jewels and let's go. We're burnin' daylight."

For a moment Charwell stood there uncertainly. Then he laughed again. "Hey, I got me a great idea. This is just what we need."

Caitlin had time for only an instant's foreboding before Charwell reached out and grasped her by the wrist. "Get your coat, Kate. You're goin' with us."

"Have you lost your mind?" Zeke demanded. "We don't need no damn woman taggin' along. . . ."

"This ain't just *any* woman. This is Colorado Kate, and she's done more train jobs than all the rest of us put together. Besides, she recognized me. Now shut up and get the rest of the loot and we'll get outa here."

Neither Caitlin's nor the other bandit's protests swayed Charwell as he dragged her from her seat. In scant moments, with her children's screaming objections ringing in her ears, Caitlin Conrad Lassiter was off the train and astride a horse in hock-deep snow.

Breathlessly, she snarled at Charwell, "I'll kill you for this, if Devon doesn't get you first."

Charwell pulled down his bandanna and grinned at her. "I'd rather take my chances with you, Kate. Now come on. We've got some riding to do."

Two

Devon Conrad crumpled the telegram in one fist. He looked up and saw Maggie staring at him with wide eyes. He forced a smile but knew it was more of a grimace from her reaction.

"Devon—what is it?"

"Kate's been kidnapped."

Maggie stared at him blankly. "Kidnapped? From the ranch? But what—how—?"

Shaking his head, Devon muttered, "Not from the ranch. From the train." He sucked in a deep breath. "The nurse said that robbers boarded the train, and it seems that one of them knew Kate. She knew him, too. He took her with him because she recognized him."

"My God." Maggie stepped forward and put a hand on his arm. "Does Jake know who it is?"

"Yeah. Charwell. He rode with us for a while. Damn his yellow hide—I shoulda put a bullet in him a long time ago. Well, it's not too late now."

"Devon . . ." Maggie's voice trailed into silence, but he knew what she was thinking. It may have been a while since he'd handled his guns, but that was something a man never forgot. The edge might be a little off, but it wouldn't take long to regain it.

"I *have* to go, Maggie."

She nodded, but her wide gray eyes were filled with pain and apprehension. "I know. Caitlin must be frantic."

"Knowing Kate, she's probably more mad than scared. I'd hate to be in Charwell's boots if she gets half a chance to grab a pistol."

"From what I've heard," Maggie said with a faint smile, "so would I. Did Jake send for you?"

"Not exactly. He wants me to wire him the locations of possible hide-outs." His mouth twisted. "Jake and I never did get along real well. I guess he figures in this case we'd be at each other's throats before long."

"Oh." Maggie pushed a strand of dark hair from her eyes and looked down at her hands. "You two seem to get along all right when they come for a visit."

"That's because neither one of us is trying to do anything more than visit. If I know Jake Lassiter, he won't take kindly to any interference, no matter who it's from. He always has to run the show."

A faint smile curved Maggie's mouth. Devon saw it and knew the reason. He fought a wave of irritation. "Don't look at me like that, Maggie. Dammit, I know more than Jake when it comes to where they could be. I've got a good mind to just go on my own. If I mess with him, he'll be giving orders and acting like a lawman."

"Well, that's only natural. He is a lawman."

"Was a lawman," Devon corrected. "He's a rancher. Been a rancher for seven years. The only outlaws he's used to hunting now are stray cows."

"Devon, if you go to Colorado with this attitude, neither one of you will help Caitlin. Can't you join forces instead of behaving like two stubborn jackasses after the same bucket of feed?"

"Sure. As long as Lassiter does it my way."

Ignoring Maggie's exasperated comment that he was worse than a mule, Devon left the sitting room. He took the stairs two at a time, his mind already considering possible locations.

The Lost Canyon would be too easy. Charwell would figure they'd look there first. Jake had probably already scouted it out and come to that conclusion.

Damn. There were so many ravines and box canyons and hidden arroyos, they could be anywhere. Plus it was December; snow would hide their tracks. But, without summer foliage providing a natural screen, they might be easier to spot, too.

A grim smile curled his mouth as Devon opened the bottom drawer of his bureau and lifted out his pistols. Once a week he took them out to clean and oil them. It was a habit, even though now he concentrated more on business matters than survival.

But this—this was something that was ingrained in him, this business of hunting and being hunted. There was a certain exhilaration in strapping on his guns and knowing that life was reduced to the basics. Not that he would go back to what he'd been before. No, he'd hated being known as a fast-draw, a killer without conscience or remorse. As Cimarrón his days had been empty of all but the need to survive. And then he'd met Maggie.

Maggie, with the rain-gray eyes and dark shining hair; Maggie, with love and loyalty and courage all bound in the same fabric of sweetly scented skin and gentle curves. It had taken a long time to be able to trust in the reality of love that would not be quickly snatched away, and he still treasured each and every day with her and their two children.

For a moment he let himself remember how Jake must be feeling. It was hell to lose the woman you love and not be able to get her back. Yeah, he'd go to Colorado, and he'd get Kate back for Jake. Whether Lassiter knew it or not, his best ally was Devon Conrad.

"Devon?"

He looked up to see Maggie in the doorway. Her mouth was curved in a trembling smile, and he held back a sigh. She worried too much. Though he knew it didn't have anything to do with lack of faith in his ability to stay safe, still her constant concern could be trying.

"Are Josh and Annie still up?" he asked to deflect the questions he could see coming. She shook her head.

"No, the children are down for a nap. Mrs. Lamb is with them. What are you doing, Devon?"

"I'm getting my guns ready," he said, and could have cheerfully bitten his tongue when she grew pale. "Never know when I might need 'em—or might not," he added hastily. "Damn. Look, Maggie, you know I have to go."

She nodded. "Yes. I know. You will join Jake, won't you?"

He hesitated. No point in worrying her too much. "Yeah, I'll join up with him."

"When?"

"What do you mean?"

"Before or after you find Kate? Look, Devon," she said quickly when he muttered a curse, "I know you want to do this alone. I haven't forgotten how you hate riding with someone else. But this time it's best. Not only for you, but for Kate's sake. Do you see what I mean?"

He stood up. "Yeah, I see that you worry too blasted much. Come on, Maggie, I know how to take care of myself. And Kate, too, when it comes down to it."

She shut the bedroom door and turned to face him. "Promise me you won't try to find her alone."

Drawing in a deep breath, he said, "I can't promise that. I don't know what I'll find when I get to Colorado." As her eyes misted with unshed tears, he found himself saying, "But I do promise to be careful, and if it's best to ride with Jake, I will. All right?"

She sniffed. "I guess that's the best I'll get out of you."

"Right now, anyway." He went to her and drew her close, one hand pressing against the back of her head to hold her face against his chest. He could feel the damp warmth of her tears on his shirt and began to stroke her dark, soft hair.

"Maggie, love, I'd never do anything that might keep me from coming back to you."

"You'd never mean to. But you take chances. You don't think of how I'd feel if . . ."

"Don't." His embrace tightened. "Don't even think it. Aw, Maggie, you know I'll be careful."

"Do I?" She rubbed her face over his shirt. "I hope so."

Curling a finger under her chin, Devon lifted Maggie's face so that he could look into her eyes. "I'd never do anything to hurt you. I wouldn't take a chance on losing you."

She sighed softly and closed her eyes. Devon bent and kissed her, his lips lingering on hers until he felt her sag into him. He turned her slightly and edged her toward the bed. Still holding her against him, his hands began to roam over her soft curves. When she lifted her arms to put them around his neck he swung her off her feet and lowered her onto the wide bed.

"It's the middle of the day," she protested faintly, but he stopped the words with his mouth while he unbuttoned her day dress and began to peel it away.

He could feel her resistance in the taut press of her body, even when he removed their clothes and slid inside her. Kissing and stroking her, he murmured soft words, love words that could always soothe her most ruffled feelings. After a few minutes Maggie gave a languid sigh and surrendered herself to the moment, and Devon immersed himself in the heated sensuality that always existed for them.

Jake snarled a vicious curse, then caught himself when he saw little Clay staring at him from the doorway. He took a deep breath and neatly folded the telegram in his hand. "Son, go into the kitchen and ask Mrs. Baker to put on a fresh pot of coffee, will you?"

"Yes, sir." Clay turned, then stopped and looked back. His

gaze was solemn when he asked, "You'll find Mama, won't you?"

Swallowing hard, Jake nodded. "Sure I will. Run along now and see about that coffee."

When the door had closed behind Clay, Jake turned to meet Roger Hartman's amused gaze. The U.S. marshal who had been his co-worker and was now one of his best friends just stared back at him with a lifted brow. Jake scowled. "Don't say it, Roger."

"What? That you don't want to admit Devon might be able to help us out? Come on, Jake. It's not like you to refuse help, especially when it's so valuable."

Jake tossed the telegram to the top of his desk and shrugged. "I'm not refusing his help. I just haven't forgotten that Devon always wants to run the show. Kate's *my* wife."

"And his sister." Roger stood and moved to the stone fireplace that filled almost an entire wall of the study. "You may be right, though. I noticed that it was Conrad's wife who sent you the telegram, not him."

"Maggie has enough common sense to know Devon's not likely to appreciate my interference. Dammit, I just want Kate back."

Jake raked a hand through his hair. He was caught between the desperate desire to find Caitlin and the overwhelming urge to shake her until her pretty green eyes crossed. Damn her red head anyway. If she'd just stayed home where she belonged, instead of running off to Texas with some·hare-brained notion of "finding herself" . . .

He looked up to see Roger watching him. "I'll find her," he said flatly, and Hartman nodded.

"I know. I have no doubt that you will get her back. I just hope there are no . . . extenuating circumstances."

"What the hell is that supposed to mean?"

Roger's brow lifted slightly. "Now, Jake, you know as well as I do what a devil of a time we had getting Caitlin off the last time. Sheriff Morgan over in Colorado Springs remembers the Lost Canyon Gang a bit too well. Now he thinks she's joined her former gang. If she has, no jury will be inclined to clear her."

Amazed, Jake snarled, "What does Morgan think? That she left her kids alone on a train and decided that the exciting life of eating out of tin cans and riding in the snow was more attractive than raising her family? Come on, Roger, no one's going to buy that stupid story."

Frowning, Roger shrugged. "I wouldn't. But there are people who always want to believe the worst, and you know human nature. It would be preferable to some folks to think that she wouldn't mind leaving behind wealth and a husband to put on men's trousers and ride around shooting up payroll trains."

"Then those people are idiots." Jake tamped his rising frustration and took another deep breath. "Look, Roger, we had a fight before she left. I don't know what's the matter with her lately, but I do know that she wouldn't rejoin her old gang."

"Maybe you and I know that, but there are people in this area who remember the Lost Canyon Gang really well. They aren't as likely to give her the benefit of the doubt."

"Too damn bad," Jake growled. "I'll find her and put an end to all their doubts. Enough of this—I need to be doing instead of talking."

"Two days of hard riding in deep snow isn't enough for you?" Roger asked dryly, then added, when Jake glared at him, "When the men are dried out and rested we'll go out again. Too bad the last snow hid any tracks."

Jake walked to the window and looked out. The Colorado mountain peaks were deep with snow, and more snow clouds moved sluggishly across the sky. It would make it damn near impossible to follow any tracks left behind. He could only hope that Kate would use common sense and stall Charwell and his cohorts until he could get there. . . .

* * *

Furious, Caitlin glared at Charwell. "Do you really think you can hold me prisoner for long? You're crazy if you do. Not only Devon but Jake will be hot on our heels as soon as they find out I've been taken."

Charwell regarded her thoughtfully. Steam rose in a thin curl from the tin cup of strong coffee he held. It was cold in the cave, but not as cold as outside, where the wind howled and snow blew in high drifts. A fire provided light and warmth in the middle of the cave, and a large gray square at the mouth showed fading daylight.

"Things ain't been goin' so well since the old gang busted up," he said after a moment. "It was always you and Devon that had the good plans. There's been times lately that we damn near been caught for only a bit of loot, and one or two of our boys has been shot."

"That's the hazard of your occupation," Caitlin observed tartly. "Why do you think Devon and I wanted to quit?"

"Hell, don't try and kid me. I know why you two quit. All you ever wanted was Durant. Once he was dead you didn't care about the rest." Charwell took another sip of coffee and grimaced. "And after Lassiter got on our trail we did good to stay alive and out of jail. Hell, I had to hightail it to Mexico for a while to stay out of his way."

"Then what do you think he's going to do now that you've taken his wife?" she taunted. It was cold, even with a fire and her coat still on. Her feet had gotten wet on the ride, and her toes felt frozen inside her boots. She tried wiggling them, and was relieved that there was still feeling in them. Eyeing Charwell thoughtfully, Caitlin tried to sort through the tangle of emotions that battled for prominence. Anger was foremost, but apprehension was rising fast. Apparently, Charwell had some sort of idea that she was certain she wouldn't like.

Shrugging, Charwell crouched down in front of the fire to pour some more coffee. He glanced up and over at the others, who were sitting a short distance away, counting the loot they'd taken.

"If it was summer," he said after a moment, "I'd worry. But not even Jake Lassiter can track men in a blizzard."

"Don't be too certain of that. I've known him to find lost calves in snow so thick I couldn't see my hand in front of my face."

"And you're just his little lost calf now, ain't you?" Charwell said with obvious amusement. "Listen, Kate, I've got a proposition for you. Like I said, things ain't been going too good. Help us out a little and as soon as we get some money ahead, we'll turn you loose. Is that a deal?"

She stared at him. "You want me to ride with you? Are you loco? I'm a mother. I have four children. What would they think if their mother turned train robber?"

"What do they think about Colorado Kate? Damn, Kate, there's still stories around about those days. Wasn't so long ago, you know."

Because she'd had the same thought, Caitlin couldn't reply. It was true. One day her children would learn the truth about some of the things she'd done. But if she was honest, she'd admit that she wouldn't change the past. At the time she'd done what she had to do in order to survive. It looked like she'd have to do the same now.

"I'll think about it," she said carefully.

Charwell looked at her over the rim of his tin cup. "You'll have to do better than that."

Shifting position on the rock, she met his steady gaze. A sense of dismay filled her. This was going to be worse than she thought.

"I'll think about it," she repeated. "Give me some time. And some coffee. It's cold in here."

Charwell fumbled in a pack for another cup and filled it for her. "May be cold in here, but it's better than being out there in the snow with a bullet in you. You might want to think about that, too."

Caitlin looked up and met his eyes. His meaning was clear enough. She curled her fingers around the tin cup and held it tightly as she lifted it to her mouth. *Never let 'em see you scared,* Devon had told her often enough when they were leading the outlaw gang. She knew better than to let Charwell see any fear.

If she stalled long enough, maybe matters would sort out themselves. Jake or Devon could find her. Or she could possibly escape. But then, she'd heard the arguments between Charwell, Zeke, and the others, too. Most of the men were opposed to her presence, resenting the suggestion that she could offer anything in the way of help. If she stalled too long, she might find herself in grave danger.

The coffee was scalding hot as she sipped it, but she met Charwell's eyes steadily over the rim of the cup. He was studying her closely, trying to gauge how far he could go. Caitlin nodded slowly.

"What would be my cut if I agreed?" she asked, and saw Charwell relax slightly.

"We'd come to an agreement. You wouldn't be cheated."

"Get me some information and I'll consider it if the take's good enough. . . ."

Maggie stared thoughtfully across the wind-scoured Texas plain. Devon had been gone for two days. A blue norther had swept past in his absence, and she thought about him being warm enough in the Colorado mountains. Of course, he'd grown up there. He knew well enough how to stay warm. His years of hiding out in caves and even less shelter had made him self-sufficient. As it had done for Kate.

A faint frown puckered Maggie's brow. She reached into her dress pocket and pulled out the last letter she'd received from Kate, announcing her intention to arrive for an extended visit. There had been something there in the carefully couched words, sentence fragments that had caught her attention and made her look more deeply into the sentiments behind the scrawled lines.

". . . am looking forward to being there for a long visit . . . need this time away from Colorado . . . Jake will do fine without me. . . ."

Maggie's frown deepened. That last sentence bothered her the most. Kate had never been comfortable being away from Jake for any extended length of time. Why this sudden change? She had fully intended to ask her that question as soon as tactfully possible after her arrival. Now, of course, she wasn't coming. Worse, a telegram from Roger Hartman had broached the possibility that Kate's abduction had not been entirely accidental. That really worried her.

"Doctor Maggie," a voice behind her said gently, and she turned to see her elderly housekeeper standing in the doorway. She stuffed the letter back into her dress pocket and stepped inside.

Mrs. Lamb smiled. "I do hate to bother you, but you have another patient. I tried to see if she could come back tomorrow as it's so late, but I'm afraid she's quite frantic about her youngest child. . . ."

"Of course. I'll come immediately. Is she in my office, or do I need to go to her?"

"Oh, she's in your office. With the child. I suspect an earache. Of course, you're the doctor."

Smiling at Mrs. Lamb's tactful diagnosis, Maggie moved swiftly down the hallway to her office. As she gently probed the screaming infant's ear and confirmed Mrs. Lamb's observation, Maggie put the thought of Caitlin Lassiter to the back of her mind. As always, the patient came first.

It wasn't until she finished and the child had lapsed into an exhausted but more painless slumber in his mother's arms, did Maggie once again turn her attention back to her sister-in-law. Alone, she cleaned her instruments and office, considering what she could do to help. If Kate had actually been kidnapped, then Devon and Jake would be the best choices to find her. But—and this was a faint, niggling worry at the back of her mind—if Kate had *chosen* to send the children on alone to Texas, then perhaps there was something she could do. After all, she had liked her sister-in-law immediately, and they'd always been able to talk to one another.

Despite the distances between them, their frequent letters to one another kept them in close contact. And she had sensed a growing discontent in Kate's letters of the past year.

Alone in her bed that night, Maggie put a hand on Devon's pillow as if to caress him. She missed him terribly. She always did when he was gone, but this time was different. He'd been determined to find his sister, but there had been another aspect of his energized determination that bothered her. For a moment, when he'd strapped on his guns, she'd remembered the Devon she had first met. The man they'd called Cimarrón had been dangerous, wild, and wary. More than once he'd frightened her. Though she did not doubt that Devon had left that part of his life behind, she did not like the cold blue glitter in his eyes as he'd made his plans to go to Colorado. It was too much like the Devon of old.

And worse—it had brought to the surface something that had been bothering her for months. She'd sensed dissatisfaction in Devon, a restless yearning that was evident in his eyes even when he didn't seem to know it himself. More than once she'd almost said something to him about it but had been reluctant to bring it to his attention if he wasn't aware of it himself. Did she tempt fate by mentioning it, or say nothing and hope it was only her imagination? God knew, she had a vivid enough imagination at times, but she also knew when her husband was discontented.

Not with her; that much she knew. Devon wasn't a man to keep something like that silent for long. Was it because he was a businessman now, his days filled with daily reports and printed figures instead of riding wherever the wind and his restless nature took him? She often wondered whether he felt tied down. If so, his search for Kate would be the perfect opportunity for him to realize it. A small thump of panic made her heart beat faster.

And then she thought of something else. . . .

It came to her, as she tossed and turned in her wide, lonely bed, that if some lawmen thought Caitlin had become Colorado Kate again, they would certainly see Devon's return to Colorado as part of a grand plan. She sat up in bed with a jerk and stared into the darkness. Dear God, it could happen all over again, mistakes and misconceptions, shots in the night, and she was so far away in Texas. . . .

Never one to delay a decision for long, Maggie knew that when morning came she would be going to Colorado on the next train. The children would be well tended by Mrs. Lamb, and she would be free to find Devon and keep him from behaving too recklessly.

Three

An icy wind blew down the collar of Devon's coat, and he pulled it more tightly around his neck. Damn cold weather. He'd forgotten how cold it could get in the Colorado mountains. Yet he was more acclimated to the weather than his poor horse, and he reined Pardo beneath the shelter of a copse of trees.

"Doesn't snow like this in central Texas, does it, boy?" he muttered, giving the animal a comforting pat on the neck. Not farther south, anyway, where he and Maggie lived.

Lifting his head, Devon squinted into the distance. Despite the drifts of snow and icy wind, sunlight glittered brightly on the slopes and peaks. It made his eyes hurt at times. After leaving the train and unloading his horse in Golden he'd immediately set out on a torturous trail through Clear Creek. Toughcuss Creek, some called it.

The narrow band of water cut a path through sheer rock walls at times, some natural and some formed by dynamite to allow iron tracks to be laid for the Colorado Central. A lot of this was new since Devon had ridden this area on a regular basis. There was new construction everywhere.

After purchasing supplies he'd set out on his own to find Kate. Though he briefly considered contacting Lassiter, he'd decided to try it alone first. Maybe one man could succeed where several would be too easily seen or heard. And Charwell would be expecting a big search-and-rescue party, not a lone man.

It was nearing dusk, and the sun would set pretty quickly this time of year. Devon decided to make camp for the night and get an early start the next morning. It would give Pardo more time to grow accustomed to the heights and the cold. And him, too.

Oddly enough, though he'd grown up in Colorado and spent a great deal of his young life here, the years he'd been gone had changed his resistance to cold and altitude. Maggie had predicted his body would respond this way, and he had to admit she was right.

After finding a deep cleft in the rocks that kept out much of the wind and snow, Devon bedded down his horse and rolled out his blankets. He kept the fire small; light and smoke would be detected too easily.

For a long time he lay in the hush of night and stared at the faint glowing embers of his fire, thinking of Maggie and Kate. Both women had had a profound effect on his life, but for the life of him, he didn't know which one had made more of an impact. Maggie, probably, because she had eventually saved him from a life he hated. God, if he thought of those long-ago days, it was always with a shudder. He'd been as close to dying then as he'd ever been—maybe more so. Even after being shot up in the same gun battle that had killed his first wife, he'd not been as close to death as he'd been walking around acting the part of a tough gunslinger. It had taken Maggie to recognize that, and to love him enough to bring him back.

But even knowing that, he'd been fighting a strange restlessness the past months that had distanced him from Maggie. He loved her, God knew, but he'd begun to feel tied down. Always before, when he felt like moving on, he had. Now he was bound by responsibilities to a wife and two children, and it had begun to weigh heavily on him. There were times he'd wanted to mount his horse and ride off for a while, and not look back. He couldn't tell Maggie, but this opportunity to work off some of that restless energy had come at a perfect time. He'd jumped at the chance to ride out alone, using ingenuity and skill to get Kate back safely. The past years had been good—probably better than he deserved—but he'd grown too soft. Too complacent. He needed this.

Pardo snorted, ears pricking forward as he stared into the night. Devon tensed. He always trusted his horse's instincts when it came to noises in the night. A keen sense of hearing and smell could detect wild animals and enemies much better than his own ears or eyes.

Leaning forward slightly, Devon shifted so that the handle of his pistol was easily accessible. He wore his .45s in a double holster low on his hips, within easy reach. It had felt normal and comfortable when he'd strapped them on again, as if he'd never taken them off and put them away.

Now he palmed his left pistol carefully, easing it from the holster to hold it down at his side. Slowly thumbing back the hammer, he waited with half-closed eyes, as if asleep in front of his fire.

He didn't have to wait long.

There was a slight noise, then a blur of movement just beyond the shelf of rock that provided Devon's shelter. He reacted instinctively, drawing his pistol to fire a warning shot. The blast of noise reverberated around him in deafening echoes that almost drowned out a faint, rasping curse in the dark shadows. At almost the same instant as he fired, Devon had rolled from his supine position in front of the fire toward the back wall. It was tight and narrow and dark there, and he lay waiting and watching.

Snorting, Pardo gave a nervous whinny. His shod hooves clattered loudly on the rock floor. Devon focused on the snowy slopes outside his small shelter. Moonlight silvered the ground and would reveal an unwary intruder.

Then he heard another faint snarling oath, and recognized

the voice. Damn. There would be hell to pay if his bullet had hit the target accurately.

"Lassiter—that you?"

"Damn right it's me, you sidewinder. What the hell are you doing throwing lead at me?"

"If you don't want to get shot, announce yourself." Devon holstered his pistol and crawled out from the narrow spot where he'd been wedged. "You alone, Lassiter?"

"Yeah, but not for long. Roger will catch up in a while."

As Jake stepped into view, a large dark shadow against the paler contrast of moonlit snow, Devon eyed him warily. Even with the years of trust and family ties binding them in a guarded camaraderie, he'd never quite forgotten those first days when Lassiter had been a hired gun sent to bring in the leaders of the Lost Canyon Gang.

Apparently, Jake hadn't either.

"Damn quick-draw still, ain't you, Cimarrón?" he muttered, stepping into the light and fingering a new hole in his coat.

"More quick than accurate. You still move fast, I see." Devon motioned to his fire with the barrel of his pistol. "Have a seat."

Jake stared pointedly at the .45 in Devon's hand. "I'll feel a sight better when you've put your iron back in leather. Never have quite trusted a man holding a gun on me."

As he obliged, Devon said, "Guess there's no word on Kate."

"What makes you say that?"

"If there was, you wouldn't be wasting time here with me," Devon said dryly. "You'd have her and be headed home. Any news?"

Jake grunted. "None good. There was a hold-up on the Denver and Pacific line yesterday. A mine payroll, I might add. An article in the local paper said it was members of the old Lost Canyon Gang who were responsible."

Drawing in a deep breath, Devon sat down on a rock and

met Jake's narrowed gaze. "If you're thinkin' I had anything to do with it, I just got to Colorado this morning."

"Hell, I know you didn't have anything to do with it." He opened his coat, pulled out a folded page of newspaper, and held it out.

Devon took it, already knowing what he would read. He was right. A headline in large type proclaimed that the infamous Colorado Kate was said to be pursuing her former profession of train robbery. One of the masked bandits was noted to have long red hair and feminine curves beneath male clothing.

"A little one-sided, ain't it?" Devon muttered as he handed the newssheet back to Jake. "Says she enjoyed taking money from folks and stuffing it in a canvas tote bag. How the hell would anyone know whether she was enjoying it?"

"How the hell would anyone know it was her?" Jake countered. "They were all masked. No one saw their faces. Only her hair."

Devon didn't say the obvious. Despite his natural wariness around Jake Lassiter, he recognized his brother-in-law's concern and decided to change the subject.

"How'd you know where to find. me?"

Jake grinned, a flash of white in the dim light. "Followed you from the station in Golden. You're either getting old or careless."

Devon gave him a disgusted glance. "Damn. Both, probably. How'd you know where I'd get off the train?"

"Natural deduction. Charwell sure can't hole up in the Lost Canyon. I checked that. Golden is kinda in the middle of where the gang used to range. Good starting point."

"Hope that don't mean I'm beginning to think like a lawman," Devon observed sourly. "If you and Hartman are riding together, where is he?"

"Uh, I lost you a few times, and so we had to split up earlier. He must have heard that shot, though. Ought to be along anytime now."

Devon grinned. "If I lost both of you, I ain't doing as bad as you'd like to think."

"Maybe not. Hell—the truth is, it was blind luck that I spotted you at all. If I hadn't been checking out a likely place to bed down for the night, I might have missed you altogether."

"That would have been a shame." Devon eyed him for a moment, then said, "Look, Lassiter, I know Kate's your wife, but she's my sister. If you'll back off, I can find her without getting her killed."

For a moment Jake didn't say anything. Then he said softly, "Not a chance, Cimarrón."

"Don't call me that." Dislike flashed through Devon, and he glared at his brother-in-law. "You know I never did like that name."

"You earned it."

"That was a long time ago. Maybe then I was Cimarrón. I haven't been him in years."

"Then don't act like a two-bit gunny if you don't want me to call you that."

"What, wanting to go after my sister makes me a gunslinger?"

"She's my wife. What if it was Maggie in danger? What if it was *your* wife being held hostage and forced to participate in hold-ups that are likely to get her killed?"

Jake's dark eyes were furious, and there was an edge to his voice that warned Devon to take it easy or risk a fight. He drew in a deep breath to calm his own temper.

"Us fighting won't help her, I know that much," he said flatly. "But I will tell you this—if it was Maggie, I'd let the best-qualified man handle it."

"Oh, you would? I bet." Jake shook his head and unbuttoned his coat. He stuck his index finger through the charred hole shot into the sleeve of his coat and looked up at Devon. "I don't think so. You would feel just like me and you wouldn't want to take any risks with someone that important to you."

It was quiet for a moment, only the faint popping of the dry wood in the fire making any noise. Then Devon asked softly, "You don't think she's really let herself be talked into joining them, do you?"

Anger flashed through Jake's eyes and he said through clenched teeth, "Kate may be mad at me right now, but she's not crazy. She'd never join up with Charwell."

"What's she mad about?"

"Damned if I know. Some stupid woman thing, probably. I tried to get her to talk to me, but all she'd do is say that I don't understand her. Hell, she's right. One minute she's fine, and the next she's acting like she's eaten loco weed."

"What'd you do to make her mad?"

Jake glared at him. "Nothing. I told you, I don't know what's the matter with her."

For a moment Devon didn't say anything. Then he gave a slight shrug. It wasn't his business. Hell, there were times he didn't understand Maggie, either. He'd say something wrong—or not say something at all—and then she'd accuse him of not listening or caring about her feelings. It was a woman thing, as Jake had said. Apparently, not even being brought up around a bunch of men, as Kate had, could make women immune to female quirks that drove a man crazy.

"She'll get over it," was all he could think of to say.

Jake nodded, then rose and said he needed to get his horse bedded down. "I'll fire a shot to let Roger know where we are."

"Great. Then we can expect to see Charwell and his men dropping in for a visit before morning. Haven't you got enough sense to wait until daylight to find Hartman?"

"Are you trying to tell me how to track outlaws? I was doing this before you were dry behind the ears."

"Yeah, and look how long it took you to find the gang when I was their leader, mister lawman."

"But I did manage to track you down—"

"Only because you tricked my sister into leading you to us—"

"That's a damn lie."

Jake took a step back into the rocky shelter, and Devon met his furious gaze with matching anger. If Roger Hartman had not chosen that particular time to arrive, tempers would have led to a blazing fight.

But Roger stepped in and observed with characteristic mildness, "Ah, I see you two gentlemen are discussing old times. How pleasant. And how loud. Good thing I was within three miles, or I wouldn't have found you until morning."

Both men turned to look at Roger, but it was Devon who said rather sheepishly, "Guess we both lost our tempers."

Jake met his gaze and slowly lowered the fists he'd brought up. "Yeah, guess we did. Glad you're here, Roger."

"So am I." Roger Hartman's eyes moved toward the fire, and he gave a pleased sigh as he stepped closer to it. "I hate cold weather. One day I think I'll go to southern California. I hear it's always warm there." He looked around at them. "Now, if you two will settle down and take care of business, it's time we figured out how to get Kate back. . . ."

Maggie shifted to a more comfortable position on the hard seat of the train. Thank heavens the stove was well stoked, or she'd be frozen by now. Even with the small iron stove at the front of the rail car, it was still chilly inside. Especially by the windows that looked out over miles and miles of snow-covered slopes and high mountain peaks.

But by nightfall she should be departing the train. She'd sent ahead a telegram informing Jake of her imminent arrival. Someone from the ranch would be at the station to pick her up, and with any luck at all she could soon join Devon. It was silly, but she couldn't escape a feeling of dread, of possible danger.

Devon wouldn't be careful, she knew. He'd think she was being foolish or overprotective if she told him to be cautious. Why must men always think they were immortal? Maybe because of the many gunshot and accident victims she'd treated in her career as a physician—and even before, when she'd lived on a ranch—she knew that a great many of their injuries were caused by recklessness and arrogance. Men just never thought they would be hurt. They either didn't realize or ignored the dangers. And Devon was one of the most reckless, arrogant men she'd ever met when it came to danger. It was a good thing she would be with him shortly.

Stretching out her legs, Maggie leaned back and observed the other passengers in the half-empty car. Most of them were men in suits with watch fobs, obviously businessmen. A few women were seated close to the iron stove with their children. It was crowded close to the heat, and so Maggie had chosen a more distant seat for privacy. After boarding this train in Golden for the last leg of her journey she was finally beginning to feel fatigued. The ride had been long and arduous, filled with either crowded cars and the smell of wet wool or screaming children who made her head ache.

Still, it was better than riding in the baggage cars, as she'd noted some passengers were forced to do. At least here she had a reasonable amount of peace and comfort. It occurred to her as she gazed idly at the empty seats to wonder why those in the baggage cars were not allowed to ride up front when the train wasn't crowded with passengers able to pay more. It would seem to be a humanitarian act, and she decided to ask Devon about the policy on the Texas and Pacific lines, which he dealt with on a regular basis.

Maggie settled back into her seat and turned to look out the window at the passing scenery. They had just crossed a high bridge over a deep ravine and she'd begun to breathe easier when she felt the train give a hard jerk. It happened again, and then there was a hissing and a screech as the brakes were applied.

Before she had time to wonder why the train was stopping the back door burst open and masked men swarmed into the car. One stood guard at the far end by the stove, watching his cohorts as they worked. Orders were barked to hand over valuables, and the men moved down the narrow aisles with swift efficiency.

Maggie watched in horrified shock. When one of the men reached her there was a short pause before the bag was thrust toward her. Maggie was shaking. She'd heard the bandits demand jewels as well.

Putting a protective hand over the bump beneath the glove on her left hand, she looked up at the robber holding out the bag and hoped he hadn't noticed. Devon had given her that ring after a series of shattering events, and it meant the world to her. She had neither asked for nor expected it, and it meant more to her for all of that.

When she met the robber's intent gaze her stomach did an odd little flip. Over the colorful edge of the bandanna covering the lower part of the robber's face, a pair of familiar green eyes met hers with an imploring intensity. A telltale curl of red-gold hair could be seen beneath the hat pulled low. *Caitlin*. Maggie's jaw drooped slightly with amazement. Was her own sister-in-law robbing her?

Then Kate said gruffly, "No funny stuff, lady. Put your money in here before I get mad."

There was such an intense light in her gaze that Maggie understood. Of course. Kate was being forced to do this. Maggie fumbled with the money clasp in her small velvet reticule, deliberately delaying as she stared down at her lap and said softly, "Are you all right?"

In a whisper came the words, "Devil's Den. Devon knows it."

Maggie didn't reply. She removed the folded currency from the money clasp and held it out, looking up as she did. "Take this and leave me alone," she said loudly. "And shame on you, sir, for robbing innocent women."

Kate's eyes crinkled softly, and Maggie knew she was smiling beneath the mask. Then she stepped back and moved to the next passenger. Maggie drew in a deep breath of relief. Apparently, the masked man at the end of the car, who had been watching them so closely, had not noticed anything unusual.

When Kate drew close to the guard he said something to her in a short, hard tone. She shot back a reply, and he grew furious. Maggie watched with growing anxiety as they quarreled in low tones; then the man was striding toward her and dragging Kate along with him. He jerked to a halt near Maggie, swinging Kate 'round by one arm.

"Hell, she's still wearin' all her jewelry. Are you blind or just stupid?"

Kate uttered a short, pithy comment that made the bandit's eyes narrow with fury. As Maggie watched helplessly, the man struck Kate across the face with the back of one hand. She staggered and almost fell, and he caught her cruelly by the back of her neck.

"Kate!" Maggie cried out, half rising, then halted in horror as she realized what she'd done.

The tall bandit immediately swung toward her, eyes piercing her with cold enmity. "Yeah, I thought there was something funny goin' on here. Come on, little lady. You can just step out here and do some explainin'. . . ."

"Let her go," Kate said in muffled tones. "She doesn't know anything."

"Yeah, I bet. I ain't willin' to take that chance, and I don't give a damn what Charwell has to say about it. Come *on.*"

Reaching down, he yanked Maggie up by her arm and, before she could form a protest, hustled her out the open back door and into the cold. She had the brief thought that now she couldn't tell Devon where the robbers were hiding out; then she was lifted onto the back of a horse and they were leaving the stalled train behind.

This was not good. No, not good at all.

Four

"They hit another mine payroll," Roger Hartman said with a dark frown. He moved to sit on the edge of the desk placed in one corner of the superintendent's office of the Colorado Central railroad. Then he looked from Devon to Jake and back. "Seems that this time the bandits were hidden in the baggage car waiting for the right time to hit. It was pretty carefully executed, but there was a hitch in their plans. . . ."

As Devon lifted a brow, Jake saw the faint spark in Roger's eyes and braced himself. He knew Roger well enough to realize that something bad was coming, but he still wasn't quite prepared for what came next.

"Looks like there was an unexpected passenger riding two cars back from the engine," Roger said slowly, his gaze still fixed on Devon. "One of the bandits recognized her, and reports say she was taken as hostage. From all indications the lady had boarded the train near Belton, Texas."

For an instant Devon's expression didn't change. But Jake was watching him closely and knew when realization struck.

"Maggie?"

Hartman nodded. "Yeah. Sorry, Conrad. Seems like she was on that train, and apparently Kate recognized her."

With slow disbelief in his eyes, Devon said, "And Kate dragged her along?"

"Well, according to the report I just received, it wasn't

quite like that. There was a quarrel between two of the robbers—one of whom was a woman—and a brief skirmish before Maggie was abducted. Of course, as always, there are conflicting stories. I've got men trying to sort out fact from fiction and get the truth now."

Jake was ready when Devon pivoted on his boot heel and stalked toward the door of the small office. He caught him by the arm, then quickly released him when Devon swung around with murder in his eyes.

Holding up his hands to show he was unarmed, Jake said, "Easy, Devon. I'm on your side, remember?"

"Then keep your damn hands off me. I'm wasting time standing here when those men have got Kate and Maggie. And come to think of it—why are *you* just standing here?"

"I'm as worried as you are, but I've got enough sense to know we have to take this slowly. We're not fooling with amateurs here. Charwell and Lincoln have been doing this a long time. Now that they're raking in even more loot, they're bound to get too greedy. It always happens with men like that. When they get greedy they'll get careless. Then we'll have 'em."

"A lot can happen before then."

"Yeah, but if you'll take a look at this map Roger's been working on, you'll see a kind of pattern. Come on, Devon, you may recognize some of these places. Their strikes have all been within a twenty-five-mile radius. There are a lot of canyons and arroyos in there, and you may be familiar with some of 'em."

Devon hesitated, then took a deep breath. Jake could see some of the tension ease as he nodded. "All right. I'll take a look."

Jake glanced up and met Roger's eyes, seeing the relief there. He felt the same way. Though he may not always want to admit it, once Devon Conrad focused his considerable energies on a project, there was an almost certain guarantee of success.

Coughing, Jake said, "By the way, a man who once rode with you should be meeting us soon. He's pretty familiar with the old hiding places, and has been checking them out."

Devon smiled faintly. "Doug Morton."

Jake grinned. "Yeah."

"Can't think of a better man to have along. Ol' Doug's got a sharp eye and a good ear. Makes me think of a hound dog when he gets on a man's track."

Devon bent over the map, studying it intently while Roger pointed out the locations that had been rejected as possibilities. Within an hour and a half they had narrowed the possibilities to only three that were feasible.

Straightening, Devon raked a hand through his pale hair and muttered, "Toughcuss Gully, Devil's Den, or below Arapahoe. What a choice. Arapahoe's a ghost town, and there are lots of empty placer mines spread out like badger tunnels. It could take weeks to search all those."

"What about Devil's Den?" Jake asked. He leaned forward to put a fingertip on the map. "It's the farthest from here. We could check there first."

Roger Hartman looked thoughtful. "That's rough country out there. Snow has blocked a lot of those passes. But, like Devon said, Arapahoe would take a lot of time. We could split up our forces, send some to each place."

Looking up, Jake met Devon's ice-blue eyes and smiled faintly. "I think I'll take Devil's Den."

After only an instant's hesitation Devon said, "So will I."

"Oh, no," Roger protested. "You two are likely to kill each other before you do Kate and Maggie any good."

Jake slid Roger a quick glance. "In different circumstances we just might do that. But both our wives are out there somewhere, Roger, and the weather's not getting any better. If Charwell and Lincoln decide they've got enough loot stashed away, they might just decide to get rid of their two biggest liabilities. And you know what that means."

Roger swore softly but offered no more objections. It

would have been a waste of breath, and even he seemed to realize that.

Snow piled up so high it obscured the entrance of the cave tucked into the rock shelf of the box canyon. Shivering, Caitlin huddled more deeply into the folds of her wool coat and exchanged a miserable glance with Maggie. A wash of guilt flooded through her at the thought that she had somehow dragged her sister-in-law into this. If she'd only refused to go along with Charwell's plan, Maggie would be safe now.

As if reading her regret, Maggie leaned forward and whispered, "I'm glad I'm with you. If there's trouble, at least we're together."

Faintly surprised, Caitlin glanced toward the gang members before replying. They were huddled together, counting out the haul they'd taken that day, and she could hear the clink of coins, the thud of heavy silver bars, and laughter. She looked back at Maggie.

"If I hadn't talked to you, you'd be safe now."

"We can't think about that. And really, two heads are better than one at times. If we concentrate, we can figure out a way to get away—a back exit, maybe?"

Caitlin shook her head. "Didn't you notice that this is a box canyon? There's only one way in and one way out. Even these idiots have sense enough to post guards at the mouth to the canyon." She shifted position slightly, trying to get comfortable. Remnants of earlier inhabitants were still scattered about the floor of the cave and along the walls. Tattered rugs, blankets, cooking utensils, and even chairs and a few mattresses were evidence that this was not the first time the cave had been used as a hiding place.

Once, years before, she and Devon had hidden here when the law was too close on their trail. Devon hadn't really liked it because of the lack of convenient exits. He'd never liked the feeling of being boxed in or trapped, even when he had the advantage.

Smoke rose from the fire to form heavy layers just below the cave's roof. The smell of wet wool, leather, and horses mixed with the acrid stench of burning cloth. The printed burlap coverings for the silver were being destroyed, and the heavy bars divided and placed in leather saddlebags. Each man received a certain allotment, and Caitlin could hear an occasional loud burst of dissension concerning the distribution of the loot.

She watched in disgust. Four of the men had ridden with them a long time ago, but Charwell was the only one she could bear to talk to. Lincoln, Hogan, and Dobbs had always seemed furtive and made her uneasy. And Zeke—she shuddered. He was the one who'd hit her, and her lip still throbbed from the blow.

"Kate," Maggie whispered, "do you suppose we could slip out when they fall asleep?"

"Even if we could," Caitlin murmured, "we don't have horses or weapons, and the snow's higher than a steer's back. We'll have to be patient and wait. Maybe on the next job . . ." She didn't say the obvious. No point in frightening her.

Maggie's clear gray eyes met hers, and she said in a steady voice, "You don't think we can escape, do you?"

There was more certainty than inquiry in her voice, and Caitlin took a deep breath. "It's not likely. But anything can happen. Jake and Devon may come, or—"

"No. Don't. I understand." Maggie turned her head slightly to study the men still grouped around their stolen goods. "If nothing else, I have learned to be a realist. Paint me no pretty pictures. I deal much better with the truth."

Caitlin was silent. The truth was often hard to swallow, but she'd learned that there was no substitute for it. Dear God, how she wished Jake were here. She'd tried and tried to remember in the past two weeks just why she'd wanted to get away from him so badly, but no reason seemed clear to her now. Oh, he had a way of losing his temper at times, and he could growl and snarl at the most inconvenient times, blowing like an enraged bull when he didn't get his way, but that seemed so unimportant now. What was important was seeing him again, and her children. Clay's howls of outrage at his mother's abduction still haunted her fitful slumber, but at least the children were safe. God—why had she *ever* wanted to leave?

When Maggie reached out and put a hand over her clasped hands, Caitlin looked up. Her vision was blurred by tears, but she heard her sister-in-law whisper, "I have faith that all will be well. . . ."

Devon reined in atop a snowy crest overlooking Devil's Den. It had been aptly named. Even in good weather it was hard to navigate the steep trail into it, with huge rocks and boulders strewn in the path by rock slides, and always the chance of another. He surveyed the area slowly. He didn't like this. No, he didn't like it at all. Too much snow had fallen, burdening aspens, pines, and cedars with heavy layers that weighted the topmost branches until they scraped the high level of snow that covered the ground in drifts. Drifts which often hid deep gullies.

"I remember now why it's called Devil's Den," Jake muttered. "It's been a while since I've been here."

"Me, too." Devon turned slightly in his saddle to look at the highest outcropping of rock on one side of the mouth leading into the canyon. "But it's the only logical choice to hide. I've used this place before. It was my favorite. It's hard to find, and any posse that does make it this far stands a good chance of getting shot—I'm willing to bet they've got a guard stationed there," he said, and pointed to the high rock guarding the pass.

"In this weather?"

"There's a rock shelter. With any luck he'll be in it. If he is, then his view is restricted to a narrow scope." Devon indicated an area close to the high rock wall. "If we go that way, he can't see us. But a guard on the opposite side can."

"Damn. Do you think there are two guards posted?"

"If you were in the business of robbing trains and had taken two women hostage, wouldn't you post as many guards as you could?" Devon shot back.

"I might," Jake said coolly. "Or I might figure that having two women as hostage would give me a certain amount of leverage over anybody coming after me."

"Yeah, but it doesn't always work that way." Devon's jaw tensed at the brief memory of lawmen and G. K. Durant storming a hideout that held two women. Apparently, Jake remembered it, too.

"Damn, I know that. But the circumstances were different then. Kate and Molly weren't hostages."

"Not so very different," Devon said with a shrug. "And it ended with both of them shot. I don't intend for it to happen again. Kate barely made it." He didn't remind Jake that Molly hadn't. Neither of them would ever forget that.

"Yeah. So what do you suggest?"

"Split up. You take one side; I'll take the other. Odds are that one of us might be spotted, but the other will make it. There's a cave in that back wall. Up about six feet off the canyon floor. It's not easy to spot. Look for twin pines at the left side, oh, about four or five feet from the mouth. With any luck I'll meet you there in about a half hour to an hour."

It took two hours before Jake and Devon were positioned on the canyon floor in a clump of snow-covered brush. They'd left their horses in a small copse of sheltering trees near the mouth, both quickly realizing that two men on foot would be less visible. Visibility was poor anyway; thick gray clouds had begun to release a blinding torrent of snow mixed with rain.

"Great weather," Jake muttered, and Devon grinned.

"This is why I live in Texas now. I spent too many years

shivering in snow not to appreciate the sun." He drew in a deep breath that felt riddled with needles. The temperature was dropping fast. The rain/snow mix would soon be nothing but a blizzard.

Motioning with his drawn pistol, he said, "You take the left. I'll go in from the right."

Jake studied the entrance to the cave for a moment, then shook his head. "Too dangerous. They'd pick us off as easy as sheep from a train. I think we should create a distraction, draw 'em out."

"Yeah, as if they would all rush outside into the snow to see what was making a racket? Damn, Jake. I thought you could come up with something better than that."

For an instant they glared at one another as the snow hit their faces with growing intensity. It was blowing sideways now, up under the brims of their pulled-down hats. Finally Devon shrugged.

"It's worth a shot, but it sure blows the element of surprise. What do we do if we still can't get inside?"

"Well, we can stand here in the snow and argue about it until we freeze to death, or we can give *some*thing a try and take it from there."

Devon tugged at the brim of his hat. "What have you got that will bring 'em out?"

Reaching under his heavy coat, Jake brought out a wrapped bundle. Devon watched curiously as he unwrapped it, then let out a soft whistle of amazement.

"Damn . . . dynamite?"

"Enough to bring this canyon down around our ears if I didn't know how much to use." Jake squinted upward in the snow. "Lucky for us, I've worked with this stuff before."

Devon followed his gaze, staring at the blur of shadow that was the mouth of the cave. "I sure as hell hope you know what you're doing."

It wasn't comforting to hear him say, "So do I."

Five

Maggie leaned forward to warm her hands at the fire. She slid a glance toward Kate, who was gazing into the flames with brooding intensity. Their conversation had been soft and personal, with frequent wary glances at the men drinking whiskey near the mouth of the cave. A few of them had become rowdy and loud, and Kate had grown increasingly nervous.

"Kate, has there been trouble between you and Jake?" she asked, to get her sister-in-law's mind off the brewing tension. "From the tone of your letters this past year, I've wondered."

Kate looked at her with a surprised lift of her brows. "Why, yes, there has. I don't know why. And Jake—he doesn't even realize I've been unhappy."

"Has he mistreated you? Stayed away too much and too long, perhaps?"

Shaking her head, Kate answered softly, "No. He hasn't been any different than he's always been. He's just—Jake. Everything he does is perfect. He doesn't make mistakes. None that he'd admit, anyway. But everything I do seems to turn out wrong. I mean, the kids are well behaved, but sometimes they get on my nerves. I want to scream at them even when they aren't doing anything more than being children. And then I feel ashamed of myself when I do yell at them.

Even little Devon, and he's no more than a baby, gets on my nerves." She sighed. "I'm a terrible wife and mother."

Maggie couldn't help a smile. "Kate, you're not terrible. This is all normal. I've seen it too many times. Heavens, I've felt that way myself more than once. It's the burden of trying to cope that begins to overwhelm us, I think. It's not easy being everything to everyone. Turning from wet-nurse and mother into a seductive wife in the bedroom is a long jump at the end of a very trying day."

Kate looked startled. "Why, that's exactly how I've felt at times. It's difficult making the shift in emotion from mothering a child to seducing a husband, yet that's what Jake expects. I can tell he doesn't understand why I don't always leap eagerly into bed as I used to."

"And that's when there's a fight, I'll bet."

Laughing, Kate nodded. "Usually. And I start it more often than not. It's easier to fight than it is to pretend something I'm not feeling."

"Then you need to tell Jake the truth. He's not stupid. He may not understand exactly why you feel the way you do, but he'll certainly understand that there are times you need to be by yourself. After all, men always seem to find the time to go off alone, don't they?"

"Jake calls it looking for stray cattle, but there's been a lot of times he's ended up in town or off in a line shack with Doug Morton for some fishing or hunting." Kate took a deep breath and glanced again toward the mouth of the cave. A burst of raucous laughter made her frown. "I wish Charwell would take Zeke, Lincoln, and the others for some ice fishing. Anything to get them away from us."

"You've known some of them a long time."

"Unfortunately. Train robbery doesn't always draw the choicest companions."

"Do you think they'll let us go once they've made enough money?"

Kate shook her head. "Men like that never make enough

money. If they do happen to get a rich haul, they spend it in saloons and whorehouses, or lose it at the poker table. No, it's not likely to be any time soon."

Dismayed, Maggie looked toward the mouth of the cave again. The man named Charwell had not been overly rough, but neither had he instilled any confidence in her, either. If the others decided that Kate's usefulness had come to an end, Charwell wouldn't put up too much of an argument to save either woman.

Kate and Maggie lapsed into silence, both of them casting worried glances at the outlaws. They'd grown even louder. Two of them were quarreling heatedly. Then one struck a blow. She had no idea who threw the first punch, but when Kate got to her feet and stepped back into the shadows, Maggie followed immediately. She'd seen men fight before, so it was no shock, but she thought she'd never get used to the sound of solid blows and harsh grunts as fists made impact on the human body.

Glancing at Kate, Maggie started to ask whether they should try to ease past the men and into the open but was stopped by a thunderous roar. The percussion rocked her back on her feet and sent her slamming into the hard rock wall. It was followed by a distant rumbling that made the floor vibrate with growing intensity.

Confused, Maggie turned blindly to look for Kate. She wasn't where she'd been standing a moment before but was several feet away. Maggie started toward her.

"Dynamite." Kate's face was pale, her green eyes wide and luminous in the dim shadows. "I'd know that sound anywhere."

"Is someone trying to seal us in?"

Kate shook her head. "I don't know . . . I don't know if that fool Lincoln set off the charges they have scattered around here, or if it's someone else." She turned to Maggie, her fright evident. "Pray that whoever is out there is on our side and knows we're in here."

* * *

"What the hell are you trying to do?" Devon yelled over the avalanche of snow and shattered tree limbs raining down on their heads. "Blow up the damn mountain?"

Jake blew out a mouthful of snow and shook his head. "Must be more charges set up around here. The little I set off wouldn't cause this big an explosion."

"Great, just great," Devon snarled. He floundered through waist-high snowdrifts, cursing as he searched for his rifle in the powdery debris.

Jake eyed him for only a moment before leaning forward to pluck a snow-clogged rifle from a drift. "Here. You'd better clean it quick, 'cause those boys will be out here before you get a chance to reload and aim."

"Thanks for the advice," Devon muttered as he grabbed his rifle.

Jake was right. Before either man had time to do much more than dust off loose snow and ready their weapons, a throng of bandits were at the mouth of the cave. Jake could see their shadows, dark against the pale outline of a snowdrift and fire-glow from inside the cave. He glanced at the sky and quickly figured they had maybe two hours until dusk. Visibility was limited because of the weather, and would be totally eliminated once the sun set.

"Step to your right," he said softly to Devon, who nodded his understanding. There was a slight incline to the right, studded with thick bushes that would provide some sort of covering.

Unfortunately, it wasn't enough to hide them from view. A bullet whistled past Jake's head, close enough that he felt the heat. Ducking, he turned slightly to see that the bullet had plowed a steaming furrow in the snowdrift directly behind his head. He glanced toward Devon to see that he was sprawled on his belly and looking around cautiously. They lay motionless in the snow for a minute, then snaked toward the foot of the slope, where those above would have to step out from behind their protective ledge in order to get a clear shot.

Another bullet spanged into the rock behind them, this time spraying granite splinters in all directions. Jake didn't draw an easy breath until they had their backs pressed against the ridged layers of rock wall and were out of sight from above.

"Damn good shooting," he muttered as he fumbled with a cartridge for his rifle. "Couldn't have done better myself."

"I'm glad to hear it." Devon's breath formed frost clouds in front of his face as he peered at Jake. "See if you can't shoot him off that ledge before he actually hits us this time."

"Yeah, I thought about that."

"Don't just think about it—do it."

Jake slanted him a quick look. "If you're in such a big hurry to give 'em our exact position, you do it. Just let me move a little bit farther up the wall first so if they throw down a bunch of lead or one of those little firesticks, I won't get hit accidentally."

"I take it you've got a better idea."

"I think so." Jake leaned back to look at the ledge, high up and to their right now. "Do you remember the way into the cave?"

Devon pointed several yards farther down. "A kind of trail goes from there to the ledge. Big enough for a single horse." He paused. "Or two men at the same time."

Even though she was braced for it, Caitlin was still startled by the next explosion. This one made the cave walls shudder, and she grabbed Maggie's hand.

"Let's take cover. . . ."

A hand descended upon her shoulder, clenching her by the coat and lifting her to her feet.

"Hell no, little lady," snarled Zeke. "You're comin' with me."

Caitlin's immediate reaction was an elbow to his stomach, catching the outlaw by surprise. He gave a "Whoof!" as she knocked the air from him and, taking advantage, she whirled around and snatched the gun from his holster.

Zeke's eyes widened with incredulous fury. "What the hell do you think you're gonna do with that?"

She looked at him. Cocking the hammer with an expert thumb, she leveled the pistol. "Care to find out?"

Behind Zeke, she could see that Charwell was coming toward them. He jerked to a halt when he saw that Caitlin held a pistol, and said warily, "Aw, Kate, what are you doin'?"

"Exactly what it looks like. Tell your stupid friend to back off or he'll be sporting some new holes in his head."

"Better do as she says, Zeke." Charwell glanced over his shoulder when a volley of gunfire sounded outside the cave. "Kate's a dead shot, and I got a feeling that's Devon out there. I don't wanna get caught between the devil inside and the devil outside."

Gesturing, Zeke growled, "These two are our hostages. How do you expect to get out of here alive if we don't use 'em?"

"Look, I can't tell how many guns are out there, but I do know how many are in here. Some damn sharpshooter has already picked off two of our men. Hogan's set to toss out a few sticks, and we can make a run for it while the men outside are dodging rocks." He shot Caitlin a glance. "You know you're more of a liability than an asset now. Here's the choice—you can shoot him, but there's enough of us in here to get both of you if you do. Or you can stand back and take cover while we make a run for it. Which is it?"

Caitlin held the pistol steady. She looked from one to the other and saw the nervous impatience in Charwell's eyes. There really wasn't much of a choice.

"You better hurry, Charwell. Sounds like those men out there are getting a bit anxious."

Charwell grinned slightly. "See you 'round, Kate."

"Not if I can help it."

She didn't take a deep breath until Zeke had backed away, his furious gaze trained on the barrel of the pistol. "With any luck," he snapped, "you'll get shot before the day's out."

Caitlin didn't bother to reply. She just motioned with the pistol toward the cave's mouth, and Zeke joined his companions. Maggie sidled close to Caitlin as the men huddled at the front, and both of them flinched when another stick of dynamite was tossed out the entrance. There was a blur of snow and rocks, and under cover of the explosion the outlaws fled.

Caitlin and Maggie crouched in the shelter of a rocky ledge and waited, cringing as the cave walls shook and more rocks slid down around them. After a short time the gunfire slowed, then stopped. No other sound could be heard, and the silence grew thick.

Though she didn't want to worry Maggie, Kate knew that it could be anyone outside the cave. Several gangs roamed the Colorado hills, at times preying on one another. Who would step into the cave when the smoke cleared? If not lawmen, it could be a rival gang, or even Charwell's outlaws.

She kept a tight grip on the pistol, determined not to be too trusting when she heard voices at the front of the cave. "Stay down," she told Maggie. "Wait to see who comes in."

Maggie nodded wordlessly. Her face was pale beneath the dark tangle of her hair. Both women waited tensely, and when she saw the dark form of a man cautiously enter the cave's mouth, Caitlin took careful aim. From this distance and with the light behind him, she couldn't make out the man's identity.

"Slow down there, mister," she called. "You make an easy target and I'm feeling kinda nervous right now."

There was an instant's silence; then she heard an exasperated, "Damn, Kate. You still mad at me?"

The barrel of her pistol wavered, and Caitlin didn't know whether to laugh or cry. "A little," she retorted, and rose to her feet. "But I have to admit that I'm glad it's you, Jake."

"Yeah, you sound real glad."

And he definitely sounded disgruntled. Caitlin sighed. She looked at Maggie, but she was already running toward the front to greet a second man. When they embraced she knew it had to be Devon. Oddly, Caitlin felt awkward about going to Jake. After all, she'd left him with no real explanation. Would he forgive her?

Uncertain, she didn't move when Jake came toward her. He walked with that easy, graceful stride that was half-unnerving, half-reassuring. When he reached her, he halted and stared into her eyes. Caitlin's heart lurched. Handsome, familiar Jake, wearing that look on his face that she'd seen often enough to know it hid deep emotion. Her throat tightened.

"Did you two come after us alone?"

"Yeah—and no, I'm not wounded in case you're interested."

Gesturing rather sheepishly with the pistol she still held, she said thickly, "I really am glad to see you."

"Can't tell by the reception." A muscle in his jaw clenched as Jake held her gaze. "Most wives don't greet their husbands with a loaded pistol, but then, you're not like most women."

"True." She lowered the pistol and lifted her chin, determined not to allow this to degenerate into an argument. "Where are Charwell and the others? Did you let 'em get away?"

"You know me better than that. Those who aren't dead are about to run into a posse on the track out of here. They won't get far, if I know Roger."

"Roger." Kate smiled slightly. "I should have known he'd be with you."

"You should have known a lot of damn things, Kate."

She took a deep breath. "You haven't said you're glad to see me, Jake."

"An obvious oversight." His ironic tone did nothing to lessen Caitlin's tenuous grip on control. "I suppose you think I came through a blinding snowstorm and over some of the roughest ground in all of Colorado just to finish an argument."

Her eyes narrowed with exasperation. "You usually don't mind that too much."

"Damn, Kate, you can make me so blamed mad. . . . Did you ever stop to think I might be worried sick about you?"

Amazed, she said, "Do you think I *chose* to be kidnapped from that train? Is *that* what you think?"

"I'm not talking about that—I'm talking about you taking off like you did, and taking my kids away at Christmas when you know I didn't want you to go at all—"

"I didn't notice any great effort on your part to find out *why* I wanted to leave you in the first place—"

Jake took a step forward. His dark eyes narrowed hotly. "You left me, and if I'm guessing right, you didn't intend to come back. True?"

"Yes." Caitlin swallowed hard at the look on his face.

Jake swore softly, then took a deep breath and said more calmly than his expression indicated, "I'm listening now. So tell me—why did you leave?"

"You never listen to me."

"Never lis—not that again. I listen to you when you say something that makes sense."

Caitlin breathed deeply to calm her mounting irritation and said, "I may not always make sense to you, but you never stop to ask what I mean, either."

For a moment Jake just looked at her; then he shook his head. "I knew it would be all my fault. It always is."

"Listen," she began angrily, but a muffled sound outside the cave drew their immediate attention.

Devon began swearing and bolted outside the cave. Caitlin stared after him, realizing what the sound had been.

After a moment Devon came back in, his face grim. "Damn them, they dynamited the entrance to the canyon. A few tons of snow are blocking it. We're stuck here for a while."

With a frightened face Maggie asked, "Can't we dig our way out?"

"We might if it wasn't snowing so hard we'd be risking getting buried in the stuff." Devon raked a hand through the snow dusting his pale hair and said disgustedly, "Looks like we're going to spend Christmas together after all."

"Christmas?" Caitlin blinked. "What's today?"

It was Jake who replied, "Christmas Eve."

Six

December 24

Jake and Devon had gone out into the worsening weather to bring in the horses. While the men were checking out the damage from the blast and retrieving the horses, Caitlin and Maggie set about investigating their resources. Surprisingly, the cave was fairly well stocked with supplies.

"Charwell must have used this place a lot," Caitlin murmured, and Maggie smiled as she held up a tin can.

"Tinned beef. And there are canned vegetables and fruit, even a few bottles of wine tucked into some of these crates. If necessary, we could exist quite handily for a while."

"Good thing," Caitlin muttered as she dug into a dusty crate, "because we may have to. That pass is narrow, and if they used enough dynamite, it will take a long time to dig our way out."

Maggie gazed at her thoughtfully. "You know, things aren't as bad as they could be."

Caitlin looked up, a smudge of dirt on her cheek and her green eyes wide with surprise. "Oh? How do you figure that?"

Shrugging, Maggie said, "You and Jake obviously need some time alone together to talk things out. Here, there are no distractions to pull you away until you two have done so."

Caitlin smiled. "You must not have any objections to listening to two adults yell at one another. That seems to be our favored method of talking things out."

"It doesn't have to be. Look—" Maggie stood up and gestured. "This cave is big enough so that we all fit in here quite comfortably and still have privacy. There's a little nook over on that side, and one on this side. Drag some of these mattresses over there, spread a few blankets on them, light two fires, and there you go—two instant cottages. You can talk to Jake, and I can talk to Devon."

"What do you and Devon have to argue about?"

Maggie sighed. "Whatever's been bothering him lately. It's time we were honest with one another. Don't you think that's true for all of us?"

After a moment Caitlin said, "It's Christmas—what do you think about cutting down one of those small pines outside and bringing it in here?" She held up a small hatchet. "I'll get the tree—you start our Christmas dinner."

When Devon stepped into the cave with his horse he paused in surprise. A pine tree stood in the middle of the cave floor, bits of brightly colored material clinging to the damp branches.

"Hey, you're blocking the entrance," Jake muttered behind him, and Devon led Pardo a few more steps inside. He could hear Jake's murmur of surprise as he saw the tree also, and grinned.

"Trust two women to set about decorating a place the minute our backs are turned," he said, and Jake laughed.

"Yeah, but at least they started cooking dinner."

The tantalizing fragrance of meat and vegetables drifted in the close air of the cave, mixed with the scent of pine and wet wool. It was an interesting blend of odors, and Devon shook his head as he began to unsaddle his horse and rub him down. The snow hadn't harmed either animal, and he was glad Charwell hadn't seen the horses. If they were ever able to dig out, they'd need them.

When he'd finished tending Pardo and given him some grain from his saddlebag Devon moved to the fire and looked at Maggie. She glanced up at him. Her face was flushed from the steam coming from a cooking pot, and her eyes were bright.

"Welcome home, Devon," she said softly, and he felt her tone all the way to his toes. Funny how she could do that to him with just a few words or a meaningful glance. And, oddly enough, he realized that anywhere she was, was home. This cave, with all its musty odors and stark rock walls, was cozy when she was here. Why had he ever felt restless?

Rising to her feet, Maggie leaned over to pick up a glass, then held it out to him. "Give me your coat so I can dry it out, and have some wine."

"Wine?" Devon shook his head, already unbuttoning his coat. "Charwell never seemed the type. Hard whiskey was more his kind of drink, I'd think."

"Yes, well, people are often surprising."

Devon handed her the coat and smiled. "Yeah, I guess I have to agree with that." He drank his wine, then gestured to the tree. "I don't have a gift for you."

Maggie's smile grew wider. "Oh yes you do, Devon Conrad. It's the best gift a woman can ever get from her man."

Puzzled, Devon considered a variety of meanings, then gave up. "All right. I'll bite on this one—what is the best gift?"

Maggie wiped her hands on a cloth, then came to him and put her arms around his waist. Rising to her tiptoes, she whispered against his cheek, "Unconditional love."

"Ah. That's a lot like unconditional surrender, ain't it?"

She rubbed her forehead against his jaw. "Yes. No terms. No compromise. No reservations."

Devon slid his arms around Maggie and held her against

him. "Too bad," he said huskily, "that we don't have any privacy."

Maggie tilted back her head and said, "Oh, I've already taken care of that."

Laughing, Devon said, "You are the most efficient woman I've ever known, Maggie Conrad. I'm willing to bet that you've managed to set up beds and silk sheets while I've been gone."

Maggie snuggled against him. "No silk sheets. Just beds."

"You know, I must be the luckiest man alive. I may have forgotten that for a while, but you certainly have a way of nudging my memory."

"Yes," Maggie said as she lifted her face for his kiss, "you are absolutely correct."

Caitlin felt awkward and shy as she watched Jake remove his coat and hang it by the fire. Silent, she filled a plate for him, and smiled at his surprise.

"I don't know how you two did so much in so little time," Jake said as he took the plate. He peered at the food in mild surprise. "Beef? Potatoes and peas?"

"Not exactly the Christmas dinner we usually have, but it's better than melted snow and pine branches. I hope."

Jake laughed. He sat down on a rock near the fire and glanced over his shoulder toward Devon and Maggie. Apparently, they had decided to forgo dinner for privacy. They disappeared into a rocky cleft in the cave and out of sight. When he looked back at Caitlin she wondered what he was thinking.

"Any sign of Charwell or the others?" she asked when the silence stretched out.

"Just their farewell gift—three tons of snow. If Roger missed 'em, they might be halfway to the Badlands by now. Or Mexico."

"At least they're not here." Caitlin sat down with a plate of food but found that her appetite had vanished. However

Jake's hadn't, and he polished off two helpings of tinned beef and vegetables before setting aside his plate. She managed a faint smile that quickly faded when he just stared back at her.

"Kate—if you aren't happy with me, I won't try to make you stay."

Hot tears stung her eyes, and she looked down at her hands for a long moment. His blunt words seared to the heart, and she struggled for control. A few weeks ago she might have wanted to leave. But now—now she knew that all she wanted or needed was this strong man who held her love in his hands. How did she confess that without sounding completely foolish?

"Kate." She looked up, flinching at the expression in Jake's dark eyes. "Kate, I know I haven't always listened to what you were saying. I'm not real good at that sort of thing. Sometimes . . . sometimes I wish I could say what's bothering me as easily as you do. I can't. But sweetheart, don't ever think that it's because I don't care how you feel." His voice was rough and raspy when he said, "It's just that I love you so damn much. Hell, maybe too much. Maybe I've made you feel tied down. I never meant to."

When he stood up, raking a hand through his dark hair, Caitlin stood, too. "Jake—I can't say that I haven't felt tied down. I have. But these weeks without you, I came to realize that the things I thought I resented the most are the very things that are the most important to me. You. The children. They're all that really matter to me in this world."

She took a step toward him and saw his black eyes narrow slightly. Reaching out, she curled her fingers in the edge of his shirt. She could feel his strong, steady heartbeat beneath her palm. "Maybe what I need—what *we* need—is some time alone together. I think our lives have been so busy that we've lost touch with those things that drew us together."

Jake smiled slightly. "Yeah, like outlaws and bullets. Well, if that was what was missing in our lives, this recent dose of it is more than enough for me." He moved to embrace her, and his voice was rough when he said, "Hell, Kate, I was afraid that even if I found you unharmed, I'd still lose you."

Shaking her head, she pressed her face against his chest. "I knew you'd come for me. I never doubted it. You always seem to be rescuing me, even when I don't know I need it." She took a deep breath. "But I need more than just love from you, Jake—I need to know that we're partners. That you value me just as much as I do you."

"Hell, Kate, what do you think all this was about?" he began, pausing when she shook her head. "Damn. What do you mean?"

"I know you love me, but I need to know that the things I do for you are as important as what you do for me. I'm not out riding the range or playing with stocks and bonds, but my job is pretty important, too. We have four children—*busy* children. I supervise all the ranch chores that you never have to think about—cooking, cleaning, making certain there are enough supplies for winter, enough flour and sugar and coffee and beans—that takes planning, Jake. Mrs. Baker is a great help, but who do you think oversees all of it? And then I try to be seductive for you when you need me."

"So that's a damn job now?" Jake snapped, his eyes flashing angrily, and she sighed.

"Don't be ridiculous. That's one of the fringe benefits. But I don't always feel seductive. Sometimes I just feel—tired."

"That's a hell of a thing to hear," he muttered.

"But it's true." Her chin lifted as she met his eyes. "I love you. I want you. But I want you to recognize that you're not the only one with the right to feel tired or grumpy."

"Aw, Kate, have I been that bad?"

"Sometimes." She rubbed her hand down over his chest. "Those are little things, Jake. But they're important."

"Sweetheart, you're the most important thing. Guess I never knew that you might think differently. I swear, I'll try not to forget that you need reminding how wonderful I think you are every now and then." He hesitated, then slid his hands up her back to her shoulders. His voice was husky when he murmured, "I love you so much, Kate. I don't want you to ever leave me again."

"No," she agreed softly, "I won't. We may argue at times, but making up isn't so bad, is it?"

His chest rumbled with laughter. "I can remember quite a few times when making up was a lot of fun. . . ."

She tilted back her head to look up at him and recognized the light in his eyes. He held her tightly against him, one hand curving over her back and hips to press her closer. She closed her eyes when he bent his head to kiss her, and she dissolved into his embrace with a longing that surprised her.

When Jake finally lifted his head she was clinging to him weakly. He made a sound in the back of his throat and muttered, "Too bad we don't have a bed handy."

"Oh, but we do," she said, looking up at him with a smile. She pointed, and he laughed softly.

"Ever resourceful Kate." He bent slightly and scooped her into his arms. As she laid her head against his shoulder and he started for the bed in the rocky niche at one side, she heard him say, "Sweetheart, this will be the best Christmas yet. . . ."

It was almost noon a few days after Christmas when Roger Hartman stopped outside the cave tucked into the box canyon. There was no sign of life, but the faint drift of smoke coming from the cave was a certain indication of inhabitance. He turned to Doug Morton at his side.

"I'm not sure I want to go inside. No telling what we might find."

Doug squinted up at the ledge with a thoughtful frown. "Y'know, I've known Devon a long time. Jake almost as long. Somehow, I'd be willin' to bet that they made it all right."

"Charwell seemed to think so." Roger's mouth twisted grimly. "Damn varmint. Sealing them in here like that with dynamite. If we hadn't caught him and made him tell us where they were, we might never have known what happened to them."

Rubbing at his chin, Doug shook his head. "Reckon we'd have found out soon enough. I have a feeling that if they ain't in there, they'll be ridin' into town soon."

Roger started up the slope with Doug close behind. More men were with them, struggling through the clogged pass that had taken two days of intensive work to penetrate. His breath came slowly, and deep snow slowed his progress, so that it took several minutes to go only a few yards.

By the time he reached the ledge at the mouth of the cave he was breathing heavily. Gloves made his hands clumsy as he cocked his rifle and stepped cautiously inside the cave. He didn't know what to expect. If they were alive, surely they'd have called out a warning or a greeting.

Right behind him, Doug Morton burst into laughter, and Roger tensed. "What is it?"

Still laughing, Doug uncocked his rifle. He slid his pistol into its holster, then pointed. Roger peered into the gloom and shook his head with a mixture of relief and exasperation.

"The least you could have done," he said shortly to a half-clad Jake, "is call out and let us know you were alive."

"We're alive." Jake rubbed his bare arms briskly. "And you men have been disturbing our peace and quiet with the racket you've been making these past two days. If you don't mind, you can go right back to town now that you've cleared the pass."

"What the hell—?"

"Uh, Mr. Hartman," Doug said with a gentle prod, "I think I'd oblige him if I were you. Somehow, I don't think he wants to be rescued right now."

Jake grinned. "We've got enough food to last two more days. Tell Mrs. Baker we'll be home then."

Roger sputtered for a moment before the reason for it dawned on him. Then he paused, shook his head, and pivoted on his heel. "Be damned if I ever try to rescue you again, Jake Lassiter. You've got more lives than a cat."

"Roger?" Jake called after him, and said when they paused and turned around, "Merry Christmas."

Doug Morton was still chuckling when they reached the pass, and Roger finally grinned. "Well, I guess Jake and Kate made up."

"Yep. Reckon they did at that."

Roger tilted his head to look at the sun shining on the treetops and pristine snowbanks. The air was crisp and cool, and he felt invigorated. He drew in a deep breath of fresh air and let it out again. "You know, Doug, taking some time off at Christmas isn't such a bad idea after all."

"Nope. Not a bad idea at all."

To My Readers:

I hope you enjoyed *Colorado Christmas*. It was written for those of you who wrote asking for another story about Jake, Caitlin, Devon, and Maggie. Jake and Caitlin first met in *Wildflower* (1992), and *Wildest Heart* (1994) was Devon and Maggie's story. Even though the course of true love may not always run smooth, with a little work there's always a happy ending. . . .

—Virginia Brown

A New Beginning

Colleen Faulkner

Prologue

Bolton Castle, England
August 1783

Brenna parted the branches of the blackberry bush and peered cautiously through the tangled bramble.

"Ye see him?" asked her sister excitedly. "Ye see the beast? Hester Marble says he's got horns and a forked tail!"

"Hsst, Abby! He'll hear you and gobble us both up."

Abby giggled. "Will not." She stood on her tiptoes to try to look over Brenna's shoulder. "Well, is he there or ain't he?"

"*Isn't* he. You know Mama will have your head if you don't speak properly."

"*Isn't.*" Abby giggled again. "Hester Marble says he covers his face from the sunlight with that black scarf, else it would melt."

Meg stared at the blackened remains of a southern wing of Bolton Castle. Rag weed had grown up through the cracks in the crumbled stone, fighting not just to take the wall but the unkempt garden that lay beyond it. "I don't see a thing," Brenna whispered. "I told you he wouldn't be here."

"I told *you* he wouldn't be here." Ten-year-old Abby picked up her berry basket and returned to the task at hand. "You best get back to picking, Brenna, else Mama will be terrible mad."

With a sigh, Brenna let go of the blackberry branch and

it snapped back into place, obscuring her vision of the castle once more. "I didn't say I *wanted* to see him." She lifted her basket from the grass and reached over her little sister's head to pick a handful of berries. She feigned disinterest with a shrug of her shoulders. "I was just curious."

"Ha! I heard you asking Mama the other day about his lordship. You asked Mama if she thought he needed kitchen help!"

"You sneaky witch!" Brenna tugged on her sister's thick braid, which was precisely the same russet color as her own.

"Mama said she'd rather sell herself on the streets of London than let you near the beast." Abby plucked a berry from her basket and popped it into her mouth thoughtfully. "What I didn't get was why would someone in London want to buy Mama? What would they do with her?"

Brenna pushed past her sister, picking berries faster. It was getting late, and time they started home. If Mama knew how close to the castle Brenna had taken her sister in search of berries, she would definitely be displeased. "You shouldn't be listening in on adult conversations not meant for your big ears."

Abby set her jaw. "I'm big enough! I'm almost as big as you!"

"You might be almost as *tall* as me," Brenna corrected, eyeing the lanky ten-year-old, "but I'm an adult and you're just a hatchling." She lifted her patched homespun skirt, pressing deeper into the blackberry bramble, where she spotted clusters of fruit just out of reach.

"It isn't fair." Abby pouted. "You and Mama are always talking behind our backs, saying we're too young to hear. I'm not an addlepate, you know. I know we've got no money and not much food for winter. With Papa gone, and Jaime being only five, we've got no man to work the fields for us. You think I don't know that?"

Brenna sighed, reaching back to touch her sister's shoulder. "It's all right, Abby. We're going to be all right. We've enough food for this winter. Think of all those turnips Mama put in that old root cellar under the bed."

Abby stepped out of her sister's reach, crossing her arms over her chest, and thrusting out her lower lip. She was fighting back angry tears. "I don't see why God had to take Papa to heaven. Stupid pitchfork." She kicked the basket she'd set on the ground. Berries spilled everywhere. "Stepping on a pitchfork isn't supposed to kill a man. Not a big, strong man like Papa."

Brenna felt the tears well up in her own eyes. Mama said theirs was not to reason why God would take such a fine man as their father, Jack Abbott. But there were times when it was hard not to question the good Lord's intentions. Abby was right; food would be scarce this winter. They'd barely dragged enough out of their stump-ridden field to feed the seven of them. Her three married sisters gave what they could, but they had their own families to feed. This year the crops had been good. What about next year, and the year after that? What if there was a drought? What if seed was too high come spring?

Brenna picked blackberries faster, pushing deeper into the bramble. Mama said not to worry, to trust in the Lord. To have patience. But Brenna was never one for patience. She liked action.

Stepping through a break in the blackberry hedge, she suddenly found herself in full view of Bolton Castle. Letting her basket swing on her arm, she stared at the magnificent gray stone walls that seemed to stretch into the heavens. It was a beautiful structure of varying roof lines and domed towers. Even to the uneducated Brenna, the architecture was impressive, with its arched windows and carved stone. It was splendid, all but the southern wing, which was nothing but charred walls and choking weeds.

Lord Bolton had lived here for as long as Brenna could recall. As a child she remembered his face, handsome and laughing. His wife had brought gifts of tangy oranges and sweet candies each Christmas Eve. Brenna smiled at the memory, but then her smile faded.

Then came the fire. No one knew how it started, only that it swept through the family quarters in the south wing, killing the beautiful Lady Bolton and her three children. Only Lord Bolton had miraculously survived, and he, the villagers said, was terribly scarred by the blaze.

Brenna hadn't seen him since the fire. He rarely left the castle. They said that when he did he was cloaked in black, with a veil to hide his hideous face. At night the villagers said he stood in the ruins of the southern wing, shouting in fury. Brenna had heard the echo of his voice at night when she was lying in her rope bed with her three sisters.

It sounded to her as if Lord Bolton cried out not in anger, but in agonizing pain. Pain of the heart.

"Brenna? Brenna, where did you go?"

"Here," Brenna whispered, mesmerized by the sad gray walls of the castle. She'd never been so close before. "Shhhh," she whispered as she heard her sister pushing her way through the blackberry bramble.

"Saints alive!" Abby blinked, looking up at the massive walls. "It looks even bigger from here than down in the village, doesn't it?"

Brenna stared at the tumbled wall closest to her. Beyond it was a small garden, obviously left unkempt since the fire. Then she caught sight of a white flower swaying in the weeds among the ruins. A rose? Could a rosebush have possibly withstood the fire and the weight of the fallen walls?

Without thinking, Brenna took a step toward the wall, fascinated by the beauty of the rose in the midst of the destruction.

"What are you doing?" Abby exclaimed in a loud whisper. "Ye lost your red head?"

"Shhhh," Brenna whispered. "I just want to see the rose."

Abby's nutmeg eyes widened in disbelief. "You're going

to pick the beast's flowers?" She crossed herself hurriedly. "He'll eat you for supper for sure!"

"Shhhhh."

"He'll spit out your bones to grind for his bread!"

"Abby, hush." Her berry basket still on her arm, Brenna crept nearer to the castle. "I won't be but a minute." The flower was just over a wall that stood no more than two feet high. All she would have to do was lean over the wall and . . .

"Arrrrggggg!"

Brenna froze in terror. The sound was more animallike than human.

Abby screamed, her voice piercing the air.

"Go away!" the deep voice growled.

Brenna stumbled backward, her gaze searching the ruins for the source of the unearthly voice. Where was he? For surely it was the beast.

"Go!" his voice boomed. "Go from here and dare not touch what is mine."

Instead of turning and running after her sister, Brenna backed her way through the blackberry bramble, still trying to catch a glimpse of the man the villagers called the beast.

Just as she was about to lose sight of the castle through the bushes, she spotted him, high above her head, balanced on a charred stone wall.

"Go! Go!" he bellowed, shaking his fist at her. "Run for your life!"

Brenna was disappointed that she could see no more than his silhouette. His face was lost in the shadows of the setting sun and the high walls of the castle.

"Arrrrggggg!" he shouted again, his voice echoing off the stone.

With one last look at the dreadful apparition, Brenna turned and ran to catch up with Abby, who was already half-way down the hill.

One

One Year Later
September 1784

Brenna rolled over on her feather tick on the floor near the fireplace, tossing in her sleep.

She could feel the snow falling, tickling her nose. It was so cold out, and yet her cheeks were warm with excitement.

Brenna found herself trudging through the snow. Hurrying. It was late at night, but the moon shone brightly in the sky, the snow reflecting its light. She was going somewhere . . . looking for someone. The wind was frigid. It whipped her hair and her cloak, chilling her to the bone. Yet she hurried on.

Something huge loomed ahead of her on the path. Some kind of structure. A house, or maybe a church. She should have been afraid of the darkness and the unknown, and yet she wasn't.

"Brenna . . ."

She heard her name on the wind. It was a man's voice, rich in timbre and filled with emotion.

"Brenna."

His name was on the tip of her tongue and yet she couldn't say it. . . .

Then she saw him wrapped in a dark cloak, his face masked by the shadows of the woolen hood. He appeared out of nowhere.

"Brenna . . ." he called, taking her into his arms, so strong and warm.

And then he kissed her, his warm lips pressing against her cold mouth. She sighed. It was a kiss a woman waited a lifetime for.

"Brenna. Brenna."

A voice called her name again, but it wasn't the man's voice. It wasn't her lover's. It was Abby's.

"Brenna, wake up! Today's the day. Today you go to the hiring fair."

"Mama, we've been 'round and 'round with this. We've got no choice."

Brenna walked along the dusty road beside her mother. Her brothers and sisters trailed behind, kicking a leather ball. Abby carried baby Ann.

Mildred Abbott shook her head dismally. "I never thought the day would come I'd sell one of my children into slavery."

Her face was etched with the lines of years of childbearing and hard manual labor. Her hair, which had once been bright red, had turned gray prematurely. She looked a decade older than her thirty-eight years.

"Mama, it's not slavery. It's a job. I'll be a servant, not a slave. And I'm not a child. I'm old enough to be wed and have my own babes."

Mildred touched one of Brenna's copper braids, looking into her blue eyes. "You'll always be my child, as long as I live in this world and the next."

Brenna took her mother's hand and brushed it against her own cheek, wondering if her mother had ever once been pretty. Born a parson's daughter, although not educated, Mildred had been brought up in a fine two-story brick house, with plenty of food and clothing. But she'd married a poor peasant farmer out of love, and all she had been able to bring to her children was a sweet singing voice and the proper speech her father had taught her.

Looking into Mildred Abbott's face frightened Brenna. She didn't want to be her mother in fifteen years. She didn't want to feel the desperation she knew her mother felt.

That was why Brenna hadn't married Albert Sooner or Johnny Pine. That was why, when the marriage proposals stopped coming a year or two ago, she'd breathed a sigh of relief. Settling down to marry a peasant farmer and breed his children just wasn't what she wanted. She deserved better. Not that Jack Abbott, Brenna's father, hadn't been a good man, but her mother had deserved an easier life.

Brenna scuffed the toe of her worn shoe against the hard-packed dirt of the road. She knew it was foolishness, idle dreaming, but Brenna wanted something better for herself than this simple village of Werster. She wanted more than had been her mother's lot. She wanted more than a suitable match. She wanted love.

"My service'll most likely be bought by a lord or a lady nearby, Mama. I'll come home every Sunday afternoon." She caught her mother's hand and swung it. "I swear by all that's holy I will."

"Don't swear." Her mother tapped her. "Quick, Brenna, cross yourself and knock the devil off your shoulder. It would be bad luck to carry him to the hiring fair."

Mildred crossed herself superstitiously, and Brenna did the same, not because she shared the same beliefs as her mother, but because she didn't want to quarrel with her. Not today.

Brenna looked up at the trees that hung overhead, the sunlight that poured through the dry, brittle leaves that were falling like rain. The air was cool, the wind brisk. Winter was coming swiftly, and with very little food in the tiny root cellar beneath the only bed in their cottage, Brenna had no choice but to sell herself into servitude. Mildred had no choice but to allow her eldest daughter to do so, and take the money to feed her other children.

"Come, Mama." Brenna tugged on her mother's hand. The children had passed them with their leather ball and were running ahead. "We have to hurry. It's almost noon. It's now or not until spring, and by then it'll be too . . ."

"Too late?" Mildred finished for her, her soft brown eyes sad. "That's what you were going to say."

Brenna smiled, relieved that she was able to do something to help. "But, see, it's *not* too late. Not with the money Mr. Jackard will give you for my services. No one will starve in the Abbott house."

"Daughter, by doing this for me, for your brothers and sisters, you give up any chance of ever wedding. Of ever having your own babies."

Brenna shrugged. "Never met a man I wanted to marry, Mama. You know that. Besides, what if I'm saving myself?" She gave her mother a saucy grin, swishing her skirt in front of her, dancing a quick two-step. "What if I'm saving myself for a lord?"

Mildred laughed, her brown eyes dancing now. "You always were my dreamer, Brenna."

Brenna walked backward in front of her mother so that she could face her, her blue kerchief of meager belongings flung over one shoulder. "Mama, this is going to be a great adventure for me. Truly it is. I'm going to sleep in a fancy house."

"In the attic over a kitchen."

"I'm going to eat fancy foods."

"Scraps from the master's table."

Brenna scowled. "I'm going to see great ladies and lords."

"And scrub their necessaries," Mildred injected.

Brenna dropped her hand on her hip. "And what, pray tell, is the difference between cleaning ours or theirs?" Before her mother could answer, she went on. "Just think, Mama; whoever buys my service has to give me a warm bed, clothes, new shoes." She wiggled the toe that protruded from her left shoe.

Mildred looked up at her daughter, her tired face brightening. "You really want to do this?"

Brenna nodded. "I do. For you. For the little ones. For myself." Then she linked her arm through her mother's and led her into the tiny town square. "Now, come on, Mama, else we're never going to get there."

The hiring fair was in the center of town, though it really wasn't much of a fair at all. Twice a year Mr. Jackard brought an auctioneer into Werster, and the lords and the ladies of the county came to buy their household servants. There were a few booths set up around the hiring block. Women sold bread and sweet cider. Men hawked the tools or leather goods they'd made with their own rough hands. There was a booth of fine fabrics and ribbons and another of raw whiskey, but most of the men and women of Werster couldn't afford such extravagances, so those booths saw little patronage. One year a puppeteer had come, and that had been the talk of the town for weeks after. But the puppeteer had never come again, and the poor folks of Werster were left with nothing but their memories.

The peasants who lived in Werster and worked the nearby fields came to the hiring fair in their Sunday best clothes, their faces scrubbed, their eyes dancing with excitement. They came to visit with friends, to purchase an item or two, but mostly they came out of curiosity. They came to see who, among their neighbors, had the worst crops this year. They came to see who would sell themselves or their children on the block. It was an odd curiosity, especially considering the fact that each man and woman knew that it might be his or her child on that block come next year.

They all led precarious lives here in Werster. Their livelihood depended upon the rain, the price of seed, and the generosity of their benefactor, Lord Bolton. Which, of course, since the fire, had been nearly nonexistent. It was Lady Bolton who had seen to their welfare, and since her death his lordship hadn't cast a glance in their direction.

Brenna walked beside her mother into the town square. Spotting Johnny Pine, she lifted her chin stubbornly. There he was with his new pie-faced wife, the miller's daughter. They'd married on May Day, and already her belly was ripe with his seed. He tipped his hat when he spotted her, a silly grin on his face. Brenna looked away, glad she hadn't married him. Suddenly she was glad she was about to sell herself into the service of another. At least now she would have an opportunity to change her life. Had she married Johnny, there would have been no chance. Her life would already be set on a path she could never change. She'd have been as plump as the miller's daughter by now, and already losing her first teeth.

"Hurry, Mama." Brenna led the way, circling a team of oxen, lifting her skirt to avoid a pile of dung. "Careful, Mama." She headed straight for the center of the town square, where the raised platform stood year-round in anticipation of the hiring fair.

"There he is. Mr. Jackard." Brenna pointed.

With a sigh, Mildred smoothed the bodice of her faded gown and walked straight toward Jackard. "Sir."

Mr. Jackard, a tall, thin man with greasy black hair and tobacco spittle on his chin, turned. Seeing Mildred and Brenna approaching, he broke into a blackened-toothed grin. "Mrs. Abbott, so good to see ye." He peered over her shoulder, hiking up his breeches with one hand. "And what you brought with ye here? The young lady we was talkin' 'bout?"

Mildred bobbed a perfunctory curtsy. "Mr. Jackard, you know my eldest daughter, Brenna."

He wiped his mouth with the back of his dirty hand. "Purty thing for an old maid."

Mildred turned to her daughter. "You don't have to do this."

Brenna sighed, stepping in front of her mother to take over. "I wish to sell my services. As you agreed, the money will go to my mother."

Mr. Jackard looked down at Brenna. "That could be arranged. Payment could be delivered—"

Brenna crossed her arms over her chest. She'd not have Mama cheated. "Today. She gets the money today."

"I got me fees, you know. This arrangin', it's hard work. I got to—"

Brenna looked him straight in the eye, ignoring his sour breath. "You'll get your fee, but my mother will have her coin today, else there'll be no sale. I won't go nowhere with no one if my mama's not paid proper."

"Well, ain't you the high an' mighty one." He lifted a brow but backed down. "All righty." He looked back at Mildred. "We'll see what she brings, and then you'll be paid, Mrs. Abbott. Fair 'nough?"

"Fair enough," Mildred echoed.

"Right this way, then, missy." He put his hand on her sleeve, directing her toward the steps that led up to the platform. "We'll be gettin' started any minute. Ladies and gents don't like to wait, they don't."

"Brenna . . ." Mildred put out her hand to her daughter, looking as if she was going to cry.

"There be time enough for good-byes after the business is done." Mr. Jackard waved a hand as he followed Brenna up the rickety stairs separating mother and daughter. "This way."

On top of the hiring block, Brenna felt conspicuous. Six feet off the ground on the platform, she could see over the heads of the people who milled about. She could see the colored banners tied to the booths. She could see the carts and carriages in which the wealthier fairgoers had arrived. Off to the left, near a gingerbread booth, she spotted her brothers and sisters. Her mother was walking toward them, dabbing at her eyes with the corner of her apron. Brenna clutched her kerchief of belongings to her chest, afraid for the first time.

"Right here. Ye can stand right here, a prime spot."

For the first time Brenna looked at the other men and

women standing on the hiring block for all to see. There was a big man with beefy hands and a wide grin, a boy of no more than seven or eight, an older woman with graying hair and a hunched back. Then there were several young women like herself, ranging in age from fifteen to perhaps twenty-five. Everyone on the block looked fearful, except for the big man, and he looked to be so dimwitted that he didn't understand why he was there.

Mr. Jackard left Brenna standing on the front corner of the platform, near the old woman. "Attention! Attention!" he called over the din of the crowd. Immediately the men and women grew quieter; even the children piped down.

He drew himself up, suddenly full of self-importance. "The biddin' is about to begin, so if ye be looking for a good housemaid or barn hand, draw near." He waved them toward him. "Draw near and see the best hired help in all the county."

The crowd began to move away from the booths and toward the hiring platform. Mr. Jackard turned to the men and women who were about to be sold into indenture. "Let's go with ye. Down the steps to wait yer turn."

Brenna fell into line behind a young girl with wispy blond hair and a scar on one cheek. Behind Brenna was the old woman, who shuffled her feet as she moved along. Mr. Jackard had to help her down the steps.

A portly man in a black coat and a feather cap walked up the steps to the platform. He had to be the auctioneer. Mr. Jackard pushed one of the young women after him.

Brenna barely heard the auctioneer's chattering voice as the first woman was auctioned off as a kitchen maid. Brenna only caught bits of what he said. "Good teeth. Big, steady feet. Not so pretty as to lure men, but not so ugly she has to wear a feed sack over her head."

Brenna fidgeted, wondering what the auctioneer would say about her. *Old maid* kept ringing in her head.

The bids closed on the young girl and she was sent off

the platform on the other side. Brenna tensed as Mr. Jackard scanned the tiny knot of nervous soon-to-be indentured servants. "You." He pointed to the big man. "You go, Albert."

The man lumbered up the steps. The platform swayed as he walked toward the auctioneer. The chatter of the common folk grew softer as the auction began.

The big man brought a hefty price. Two lads went next, then four more young women. Brenna was getting more nervous by the moment. She could feel her palms sweating. Good God, she prayed. *Let's just get this over with and be done with it.*

Then Mr. Jackard was studying the group again. There were only two left, Brenna and the old woman. "You, Mildred's girl."

Brenna touched her breast, stalling for time. "Me?"

Jackard nudged her shoulder. "You. Go on."

Brenna started up the steps before she could give herself the chance to change her mind. She made herself focus on the thought of bread on the supper table and wood in the fireplace of her mother's cottage come this winter. She tried not to think about all the people staring at her, whispering. Clutching her bundle close to her chest, she didn't look at her mother as the auctioneer had her turn around once and then face the crowd.

"Put you arms down," hissed the auctioneer in her ear. "They'll think you're hiding some deformity."

Slowly Brenna lowered her bundle to her side so they could get a good look at her. She stared straight out, over their heads, focusing on a black carriage behind them.

Black carriage. *How odd,* she mused, her thoughts disjointed. *Wasn't that Lord Bolton's carriage?* Brenna hadn't seen it since the fire, but she was almost positive it was his lordship's.

As Brenna stared at the black coach, the auctioneer pitched her attributes. "Pretty enough to serve dining guests, strong enough hands to scrub floors, smart enough to learn new tasks," he chattered.

Brenna felt sick to her stomach.

Someone in the crowd spoke up and the bidding began. A fragile old woman with a middle-aged companion bid for Brenna, but a stocky man in a black coat bid higher.

Brenna's gaze strayed from the black coach. Not Lord Cater, she thought. Everyone in the town knew of Lord Cater. He was a pious man with a string of daughters and no hope of a son in his future. He'd wed and buried four wives and had only recently wed a fifth, this woman twenty years his junior. Lord Cater liked to appear to be a religious man of high moral standards, but everyone in Werster knew he beat his wives and servants, as well as his daughters.

"Not him, please," Brenna prayed under her breath. *Don't give up, keep bidding,* she directed silently to the old woman.

Then the old woman fluttered her hand, signaling to the auctioneer that she had withdrawn. Brenna's gaze met Lord Cater's. She didn't like the way he looked at her with those cold black eyes of his.

"Last bid for the girl in blue . . . going, going—"

"I'll take her," came a voice from somewhere behind the crowd. Immediately everyone turned to look behind them. From Brenna's place on the platform she immediately spotted the man who had spoken. He was climbing out of Lord Bolton's coach!

"You wish to bid higher than Lord Cater?" the auctioneer questioned.

The man slammed the coach door shut before anyone had a chance to see who else was still inside. The crowd immediately broke into a hush of whispers.

The man from the coach cleared his throat, making his way toward the platform. "I'm Mr. Jessop, Lord Bolton's secretary."

Brenna could only stare, her mouth agape, as Mr. Jessop

approached the auctioneer. "And on behalf of my master, I'd like to purchase the services of the redhead."

"Your bid then, sir, is . . . ?" the auctioneer asked.

Mr. Jessop waved his hand. "Lord Bolton is not interested in bidding. He'll take the young woman with the red hair for twice what Lord Cater offered."

Exclamations of surprise rippled through the crowd.

"Is that acceptable to whomever is running this sale? If not," he started to turn way, "Lord Bolton will take his business elsewhere."

Mr. Jackard came stumbling up the platform steps. "It . . . it is accep . . . acceptable, sir."

"But I won the bid," protested Lord Cater, waving his gold-tipped cane. "I took the bid. The chit is mine."

Mr. Jessop turned on his heel to address Lord Cater. "Would you care, sir, to step into the coach and discuss the matter with Lord Bolton?"

Everyone immediately turned to look at the carriage, in awe of the implication that the mysterious earl was inside.

"N . . . no, that . . . that's well enough. I . . ." Lord Cater waved his cane. "I didn't really need another kitchen girl this fall anyway."

"Excellent." Mr. Jessop turned to face the platform again. "Come, girl."

Brenna held her breath, realizing the secretary was speaking to her. "Me?" Her own voice sounded odd in her ears.

"Yes, you. Come, come." He signaled for her to walk to the edge of the platform so that he could help her down. "No one keeps Lord Bolton waiting."

Brenna hurried to the edge of the platform. With the aid of the secretary, she jumped down. The crowd parted, and before she knew what was happening she was walking toward the foreboding black coach.

Brenna glanced over her shoulder, looking for Mildred. "I . . . I didn't get . . . get a chance to say good-bye to my mother."

"If his lordship loses his temper, we'll both pay; now hurry," Mr. Jessop said, ignoring her protests.

Brenna looked hurriedly over her shoulder once more. They had almost reached the coach. She caught a glimpse of her mother, and when Brenna saw how concerned she was Brenna forced herself to smile. "I'm all right," she mouthed. "I love you. See you Sunday."

The black coach door swung open and Brenna was pushed into darkness.

Two

It took a moment for Brenna's eyes to adjust to the darkness. She dropped onto the leather bench across from a tall cloaked figure. *Lord Bolton?* Fear trickled through her veins.

Inside, it smelled of oiled leather and of *him*. It was a pleasant masculine smell, of pine, shaving soap, and good wool. The coach door slammed shut and she gave a start. She was alone with Lord Bolton and his secretary. She felt the coach lurch forward and roll out of the village square.

Brenna clutched her kerchief of belongings to her breasts, staring straight ahead into the darkness. The window shades had been rolled down so that only the barest pinpricks of light filtered in.

"I didn't get to say goodbye to my mother," she said softly.

"What?" the cloaked figure bellowed. Lord Bolton, for surely it was he, turned to Mr. Jessop seated beside him. "Tell her she's not to speak unless asked a direct question. I want no prattling women in my household." He brought his hand down swiftly on the seat, leather slapping leather. It was a monstrous hand, covered by a black glove. "I won't tolerate it."

Mr. Jessop spoke calmly. "Lord Bolton says—"

"I didn't get to say goodbye to my mother," Brenna repeated a little louder, speaking directly to *him*. "I was told I would have time to say goodbye." She was staring at him now, trying to see his face. She couldn't.

"I'm a busy man," Lord Bolton grumbled. "I haven't time

to wait on fond farewells." He waved one hand impatiently. "You have been hired as a companion to my son."

Son? What son? Brenna wondered. *Hadn't his lordship's children died in the fire?* Everything was happening so quickly, she couldn't think clearly. She pressed her fingers to her temple. Never in her wildest dreams had she thought Lord Bolton would purchase her indenture. She looked up. "I was offered as a kitchen maid, my lord. I haven't any experience—"

"You speak well for a peasant."

"My mother's father was a parson. Mama saw fit to teach all of her children proper—"

"Silence!"

He shouted so loudly that Brenna leaned back, cowering against the smooth leather seat. The man . . . his voice was so imposing that it seemed to take up every bit of space in the coach until Brenna thought there might be none left for her.

She gritted her teeth. She was afraid, but she could feel her anger building . . . burning.

She heard him draw in his breath, as if he was giving himself a moment to calm his temper. "My son is lonely. You spoke of family. Surely you have brothers and sisters?"

"Aye," she said softly.

He lifted one great shoulder. In the black cloak he was a massive man, with shoulders like a drover's. "Then you have experience. Play with him, teach him a game or two. Sing, dance, bloody hell, I don't care what you do. Make him laugh." He looked away. There was a bitterness in his voice that Brenna could taste on her own tongue. "God knows the boy needs to laugh."

Brenna scooted forward on the seat a little. "How . . . how old is he, your son?"

Lord Bolton whipped his head around. "Didn't I say you were not to speak unless asked a direct question?"

"How am I supposed to do my job if I know nothing of the boy?" Brenna snapped back. Then her eyes grew wide with shock at the realization of what she'd done. She didn't know what had gotten into her. She slid back on the seat again, covering her mouth for fear something else would come out.

It was just that he didn't have a right to shout at her like that. What had she done wrong to displease him that he had a right to bellow like a bull?

He deliberated again. "He's eight," he answered finally, his patience obviously stretched.

"His name is Alexander," Mr. Jessop offered, seeming to know what Brenna's next question would be, whether she was spoken to directly or not.

She nodded. "Care for the boy? I can do that. I can be a companion." She hesitated. "I'm willing to do light house-keeping as well." Her gaze darted from the silhouette that was Mr. Jessop to the giant silhouette of her employer . . . her master. "I assume I'll have Sunday afternoons off to visit with my family?"

"You assume incorrectly!"

This time he snapped at her so harshly that, against her will, tears sprang to her eyes.

"No one leaves Bolton Castle." Then he banged on the coach roof. "Driver, let me off here," he boomed. "I'll walk the rest of the way." He stood, holding on to the leather strap as the coach rocked to a halt. "Jessop, show her to her room. You know the drill. I don't want to be disturbed again to-night."

"Yes, my lord."

The door opened and blinding light poured in. His lordship was so quick that Brenna caught only a glimpse of the back of his dark head and the swish of his wool cloak. Suddenly he was gone, the door slammed shut, and it was dark again.

Brenna leaned back against the seat as the vehicle rolled on again. "Guess I didn't make such a good impression on him, huh?" she asked the secretary.

He grabbed the hanging leather strap to steady himself as

the coach was jolted to and fro. "Oh, I don't know, miss."
She could hear the smile in his voice. "I think he likes you
just fine."

Brenna sat on the edge of the massive bed covered by a
white counterpane, afraid to move for fear she would muss
something. She stared at the huge bedchamber made warm
by the great fire in the fireplace and filled with the light of
candles. If only Abby was here to see this. . . .

Brenna stared at the flower-papered walls, at the polished
redwood furniture, at the heavy brocaded burgundy drapes
that covered the windows floor to ceiling, blocking out the
chill of the wind. It was beautiful. And yet at the same time
it was a little frightening.

Yesterday afternoon she'd been escorted to this bedchamber
by Mr. Jessop. At first she had thought she was to wait for
the young Alexander. But when the hours stretched into evening and a male servant brought her a supper tray, he explained that the room was hers. Lord Bolton had ordered it
so. If there was anything she wanted or needed, she was to
come find him in the kitchen. His name was Patsy.

When Brenna asked about the little boy Patsy could tell
her nothing. He didn't know when she could see him. It was
up to Lord Bolton's whim, he explained. As was everything
else in the household, it appeared. . . .

Brenna got up from the bed, smoothing a wrinkle in the
embroidered counterpane. She still couldn't believe this room
was hers. She walked to the fireplace and ran her finger along
the polished mantel. Why, this bedchamber was bigger than
the whole cottage she had shared with her mother and five
brothers and sisters. She had never seen such opulence, never
dreamed such furniture, such bed linens, existed.

Brenna turned her back to the fireplace and lifted her
shabby skirts to warm herself. It had grown cold outside, and
the wind howled. Somewhere a case clock chimed three.

Brenna's mother didn't have a clock, but Mrs. Murphy did, and Brenna had sat in the old woman's cottage many an afternoon watching, waiting to hear it chime.

Brenna dropped her skirts. She was bored. She missed her mother and brothers and sisters. She wanted to see her charge. She wanted to do something, anything. She wandered to the door that was as wide as she was tall. She rested her hand on the polished knob. Patsy hadn't said she had to stay in the room. As far as she knew, Lord Bolton had given no such instructions.

She was just about to turn the knob when she heard footsteps outside in the hallway. She backed away from the door. Someone knocked.

"Y . . . yes?"

"It's Patsy, miss."

"C . . . come in." She tucked her hands behind her back, feeling guilty, though why, she didn't know.

Patsy walked in carrying a tray on one arm, a gown draped over the other. "Brought ye tea."

"Tea?" Brenna peeked over the young man's shoulder as he lifted the white napkin from the tray to reveal a teapot, a porcelain cup, and a plate of sweets. Her mouth watered. "Oh," was all she managed.

"And this." He walked across the bedchamber to lay the gown on the bed. "Himself says to make a list of what else you need." His cheeks pinked. "Lady things, and Mr. Jessop will see to them."

Brenna abandoned the tray of cakes and biscuits for the beauty of the gown. *"Himself?"*

"His lordship." Patsy stepped back from the bed. He was dressed impeccably in black and green livery. "Lord Bolton."

In awe, Brenna lifted the hem of the blue and green floral day gown. Its lines were simple, but the fabric was exquisite. Even her untrained eye could see that. She looked up at Patsy. "Lord Bolton wants me to have this gown?" She was caught between the excitement of the idea of putting on such a gown, and the self-consciousness of realizing what she was wearing. Her own dress had seen better days.

"Aye. So he told Mr. Jessop, who told me."

Gingerly, she lifted the dress to hold it up against her. Patsy was retreating to the door. "But where did it come from, Patsy?" *Was it his wife's?* she wondered.

"Don't know." He opened the door. "Even if I did, I wouldn't say. *Himself* don't like prattle. 'E pays me good to keep my mouth shut, and so I do." He nodded. "Ye need anything else, you just pull that rope." He pointed to the cord that ran along the wall behind the bed.

Still holding the beautiful gown up against her, Brenna watched Patsy go. She was so lonely that she would use any excuse to keep him from leaving. "Patsy?"

He stopped in the doorway, now impatient with her. "Miss?"

"I still haven't seen my charge. I've been here a day and I haven't seen Alexander, or . . . or even heard him. Where is he? Why hasn't he come to me? Why haven't I been sent—"

"Told you, miss. It isn't up to me. It's up to *himself.* You'll see the boy when *he* says so. Not before." He closed the door behind him, ending the conversation.

"So I'm supposed to put on this beautiful gown, drink my tea alone, and wait?" She turned to an oval, full-length mirror that rested on the floor near a clothespress. "Is that what I'm supposed to do?" she asked her reflection. Then she scrambled to disrobe, anxious to try on the gown.

It fit nearly perfectly. It was just a little wide in the hips and perhaps an inch or so too short. So Brenna sat in the beautiful gown alone and drank her tea and ate her cakes. And when supper was served that evening she sat alone again in the gown and ate. All through the meal she kept hoping she would be summoned by Lord Bolton. After all, why had he sent the gown if he didn't intend to see her tonight? But finally, when the case clock somewhere beyond her room chimed ten o'clock, she took off the gown and climbed into the warm feather bed.

In the morning Brenna dressed in the gown again and waited patiently for Patsy to bring her a breakfast tray. She stared at her shabby shoes under the hem of the gown. "Patsy?"

"Miss?" He served her a plate of coddled eggs, sliced beef, fresh raisin bread, and porridge.

"Am I a prisoner here? In this room, I mean?"

He tucked the empty tray under his arm, thinking for a moment. "Not as I been tole."

"Good." She smiled, taking a bite of the bread. "Thank you, Patsy."

Looking slightly befuddled, Patsy took his leave. But then he stopped in the doorway. "If you have a mind to look around, there's just one place you don't go. None of us. Not even Mr. Jessop, unless he's called."

She looked up. "Oh? And where is that?"

"The south wing. 'E said 'e'd rip off our arms and beat us with the bloody stumps ifin 'e catches us there." He blew the blond cowlick on his forehead back. "So we don't go there."

Brenna frowned. "But I thought the entire wing had been burned out in the fire."

"Not all of it. There's still a hallway. Part of a room, and his laboratory in the tower."

"Thank you."

Patsy left, and Brenna finished her meal. Then she ventured to the door. She couldn't stand being in this room another minute. She wasn't used to idleness, and it was doing nothing but making her more uneasy. If Alexander wouldn't come to her, perhaps she could go to him. Perhaps his hideously scarred father cared nothing for the boy. Perhaps the man was so traumatized by his family's death and his own injury that he left the boy alone to his own devices, just as he had left her.

In the hallway Brenna looked left and right before she closed the door softly behind her. Her old shoes made a clacking sound on the polished floor as she made her way to the winding staircase. At the top she gripped the banister, looking down the spiral. The staircase was so wide that two coaches could have made their way up, side by side, and not touched at the axles.

Down the stairs she went and into the central hallway. This was the way she had entered two days ago. Mr. Jessop had brought her in the front door, through the hallway, and right up the stairs to her chamber. She'd not seen him since.

Brenna turned left, walking through a parlor of some sort, its furniture draped with ghostly covers. The house seemed to stretch on forever, room after room. They were all unused, apparently unoccupied for many years. It was eerie passing through the rooms with portraits draped, spinets covered, windows tightly shuttered. But by the time she reached the library Brenna walked with confidence. There was nothing to be afraid of here, she told herself. It was just an empty—or nearly empty—house left neglected by a wounded man.

In the library she studied the books with envy. Her grandfather, the parson, had had only a Bible. There were so many books, hundreds she guessed. This was the one room that was obviously used. The shelves were polished, the books in neat order. A candle had recently burned in a wall sconce. Brenna moved on. There was a music room, a glass sunroom, a ballroom with its chandeliers covered, its black-and-white-tiled floor left dusty. *It's been a long time since anyone has danced here,* she mused sadly.

Brenna left the ballroom. She was looking for sleeping quarters; a nursery or something. Where did Lord Bolton keep this child that no one heard or saw him?

Brenna entered a dark hallway and caught the scent of burnt wood. It was an old smell, as if the fire had been put out a long time ago. She guessed she must be nearing the southern wing. She knew she ought to turn back, but her curiosity got the better of her. *Just a little farther,* she told herself. After all, what if the boy was here? Alone?

Brenna came upon an arched doorway partially boarded up. The smell of charred wood was strong. This had to be the southern wing. It gave her the spooks. She glanced over her shoulder. She had to have been wandering around Bolton Castle for more than two hours and she'd not seen a soul.

She picked up the skirt of the gown Lord Bolton had lent her and stepped over a board, into the dark hallway. "Alexander?" she whispered. "Are you here?"

A breeze so strong that it blew her hair, gusted through the hall. She hugged herself for warmth, knowing she should turn back.

"What are you doing here?"

Lord Bolton appeared so unexpectedly, out of nowhere, that Brenna nearly jumped out of her skin. She turned around to face him. He'd come up behind her from the direction in which she'd just come.

"I said what are you doing here?" he shouted. "Get out! Didn't Jessop tell you this place is forbidden?" His voice reverberated off the stone walls and charred timber.

She cringed, still hugging herself. "I . . ." She took a deep breath. "I was looking for your son, my lord."

"Get out," he repeated, coming closer.

Brenna slowly edged her way around him. In the darkness she could only make out the outline of his body, his cloak. The hood was pulled up so that she couldn't see his face. The poor man. She felt a surge of tenderness. How hideous were his burns that he couldn't even show his face to his servants?

"I'm sorry," she whispered, hedging toward the doorway from which she'd come. "I only wanted to see the boy. I . . . I'm lonely up there all by myself. I'm used to my family, my mother, my brothers and sisters. I thought I could—"

"I said I would send for you when I wanted you!"

"I don't understand. You bought my indenture so that I

could be a companion to your son. Then I don't see your son."

He watched as she backed through the doorway, stepping over the wood planks. "He doesn't want to see you! It's his choice."

"An eight-year-old, alone, without a mother, makes such choices in your household, my lord?"

Responding with something that sounded much to Brenna like a growl, his lordship stomped off into the cold darkness of the burned-out southern wing.

Brenna stood there for a moment, now thoroughly confused. "Well," she huffed, calling after him, "if you don't need me, or want me, then why not just send me home?" She turned to go, frustrated nearly to tears. She didn't know whether his lordship had heard her insolence or not. But she felt better just the same.

Hours later, Brenna stood in her bedchamber staring out her window. She was lonely and miserable. It was dusk and a storm was brewing. She could hear the patter of rain on the slate roof and feel the force of the wind as it grew in strength, battering the glass panes.

A knock came at the door and she turned anxiously. It was too early for supper. If there was one thing she had learned about Bolton Castle, it was that Patsy kept a tight schedule. "Yes?"

"Patsy, miss."

"Come in."

Patsy stuck his head in the door. *"Himself* requests your presence in the dining room. Eight o'clock. On the chime."

Brenna felt a surge of excitement. For all his lordship's bellowing, had he given thought to her words? "Will Alexander be there?"

"Don't know."

She was immediately suspicious. "Because if he won't be there, I won't come to supper."

"All I know is *himself* has called. If ye know what's good fer ye, you'll do as yer told."

Before Brenna could answer he was gone.

"Supper?" Brenna said to herself in the mirror. "What an odd way to treat an indentured servant."

For the next two hours Brenna fidgeted in her room. She brushed her hair and piled it up on her head. She pulled it down and brushed it over her shoulders. She had no choice in what to wear—it was her old gown or the new blue and green floral one his lordship had sent—but she could decide for herself how to fix her hair. She wanted to look nice for her charge. Brenna experimented with several elaborate coiffures, but finally decided to just wear her hair down her back with one plait twisted around her head like a crown.

Brenna waited hesitantly by her door for the case clock down the hall to chime eight, and when it did she stepped out of her chamber. She was shaking inside with fear and excitement, but she walked casually, refusing to let Lord Bolton know he intimidated her.

Patsy met Brenna at the bottom of the long staircase. "This way, miss."

She followed him to the right, down a section of hallway she hadn't explored earlier that day. He halted at a paneled door that slid into the wall. He stepped back and opened the door for her.

She could see the long dining table set for three on the far end. Candles burned in a massive crystal chandelier overhead and a fire crackled in a fireplace to her right, just out of view. But she couldn't see *him.*

Brenna straightened her back and clasped her hands. She prepared herself for the sight of his lordship, promising herself that no matter how hideous his scars were, she would not react. She glanced at Patsy nervously. "Aren't you coming with me?" she whispered.

"I'm a servant, miss." Patsy fluttered his lashes with reproach. "I serve; I don't dine with 'is lordship."

Brenna still hesitated in the doorway. "Where . . . where is he?" she whispered.

"Inside."

The moment she stepped through the doorway, the door ominously slid shut behind her. Brenna took a deep breath. He stood in front of the fireplace, his back to her.

Brenna dropped one hand to the upholstered dining chair in front of her. Lord Bolton was wearing no cloak this time. There were no shadows in the room in which to hide. She bit down on her lower lip in readiness to see his hideous face.

"Ah, you're here." Lord Bolton turned.

Brenna's breath caught in her throat. She knew she must have gasped.

Lord Bolton was the most handsome man she had ever laid eyes on. . . .

Three

Lord Bolton stared back at her. "What were you expecting?" His tone was dry, sarcastic. "A beast, no doubt?"

She took a step back. Her cheeks felt flushed. Nothing here at Bolton Castle was what she thought it would be. Why would the earl conceal his face with scarves and cloaks and shadows when he had nothing to hide?

Lord Bolton was indeed attractive, with broad cheekbones and a graceful, aquiline nose. His mouth was full, sensual. His hair was as black as a raven's wing, hanging shiny and thick at his shoulders. His eyes were so gray they were almost silver. In his eyes, at a glance, she saw sadness.

She finally came to her senses enough to curtsy. "My lord."

He had a glass of blood red wine in his hand. He lifted it casually. "And this is my son, Alexander."

Brenna hadn't even noticed the boy in the room, she'd been so shocked by Lord Bolton's unscarred face.

When her gaze met Alexander's she didn't know what kept her from making a sound. She didn't know how she controlled her facial features, how she kept the smile on her face.

It was Alexander. It was the child who had been scarred by the fire. An entire side of his face was ridged with ugly ripples of hardened skin. He had his father's hair. His father's frown. His father's eyes, and in those gray eyes she saw the same pain she saw in Lord Bolton's.

"Good even', Alexander." She walked toward him, offering her hand. "I'm so glad we could finally meet."

The boy turned the unscarred side of his mouth up in a sneer. "I don't want you here. I don't need a companion." With that, he trounced off toward the opposite end of the dining room.

Brenna looked up at Lord Bolton. He was watching her, waiting to see how she would handle his son. She could see it in those gray eyes.

"Well, I'm sorry you feel that way," she said, following Alexander. "Because I was hoping we could be friends."

"I don't need any friends." The boy dropped into a chair that was taller than he was. "I told Papa I didn't need a friend."

Brenna walked slowly to the chair opposite the boy, leaving the head of the table for his lordship. "Don't need a friend? Well, everyone needs a friend." She kept her tone light and was careful to look directly at him. Her heart ached for his physical wounds, but she didn't want him to think she was repulsed in any way. "I can tell you, I'm sore in need of one now."

"Well, I'm not." He dropped his chin into his hand to sulk. "And even if I did want a friend, it wouldn't be you."

"You don't need a friend to play hide and seek?"

He cut his eyes at her.

She almost smiled. "And what of ball? You don't need a friend to toss a ball?"

He lifted one shoulder in a shrug. He was dressed as elegantly as his father in a matching sapphire blue coat and breeches.

The boy thought on the matter for a moment. "I don't know. I don't care."

Brenna could feel his lordship watching her. It made her giddy inside. She knew this was her chance with Alexander. Perhaps her only chance. "And what of a friend to teach you this?" She picked up three apples from a polished silver bowl on the dining table and tossed one after the other into the air, juggling them as her father had taught her.

Alexander sat up with sudden interest. "Wow-ee! You could teach me that?"

Brenna shrugged one shoulder, imitating the boy. "Sure. Easy enough. Toss me another."

Alexander snatched an apple out of the bowl and threw it to her, purposely, just a little too far to her right.

She had to jump to catch it, but she managed. Then she was juggling all four apples, tapping her foot to keep the rhythm.

"Wow-ee! See that, Papa?" He looked at his father. "Where'd you get her? A fair?"

Lord Bolton did not smile as he came to the table. "I see your talents are many, Miss Abbott." He lifted his linen napkin from his plate. "The auctioneer did not do you justice."

Brenna caught the apples one at a time and deposited them into the bowl. Knowing when she was being chastised, she slipped into her chair obediently.

His lordship began serving them bowls of soup from a fancy blue and yellow tureen.

"I . . . 'Twas only an amusement for the boy." She twisted her hands in her skirt beneath the table. "I did as much for my brothers and sisters."

Lord Bolton lifted a haughty eyebrow as he passed her a bowl of some kind of white soup. "No doubt."

Brenna lowered her gaze to her bowl.

His lordship handed his son a bowl of soup. "Alexander, say the grace for us."

The boy looked straight at Brenna. "I don't wanna."

"Alexander."

"Make her." He pointed. "She's the servant. She's my servant, so I can make her do what I want. Say grace, wench!"

Brenna kept her gaze down, waiting for his lordship's explosion, for surely he would not allow his son to speak so rudely. Even in Brenna's meager home, no one would have dared refuse to speak the grace at their father's suggestion.

But instead his lordship merely folded his hands and began grace on his own. Brenna clasped her hands and closed her eyes tightly.

While his lordship thanked the good Lord for the meal, Alexander slurped his soup loudly.

When Brenna whispered "Amen" after his lordship, she opened her eyes to see Alexander drinking his soup directly from his bowl.

Lord Bolton picked up a big spoon next to his plate. Brenna imitated him.

After the first mouthful Lord Bolton retrieved a small, red leather-bound book from his coat and began to read as he ate his soup. Apparently there was no supper talk here at Bolton Castle.

Brenna tasted the soup to find it creamy and delicate. It had potato and cheese and some herb she didn't recognize. She finished the bowl, as did his lordship and the boy.

Next Lord Bolton lifted the lid of another elaborately painted china dish and doled himself a portion. "I prefer to have as few servants as possible, so we serve ourselves our meals, Miss Abbott." He looked at her with that mocking frown again. "Shocking, is it not?"

She wasn't certain what he wanted her to say. It was hard for her to look at his handsome face and sound even half intelligent. "Obviously we had no servants in my home," she said softly. "My mother always served my father. I know no other way but to serve myself."

He slid the large china serving dish toward her. Following his lead, she took a slice of roasted pork, some tiny red-skinned potatoes, and a spoon of peas with leeks. Then she slid the bowl across the table to Alexander and accepted the plate of freshly baked rye biscuits his lordship pushed toward her.

Brenna was just lifting her fork when she saw the boy

reach into the serving dish with his hand and come up with a potato. He dropped it onto his china plate and dug with his hand for another morsel.

Brenna knew her eyes must have widened. Brenna had no education, no training of elegant manners, but she knew that even in the humble cottages down the hill Alexander's conduct would have been considered unacceptable. The fact that he was a lord's son only made his behavior more appalling.

His lordship said nothing, but went on reading his book. With an audible sigh, Brenna returned her attention to her meal. After all, in his father's presence, surely the boy's table manners were not her responsibility. As far as she could tell, this was normal behavior, the child eating with his hands, the father ignoring him, his nose in a book.

Brenna was not halfway through her meal when Alexander jumped up from his chair. "Done." He wiped his mouth on his sleeve. "Come on. Show me again. I want to juggle."

Brenna laid down her fork, glancing at his lordship who, like her, was still eating. "As soon as I'm done, I could—"

"Now." He thrust out his upper lip. It was odd, but it was now the boy's frowns that she noticed and not the burn scars.

He pointed to the fruit. "I want you to show me how to do that *now*. In my chambers."

She glanced at Lord Bolton. He either didn't hear his son or had no comment.

"I . . . I can do that." She touched her plate. "As soon as I'm done."

He crossed his arms over his chest. "Are you deaf or addlepated? I said now. I'm done; you're done."

Brenna looked down at her plate. She took a breath. She had been hired as a companion to the boy. It was her duty, Mr. Jessop had explained, to be his companion, to keep him company. It was not her duty, she decided, to encourage his rudeness and lack of regard for others.

"When I'm done, Alexander, I'll be happy to teach you how to juggle." She spoke softly but firmly.

The boy looked at his father, but Lord Bolton went on reading.

"Fine," Alexander shouted. "Then just forget it. I didn't want to learn how to juggle bloody fruit anyway!" He kicked his chair with such force that it tipped over, and then he stomped toward the door.

Brenna was astonished. She had half a mind to jump up and lead the boy back to his chair by his ear. But not knowing her position in the household, she simply picked up her fork and went back to her meal.

Alexander left the room, leaving Brenna and his lordship alone.

Brenna ate another bite or two, but the food that had tasted so good only moments before was now as dry as an old biscuit in her mouth. She glanced at Lord Bolton, who was still lost in his book.

God's teeth, he was a comely man. Such perfect teeth. Eyes a woman could lose herself in. And smart. She could tell by the way he spoke.

So why was a man like himself allowing his son to be such a wretched brat? Was that why he had brought her to Bolton Castle? Not to be a companion, as Mr. Jessop had said, but to teach the boy how to be a pleasant young man? Should she just ask him?

At that moment Lord Bolton glanced up. "If you're done you're welcome to go. You're a servant, but I have no intentions of ordering you about. Come and go as you please as long as you remain on the grounds."

"I cannot see my family?" she inquired.

"You cannot. See to my son. Come for meals. I ask nothing more." He returned his attention to his book, her dismissal obvious.

Brenna wiped her mouth with her napkin and placed it beside her plate. She couldn't believe he wouldn't allow her to visit with her mother. "My lord, I . . . I'd sorely like to see my family. If it's Alexander that's the problem, I could take him with me on Sunday afternoons. He . . . he could play with my brothers."

Lord Bolton looked at her over the top of his book. "Alexander in the village? Impossible." He looked down at the pages again. "Good night, Miss Abbott."

She slid out of her chair, dejected but not wanting to seem so. "Good night, my lord." Without another word she left the dining room and retired to her bedchamber for the night.

"It's got to get better," she said to herself as she undressed for bed. She was so unhappy that she was near to tears. She missed her mother and family, but she was unhappy about Alexander, too. The boy needed her. Needed someone. "There's got to be a way to reach him," she murmured to the empty room.

Exhausted, she climbed into bed. Surely there was something she could do for him. Perhaps he only needed some attention and his behavior would be more acceptable. He couldn't be happy, she reasoned. No one who behaved in such an ugly fashion could be happy with him or her self.

Brenna blew out the candle beside her bed and pulled the counterpane to her chin. She could hear the autumn wind howling about the window shutters, but here inside Bolton Castle she was warm and cozy. A fire crackled on the hearth.

Tomorrow was another day. Tomorrow she would find the boy and begin her work.

But as Brenna drifted off to sleep it was not Alexander she thought of. It was his father . . .

Brenna sat on the last step of the grand staircase beside her pouting charge. "You don't want to play ball? You said it was fun yesterday."

"Well, it's not today."

"And you don't want to draw pictures with ink and paper."

"Nope."

"And you don't want to play 'hide the thimble'?"

Alexander stuck out his lower lip. "Nope."

"Then what is it you want to do?" Brenna could hear the impatience in her voice as it echoed in the empty hall.

Just then, Patsy arrived, carrying a silver tray with a cup of steaming chocolate on it. "Your chocolate, sir."

Alexander wrinkled his nose. "You took too long. Take it away." He rose off the step, giving a flip of his hand. "I want lemonade now."

"Sir, we have no—"

"Did you hear what I said!" Alexander shouted, stomping his foot. "I want lemonade and you have to get it for me. You work for me." He pointed. "You do what I say or my father will put you out on your ear, and then how will you feed that crippled, ugly mother of yours, hmm?"

Patsy lowered his gaze. "Yes, my lord."

Brenna watched the manservant back out of the hall. At least a dozen times in the last week she'd seen this scenario played out and she'd had just about enough. To this point she'd held her tongue—after all, she too was a servant—but enough was enough.

This situation was simply not going to work. Brenna couldn't be the boy's companion. He wanted no companion, he wanted someone else to shout at. There was nothing for the child to do to keep himself occupied. Despite the tower of toys in his bedchamber he wandered about the castle aimlessly. He had apparently had none of the education a boy of his breeding would normally have had. From Brenna's observation the child had simply been left to run wild, mostly ignored.

"Alexander." She rose off the step, using the same tone of voice she used with her brothers and sisters when they'd been naughty.

Alexander spun around, belligerent. "What?"

"You have no right to treat another human being thusly."

"He's not a human being; he's a servant. A poor peasant."

"And you are a rude, spoiled little boy who needs to apologize."

Alexander screwed up his face. "I'll tell Papa what you're saying and he'll sell your indenture. He'll . . . he'll sell you to . . . to . . . to the whorehouse in London," the child sputtered.

"You want to tell your father? Excellent idea." She grasped him by the arm. "Come, let's do it together."

"Wh . . . what? Let go of my arm. Let go! Where are you taking me?"

Brenna half led, half carried the boy down the hallway, headed directly for the south wing. "We're going to tell your father what you said to Patsy. How rude you were to him. How rude you are to me."

"My father doesn't care!" Alexander ripped his arm from Brenna's grasp. "He doesn't care!" he shouted, his voice wavering. "He doesn't care about me at all," he finished softly.

Then Brenna saw the tears and she felt her heart wrench within her breast. There Alexander stood before her, his shoulders hunched, tears running down his face.

"Oh, Alexander," she said softly. And for the first time he let her reach out and take him in her arms. "That's not true."

"It is true. He doesn't care." The boy sniffed. "All he does is sit in his laboratory. He doesn't want to play with me. He doesn't want to read to me." His tears dampened her shoulder as he held tightly to her. "He hates me."

"He doesn't hate you." She crouched so that she was at eye level with him and took her handkerchief to gently wipe away his tears. "How can you say that? Your father loves you." She smoothed his dark hair. "He sent for me because he thought he needed help taking care of you."

Alexander only shook his head, clinging to her. It was obvious he craved physical attention. It was obvious he did need her. The boy just didn't know how to communicate it.

"Oh, Alexander," she whispered

Slowly his tears subsided, and then, sniffing, he stepped

back, away from her. "I'm sorry," he said softly. "I don't mean to be bad. It just happens."

She smiled. "I know you don't. Now I want you to do me a favor."

He wiped his eyes with his cranberry-colored coat sleeve. "What's that?"

"I want you to go to the kitchen and apologize to Patsy and then I want you to make us tea."

"Patsy makes tea."

"I know. But I want you to do it. You make the tea. You set the tray and you bring it to the library. We'll take it there where we can look out the window to the gardens."

"All right." He scuffed his feet as he walked away from her, calling over his shoulder, "Just this one time. But don't think I'm gonna serve you all the time." He pointed. "Because remember, Papa hired you to take care of me, not t'other way around."

She smiled. "All right."

He turned back. "So, where're you going?"

"To see your father," she answered firmly.

Brenna drew her wrap closer and knocked on the door to the laboratory again. Wind blew through the crumbled walls of the long southern hallway, blowing her hair.

"Go away," came a gruff voice from the other side of the door.

"So you do hear me," she said softly to herself. She knocked again.

"I said, go away, Jessop!" Lord Bolton bellowed.

Brenna took a deep breath, thinking over her choices. She'd been here a full week and since the first time she'd met Alexander this had been coming. There was no need for her to delay the matter any longer. She had to speak to his lordship about Alexander.

"Sir?"

"I said, leave me!"

So Brenna opened the door. "My lord?"

Lord Bolton was seated high on a stool, bottle and glass beakers in disorder around him. Some contraption on a table on the far side of the room bubbled and hissed, steam rising from its coils. The laboratory smelled heavily of sulfur, of burning cherry wood in the fireplace, and of him.

"You're not Jessop!"

"No, sir."

"What is the meaning of this?" Lord Bolton came down off his stool. He was without his coat, dressed simply in a black woolen shirt and black breeches, his hair tied back in a neat queue with a bit of leather. "Why have you come? You were told you must never come here!"

"I . . ." She drew up her courage. "I came to speak with you, my lord."

"You can speak to me at supper!" He turned away, shooing her with his hand. "Get out."

"No."

He whipped around. "What did you say to me?"

She looked him straight in the eyes. The same eyes that now haunted her dreams. "I said, no, my lord. I must speak with you privately. Without Alexander."

He crossed his arms, resting them on his broad chest. "What about him?" he questioned gruffly.

Brenna took a step closer.

"That's far enough," he barked. "I'll have no woman ruining years' worth of research."

Brenna stopped where she was, glancing at the stone floor, trying to slow her pounding heart.

"Yes? Well, what is it?" he barked. "You barged in on me, now tell me what it is you have to say that is of such urgency."

She lifted her gaze. "Your son is bored."

"That's why I brought you here."

"He has nothing to do all day. No friends. Nothing to

occupy his mind. That's why he's so rude and uncontrollable at times." She paused, waiting for him to deny the facts. He didn't.

"So what do you propose, Miss Abbott? What is the magic solution to a deformed boy's happiness? More juggling?"

"You cannot allow him to run like a wild boy because he has a few scars," she snapped.

"A few scars? *A few scars?* Do you know the pain that child went through? What it's like to hear a baby that has been burned cry?"

She set her jaw, determined to see this through. "I have no doubt you both have suffered, but that does not mean the child should be allowed to run without direction. He needs to be educated. A boy of his birthing should know about music, about art, about . . . about things . . ."

He shrugged, precisely the same way Alexander did. "All right. You're so clever, you know better than I. You teach him."

Brenna lowered her gaze, uncertain of what to say. Was this some sort of trap? He had hired a village girl. Surely he didn't expect her to know how to read. In Werster there was no need for a woman to read. No need for her to waste her time with skills that would be of no use to her or her husband. "I cannot teach him, my lord," she answered him quietly. "I cannot even read myself."

There was a long moment of silence. "I will think on the matter," he finally said. This time his tone had a gentleness she'd not thought him capable of.

"Thank you, sir," she said softly, with a curtsy. Then their gazes met and for some silly reason she felt a smile turn up her lips. He didn't smile back, but there was a warmth in his gaze that made her skin tingle, her heart pound Then before she angered him again, she hastened from the laboratory.

Four

Brenna sat on a chair in the warm sunshine that poured through her bedchamber window. She was darning one of Alexander's stockings. The boy lay on her bed, belly down, playing with a loop of yarn she'd knotted for him.

As the days passed she and Alexander were finding each other's company more enjoyable. It wasn't to say that the boy didn't have his moments. He could still be stubborn and belligerent, but she was becoming very attached to him. And were he to admit it, she guessed he felt the same way about her.

Having Alexander kept Brenna's mind off her loneliness and how much she missed her family. A few days ago at the dining table Brenna had tried to bring up the matter of visiting her family again, but his lordship had refused to even discuss it. He said he had paid for her indenture; therefore she was his to do with as he saw fit. His final word was that she would not leave the castle for any reason.

Yesterday when Patsy had gone to town he'd visited her mother and taken news that Brenna was well. It wasn't the same as going herself, but at least her mother wouldn't worry so.

Alexander kept Brenna's mind off something else besides being lonely, too . . . someone else. She didn't know what was wrong with her, but she often found her thoughts dwelling on Lord Bolton. Despite her anger over his refusal to allow her to see her family, thoughts of him haunted her day and night. She contemplated the way he sat each night at the dining table reading his book. She thought about the timbre of his voice when he asked her to pass the bread. She went over and over in her mind the way he had almost smiled at her in his laboratory that day. Not that he'd given her any attention since then—he'd barely said a dozen words in the last fortnight—but still, the thought of him made her warm.

Alexander got up off her bed, bored with the string, and wandered toward her. He had taken off his coat in the warm room and wore his hair in a queue tied with a black ribbon. He looked much like a small version of his father, as handsome as he. As for the burn scars, she didn't even notice them anymore. They were as much a part of him as his mischievous grin, his sense of humor.

The boy tapped on the windowsill. "You think Patsy would let us make cookies again today, Brenna?"

"I don't see why not." She looked up from her darning. "I think he actually enjoyed himself, if he were to tell the truth."

Alexander giggled. "He did, didn't he?" He toyed with the crimson window drapes. "You know what I wish?"

"What?"

"That Father would make cookies with us. Or play hide the thimble, or draw dogs with us. That's what I wish."

Brenna looked at Alexander. She yearned to reach out and take him in her arms, but she had learned very quickly that she had to allow him to make the first move whenever it came to physical contact. "Your father is a very busy man," she said casually.

"But for just half an hour." He sighed, pulling back the drape to look out the window. "I don't see why—" He stopped suddenly. "Brenna . . ." he breathed in awe. "Look."

Brenna glanced out the window. To her surprise she spotted a hired coach laden with trunks approaching Bolton Castle. "Who in the heavens . . ."

"Who do you think it is?" Alexander bounced up and

down on his shiny heeled shoes. "No one ever comes to Bolton. No one ever came but you." He grabbed her hand in his excitement. "Who do you think it is? What do they want?"

"I've no idea." Brenna was as surprised by the new arrival as he was. Who would dare come? Lord Bolton had no friends, no relatives, according to Alexander. They were all alone in the world.

"Let's go see!" He grabbed her hand, and before she could protest he raced out her bedchamber door, leading her.

At the bottom of the grand staircase they met Patsy and Mr. Jessop in the hallway.

"Who is it? Who is it?" Alexander exclaimed, letting go of her hand to leap down the last two steps. "Oh, Mr. Jessop, who approaches?"

Jessop tucked his hands behind his back, a smug look on his face. "Just wait and see, young master. I think you will be thoroughly surprised. And pleased." He caught Brenna's eyes. "You, too, miss."

Patsy opened the front door to meet the carriage at the steps. The carriage door swung open and men in stiff black coats came tumbling out.

"One, two, three, four," Alexander marveled aloud. "Four visitors. And so many bags!" He turned to look at Jessop. "You have to tell me, who are they?"

The secretary could barely contain himself. "Your tutors, master."

Brenna could not resist a smile. *He listened,* she thought with a grin. *Lord Bolton listened to what I said!*

"Tutors?" Alexander breathed. Suddenly his voice was more apprehensive than excited. "I've never had tutors. Who sent for tutors for me?"

"I did."

Brenna turned in surprise to see Lord Bolton standing in one of the hall's archways. She wondered how long he'd been there and she'd not noticed.

"My lord." She dipped a curtsy.

The men all bowed.

"You sent for tutors, sir?" Alexander walked to his father. "What for?"

"To instruct you. You'll learn to read and write in English, French, and Latin from Mr. Loran." He looked up, cocking his eyebrow as he did. "And which of you might be he?"

A tall thin man with a goatee bowed stiffly.

Lord Bolton extended a hand. "Mathematics, astrology, and literature, from Mr. Cache."

Another man bowed, this one shorter, more portly.

"Mr. Arbutus will teach you the gentlemanly arts of good manners and deportment."

Another bowed.

"And Mr. Luttle is your dance master."

The last in line bowed, presenting a fine leg.

Alexander looked unsure of himself. "I need these instructors?"

"You do." Lord Bolton rested his hand on his son's shoulder in a rare display of physical affection. "I must apologize, my son, for I've been remiss in not calling these gentlemen sooner."

It was then that his lordship looked over at Brenna, his gaze locking with hers. This time he had a smile for her. Actually, it was more of a grin.

Brenna broke into a smile as well, feeling her cheeks color. She was embarrassed that his lordship would pay such attention to her in front of the others, and yet she was thrilled at the same time. "Thank you," she mouthed, giving him a saucy smile.

He looked back at his son. "And so that you will not be bored, Alexander, your companion, Miss Abbott, will sit in on all of your classes, and learn what she can as well."

Alexander wrinkled his nose. "A girl, sir?"

"A woman learns as well as a man given the chance," Bolton told his son. "The arrangements have already been made."

Brenna's breath was tight in her throat. If only his lordship knew how much this would mean to her. Of course he would find out that she had lied to him, but it was only a little lie, and she'd cross that footbridge when she came to it. "Oh, my lord!" she breathed. "Thank you."

He looked at her again. This time if Brenna hadn't known better she would have thought it was something like the look a man gave a woman. A man gave a woman whom he was attracted to.

She could only stare back, thinking surely she was mistaken, or dreaming, yet never wanting to tear her gaze from his handsome face.

"Well, sirs." Mr. Jessop clapped his hands, shattering the magical moment. "Let me get you settled in your quarters and classes can begin this afternoon. Then you will meet your pupils and I can outline what Lord Bolton expects of you."

Brenna looked down to see Alexander beside her, his small hand slipping into hers. Unsure of himself, he had sought her comfort. She smiled down at him, squeezing his hand. "This is going to be wonderful, Alexander," she assured him. "You and I are going to learn to read!"

When she looked up his lordship was gone.

"Oh, please, Brenna, just a few more minutes?" Alexander jumped over an overturned stone bench. Dead, tangled vines had grown over the seat, sad proof that it had been a long time since anyone had attended to the garden.

The October air was cold and crisp, but the sun shone brightly on their faces. Bundled up in the new green wool cloak and mittens his lordship had sent to her chambers, Brenna was warm and happy. The air smelled like snow.

"I've enjoyed our walk, too, Alexander. But we have work to do, you and I," she chastised her charge affectionately. "Mr. Loran will be sorely disappointed if we come to class unprepared."

"The bloody hell with Mr. Loran." He stuck out his lip. "I'd rather stay here with you."

"Alexander!" She was tempted to laugh but kept a stern look on her face. She grasped the bench by one leg and uprighted it, tearing it from its bed of weeds. "My guess would be that that is not good manners." She plopped down on the bench.

"No. I don't guess it is. But I like being here with you." He wandered off through the weeds, dragging a stick behind him. "Papa never comes outside with me like you do."

She folded her hands in her lap, deciding to give him five more minutes. "I know. He's busy, Alexander. He—"

"Brenna! Brenna! Come, come quick!"

Brenna stood, turning to look for him. She could see Alexander's head just above the weeds near a stone fountain that had long gone dry. "What is it?"

"Oh, Brenna, it's a bird. A poor, hurt birdie!"

Brenna pushed her way through the weeds to find him crouched beside the carved fountain. He had removed his mittens. "Look," he whispered, pointing.

Brenna crouched beside him to see the little starling huddled under a pile of dry leaves. The bird was trembling with fear and cold. "Oh, Alexander . . ."

Lord Bolton leaned over the rail of the balcony to see what his son and Miss Abbott were looking at. The autumn breeze that rippled his hair was invigorating. As he guessed, the fresh air had done him good, cleansing his mind and his blood.

He'd been out here half an hour watching them, undetected. He couldn't remember when he'd begun this ritual of taking a breath of air at the same time that Miss Abbott took Alexander for a walk. They came each day to take a break from their studies.

Miss Abbott . . . *Brenna*.

Julius felt strange inside. It had been so long since a

woman's name had been on the tip of his tongue like this. He thought of Anna, his sweet Anna, the mother of Alexander, of his other children gone to their graves.

What would his Anna think of him, sneaking about their home like this, watching a servant? Lusting after her?

But he couldn't help himself. The girl was in his thoughts more than he cared to admit, even to himself. He liked to watch her bend over her books, nodding to the instructor, her thick red hair falling to frame her heart-shaped face. He liked to hear her laughter as she danced across the dusty ballroom floor, his son leading her awkwardly through the dance steps. He liked the way her blue eyes danced merrily when she answered a question correctly. And he liked the way she smiled at his son. A part of him was even a little jealous. The boy liked her so much. No, he loved her.

A part of Julius was sad to think that Alexander would never love his mother, but of course he never really knew her. He'd been an infant, not yet weaned, when she'd died in the fire with his two sisters and brother. A part of Julius rejoiced to see that Alexander had someone in his life he could depend on . . . someone to love.

Julius tried to be a good father. He loved the boy so much. But he didn't know how to be a father. He felt so damned guilty that sometimes . . . too often, it incapacitated him.

Julius leaned over the stone rail. What have they found? he wondered to himself.

He could see Alexander on his knees, reaching for something. He couldn't hear what Brenna was saying to him. All he could hear was the murmur of her gentle voice.

His son scooped up an object in his hand, and then the two started to walk toward the castle, their heads bent in conversation. For a moment he stared at the crumbling fountain. A memory flashed before his eyes. He remembered the water flowing from the lion's mouth into the pool. He remembered Anna's shy laughter. He remembered making love to her beside that fountain in the fading light of a summer's eve.

Sweet God, he'd been so happy.

"Papa?"

The sound of a stone hitting the ground below him caught Julius off guard. He must have knocked it over the edge.

"Papa?" his son repeated.

Julius blinked. Damn! He'd been caught. He looked down, feeling foolish.

Alexander and Brenna stood on the ground, looking up at him standing on the crumbling third-floor balcony.

"Papa, what are you doing up there? Look what I found. A bird." He grinned at Brenna. "Brenna says it's just an old starling, but it has a hurt leg." He looked back at his father with the scarred face that haunted Julius's dreams.

How good it was to see his son smile. Brenna had brought that smile to his face. Julius knew he had her to thank for his son's laughter, not to mention his improved behavior.

"Can I keep him and try to mend it?" The boy fidgeted. "Can I, Papa?"

The way Brenna . . . Miss Abbott . . . looked at him made him uncomfortable, but not in a bad way. It was just that he was always at a loss for words around her. Usually he just ended up getting angry with himself and shouting, even when he didn't mean to.

"Alexander, a bird?"

"Oh, please, please, Papa. I swear I'll take care of him. I'll feed him and I'll clean his cage. I . . . I . . . I'll even practice my Latin when Brenna says I have to. Please, Papa?"

He looked up with such an earnest face.

Julius sighed, leaning casually over the rail. "What do you think, Miss Abbott?"

"Well, my lord, the leg could certainly be mended." She nibbled on her lower lip . . . one of the sweetest lower lips he'd ever had the pleasure to lay eyes upon. "I see no harm in letting him keep the bird for a few weeks. It would be a good way to teach him some responsibility."

"Right." Julius nodded. "Exactly what I was thinking." He

stood straight again. "Well, I should get back to my work, and the two of you should get back to your studies."

"Yes, my lord." She curtsied to him and then, taking Alexander's hand, started to lead him off.

Julius turned to retreat as well, then stopped. He didn't know what possessed him. He heard himself call to her. "Miss Abbott?"

She backed up so that she could see him at the balcony rail again. "My lord?"

"Would you care to dine with me this evening?" As soon as the words were out of his mouth, he wanted to wince.

She blinked. "My lord, I dine with you every evening."

He felt stupid. Of course she did. Not that they actually talked or anything, but . . . "Right. It's just that I . . . I wanted to talk to you about Alexander. To see . . . how well you think he's doing."

There was the tiniest hint of a smile on her lips. "We could certainly discuss the matter were you not so consumed by your books, my lord."

He looked away and then back at her. "Touché," he said, as much to himself as to her. He leaned on the rail again. "In private. I meant to talk privately. Without Alexander."

She looked at him, her pretty face frowning in confusion. "You want to dine alone to speak about Alexander?"

"Yes." He shook his head. "I mean, no. The tutors join us tonight as well." He could feel his palms sweating despite the chill in the air. "Well, what . . . what of a turn through the gallery after we sup? We could talk then."

She curtsied. "Yes, my lord."

He watched her until she disappeared from sight and then clamped his hand over his forehead, amazed at his own foolishness. " 'Would care to sup with me?' " he mimicked himself, making his way across the precarious balcony. "What an addlepate she must think I am now."

Five

"I'm sorry. I didn't mean to disturb you, my lord." Brenna hung back in the doorway of the library. She hadn't expected to find him here in the morning. It was a pleasant surprise that she knew made her cheeks color.

Lord Bolton turned from the bookshelves, a book cradled in his big hands. "You're not disturbing me. Please, come in and . . ." He looked at Brenna with those gray eyes that made her legs shaky. "And I told you, I'd really prefer you just called me Julius . . . Brenna."

She looked down at the black-and-white tiled floor. "Julius," she whispered, liking the sound of his name on her tongue.

Time was flying so quickly that Brenna could barely keep track of the days. In one week it would be Christmas. In the last two months so much had changed, and all of it had started with that walk in the gallery shortly after the tutors had arrived. It was not that there was anything spectacular about that night. Brenna and Lord Bolton had discussed Alexander and his improvement in behavior. They had talked about how quickly he was learning under his tutors' watchful eyes. What was significant about that night was that Lord Bolton had listened to Brenna's opinions, honestly interested in her thoughts and impressions. He treated her as an equal. He inquired about her own academics and congratulated her on her accomplishments. After they talked he walked her to her chamber and kissed her hand, thanking her for all she'd done.

After that night it seemed to Brenna that Lord Bolton had changed. It was subtle at first. Those first few weeks after the tutors arrived, Julius hung back in the shadows, watching her and Alexander, but now he was actually beginning to participate in his son's life. At supper, most evenings, he no longer brought his book with him. Instead, he engaged Alexander and Brenna, and sometimes even the tutors, in lively conversation. He was teaching the boy to fence. He often sat in on their Latin lessons in the afternoon, and yesterday, Lord Bolton had actually played hide and seek in the east wing with Brenna and Alexander.

Brenna was thrilled with the growing affection between father and son. And, she had to admit, she was thrilled with his lordship's attention, even if it was only due to the boy. Just to be in the same room with Julius made her heart flutter. It made her think of things that she knew could never be.

"I . . ." Brenna lifted her gaze to look at him. "I was just bringing this book back." She showed him the leather-bound volume.

"Chaucer?" he asked incredulously. "I see you've made a great deal of progress in such a short time."

Brenna avoided meeting his eye. She had known this was coming; she was surprised one of the tutors hadn't said anything to him. "Actually, I wasn't entirely truthful with you when I said I couldn't read."

"No?" He lifted his brow, but he sounded amused rather than angry.

He obviously wasn't going to make this easy on her. "No. You see . . ." She sighed. "My father was a good man, but he didn't believe in reading. He said it was a waste, especially for a woman. In Werster a woman who can read is looked down upon as frivolous." She ran her palm over Chaucer's leather covering. "My grandfather, the parson, taught me to read, but it was our secret. Even my mother doesn't know.

She thinks that knowing how to read, how to speak properly, has made her life harder. She says it's made her wish for things she can never have."

"And has it?"

"My lord?" She blushed, realizing she'd called him *my lord* again. "Has it what?"

"Made you wish for things you believe you'll never have?"

She thought for a moment and then answered honestly. "Perhaps. But I like to think I don't know what the good Lord has in store for me."

He chuckled at her answer. "Well, come in." He waved her in. "There's certainly enough room for the two of us. Return the book to its place and get another. I can make some recommendations, if you like."

Brenna came into the sunshine of the library, feeling a little awkward. She was rarely alone with Julius; it seemed that Alexander was always between them . . . her buffer. Being alone like this with Julius made her heart beat erratically. She could smell his shaving soap, the scent of his skin. She couldn't stop herself from wondering what his silky hair would feel like between her fingers.

She wandered to the shelves beside him, trying to appear casual, not wanting him to know how he affected her. She stared at the spines of the books, but her mind didn't register the titles.

After a moment he spoke. "So . . . um, how is Alexander today?"

"Quite fine."

"And . . . and the bird?"

"The leg is mended. I told Alexander he couldn't keep it in that cage in his chamber forever, that the bird belonged free. I think he understands. He's just not ready to let it go yet."

Julius nodded and then fell into silence.

After another minute it was Brenna who initiated the conversation. "I . . . I wanted to thank you, *Julius,* for the new gown. The one you sent up yesterday." She clutched a book to her breast for support, looking into those gray eyes of his. "I don't know what to say. It's the most beautiful green fabric I've ever laid eyes on. And the shoes—really, it's too much."

Julius had returned his book to the shelf and was just standing there, looking at her. "I knew when the dressmaker sent the fabric that it was perfect for you."

She watched, frozen, as he reached out and brushed a lock of stray hair from her cheek. "It will go perfectly with your hair, and with Christmastide coming—"

He was so close that she could feel his breath on her cheek. She could feel the heat of his body. It just seemed so natural that she should rest her hand on his broad chest. . . .

"Julius . . ." she whispered, feeling dizzy with the nearness of him.

"Brenna . . ."

Her eyes drifted shut. She trembled with anticipation. He was going to kiss her. God above, Lord Bolton was going to kiss Brenna Abbott.

Just as his lips brushed hers there was the sound of rapid footsteps in the hallway.

Brenna pulled away, confused, a little frightened and unsteady on her feet.

"God's teeth, what is it, Jessop?" Julius snapped, making Brenna jump in her skin. He jerked a book off the shelf. "Can't you see . . . can't you see I'm occupied?"

The secretary bowed deeply. "My apologies, my lord, for the interruption, but it's—" his gaze strayed—"it's Miss Abbott I seek."

"Me?" Brenna crossed the library on shaky legs. His lordship had kissed . . . well, almost kissed her. She didn't know what to think. What to do. "What is it, Mr. Jessop?"

Lord Bolton's secretary leaned closer, whispering.

Brenna covered her mouth with her hands as she listened. "No," she murmured.

"I'm afraid so," Mr. Jessop answered gravely.

"Thank you, Mr. Jessop." She nodded. "I appreciate you bringing me word."

"What is it?" Julius asked.

Brenna walked back toward the bookshelves, the sound of Jessop's footsteps echoing in her head. "My sister, Abby," she said softly, her thoughts in a daze. "Patsy brought word from the village that she's very ill." She looked at Julius with tears in her eyes. "My mama fears she might die."

"I'm so sorry. Perhaps I could—"

She studied his face. "I have to go home, my lord. Julius. I know you said my place is here with your son, but may I—"

"No."

She stared for a moment, thinking she'd not heard him correctly. Suddenly Julius's gentle, handsome face was hard and unyielding.

"You won't let me go to my sister?"

He slapped down the book he held in his hand. "Is anything ever enough for you, Brenna?"

She was taken aback by his anger. "Sir?"

"Is anything enough? I give you a warm chamber, beautiful clothing, French wines and cuisine. I brought you tutors so that you might be educated. For pity sake, I've got a man here teaching you to dance! Is it not enough? All that I ask in return is that you stay here—with my son—and yet you ask for more!"

"My sister," she murmured. Silent tears slipped down her cheeks as she backed her way out of the library. "But it's my sister." The book slipped from her hands and hit the floor with a bang. Brenna stared at the book through her tears for a second and then turned and ran.

Julius groaned, crossing the room to pick up the book she'd dropped. *Shakespeare's Sonnets.* With a growl of anger, he hurled the book through the air. It hit above the mantel, glanced off a candlestick, and fell beside the upholstered reading chair. "Jessop!" he boomed. "Jessop, get your ass in here, now!"

"There's nothing to discuss, Lord Bolton. You made your point clear." Brenna stood in the garden, a cold breeze whipping her hair about her face and shoulders. Snow had begun falling that morning, and there was a soft blanket covering the garden, filling in its jagged ruts and softening its landscape.

Brenna kept her arms crossed stubbornly over her chest, watching Alexander, who sat in the distance. She refused to think about their near kiss. Lord Bolton wasn't interested in her. She'd been a fool to think so, even for that instant. At the very most he was interested in seducing his house girl, out of boredom, out of loneliness, out of lust.

Brenna focused on Alexander. Cut off from her family, it seemed that the child was all she had to live for these days. Alexander had perched himself on the edge of the stone fountain. He was talking to his starling in its cage.

"Brenna . . ." Julius began again. He stood beside her in the black cloak he was known for with the old angry look on his face.

"This discussion is unnecessary. I am a servant here. You are my lord." She looked into his eyes defiantly. "I'm not such a stupid peasant girl that I don't know what that means. You are my master and you have the right to do with me as you please. I've no say in the matter. You made that clear."

Julius ran his fingers through his hair in obvious frustration. "I want you to understand that I'm not trying to be harsh. It's only that—"

"That what?" Brenna demanded angrily. "That you want to prove that you are lord and master of me and all who reside in this lonely castle? How could anyone within two leagues not know? You're certainly the loudest!"

Julius groaned. "Brenna, I—Oh, the hell with it!" He

swung a fist angrily and walked away. "Bring my son inside soon," he barked. "It's cold and the snow is falling harder."

Brenna made no response but to tromp through the snow and weeds toward Alexander. "It's time to go," she said.

"I know." The boy hung his head. He had his finger poked through the bars of the cage. The bird was pecking his finger. "I just wanted to say goodbye again."

"You're doing the right thing, Alexander." She smiled at him.

"I know."

She watched as the young boy with the scarred face opened the tiny door to the cage. "Go on, Charlie." He rattled the bars. "Go with you."

The starling needed no more encouragement than that and flew from the cage. Alexander jumped up to watch him go. "Good-bye," he called softly.

They watched the bird until it had disappeared beyond the hedge where Brenna and her sister Abby had picked berries two summers before. Then Brenna picked up the cage and put her arm around her charge to lead him back toward the warmth of the castle.

"Time to get back to our studies."

"I know." He slipped his hand around her back.

"I'm proud of you, Alexander. Of what you just did."

He smiled up at her. "Thank you." Then, after a moment, he spoke again. "I heard you and Papa. Are you angry at him?"

Brenna sighed. She was determined not to bring Alexander into this matter. She wouldn't let her anger with Julius alter the relationship she and Alexander had built. "It's no concern of yours, sweet. I'm just worried about my sister."

"Well, I'm sure she's much better now that the physician has been there. That and the food Patsy took your mama."

Brenna stopped dead in the snow. "What physician? What food? What are you talking about?"

Alexander went on walking, and Brenna had to run to catch up to him.

"You know, the physician Papa had sent from London. The food he had Patsy take from the larder in the cellar. You know, that stuff."

Julius sent Abby a physician? And food for my family? Brenna marveled silently. *Why didn't he tell me? Why would he go to such trouble, spend so much of his coin for me like that, and yet refuse to allow me to walk down the hill?*

Inside the castle, Brenna and Alexander stomped the snow from their feet. "Go take off your wet boots and—"

"Alexander," Julius's voice called from down the hallway.

Brenna kept her back to him. Now she was truly confused. How could he have been so cruel as to prevent her from visiting her ill sister, and yet taken such care to see that she and the family were provided for?

"Alexander, do you want to come to my laboratory? I've an experiment I've been working on. I want to show you."

Brenna turned to look at Julius, Alexander's snowy cloak in her hands. "Julius?"

"You said the discussion was unnecessary." He stood in the darkness of the hallway so that she couldn't see his face.

She walked toward him. "Julius, did you send a physician for my sister? Did you send food to my family?"

He lifted one broad shoulder. His cloak was tossed over one arm, his hair damp and disheveled from the snow and wind. "It was nothing."

She stopped right in front of him, forcing him to look her in the eye. "It's something to me. To my mother. To my sister. To those I love."

He ran his hands through his hair, glancing away, then back at her. "I cannot let you leave," he said, so softly that she could barely hear him.

Was that a tremor in his voice?

"I cannot let you go, but I ask that you forgive me. Stay here with my son. Care for him. Love him as you do and I

will see that your family is always taken care of from thi
day forward."

Her eyes searched his. "I don't know what to say."

"Say you forgive me. Say you will not try to run away
Say you will be mine and Alexander's guest tomorrow nigh
for supper, and dancing in the ballroom."

"I can show you what my dance master taught me, Papa,"
Alexander said, carrying his wet boots under his arm. "Let'
go. I want to see how the experiment turned out!"

"Dancing?" Brenna asked, ignoring Alexander, still look
ing at Julius.

"Well, it's Christmas Eve." He raised his brow. "Surely
you dance in your house on Christmas Eve?"

Then, before Brenna could respond, he and Alexander were
gone. Down the hallway they went, Alexander chattering and
Julius listening as all good fathers did.

The next evening Brenna dressed in the velvet green gowr
Julius had given her and slipped her feet into the matching
heeled slippers. Because it was so cold this Christmas Eve
she added a black velvet cape he had also given her.

Brenna turned before the mirror, smiling to herself. The
first gown Julius gave her might have been Lady Bolton's.
but this was Brenna's. He'd bought the material himself and
had had the gown fashioned for her. She smiled at her own
reflection. She still didn't understand Julius. It made no sense
to her that he could be so kind in some ways and so thought-
less in others. But she understood him a little better since
she'd talked to Mr. Jessop.

Yesterday, after the odd exchange she'd had with Julius in
the hallway when he'd asked her to dine and dance with him.
she'd sought out Mr. Jessop. She wanted to know what had
happened in the fire. At first Julius's secretary was hesitant
to say anything, but finally he gave her a brief account of
the tragedy.

Apparently the fire had begun in the family's sleeping quarters. Julius had been working in his laboratory late at night. Neither the servants nor Julius had smelled the smoke until the blaze was raging through the bedchambers. Julius managed to save the infant Alexander, but the others had been consumed by the flames. It was a sad story that made Brenna's heart ache for Julius's loss, and for the guilt she knew he must feel. Knowing his lordship as she thought she did now, she understood that he must blame himself, thinking that if he'd not been in the laboratory that night he might have saved his family.

The case clock in the hallway struck seven. Not wanting to be late, Brenna grabbed a lighted candle and hurried from her bedchamber. Julius met her in the doorway of the dining room, a glass of wine for her in his hand.

"Brenna." His gaze met hers.

She took the glass he offered, feeling like a princess. "Julius." She brought the glass to her lips, watching him watch her. It was the most delicious feeling.

"Brenna! Brenna!" Alexander came bounding over to her. "Patsy made pheasant with stuffed oysters, and bread pudding, and buttermilk biscuits, and all my favorites. Come see!"

Brenna begged Julius for forgiveness for abandoning him, using only her eyes. Then she allowed Alexander to lead her off to see the dining table laden with food and decorated with greenery and fruit. Candles burned in every wall sconce, every candelabra, and the chandelier high above the table. The dining room was beautiful. Someone had even taken the time to drape greenery over the mantel, and the fireplace smelled of fresh burning pine.

The tutors entered the dining room one by one, Mr. Jessop joined them, and the meal was served by Patsy. When he had completed his tasks and gone to make his retreat from the dining room Julius called after him. "Patsy!"

The servant held a tray in his hand. "My lord?"

"Sit with us?" Julius indicated an empty chair.

"My lord?"

"I said, join us."

Patsy blinked. "At your dining table, my lord?"

"Why not? It's Christmas, and who else will you spend the evening with but the rats in the larder? Sit. Sit."

The meal was a delightful one, with appetizing foods, good wine, and lots of talk and laughter. Brenna said very little, seated in her place beside Julius, across from Alexander. She was afraid to. She didn't want this night to end. She didn't want the dream to end.

After a dessert of fruit and nuts and nut cakes the group retired to the ballroom. Julius invited Patsy to join them, but the young man declined, saying he'd had quite enough joviality for one night.

Brenna was thrilled to find that the two great fireplaces on opposite ends of the ballroom had been lit. The floor had been swept. Gilt chairs with red and green upholstery had been placed here and there. Fresh candles had been placed in all the wall sconces. The covers had been removed from three massive chandeliers, and their crystal teardrops polished. The candles in the ballroom glimmered like stars in the heavens.

Mr. Luttle began a lively tune on the spinet and Brenna found herself across from Alexander, doing a jig, showing Julius what the boy had learned. The tutors all took their turns dancing with her. The good meal and the free-flowing wine relaxed the tutors and Mr. Jessop, so that they laughed and talked with her as if she belonged to each of them. At some point in the evening she stopped being "Miss Abbott" and became "Brenna" to them.

Finally, after more than two hours of dancing, singing old Christmas ballads, and more wine, the tutors began to take their leave, one by one.

"Just one more tune, Mr. Luttle," Julius begged. "For I fear I've not had my turn at dancing with our Brenna."

As Julius took her hand, Brenna's gaze met his. "I was afraid you wouldn't ask for fear I would step on your toes."

He smiled, pulling her closer into his arms than was appropriate for the minuet the dance master played. "I didn't know whether you would want to dance with me," he murmured.

Her reply was a smile as she danced out of his arms, counting to follow the correct steps.

Of course, Julius was a superior dancer, dressed in his sapphire blue breeches and matching waistcoat and coat. Every time their fingertips touched, she felt her heart in her throat. Brenna had no idea what his lordship's intentions were toward her. Did he want her for his mistress? For surely that was lust that burned in his eyes. He ran so hot and cold that she wondered if he was wrestling with the same thoughts himself.

All Brenna knew for sure was that there was something between them, something strong, overpowering, a feeling that overwhelmed her. The word *love* bounced around in her head.

Mr. Luttle lifted his hands from the keyboard of the spinet on the last note. Julius bowed deeply. She curtsied, and then they both clapped.

Hearing no sound from Alexander, Brenna turned to look for him. "Look," she said softly to Julius.

The two stood for a moment, looking at the little boy they both loved so deeply. The scars on his face meant nothing to them. All they saw was the child's intelligence, his humor, his sense of awe of the world.

Alexander lay curled on a bench against the wall sound asleep, covered by one of his tutors' stiff black coats.

"Another song, my Lord Bolton?" asked the dance master.

"No. Thank you, Mr. Luttle. It looks as if I have another matter to attend to." He indicated the sleeping boy.

"Then I will take my leave." Mr. Luttle rose from the spinet bench and bowed. "My Lord. Brenna. Good night."

"Good night," Brenna called after him. "And thank you."

Julius lifted the sleeping boy in his arms. "Let's put him to bed."

Brenna's gaze met his. "Me?" The two had never put Alexander to bed together. It was always either Brenna or Julius, never both. That would have been too intimate for master and servant.

"Yes, you, and then if you would, join me in my study." He looked down at his son, avoiding her eye. "I've something for you."

Six

Brenna and Julius tucked Alexander into bed in his chamber beside his father's and then retired to Julius's private study, off his own bedchamber.

"Wait here." Julius added a log to the fire Patsy must have started and made a hasty retreat from the room. "I have to get the gift."

"I have nothing for you," Brenna called after him. "I really don't need a gift."

"Pour us some wine," he said from the doorway. Then he disappeared into the darkness.

Brenna walked to a side table and poured Julius a glass of wine. She was nervous. She had never been in his private chambers before. The room smelled so much like him; it showed so much of his personality. There were books everywhere, mostly scientific . . . except for a copy of Shakespeare's sonnets.

There was a discarded coat tossed on a chair. She ran her hand over the sleeve. A pair of damp boots had been left by the door to dry. Along one wall were several small painted portraits. Brenna set down the wineglass and crossed the room to study them.

A lump rose in her throat. These were his children. She remembered them vaguely. There was a little boy just Alexander's age who looked so much like him it was eerie. There were also two sweet little girls in white dresses, wearing blue ribbons in their hair. And then his wife . . .

Brenna heard footsteps behind her. Julius came into the study and closed the door.

"She was very pretty. . . ." she said quietly. She didn't know what else to say. She *was* pretty. Beautiful. And wealthy. And well educated. Brenna knew she paled in comparison.

"She was," Julius answered in his strong tenor voice.

"You loved her a great deal?"

He took his wineglass and walked toward the fireplace. "A great deal."

She watched him spread out a quilted blanket on the floor before the fireplace. He added several large, overstuffed pillows.

"Join me, Brenna?"

Brenna could feel her heart pounding. Was he going to seduce her? Could she possibly resist him if he did? She knew she should excuse herself, now while she had the chance. But she couldn't. All she could think about was the kiss they had never completed.

"It's all right," he said quietly, offering his hand. "You've nothing to fear, sweet. My intentions are nothing but honorable."

As she walked to him and took his hand, she found herself a little disappointed. Perhaps she really wanted to be seduced.

Julius took her cloak from her shoulders and tossed it on a chair. He added his own coat. "It's warm down here. Come, sit with me."

Julius sat on the blanket facing the fire and Brenna sat beside him. When he slipped his hand around her waist she gave no resistance. It felt right. Natural.

"Brenna . . ."

She looked into his eyes. It was obvious he wanted to say something to her. It was also obvious that it would be difficult for him. "Julius—"

"No." He held up his hand. "Let me speak. I know what I want to say. And if you don't give me the chance now, I may never be able to say it. I've been rehearsing since this morning."

She nodded, her gaze never straying from his.

"Brenna, when I brought you here it truly was to be my son's companion. It was only due to Mr. Jessop's urging. I had no other intentions. I didn't really even want a woman in the house. I was afraid it would be a dishonor to my wife."

Brenna wanted to protest, but she could tell by the look in his eyes that it was best that she remain silent and let him talk.

He went on haltingly. "I knew Alexander needed someone." He took her hand in his. "I knew he needed a woman's influence." He looked into her eyes. "Somehow I knew he needed you.

"Then you brought so much more than companionship for my son. You became his friend, the mother he never knew. But that's not all you did. You brought me out of a long sleep. You brought all of us at Bolton Castle out of a long sleep. You made me realize that life had to go on for Alexander, even though his mother and his brother and sisters were gone." He lifted her hand to his lips and kissed her knuckles. "You made me realize it had to go on for me." He shook his head. "I'm not a cruel man. Or evil."

"I know you're not." This time she dared to kiss *his* hand.

"It's just that I had so much guilt inside me," he went on. "So much bitterness. I felt so badly for Alexander, for his injuries, that I made them more important than my son himself. That's why he had no discipline."

Brenna felt tears brim in her eyes. "You have a beautiful son, Julius. And when the time comes for him to leave Bolton Castle no one will notice the scars for more than a moment's time."

"I think I know that now."

"And as for the guilt," she said, "I cannot say that I wouldn't feel some of the same were I in your place, but . . ."

She smiled. "The time has come to let it go, for your sake and for Alexander's, and I think you have."

From behind his back Julius brought out a square box wrapped in gold fabric and tied with a bow. "This is for you."

It was the most exquisite gift Brenna had ever seen. The box was wrapped so beautifully, she didn't want to open it.

Julius took his arm from around her waist and reached for his glass of wine. "Go ahead. Open it."

Brenna untied the bow and pulled back the cloth to reveal an ordinary wooden box. She touched the lid, and he nodded for her to open it. When she pulled off the top a glimmering round ball with ribbons tied 'round it, floated upward.

"Oh . . ." she breathed, watching it hover just above the box. "Magic."

He chuckled. "Science, actually. And it won't last long. I've been working in my laboratory for months, and the process still isn't perfected."

"What is it?" she breathed, batting at the tiny floating balloon with her finger.

"A gas."

"It's wonderful, Julius." She looked into his gray eyes, wondering if she would dare seduce him herself. "Thank you."

"You're welcome. I'm glad you like it, but actually that's not your gift."

She watched the balloon bounce on the end of her finger. "No?"

"No." He untied the ribbons at the bottom of the balloon and it floated out of her hands. "Your gift . . ." His voice was suddenly husky. "Your gift is . . . is your freedom."

Brenna stared at him, still not understanding. "My freedom?"

He watched the ball float over their heads, upward, crawling toward the high ceiling. "I want to return your term in-

*We have 4 FREE BOOKS for you
as your introduction to
KENSINGTON CHOICE!
To get your FREE BOOKS, worth
up to $23.96, mail the card below.*

FREE BOOK CERTIFICATE

Yes! Please send me 4 Kensington Choice (the best of Zebra and Pinnacle Books) Historical Romances without cost or obligation (worth up to $23.96). As a Kensington Choice subscriber, I will then receive 4 brand-new romances to preview each month for 10 days FREE. I can return any books I decide not to keep and owe nothing. The publisher's prices for Kensington Choice romances range from $4.99-$5.99, but as a preferred subscriber I will get these books for only $4.20 per book or $16.80 for all four titles. There is no minimum number of books to buy and I may cancel my subscription at any time, plus there is no additional charge for postage and handling. No matter what I decide to do, my first 4 books are mine to keep, absolutely FREE!

Name _____

Address _____ Apt. _____

City _____ State _____ Zip _____

Telephone (_____) _____

Signature _____

(If under 18, parent or guardian must sign)

Subscription subject to acceptance. Terms and prices subject to change.　　KF1296

AFFIX
STAMP
HERE

KENSINGTON CHOICE
Zebra Home Subscription Service, Inc.
120 Brighton Road
P.O.Box 5214
Clifton, NJ 07015-5214

denture to you. I have no right to keep you here. No more right than Alexander had to keep his bird."

"Julius—"

"Please let me finish."

She reached out and brushed her hand against his cheek. He caught it and rubbed his face against it, again and again.

"I wouldn't let you go at first because I feared you wouldn't come back. That you'd run away because Bolton was such a dreary place. Because my son was so ill-behaved. Because I—you know. I was such a *beast*." He frowned. "I wasn't born a lord, you know. I was born plain Julius Irons, son and grandson of a common soldier. I followed in my father's footsteps and had the good luck to save the king's life in a hunting accident. He rewarded me with a title and a wealthy wife, but I had to learn to be a gentleman—as you have learned to be a lady."

Her eyes widened at his confession. "You always seemed a gentleman born to me. But you know I wouldn't have fled. I sold myself. A bargain was made. I would have come back."

"I know that now." He kissed her fingertips one by one. "After a while the truth is, I wouldn't let you go because I couldn't bear the thought of losing you. Not forever, not for a day, not even for an afternoon."

"Oh, Julius . . ." she whispered.

Then he kissed her. His mouth touched hers and she wrapped her arms around his neck with sudden urgency. Her lips parted. She moaned softly. He felt . . . he tasted so good. It was the kiss a woman dreamed of her entire life.

And when it ended—too soon for Brenna—Julius rose and took her hand. If he had led her toward his bedchamber, she would have gone. But instead he picked up her cloak, placed it around her shoulders, and lifted the hood, tucking in her red curls.

"The carriage waits to take you home."

"Now?"

"Yes, now. It's nearly midnight. Christmas. You don't want to disappoint your mother on Christmas Day, do you?"

Tears sprang in her eyes again. She didn't know what to say. Home. *Home to Mama, home to Abby, home to her brothers and sisters?*

She turned to go, then turned back. "Wait . . . my gift." She stretched out her hand.

The balloon had already begun to lose its magic gas. It floated just off the mantel.

Julius retrieved it and pressed it into her hands. "Good-bye, Brenna."

She feared she would break into tears. "Good-bye, Julius." She rested her hand on his chest. "Alexander—"

"I'll tell him good-bye for you."

He kissed her again. This time it was a farewell kiss, light and quick. "Mr. Jessop waits downstairs. He will see you home safely." Suddenly Julius's tone was brisk and businesslike. "You'll forgive me if I don't go myself."

Brenna nodded because she was afraid to speak; then she hurried down the hall toward the waiting carriage and home.

Christmas Day was delightful. Brenna visited with her mother and the recovering Abby, and her other sisters and brothers. They celebrated Mass in church. They had a fine feast of pork and leeks and fish and turnips, sent from Bolton Castle. There were even small gifts of oranges and ribbons for the girls and plaster marbles for the boys.

In the afternoon friends from the village came. There was music and dancing and laughter in the tiny cottage. Everyone seemed so pleased to have Brenna back again. They all marveled at her tale of the magic gas in the ball and passed the now flat balloon around. They all wanted to know what it had been like to live in the beast's den. But when she tried to tell them what Lord Bolton was really like they seemed more interested in the tales that had circulated around the village for so many years. No one really wanted the truth; the legend seemed far more exciting.

The afternoon passed and evening approached. The visitors went home. Abby was tucked in for an afternoon nap and the house grew quiet. Brenna sat with her mother at the only table in the single room.

"I'm glad to have you home, daughter."

Brenna smiled at her mother, the balloon Julius had given her safe in her hand. "I'm glad to be here."

"Are you?" Her mother picked up her darning needle.

"Of course. Why wouldn't I be?"

"Brenna, can you be content here? Can you be content now that you have drunk good wine, eaten stuffed oysters, and danced with a lord?"

Brenna stared at the scarred table, surprised that her mother could understand so easily what Brenna didn't understand. She shook her head sadly. "It's not that I don't love it here with you and the children, but I fear not."

"Then have the courage to seek the life you would choose."

She looked at her mother, truly in need of advice. "I don't know what you mean."

Mildred bit off the thread in her darning needle. "You've now had experience caring for a child of wealth. Go to London. Become a governess. I would bet one of those fine tutors would help you seek employment."

Brenna stared at the flickering flame of the tallow candle on the center of the table. *Have courage to seek the life you choose. . . .* Her mother's words echoed in her mind.

There was a moment of quiet as Mildred went on darning a stocking.

Suddenly Brenna rose. She made her decision in an instant. She had to go back to Bolton Castle. She missed Alexander. She missed Mr. Jessop, Patsy, even the tutors. Most of all she missed Julius. She didn't know what she would say when she got there. Beg for her job back, she guessed. All Brenna knew was that she had to go.

"Where are you going?" Mildred jumped out of her chair.

"Back to Bolton Castle." Brenna took her velvet cloak from the peg at the door.

"Tonight? How will you get there? Daughter, I don't understand." Mildred followed her to the door.

"Mama, I'll be back tomorrow, I promise. I just have to . . ." She brushed her mother's cheek with a kiss. "I have to have the courage to seek the life I would choose, or as close to it as I can find." She didn't dare tell her mother the truth about her feelings for Julius. She would never understand.

"Brenna, daughter, I didn't mean go tonight. I didn't mean go back to Bolton."

"I'll be all right. Truly I will." Brenna stepped out into the cold darkness. It had begun to snow again, but there was a bright half moon in the sky. The light of the moon reflected off the snow, illuminating the road up the hill toward the castle that loomed in the darkness.

"I can't explain myself, Mother. I just know that's where I belong." She kissed her mother again and hurried away.

As Brenna approached Bolton Castle, she saw no light in the windows, only an empty darkness. The castle looked just the same as it had all these years, but it didn't feel the same anymore. Brenna was not afraid. This was where she wanted to be; with Alexander, with Julius, in any capacity he chose. As she walked in cold darkness, the snow pelting her face, she had the strange feeling she had done this before. And yet, of course, she knew she hadn't.

Brenna approached the castle from the ruins of the southern wing. She intended to pass there and go to the front door in the main house.

"Brenna?"

Julius's voice came out of the darkness, so unexpected that
t startled her.

She stopped where she was to stare up at the wall.
"Julius?"

"Brenna? You came back? Why?"

She watched by the light of the moon as Julius leaped
over the balcony rail and shimmied down a wall left partially
standing. He came to her as a shadowy figure, and again she
felt a familiarity about what was happening.

"Why?" he repeated.

She bit down on her lower lip, not knowing what to say.
He *seemed* pleased to see her. "I came back because I don't
belong in the village any longer. I don't belong with my
brothers and sisters. I belong here at Bolton, with Alexander."
She wanted to say *with you,* but she was afraid to. "If you'll
have me," she finished lamely.

"If I'll have you?" With a sweep of his cloak, he took her
into his arms. "Brenna. You would choose Bolton over your
home?"

"I fear this is my home."

He brushed her cheek with his cold hand, and then the
nape of her neck. He stared into her eyes. She could have
sworn he had been crying.

"Why were you out here?" she whispered. "It's so cold."

He smiled. "Waiting for you, I think." Then he kissed her
hand. "So, will you have me?"

Brenna blinked. "My lord?"

"Really, darling, you should call me by my given name.
That is what wives call their husbands, is it not?"

"Wife? Husband?" She grabbed a handful of his wool coat
for support and looked into his eyes, knowing she must have
heard something wrong. "Are you asking me to marry you?"

"I am." He pressed his mouth to hers. "Will you have
me?" he asked against her lips. "Will you be my wife?"

Tears sprang into her eyes. This couldn't be happening.
Not to Brenna Abbott. It had to be a dream. And then she

remembered the dream she had had the night before she went to the hiring fair. This was it. The man . . . it had been Julius!

"Yes," she whispered. "And if this is a dream, I pray I never wake up."

"A dream in which the beautiful maiden marries the beast." Julius's laughter echoed off the walls of the castle. "I think not, for I am as real, as real as this. . . ."

And then he sealed their love with a kiss.

The Christmas Portrait

Holly Harte

Prologue

Galveston, August 1863

Meghan ran her fingers over the glass in the picture frame, tears stinging the backs of her eyes. She swallowed hard. How excited Drew had been when he presented the portrait to her as a Christmas gift in '61, just a month before he left to join the Confederate Army, and only six months after their wedding. She managed a small smile at the memory of that Christmas. She'd treasured the photograph, placing it on her bedside table, where she could gaze at Drew's beloved face upon awakening every morning and before falling asleep every night.

But now there was nothing left to treasure. Ever since she'd received the awful word of Drew's death at Gettysburg, the image in the photograph had begun to fade. Now there was only the photographer's backdrop visible beneath the glass.

"Oh, Drew," she whispered, her voice breaking with emotion as she ran her fingers over the glass a second time. *You were supposed to come back. You promised you would. You said no matter what happened, you'd find a way to come back to me.* She drew a shaky breath, then exhaled on a sigh.

A mournful meow pulled Meghan from her painful musings. She looked down to find McTavish, a long-haired, slightly pug-nosed, gray cat staring up at her.

"I know. You miss him, too." Though Meghan liked cats

well enough, Drew had been the real feline lover. He'd raised many cats, but he claimed McTavish was his favorite.

McTavish meowed again, then rose and rubbed his arched back against her skirt. After running a hand over the cat's head, Meghan shifted her attention back to the picture frame in her lap.

Unable to part with the frame despite the faded portrait of Drew, she carefully wrapped it in several layers of tissue paper then tucked it beneath the clothes in the bottom drawer of her dresser.

One

November 1865

Meghan walked along the beach, relishing the warmth of the winter sun on her head and shoulders. The days were much too short for her to spend as much time watching the ocean as she did the rest of the year. Drew had enjoyed the ocean, but not nearly as much as she. Meghan loved the salt spray, the wind in her face, the white foamy waves breaking over the beach and rushing ashore, then retreating in a never-ending cycle. She stopped to stare out over the vast stretch of water. Was it possible Drew had been gone over two years?

She sighed. She should get on with her life, start keeping company with the men who'd expressed interest in her, as her friends and employers, Moira and Grady Donovan, kept telling her. Now that the war had ended, Galveston was on the grow. Each day more and more single men arrived on the island. Like the army captain Moira and Grady had invited to share Thanksgiving dinner with the three of them just a few days earlier. The man was nice enough, and Meghan knew the Donovans were probably right, but she just couldn't bring herself to become involved with anyone. Something held her back, something she couldn't put her finger on, yet it was there nonetheless.

"Meghan?"

A male voice carried to her across the beach, startling her from her thoughts. She swung around to face the man who'd called her name. He was tall, perhaps a little over six feet, and lean, though he appeared to be well muscled beneath his jacket. His face and hands were tanned, his jaw square, his nose straight. His hair held the color of the sun, burnished gold with silver highlights; his eyes reminded her of the sea, a deep blue-green.

Meghan's heart speeded up from just looking at this stranger. Unable to speak, she could only stare as his brow furrowed.

"You are Meghan, aren't you?"

"Yes," she finally managed to say. "I'm Meghan Tompkins. Have we met before?" Now her brow wrinkled in confusion.

"No, we haven't met." He lifted one hand and ran his fingers through his thick hair. "At least, I don't think we have."

Meghan tipped her head to one side, studying him through narrowed eyes. "Who are you?"

"I'm Travis Garner. My ship, the *Empress*, dropped anchor in the bay late this morning, and I've been searching for you ever since I came ashore."

"How did you know to look for me at this beach?"

"I just . . . I can't explain it. But when you weren't at the store I knew to come here."

"Have you visited Galveston before?"

"No."

"Then why are you looking for me?"

"As I said, I'm not sure. I only know I had to come to Galveston and find Meghan. You." He ran his fingers through his hair again, turning his face into the cool winter breeze. He drew a deep breath, then turned his tortured gaze back to her. "Listen, I know this must sound crazy, but I've been thinking about finding you for months. I had to come here. I had to find—"

Meghan held up one hand. "I don't want to hear anymore. You're not making any sense, so if you'll excuse me, I have to get back to town." Grasping her skirt with both hands, she turned to leave, resisting the urge to run.

Travis watched Meghan hurry away, her dark auburn hair, high cheekbones, turned-up nose, and full mouth still lingering in his mind's eye. He could also recall how her pale green eyes had widened with fright at his claim of looking for her. He couldn't blame her. Hell, who wouldn't be frightened after hearing his reason for coming to Galveston: to search for a person he didn't know but couldn't get out of his mind?

A few minutes later he left the beach and headed back to the wharf. He'd give Meghan a little time; then he'd try to talk to her again. He couldn't head back to St. Croix until he settled whatever it was that had drawn him to Galveston.

The rest of that evening and well into the next day, Meghan's thoughts continued to dwell on the man at the beach. What could have caused his odd behavior, or made him say such strange things? Surely he must have fought in the war and as a result suffered from battle fatigue or some sort of fever or other brain disorder. Nothing else could explain his presence on the island or his claim to be looking for her.

The door of Donovan's Mercantile opened, drawing Meghan's attention away from her thoughts. She turned toward the front of the store only to have her mouth fall open in shock. The very man who'd been filling her thoughts stood just inside the door.

She closed her mouth with a snap, then marched over to him. "What do you want?" she said in a voice more curt than she had intended.

"Meghan, you have every right to be leery of me. But I swear, I only want to talk to you. Please."

He looked so genuinely troubled that Meghan didn't have the heart to refuse him. "All right. I'll give you five minutes."

"Actually, I'd prefer going for a walk, if you can leave the store. We won't go far."

Meghan stared at him for a moment, then nodded and headed for the back room. She returned a minute later, a woman in her early forties with black hair and bright blue eyes following behind her.

"I'll be back soon, Moira," Meghan said, taking her shawl off the peg behind the counter. She wrapped the dark blue wool around her shoulders, then turned back to her friend. "As I said, I won't be long. I just need to speak with Mr. Garner for a few minutes."

"Take all the time you want," Moira replied, her eyes sparkling with pleasure. "Today's not all that busy anyway, so there's no need to be hurrying back. Go on with ye, and have a good time."

Meghan sent Moira a glare of warning, then turned to step through the door Travis held open for her.

The sky was clear again, the wind a little less brisk as Meghan led him down the street. With Christmas just a month away, the folks in Galveston were anticipating the holiday season—the first no longer tempered by the pain of war. Even though Union troops still occupied the city, everyone was busy making plans for the most exuberant time on the island. This year Christmas would be joyfully celebrated, the stores beautifully illuminated with gaslights, every church edifice aglow with candles.

After they'd walked for a few minutes Meghan said, "What was it you wanted to say to me?"

Travis cleared his throat, uncertain how to begin. At last he said, "I was born and raised on St. Croix, in the West Indian Islands. My family has been in shipping for generations, and I've captained my own ship since I was just past twenty. I've always loved the sea and can't imagine doing anything else with my life."

When he fell silent Meghan said, "You still haven't told me why you came here to find me. That is what you said yesterday, isn't it?" At his nod, she added, "Then tell me why."

"It started over two years ago. In June of '63 the *Empress* was just a few days out of port when I was stricken with a sudden fever. I'd never been sick a day in my life, so my crew was baffled at how quickly I'd been taken ill. Jason Le Clair, my first mate and best friend, ordered the crew to return to St. Croix, where he summoned my family's doctor. By the time they settled me in my room I had slipped into a coma."

"What illness did the doctor say you'd contracted?"

"He wasn't sure. But since I was running a very high fever and remained unconscious he told my family he was afraid I had no chance of surviving."

"Obviously he was wrong. What did he do to save you?"

"Nothing. Whatever saved me had nothing to do with his medical skills."

She stopped and turned to look up him. "What do you mean?"

Travis ran a hand through his hair in a gesture Meghan was beginning to recognize as a nervous habit. "When the doctor's treatments didn't reduce my fever he told my family there was nothing more he could do, that my survival was out of his hands."

"So why do you think you survived?"

"That's really hard to explain. Other than the first few hours after the sickness hit me, I don't remember anything about the weeks of my illness until just before I awoke from the coma."

Meghan stared at him thoughtfully, her curiosity piqued by the story he related. When he remained silent she touched his arm. Her fingers tingled at the contact, sending a ripple of pleasure over her body. Ignoring her reaction, she said, "Travis, tell me what you remember."

He started at her voice, then turned his gaze to meet hers. "I remember being unconscious and feeling myself being pulled through a dark tunnel, moving closer and closer to a bright light at the end. I knew I was dying, but I wasn't afraid. As I began to slip into the arms of death, I felt as if I was floating above my body. But then, before I entered whatever afterlife awaits us, I experienced a sensation of being jerked away from the light, back into the tunnel of darkness and back into my body. The next thing I remember is awakening from the coma, weak but lucid."

He drew a deep shaky breath, his dark blond eyebrows pulled together in a frown. "Your name was the first word I spoke."

Meghan stood beside him, wide-eyed but silent.

When she made no comment he continued with his story. "I couldn't figure out why I was thinking about a woman I had no recollection of meeting and of a place I'd never visited. I thought perhaps my fever had impaired my memory, but Jason assured me I didn't know a Meghan. I finally dismissed my preoccupation with both you and Galveston as an inexplicable aftermath of my illness and close call with death."

Meghan tightened her grip on his arm. "But you came here anyway."

"Yes. Even after I fully recovered and returned to my ship I couldn't stop thinking of coming here and finding you, though I had to wait for the war to end before making the trip. I knew your name, where you worked, and that you loved to walk along the beach, yet I still can't explain how I knew such things.

"Jason thinks the fever must have permanently damaged some part of my brain." Travis looked up the street, the muscles in his jaw working. "He might be right."

"When . . ." Her voice broke. "When did you come out of the coma?"

"I was unconscious for almost two weeks. I came to on the third of July."

July third. The day Drew had been mortally wounded at Gettysburg. Meghan jerked her hand from his arm and pressed her fingers to her mouth to stifle a gasp. The blood rushed from her head, making her sway on her feet.

Travis grasped her shoulders, steadying her. "What is it? You look like you've seen a ghost."

Meghan wanted to reassure him, but she couldn't utter a sound. *Dear God, was it possible? Were Drew's death and Travis's recovery somehow linked?* Drawing a deep breath, she gave her head a little shake. The notion that there might have been some sort of soul transference was, to say the least, shocking; the possibility totally preposterous. Dismissing the bizarre turn of her thoughts, she finally said, "I'm fine. It's just that your mentioning July third gave me a start. That's the day my husband was killed in the war."

Travis stared down at her for a long, tense moment. "Do you think the date is more than a coincidence?"

"No . . . no, I don't think so," she said, shrugging off his hands. Turning in the direction they'd come, she said, "If you'll excuse me, I have to get back to the store. Good day, Mr. Garner."

"Good day," he murmured at her retreating back, his face drawn into a puzzled frown.

Two

Meghan tucked a strand of hair back into place among the cluster of curls piled atop her head, then heaved a heavy sigh. Why she had agreed to go with Travis to the first of Galveston's Christmas balls at the Tremont Opera House baffled her. There was just something about him that tugged at her insides, something wholly appealing and somehow familiar. She halted that line of thinking. After coming to the startling yet totally absurd conclusion several days earlier that Drew's spirit might have returned to her in Travis's body, Meghan had admonished herself to stop such fanciful thoughts. Such an occurrence wasn't possible. Still—A sharp knock on the door jerked her back to the present.

Pasting a smile on her face, Meghan moved across the parlor of her small house and opened the door. If Travis had been handsome before, dressed like a ship's captain, he was even more so in formal evening attire. The crisp white collar of his shirt was a bold contrast to his deeply tanned face, his deep green cravat a perfect complement to his eyes, his long black frock coat an ideal means of accentuating his wide shoulders.

Her heart beating a wild rhythm against the tight bodice of her dress, Meghan met his hooded gaze.

"You look wonderful," she said, her voice sounding slightly breathless.

"And you're beautiful." He took a step closer and bent to brush his lips across her cheek.

Though her yellow taffeta gown was several years out of fashion, Meghan was pleased by his compliment. Feeling the heat of a blush climb up her face, she dropped her gaze and whispered, "Thank you."

"You're welcome, Meggy."

Her head snapped up, delicate brows pulled together in a frown. "Who told you my nickname is Meggy?"

He shrugged. "No one. Meggy just seemed a natural shortening of Meghan."

After a moment of searching his gaze for a hint of some sort of deception she accepted his explanation, then reached for her evening shawl. Travis took the garment from her and dropped it over her shoulders. When his fingers grazed her skin through the sheer netting of the dress's upper bodice, a familiar flash of desire skittered up her spine—the same reaction she'd had to Drew's touch.

She squeezed her eyes closed for a moment, remembering how much she'd ached for Drew's touch, longed for his kisses and caresses after he enlisted. And now she'd never experience either one again. Biting her lip to hold in a moan of protest, she finally managed to regain her composure.

On the walk to the Tremont House, Travis said, "Did you stay on the island during the war?"

"Yes. I thought of leaving several times. Food was scarce, and since so many of the mercantile's customers moved to the mainland until the war ended, business dropped off to almost nothing. I felt like I wasn't earning my salary, so I told Moira and Grady I was thinking of moving to Houston. They put up a fuss and insisted I was doing no such thing. Since the two of them are the closest I have to real family, I agreed to stay."

"Obviously their business survived. From what I've been told by some of the folks here, a lot of businesses didn't make it through the war."

Meghan nodded. "With the harbor closed, stores weren't receiving merchandise. They had no choice except closing their doors. At one point there was only a handful of businesses still open. Moira and Grady were lucky to survive. Grady says it was his good business sense that saw them through the war, but Moira insists it was luck. She found the back tooth of a horse while she was visiting a friend not long after the war began and she's carried it with her ever since. She claims the tooth is an old Irish omen for never wanting for money."

Travis chuckled. "You always said Moira was a bit superstitious."

Meghan cast a sidelong glance in his direction. He was doing it again—making reference to things she'd supposedly told him. How did he know such things when they'd only met a few days before?

Arriving at the Tremont Opera House, Meghan put aside such confusing thoughts and resolved to enjoy the evening. Christmas was her favorite time of year, though the previous two had lost their appeal after Drew's death. But tonight she hoped to recapture some of the magic of the season.

There was already a crowd in the ballroom. Some were familiar faces, but most were strangers to Meghan. Smiling up at Travis when he asked if she'd like to dance, she forgot about the others in attendance and let her senses bask in the attentions of the handsome man holding her.

Travis couldn't take his gaze off Meghan. Though there was no denying she was incredibly lovely, there was something about her beyond the physical that he found appealing, a sense of feeling whole while in her company, a sense of rightness with her at his side. And of course she also appealed to him on the most basic of levels: sexually. He desired her more than he'd ever wanted a woman, and he'd certainly had his share of intimate relationships in his twenty-nine years. But his feelings for all those women didn't come close to what he felt for Meghan.

Ever since he'd awakened from his coma he could think

of only one woman; he wanted only one woman. The woman he held in his arms as they moved across the dance floor.

He longed to taste her full mouth in a slow, deep kiss, instinctively knowing her lips would be as sweet as the ripest peach, as potent as the strongest whiskey. He longed to pull the pins from her hair and run his fingers through the silky auburn locks. He was already half hard from his provocative thoughts. Forcing himself to take slow, steady breaths, he tried not to think of the things he'd like to do to Meghan, or have her do to him.

By the time the song ended a few moments later Travis had managed to gain control over his traitorous body.

"Would you like a glass of punch?" he asked, noting her flushed cheeks.

She gave him a grateful smile. "Yes, I certainly would."

Travis escorted her to the refreshment table and poured two cups of punch. He handed one to Meghan, then lifted the other and took a sip. "Wait," he said, reaching out to grab her arm as she raised the cup to her mouth.

"What is it?"

"There's whiskey in the punch."

"I know."

"But you don't drink whiskey."

Meghan stared up at him with wide eyes. "Why would you say that?"

"Well, I . . ." He cleared his throat, the corners of his mouth turning down. "That is . . . er . . . most ladies don't drink spirits."

After a moment she lifted the cup and took a long swallow. "Actually, I didn't drink whiskey until two years ago. I acquired a taste for Irish coffee, which contains a full jigger of Irish whiskey, when Moira and Grady served it after Christmas dinner. Now I enjoy the taste every now and again." She took another swallow. "This isn't nearly as smooth as Grady's Irish whiskey, but it'll do in a pinch."

Travis shook his head, a smile replacing his frown. "You're

one of a kind, Meghan Tompkins." With a chuckle, he lifted his cup in a salute, then downed the cool drink in one gulp.

"Shall I fetch you a refill?" he asked, a twinkle in his blue-green eyes.

She batted her eyelashes at him. "Would you be trying to get me drunk, Mr. Garner?"

"Me, ma'am?" He affected a perfect horrified expression. "Why, how could you even think such a thing?"

Meghan burst out in gales of laughter. "You always could make me laugh," she managed to get out between giggles.

His face sobered. "What?"

She dropped her gaze, appalled at what she'd let slip. "Nothing. I was just . . . it was nothing." Pretending great interest in smoothing the skirt of her dress, she scolded herself for voicing her suspicions—that Travis and Drew were somehow connected. The idea still seemed completely ridiculous, and yet . . .

Hoping to ease the uncomfortable moment, Meghan lifted her head and glanced at the other guests swirling around the dance floor. "Now that my thirst has been appeased, would you care to partner me again in another dance?"

"My pleasure," he replied, holding out his arm to her.

By the time the ball ended much later, Meghan's face was flushed, several curls had worked free of her upswept coiffure to dangle onto her shoulders, and her legs and feet ached from the constant dancing. In spite of the discomfort she was happier than she'd been in a long time.

"Are you sure you want to walk home?" Travis asked, escorting her from the opera house. "You barely sat down all evening."

"Yes, but my house is only a few blocks away. And besides, the night air feels wonderful."

They crossed Tremont Street, Travis's boots crunching on the crushed oyster shell pavement, then headed east on Market. After a few minutes he said, "Galveston is a beautiful town."

"Yes, I've always thought so. But when the oleanders are in full bloom, that's when the island is truly magnificent."

"Have you considered living anywhere else?"

"I used to think about it, especially after losing my parents and my brother and sister to yellow fever seven years ago. I even thought of going back to Ireland. But then I met Drew, and after we were married I figured Galveston would always be my home. And when I learned he'd been killed, I was too busy helping Moira and Grady to think of leaving." She drew a deep breath. "I do love the scent of the ocean, and I would miss it terribly if I lived very far inland."

Arriving at Meghan's house, Travis turned toward her. He lifted one hand to touch one of the long curls brushing her shoulders. Rubbing the lock of hair between his thumb and forefinger, he said, "Would it be too bold of me to ask for a kiss?"

Meghan's breath caught in her throat. She longed to experience his kiss, to feel his lips pressed to hers. But agreeing would be highly improper—having known him for so short a time. Yet, she couldn't form the words to refuse. Swallowing hard, she shook her head. Her heart pounding heavily against her chest, she kept her gaze locked on his mouth as he closed the distance between them.

Travis released the lock of hair and moved his hand to cradle the back of her head. He brushed his mouth ever so gently across hers, eliciting a moan from deep in her throat. "Meggy. Meggy," he groaned, nibbling at her lips before settling his mouth firmly on hers.

He widened his stance, pulling her more tightly against him. Everywhere their bodies touched a flare of desire ignited and then sizzled through him until he was afire with need. His pulse thundering in his ears, Travis lifted his head. He sucked in a deep breath, hoping to cool the tide of desire before it surged out of control.

When Travis made no move to kiss her again Meghan allowed her eyelids to drift open. Her breath coming in rasping pants, she stared up at the man holding her. Every nerve ending in her body screaming with longing, she pushed her hips more tightly against him. His groan at the contact and his arousal, evident even through the layers of her skirt and petticoats, made her dizzy with desire. She licked her lips, relishing the taste of him on her tongue. Lifting one hand, she smoothed the deep furrows of his forehead with her fingertips. "Is something wrong?"

"No," he said, his voice a croaking whisper. "I've just . . . I've just never wanted anyone as much as I do you."

She gave him a bright smile. "Should I take that as a compliment?"

"You may, because that's how I meant it. Kiss me one more time and then I have to head back to the *Empress* before I forget I'm a gentleman."

Rising up on tiptoes, Meghan looped her arms around his neck and pressed closer. Just as her lips found his, he opened his mouth and laved his tongue over the silky underside of her bottom lip. She stiffened at the intrusion, then immediately relaxed against him, her fingers tangling in the golden hair at his nape as she tried to pull him even closer.

Feeling his control slipping away again, Travis stroked his tongue over her lips one last time, then broke the kiss. His forehead pressed to hers, he struggled to breathe. "Jesus, Meggy, you take my breath away." Giving her nose a quick kiss, he straightened. He pulled her arms from around his neck and took a step back.

"Can I see you tomorrow?"

"I can't. I volunteered to help with the children's Christmas program. I'll be at the church most of the day, and in the evening I'm helping Moira make cookies."

"Okay; how about Monday?"

"Monday's fine, but it will have to be late. The stores are starting to stay open until nine for Christmas shoppers."

"How about a late supper?"

"I'd like that."

Travis turned to open the door of her house, then stepped aside so she could pass in front of him. " 'Night, Meggy," he whispered as she crossed the threshold.

" 'Night, Travis."

She watched until he disappeared down the street, then closed the door and turned toward her bedroom. She stopped at McTavish's basket.

Bending to run her hand over the soft gray fur, she said, "And good night to you, McTavish."

The cat blinked up at her, yawned, then curled back into a ball. Meghan smiled, then straightened and entered her bedroom. Undressing quickly, she slipped a nightdress over her head, then pulled the rest of the pins from her hair and carefully brushed out the snarls. She climbed into bed and lay down with a sigh.

Against her will, comparisons of Travis and Drew niggled their way into her thoughts. As she drifted into the arms of sleep, she wondered what the chances were of two men being so much alike.

Three

Travis stood at the rail of his ship's bow, staring at the city of Galveston. Five days had passed since he first kissed Meghan, and he was still having trouble coming to terms with his growing attraction to her. He'd had his share of women in the fourteen years since he lost his innocence at the age of fifteen. But he'd never cared for any of his partners the way he was beginning to care about Meghan. He was completely astounded at how he could experience such a depth of emotion for a woman he'd met just two weeks earlier.

Perhaps that was the crux of the matter. Perhaps having known Meghan for so short a time made caring for her all the more difficult to accept. He heaved a weary sigh. Or maybe he hadn't come to terms with the fact that he'd sailed to Galveston to search for her because he couldn't stop thinking about a woman he didn't know who lived in a city he'd never visited.

Frustrated at being unable to find the answers to his troubling questions, he curled his hands into fists atop the ship's rail. Squeezing his eyes closed for a moment, he forced his fingers to relax, then blew out a weary breath. *Ah, hell, what difference does it make? I'm here, and I enjoy being with her.*

He pushed away from the rail and headed for his cabin. He was having supper with Meghan and the Donovans; then he planned on figuring out a way to have Meghan all to himself for the rest of the evening.

* * *

Meghan opened the door of the Donovan house in response to Travis's knock, then tipped her face up to accept his hello kiss.

"Hmmm, I missed you," he murmured against her mouth.

Her eyes alight with mischief, a dimple appeared in her right cheek. "Aw, be gone with ye. It's barely been twelve hours since you walked me home."

"I know," he replied, one hand pressed dramatically over his heart. "And every one of them pure misery without you."

Her smile widened. Giving him a gentle swat on the arm, her voice dropped to a whisper. "I missed you, too."

Meghan looped her arm through his and led him across the parlor. "Grady, I'd like you to meet Travis Garner. Travis, this is my dear friend and employer, Grady Donovan."

Travis accepted the older man's hand. Grady looked to be in his late forties, of medium height and stout build, his grip firm. "Pleased to meet you, Mr. Donovan."

"That's Grady to you, young man. Mr. Donovan was me da."

Travis chuckled. "Okay, Grady it is."

"Well, sit yerself down, Travis. Dinner won't be ready for a while yet."

"I'll go help Moira," Meghan said, flashing a smile in Travis's direction, then hurrying from the room.

After Travis made himself comfortable on the sofa, Grady said, "Meghan tells me you're in shipping."

"Yes, that's right. My ship is the *Empress*, part of a fleet of ships owned by my family in St. Croix."

"You must've seen a lot of the world then."

"A good share of it. I started sailing as a lad with my father, who put in at nearly every major port. But since I became captain of my own ship, most of my trips have been between the United States and Great Britain."

"And what brought you to Galveston?"

Travis shifted on the sofa. Though he knew he'd be asked the question, he still wasn't sure how to answer. Finally he said, "I heard Galveston has a deep harbor, and with the war finally over I thought it might be a good time to check out the possibility of picking up some business for Garner Shipping."

Grady nodded. "Aye, things are improving here each and every day."

Before Travis could say any more, Meghan announced that dinner was ready.

Travis enjoyed the meal and chatting with Moira and Grady, both of whom treated him like an old friend. But in spite of feeling comfortable in the Donovan home, his mind raced ahead to after supper. How long would he have to wait before he and Meghan could make their excuses and leave without appearing rude?

He glanced over at Meghan, his eyes widening at the desire he saw reflected on her face. When she realized he was watching her, she quickly averted her gaze, making him wonder if he'd only imagined the longing in her expression.

As it turned out, Travis didn't have to worry about coming up with an excuse to take his leave. After coffee and dessert Moira turned to Meghan and said, "I hope you don't mind, dear, but Grady and I agreed to help decorate the church this evening. Father O'Brien wants everything finished for tomorrow's service. I'm afraid we have to leave right away. I don't even have time to do up these dishes."

Meghan shot a quick glance in Travis's direction, then turned back to her friend. "Of course we don't mind." She pushed her chair away from the table and rose. "I'll help you clear the table; you two can be on your way that much sooner."

Travis coughed to cover the laughter threatening to erupt from his chest. He hadn't been wrong; Meghan *did* want to be alone with him.

A few minutes later Travis thanked the Donovans for the

invitation and the fine meal, then cupped Meghan's elbow firmly with his hand and led her from the house.

"Is there somewhere you'd like to go?" Travis asked several minutes later, his pulse pounding in his ears.

She tipped back her head and met his gaze. "I'd like to walk on the beach." Seeing the disappointment in his eyes, she smiled. "Just a short walk; then we'll head for my house."

Travis nodded, hoping the ocean breeze would cool the heat of his desire. Telling himself the delay would only heighten his anticipation of tasting her sweet lips, he returned her smile.

When he stepped into her parlor a short time later Travis felt an instantaneous sense of belonging, as if he'd been there before. Yet he'd never set foot inside Meghan's house—she had never invited him inside on the several occasions he had called for her or escorted her home. Shaking off his strange reaction to the Tompkins house as a product of his overactive imagination, he turned his attention to Meghan.

"Come, sit beside me," he said, lowering himself onto the small settee and patting the cushion beside him.

Before Meghan could react McTavish came running into the room and leaped up onto the settee beside Travis.

"Who do we have here?" Travis asked, rubbing his fingers under the cat's chin.

"This is McTavish," Meghan responded, her brow furrowed. McTavish was a very aloof cat, seldom leaving the kitchen when she had visitors. Yet it was almost as if the cat knew Travis. But that wasn't possible. Travis had never been in—

A deep male chuckle pulled Meghan from her thoughts. Travis smiled up at her, then said, "He's sure a friendly fella."

"I don't understand. McTavish isn't much of a people cat. But he certainly likes you." Meghan was baffled by the cat's reaction to Travis. Drew was the only one McTavish would allow near him for more than a brief pat on the head.

Travis gave the cat one last chuck under the chin, then

whispered, "How 'bout you get down so your mistress can sit there?"

McTavish cocked his head to one side in contemplation of the request, gave his tail a haughty flick, then jumped to the floor and curled up next to Travis's feet.

The cat's uncharacteristic behavior forgotten at the blazing look Travis gave her, Meghan eased down on the settee. "Can I . . . can I get you something to drink?" Her voice quavered in reaction to his nearness and the heat she saw in his eyes.

He shook his head. "The only thing I want is to kiss you, Meggy," he whispered, leaning toward her and brushing his lips over hers.

Meghan's breath caught in a soft gasp, her heart hammering even harder at the soft touch of his mouth. She moaned, looped her arms around his neck, and scooted closer. Her tongue peeped out to rasp across his lower lip, wrenching a rumbling groan from deep in his chest.

Travis hauled her onto his lap and took her mouth in a searing kiss. His tongue dueled with hers, stabbing and parrying in perfect timing. His lungs afire from holding his breath, he finally lifted his head. Gasping for air, he stared down at the woman in his arms. Her bosom heaving, her lips swollen from his assault, and her hair cascading down her back in a wild tangle, she looked like a goddess—a love goddess.

He watched as her eyelids lifted, revealing eyes darkened with desire. "You're so beautiful," he whispered, then lowered his head for another quick taste of her mouth. He shifted one hand, moving his fingers around her side to settle over one breast. Using his thumb, he rubbed the firm mound until the tip contracted into a hard pebble, pushing at him through the layers of her clothes.

She moaned, wiggling on his lap and shifting her upper body to press more fully against his hand. He had to bite his lip to keep from crying out at the pressure of her bottom brushing his erection. Though he wanted to do more than kiss her and was certain she was aroused enough to let him, he couldn't bring himself to take advantage of her that way.

"Easy, love," he crooned, changing his kisses to soft pecks and altering his touch to gentle caresses meant to cool rather than stoke her desire. Feeling her body lose some of its stiffness, he said, "That's it; just relax. The ache will be gone in a minute."

When her breathing returned to normal and her pulse slowed to an even cadence, she kept her gaze downcast as he shifted her back onto the settee beside him.

Meghan was mortified at her boldness. No one but Drew had ever made her react in such a brazen fashion. Clearing her throat, she said, "I'm sorry if my behavior offended you. I . . . I don't know what—"

"Shh," he whispered, pressing a finger to her lips. "Don't ever be sorry about feeling desire, Meggy. It's the most natural, the most wonderful thing on this earth."

"Then . . . then why did you stop?" She still couldn't look at him, but stared at her clasped hands.

Travis watched her for a moment, his heart contracting with an emotion he had never experienced. "I stopped because I wasn't sure you were ready to take the next step."

She lifted her head at his words and met his gaze. "But I *was* ready."

He chuckled. "Yes, you were ready. Physically." His expression sobered. "But I couldn't be certain you were ready emotionally. It's been a long time since you've been with a man, and I just can't allow myself to take advantage of your . . . er . . . needs. I didn't want you to regret your actions later."

She stared up at him for a long moment. "Thank you for being concerned, but you wouldn't have taken advantage of me. And I . . . I wouldn't have regretted making love with you."

He offered her a weak smile. "I thank you for the compliment, Meggy. Maybe next time I . . ." He let his sentence go unfinished, not wanting her to feel as though she had to make some sort of commitment.

He smoothed a lock of hair away from her face, then said, "I think I'd better go." He bent to brush her lips with his, then rose from the settee and moved toward the door. McTavish followed him, rubbing against his trousers.

He bent to scratch the cat, then straightened and swung around to face her. "Can I see you tomorrow?"

"I'm going to church in the morning. Then, in the afternoon, I plan on decorating my Christmas tree. You can help me, if you'd like."

His brows pulled together. "I've never decorated a Christmas tree. The idea really hasn't caught on in St. Croix."

"There's nothing to it. String some popcorn into garlands and drape them on the tree. Then hang gingerbread cookies and a few paper ornaments and you're done. Simple."

"How about if I take you to church, we have dinner in one of the restaurants afterwards, and then we decorate your tree?"

"I'd like that. I'll see you in the morning, then." She rose and moved to stand beside him.

He lifted a hand and cupped the side of her face. " 'Night, Meggy. Sleep well."

After another soft brush of his mouth he reached down to give McTavish one last pat, then opened the door and disappeared into the night.

Four

Travis sat next to Meghan in the church pew, swamped with comforting familiarity and disturbing alienation. Trying to decipher the conflicting sensations, he decided his feeling out of place was because he seldom sat with a congregation listening to a sermon. Though he was a God-fearing man, the life he'd led rarely allowed him to spend his Sunday mornings worshipping in a church. Most of his prayers had been said beneath an open sky, standing on the deck of a ship with only the wind and ocean for company. As for feeling as though he belonged, he credited the woman sitting beside him.

He glanced over at Meghan, whose features were rapt with attention. Staring at her, his chest swelled with pride and that unnamed emotion he'd felt the night before, at having such a fine woman by his side. Sensing his gaze, she cast a sidelong glance in his direction. Her attention returning to the reverend's sermon, she slowly unclasped her hands and lowered one to the seat between them. Using her full skirt as a shield where the pale blue fabric spilled across his lap, she ran her fingers over his thigh in a teasing caress.

Travis started, the touch of her hand on his leg nearly making him leap from the pew. He stared down at her through narrowed eyes. The little imp was playing with fire—but seeing the twitch of her lips, he suspected she knew that.

He spent the rest of the service trying to devise ways to get back at her. When they rose to sing the final hymn and he reached for the hymnal he and Meghan shared he was struck with inspiration. Hoping his movements would appear as nothing more than the enthusiasm of raising his voice in song, he rubbed his elbow back and forth over her left breast. He had to hide a grin when he heard her soft gasp and saw the startled gaze she flashed up at him.

"That was no way to behave in church," Meghan said in a fierce whisper a few minutes later as they walked down the street. "If anyone had noticed what you were doing, I would have died of embarrassment."

"I was being discreet, Meggy," Travis replied. "There's no need to carry on so. And what about you? Don't you think some eyebrows would have been raised if the congregation had witnessed your hand wandering onto my thigh?" When she started to open her mouth in protest his fingers halted the words. "Besides," he continued, running the tip of his forefinger over her full lips, "don't you always say, 'If people want to look, let 'em look'?"

Meghan's pique fled, replaced by surprise. Grasping his hand and pulling it from her mouth, she said, "When did I say that?"

Travis furrowed his brow. "I don't know." Unable to remember the exact time, he shrugged. "Obviously it was some time in the last couple weeks."

Meghan nodded but didn't respond. She was certain she hadn't quoted one of her favorite sayings within the past two weeks. In fact, she doubted she'd said it in the past two years. Refusing to slip back into that confusing line of thinking, she offered Travis a bright smile. "You're right; I overreacted. Forgive me?"

He returned her smile, his teeth a stark flash of white against his deeply tanned face. "Of course." Wrapping her arm through his, he said, "What would you like for dinner?"

"I don't know. What sounds good to you?"

"I have a sudden taste for fresh oysters and fried trout. How about you?"

Meghan's head snapped up. That was the very same meal she and Drew had shared just before he left for—Shaking her head to dislodge those thoughts, she drew a calming breath. Travis lived on an island and made his living on the ocean; he was bound to enjoy seafood. "Yes, oysters and trout would be fine."

He lowered his face to nuzzle her ear. "And then your sweet lips for dessert. The perfect meal."

The meal was indeed perfect, Meghan thought later on their walk back to her house, in no small part due to her companion. Travis had to be the most courteous, most entertaining, most exciting man she'd ever known—other than Drew, of course. She inhaled a deep breath of the salty air, turning her thoughts to the small Christmas tree awaiting them in her parlor. The decorating of a tree for Christmas was not a tradition brought with her family when they sailed from Ireland. It was only after coming to Galveston that she'd been introduced to the holiday practice by the many Germans living on the island. Now Meghan couldn't imagine celebrating Christmas without the fun of decorating a tree.

Travis proved to be adept at stringing popcorn, his large hands extremely agile with a needle and thread. "I've plied many a stitch to a torn sail," he replied to her comment about his ability. "That's one of the first things sailors have to learn when they choose to make their life at sea."

But when the time came to string the white puffy garlands on the tree he deferred to Meghan's experience.

"You've done this before," he said, slouching on the settee and calling to McTavish to join him. He stretched out his legs in front of him, absently stroking the cat with one hand. "If I tried, you might be sorry. I'd get everything tied in knots."

Meghan smiled, recalling how Drew never wanted to help

decorate the tree either. "Okay. You can hand me the ginger-bread cookies and the rest of the ornaments."

After half an hour of arranging and then rearranging the decorations Meghan stood back and proclaimed the result the best-looking tree she'd ever had.

She turned to Travis and said, "Thank you for your help. How about a cup of Irish coffee?"

"I didn't do much," he replied. "But I'd like to try this Irish coffee you've been talking about. Anything I can do to help?"

"No, not yet. I'll just put the coffee on to boil." Meghan picked up the bowl of leftover popcorn, the needles and spool of thread, then moved toward the door to the kitchen.

When she returned to the parlor a few minutes later Travis was bent over the room's small wood stove. Seeing the way his trousers pulled taut across his buttocks sent her pulse into a wild rhythm. Her hands suddenly damp, she wiped them on the skirt of her dress. Her voice was slightly raspy when she said, "The coffee will be ready in a minute."

Travis straightened, then turned toward where she stood in the doorway. "I could hear the wind picking up, so I thought a fire would chase the chill."

Meghan couldn't make her throat work to respond. Snared by the intensity of his gaze, she had trouble even breathing. She finally managed a nod, then started across the room. The damper on the parlor stove was touchy and would permit smoke to fill the room if it wasn't adjusted to just the right angle.

"Don't worry about the damper," Travis said as she moved past him. "I took care of it."

She came to an abrupt halt, then swung around to face him. How did he know about—?

Travis grabbed her arms, frightened by her sudden pallor. "Are you all right?"

"Yes, I'm fine. I . . . uh . . . I guess I'm just a little chilled."

He ran his hands up and down her arms until the color returned to her face. "You need a warm drink. How's that coffee coming?"

"It should be ready by now."

Meghan went back into the kitchen. Forcing herself to concentrate on making the Irish coffee, she set out what she would need. After ladling a tablespoon of brown sugar into each cup she added a jigger of Irish whiskey, then lifted the coffeepot from the stove. She filled the cups with hot coffee and added the final ingredient: a dollop of cream flavored with sugar and vanilla.

Placing the cups on a tray, she returned to the parlor. "I didn't take the time to whip the cream, but otherwise I followed Moira's recipe."

Travis took one of the cups and lifted it to his mouth. The sweetened blend of whiskey and coffee tasted delicious. Though he and Meghan had never shared a drink in her parlor, he had the strange sensation of having done so before.

"Do you like it?" Meghan asked, shooing McTavish off the settee. She sat down beside Travis, then took a sip from her cup.

"Yes," he replied, a scowl marring his face.

She set her cup back in the saucer, then said, "Is something wrong?"

"No," he said more sharply than he had intended. Shoving aside his disconcerting thoughts, he softened his voice and forced his mouth into a smile. "No, everything is fine."

When they finished their coffee he set their cups aside, then stretched one arm along the back of the settee behind Meghan. Wrapping his hand around her shoulders, he urged her closer. When she sat pressed against his side, her head nestled on his shoulder, he whispered, "There, isn't that more comfortable?"

"Hmm, yes." The Irish coffee had warmed her insides; now the nearness of Travis was warming her on the outside. The scent of his cologne mixed with the potent musky odor of his skin drifted to her nose, making her nostrils flare. His natural scent wasn't the same as Drew's, yet it affected her just as strongly.

Though she knew she was being forward, she turned her face up to his and kissed the underside of his jaw. Intoxicated by his scent, she laved her tongue across his skin. The slight stubble of his beard sent a shiver up her spine.

"Are you still cold?" he said against her ear.

She shook her head. "Actually, I feel like I'm on fire."

Grasping her shoulders, he pulled her closer until she practically lay atop him. His eyes had darkened to a deep blue, and a vein in his neck throbbed with his increased pulse rate. "I feel the fire, too, Meggy," he murmured before capturing her mouth in a blazing kiss.

Her arms locked around his neck, Meghan pressed her breasts against his chest, wiggling her hips to lessen the distance between them even more.

When her movements brought her thighs in contact with his arousal, Travis jerked his mouth from hers. His breathing harsh in the stillness of the room, he said, "Don't keep moving like that, sweetheart, or I'll be doing more than kissing you."

Meghan opened her eyes, trying to focus on his face, her heart thundering in her ears. "I . . . want . . . you to . . . do more . . . than kiss me," she managed to get out between deep breaths.

Travis stared down at her dilated pupils. The flecks of gold swimming in her pale green eyes were a sure sign that her desire was at a fever pitch. He didn't dwell on how he came to have such knowledge, but turned her so he could wrap one arm around her shoulders and slip the other beneath her knees.

As he carried her to the house's one small bedroom, he said, "Are you sure this is what you want, Meggy? Tell me now if you aren't." He stopped at the bedroom door. "Because once we cross that threshold there's no turning back."

She lifted her head from his shoulder and stared up at the man holding her. She shouldn't be allowing this, she realized in some vague place in her mind. But nothing had ever felt more right—not since the last time with Drew. The man holding her wasn't Drew, yet she recognized that with very little effort she could fall in love with Travis. Perhaps she already had.

Smiling up at him, she said, "Yes, I'm absolutely sure."

Travis moved into the room, set Meghan on her feet next to the bed, and then pulled back the crocheted coverlet and top sheet. He stared at the bed for a moment, his brows knitted in a frown. Giving his head a quick shake, he turned back to her. He reached for the pins in her hair. "I love your hair," he murmured, his voice rough with need, running his fingers through the heavy mass.

In a slow, playful game, they took turns removing the other's clothes until finally they stood staring into each other's eyes, naked.

When Travis seemed to hesitate Meghan placed one hand on his chest. "You haven't changed your mind, have you?"

Travis clenched his teeth, struggling to control the hot spurt of desire her touch ignited in his veins. Finally he shook his head.

"Good," Meghan whispered, running her fingers through the patch of silky golden hair covering the center of his chest. "Make love to me, Travis. It's been so long, and I don't think I can wait much longer." Meghan realized her request must sound overly bold, but she couldn't—she wouldn't call back the words. In spite of knowing Travis for only a few weeks, she knew what was about to happen was absolutely right.

When he still didn't move she flashed him a smile. "Don't you think we should lie down?"

A chuckle rumbling in his chest, he bent to sweep her into his arms, then eased her onto the mattress. Stretching out beside her, he lowered his head until he could rub her nose with his. "Any more requests?" When she shook her head he ran the tip of his tongue over her lips, paying particular attention to the corners of her mouth. She moaned, threading her fingers into the hair at his nape and holding him fast.

"Don't tease," she whispered against his mouth, then tugged him closer.

"I won't," he managed to say before kissing her in earnest, his hands exploring her soft curves.

Meghan reveled in his touch, her body aflame everywhere his fingers and mouth grazed her skin. He caressed her breasts, then suckled them until her nipples hardened into tight rosettes. How he knew exactly where and how to touch with no instruction from her was a puzzle, but one she soon forgot. By the time he pushed her thighs apart and settled between them on his knees she could barely think.

"Hurry," she murmured, her eyes squeezed shut, her hands clenching into fists. "Please, hurry."

"Soon, sweetheart, soon. Hold on just a minute more." His gaze left her flushed face and settled on the tangle of dark hair covering her sex. He could see the moisture on her feminine flesh. The musky scent of her need filled his nostrils. Parting her with his fingers, he stifled a groan. She was exquisite, like hot silk.

Refusing to give in to his own desire, he rubbed his thumb over the hardened kernel of her most sensitive place. She jerked, then moaned again. "Easy, Meggy. Just relax."

When her muscles lost some of their tenseness he resumed the stroking with his thumb. Her hips came off the bed and then lowered, matching the rhythm he set. He longed to shift positions and bury himself in her hot center, but he knew she was very near her peak and refused to do anything that might prevent her from reaching the final plateau.

Continuing the circular movements of his thumb, he slipped one finger inside her. He had to bite his lip to keep from crying out as her inner muscles tugged at him, bathing him in her essence. Just when he thought he couldn't last a moment longer, that he would surely lose control before he could sheath himself in her warmth, she inhaled sharply.

Her body went rigid; then she arched against him, bucking against his fingers in a frantic rhythm, her hands moving to grip his arms, her nails biting into his flesh. She sobbed his name, then pushed up one last time before collapsing in a boneless sprawl.

Travis smiled at the way her hair cascaded over the pillow in a tousled snarl, how her breasts heaved with her labored breathing, how her thighs lay open in careless abandon. When he realized he'd never felt such incredible satisfaction at having pleasured a woman, his smile faltered. He'd always been a considerate lover, never having been so selfish as not to take care of his partner's needs. But nothing in his past sexual encounters came anywhere close to what he'd just experienced. Why was it different with Meghan?

As he stared at the woman filling his thoughts, she stirred, lifting one hand to brush the hair away from her face. When her mouth curved into a lazy smile, his thoughts scattered like smoke in the wind.

"You look so serious," she said in a husky whisper. "Is something wrong?"

"No, everything's fine." He bent and placed a kiss on the inside of her thigh.

"Umm, that feels wonderful."

"Yes, it does." Slipping his arms under her thighs, he lifted her off the bed and pulled her legs up around his waist. "I can't wait any longer, Meggy. I have to . . ." The rest of the words were choked off by the intensity of his need. He gulped a deep breath of air, then guided his hardened flesh to her softness.

He shoved into her, sinking as far as he could, wrenching a moan, an almost savage rumble from deep in his chest. She was incredibly tight and slick. "Jesus, Meggy," he murmured, leaning forward to brace his weight on his forearms. "You feel like heaven."

He began moving in slow, gentle thrusts, his lips seeking and finding hers, his tongue mimicking the movements of his hips. Meghan met him on every thrust, her hands caressing his back and shoulders, her legs locked around his waist.

When he thought his desire could go no higher, she grabbed the backs of his thighs and pulled him closer.

He pulled his mouth from hers, his lungs on fire, and continued to thrust into her. Throwing back his head, he closed his eyes and tried to delay his climax. But it was too late. Pushing into her as far as he could one final time, he gave himself over to his body's hunger for release.

With a groan, he fell forward and pressed his face into Meghan's neck. Several minutes passed before his senses righted themselves, before his breathing slowed to normal. Gathering his strength, he rolled onto his back and pulled Meghan against his side.

He thought he'd experienced all there was when it came to pleasures of the flesh. But the woman lying in his arms had disabused him of that notion. How that could be went beyond his knowledge and left him uncomfortable, and worse, vulnerable. These were feelings he didn't like.

Meghan snuggled closer, running the toes of one foot up and down his calf. She placed a kiss on his chest, then said, "A penny for your thoughts."

Five

His somber mood evaporating at the touch of Meghan's lips, Travis affected a light tone when he said, "I'm afraid you wouldn't get your money's worth."

She chuckled, her breath stirring the hair on his chest. "That worthless, huh?" Her fingers explored the heavy muscles beneath her hands until she found one flat male nipple. Circling the tiny nubbin with the tip of a fingernail, she added, "There's nothing worthless about you."

"Is that right?" he said, trying to keep the laughter out of his voice. "You wouldn't be telling me that just so you can have your way with me again, would you?"

"Have my way with you!" She pushed herself up onto one elbow to stare into his face. "How dare you say—" The twitching of his lips and the sparkle in his eyes deflated her anger before it had built up a good head of steam. "You're going to pay for that remark, Travis Garner."

Before he realized her intention, he found himself fending off her hands as she tickled his underarms, then his ribs. "Meghan, stop," he managed to say around a bark of laughter. "Enough. Enough."

He finally succeeded in grabbing her wrists and pulling her fingers away from their assault on his body. "My God, woman, you have more hands than an octopus."

Meghan stared down at him, eyes narrowed, lips pursed in a pout. The mutinous set of her mouth slowly eased, giving way to a wide grin. Laughter bubbled up from her chest and spilled from her lips. The sound settled over Travis like a puff of balmy air, making his heart cramp and his blood heat.

His hands still locked around her wrists, he lifted her arms over her head, the position forcing her breasts upward, closer to his mouth. He groaned, then raised his head enough to take one nipple between his lips. "Sweet. So sweet," he murmured around the hardened tip.

She wiggled her hands, but he refused to release her. She whimpered in protest, then sucked in a sharp breath as his teeth grazed her distended nipple. "Travis, please," she sobbed. "I want to touch you."

He dropped his head back onto the pillow. "You won't try to tickle me again?"

She shook her head, giving him a pleading look.

"Swear?"

"Yes, yes. I swear."

He slowly loosened his grip. When she could pull her wrists free she lowered her hands to his shoulders, then slid them around his neck. Her fingers threading through his hair, she lowered her mouth to his. Deepening the kiss, she pressed her full weight against him, keeping him flat on his back while she shifted positions. When she lay atop him, she finally broke the kiss. She pulled her fingers from his hair, then brought her knees up on either side of him so that she sat astride his hips.

"Hmm, I like this," he murmured, lifting a hand and running his fingers across one puckered nipple, then lower over her stomach. He stopped his explorations just short of the auburn curls pressed against his belly. She rotated her hips forward, but he moved his fingers higher. "I think you want me to touch you. Is that what you want, Meggy? Shall I touch you and make you burn for me?"

He inched his fingers lower while watching her face. When she didn't respond he halted the descent. "Tell me, Meggy. Tell me what you want."

She closed her eyes and drew a deep breath. She hated

him for doing this, just like—No! She wouldn't think about that now. Not when she was ablaze with desire. Not when she would go mad if she didn't get him to touch her and bring her the relief she craved.

She swallowed, then said in a shaky voice, "Yes, I want you to touch me with your fingers."

Travis smiled. "Good girl." He moved his hand lower, pushing through the curls. She lifted her hips, allowing him better access. He separated her tender flesh and nudged the pebble nestled there. She was already damp and swollen. She sucked in a sharp breath, her body bucking at the contact.

"Easy, Meggy. I'll make it good for you; you know I will."

She stared at him through glazed eyes, then managed a jerky nod before her lids drifted closed. When he began a slow, easy rhythm with his fingers, she moaned, a shiver racking her shoulders. Head thrown back, hands braced on his chest, she began moving her hips to match the motion of his hand.

Travis watched her strive for, then reach her climax, his own desire forgotten. Bringing Meghan satisfaction was his primary concern; his no longer mattered.

The harsh pants of her breathing abruptly caught as she cried out. Her body went rigid. Then the spasms began. She bucked against his hand time and again, until the contractions slowed, then stopped. Her legs and arms quivering, she fell forward onto his chest with a sob, pressing her face to his neck.

He brushed the hair off her cheek and tucked it behind one ear, then ran his hand up and down her back. When her breathing grew level, he whispered, "See, I told you I'd make it good for you."

She managed to move one arm enough to give him a weak punch in the shoulder. "You don't play fair. You knew exactly how—" She bit her lip to halt what she'd been about to say. She cleared her throat, then said, "I mean, you are obviously more experienced than me."

"Experience has nothing to do with it. When two people are as attuned to each other as we are . . ." He frowned up at the ceiling. *What kind of drivel am I spouting? I open my mouth and have no idea what's going to come out. I feel like I've lost control of everything.* He squeezed his eyes closed, trying to make sense of what was happening to him. *Maybe I've been on land too long. Or maybe—*

Meghan shifted, pulling him from the tangle of his musings. "I'm sorry," she murmured. "I guess I fell asleep for a minute."

He kissed the top of her head. "You have reason to be tired."

"But what about you? You didn't . . . I mean, don't you want to . . . ?"

"Shh, don't worry about it. You just rest. When you've recovered we'll take care of my needs." He eased her off his chest and onto her back next to him. Bending to press a kiss to her brow, he said, "Take a nap, Meggy. I think I'll get something to eat; maybe the rest of those gingerbread cookies."

She smiled at him, then sighed and closed her eyes. "They always were your favorite."

Travis swung back to look at her. "What?" When she didn't respond he leaned closer. "Meggy?"

She made an inarticulate sound, then rolled onto her side, facing away from him.

Thinking he must have misunderstood her, Travis rose from the bed and reached for his trousers.

In the tiny kitchen Travis pulled a chair away from the table and sat down. McTavish came into the room, stretched, then jumped up into Travis's lap. Smiling at the cat, Travis reached for the cloth-covered plate in the center of the table. He lifted the cloth and picked up one of the gingerbread cookies.

He took a bite and chewed thoughtfully. When had he come to like the taste of ginger? He couldn't remember the spice ever tasting as good as it did in Meghan's cookies. He glanced down at the purring McTavish. Come to think of it, when had he become a cat fancier?

His brow furrowed. Now that he thought about it, he realized he'd never been overly fond of cats until after his illness. Not long after he'd recovered, he'd heard about a lady on St. Croix who was seeking homes for a litter of kittens. When he arrived at the lady's house the only kitten left was the runt, a black female the owner said might not survive.

Travis was immediately taken with the tiny ball of fur. He named her Blackberry and ensconced her in his cabin on board the *Empress*. Blackberry thrived under his tender care. She became his constant companion, even sleeping on the foot of his bed, and grew up to become an excellent mouser in the ship's hold.

He scratched under McTavish's chin, thinking how jealous Blackberry would be if she could see her master fussing over another cat. She'd probably stick her nose in the air and strut away with her back ramrod stiff, the tip of her tail twitching in annoyance. He chuckled at the image. His amusement suddenly faded. He still couldn't understand how his illness had brought about his new fascination with cats.

Meghan and Travis spent the rest of the day in her bed, alternately dozing, talking, and making love—sometimes with slow playfulness, other times in a wild frenzy. And as the hours passed, Meghan's suspicions continued to grow. By the time Travis rose from bed and announced that he'd better get back to his ship, she no longer had any doubt. Her mind finally accepted what her heart had known all along.

Drew had kept his promise. He'd returned to her.

Wondering at the conclusion she'd drawn, she stared at the bedroom doorway long after Travis had turned in the opening and flashed her one last smile. As incomprehensible as it seemed, Travis was indeed her husband incarnate. She didn't question the hows or whys of such a startling revelation; she simply accepted the fact that her husband's spirit had returned in the body of another man. But there was still a major problem: While she had finally realized the truth, apparently Travis had not.

She rolled over in bed, wincing at the slight soreness of her muscles. Though physically exhausted, her mind was wide awake. For hours she stared out the window at the night sky, her thoughts in a jumble. Still thinking about her dilemma and the decision she knew she would have to make, she finally drifted off to sleep.

The sun streaming across her bed woke her, pulling her from the depths of slumber. Stretching, she drew a deep breath, filling her lungs with the scent of Travis and their heated lovemaking. The memory of the previous day brought back another memory as well. She jerked upright, clutching the sheet to her naked breasts.

Somehow, in her sleep, her mind had sorted through her options and found the answer that had eluded her the night before. Her course set, she swung her feet to the floor, then rose and reached for her cotton wrapper. Pressing her lips together with determination, she pulled clean underclothes from the dresser. After a quick bath she would head for the wharf.

She had to talk to Travis. She couldn't go on seeing him if she didn't tell him what she'd come to accept as fact. She knew that broaching what he might well label an outlandish tale meant she had to risk losing him. But she had to take the chance. She had to make him see the truth of her words.

There was no alternative.

Six

Meghan arrived at the wharf just as Travis was coming down the gangway of the *Empress*.

"Meghan? What are you doing here? Aren't you supposed to be at the mercantile?"

She took the arm he offered, then said, "I stopped by and told Moira I'd be in later. Travis, there's something I need to talk to you about."

He could see the haunted look in her eyes and something close to fear squeezed his heart. "All right. Have you eaten?"

Meghan shook her head.

"Would you like to get some breakfast?"

"I don't think so. But if you want to eat, I'll have some coffee."

"All right, let's go."

She fell into step beside him, praying she wasn't making a mistake.

Once their cups of coffee were set in front of them, Travis leaned back in his chair, one hand toying with his spoon. "What was it you wanted to talk about?"

Meghan started, then looked up to meet his concerned gaze. "Umm, I'm not sure how to say this, so I . . . uh . . . guess I'll just plunge right in." She drew a deep breath, then said, "I believe you're my husband."

Travis straightened. "What! Look at me; do I look like your husband?"

"I know you're not Drew physically. But on the inside, I think you're him."

"You're talking nonsense."

She reached across the table and grabbed his forearm. The muscles beneath her hand were rigid with tension. "I know it sounds crazy, but please hear me out."

His jaw clenched, he gave her a terse nod.

"Let me start at the beginning. When Drew left to join the Confederate Army he promised me he would return. His exact words were, 'No matter what happens, Meggy, I swear I'll find a way to come back to you.' I always thought his words were meant to give me hope if he was captured or injured. But then I got word he'd been killed at Gettysburg, and I knew he wouldn't be able to keep his promise."

"And you think my coming here is in some twisted way the keeping of his promise?"

"Yes, sort of." Seeing the tightening of his mouth, she rushed on. "You told me the date you nearly died was two years ago, on July third, which is the day Drew was killed. I don't know how it happened, but I think at the moment of Drew's death, his soul left his body and somehow entered yours."

"Are you talking about reincarnation?"

"No; at least, not in the true meaning of the word. I'm not sure what it's called. But I believe both your soul and Drew's were in some sort of limbo at the same time, and when you were called back to the living his soul merged with yours. I don't have an explanation for how something like that can happen, but I'm convinced it's true. There are—"

"Stop it!" Travis slammed his hand down so hard, coffee sloshed onto the table. "That's ridiculous."

"Perhaps. But how else do you explain your coming to Galveston to look for a woman named Meghan? How can you explain your knowing to look for me at the mercantile and the beach, how you knew my nickname, how you knew about the damper on my wood stove or that I used to be a teetotaler? Can you explain why McTavish took to you so quickly, as if he recognized you?"

When he didn't respond but continued to stare at her, she added, "There was something familiar about you from the first time we met. But yesterday everything finally made sense. When we . . . um . . ." Her cheeks warming with a blush, she dropped her gaze to the cup of coffee in front of her. ". . . When we made love, that's when I knew for sure that Drew kept his promise."

"How did our making love prove anything?"

"You knew exactly how to kiss me and touch me. Drew was the only man I've ever been with, yet you did things only he knew about. I'm not an authority on intimate relationships, so if there's another explanation for your doing what you did," she forced herself to lift her gaze and look at him, "then I'd like to hear it."

"There's no big secret," he said more fiercely than he intended. "One woman is pretty much like another. What pleases one pleases them all." The pain in her eyes was like a knife in the chest, but he refused to take back his harsh words. Her talk of souls in limbo traveling from one body to another had him so off kilter, he could barely think. His head pounding and his gut twisting, he knew he could never eat the breakfast he'd ordered. He pushed away from the table and rose. "I have to get back to my ship." Tossing some money on the table, he turned and left the restaurant without a backward glance.

Meghan bit her lip to keep from calling him back. She knew what she'd told him must have come as a shock. She was still shocked herself. He just needed time to work it all through. Once he accepted what she had come to believe, they could talk about their future. Knowing that was asking a lot of anyone, she prayed Travis would see the truth of her words.

If he didn't, she would lose Drew a second time.

* * *

Travis went straight to his cabin on the *Empress* and poured himself a glass of scotch. He swallowed the liquor in one gulp, then refilled his glass. Sinking into a chair, he waited for the warmth of the liquor to ease the twisting of his gut and soothe his frayed nerves. When he could finally breathe without feeling as if a rope was tied around his chest he slumped against the back of his chair with a weary sigh.

He slowly sipped his drink, replaying the conversation with Meghan in his head. As much as making the admission grated on him, he had to agree with her in part: He had come to Galveston looking for a woman named Meghan; he had known to look for her at the beach. And, yes, he knew her nickname. But all of those things had logical explanations.

He'd obviously heard someone talk about Galveston and a woman named Meghan who worked at Donovan's Mercantile before his illness, but his fever had erased the memory. Since she lived on an island, it made perfect sense to look for her on the beach. And as he'd told her the first time he used her nickname, Meggy was a common shortening of Meghan.

But what about the other things she claimed proved another man's soul had taken up residence in his body? Just how *had* he known about adjusting the damper on her stove, or her previous distaste for whiskey? And what about McTavish?

Travis knew animals possessed a sixth sense, an intuitive ability to distinguish friend from foe. *Was that why McTavish took to me so readily? Because he recognized me as his master?* He heaved another sigh. *Christ, listen to me. Now I sound like Meghan.* Meghan. Just thinking her name did crazy things to his insides and brought to mind her final claim. She said when they made love he knew exactly how to bring her pleasure; knowledge only a man who'd been intimate with her would have.

And since he didn't doubt her claim of having made love with only one man, how had he become privy to such knowledge?

He ran a hand through his hair, then lifted the glass for

another long draught. There had to be an explanation. But it wasn't the one he'd given Meghan. He knew all women weren't alike when it came to pleasuring them. What aroused one didn't necessarily arouse another. He'd only used that excuse because her absurd theory shocked him down to his toes.

"Damn," he muttered, setting down his glass with a thud. *Think, damnit, think!* He started to reach for the bottle of scotch, then withdrew his hand. It wasn't even noon, so the last thing he needed was trying to drown his problems with scotch. Keeping a clear head was imperative if he intended to figure out a plausible explanation to refute Meghan's claims. And he sure as hell did.

Travis stayed away from Meghan for the next several days. Instead, he spent his time at the custom house, arranging for a load of cargo. Four days later there was room left in the hold of the *Empress* for a few more crates. Once he found someone with goods to fill the remaining space he would make plans for his departure from Galveston. Knowing he was considering leaving without having resolved anything with Meghan, he tried not to think about her or their last conversation. He wasn't one to take the coward's way out, but this time he was at a loss on what to do.

He successfully kept thoughts of Meghan and her outrageous claims from interfering with his business during the day. But when he retired to his cabin each night there was no distraction to keep her from niggling into his thoughts.

On the fifth night after he'd stormed out of the restaurant he lay on the wide bunk in his cabin, staring up at the ceiling. Blackberry jumped up onto the foot of the bunk and rubbed against his crossed ankles.

Travis pulled his gaze from the shadows the oil lamp cast above his bunk. "What is it, Blackberry?"

The cat turned her face in his direction and gave a long, sorrowful meow.

His brow furrowed, then suddenly cleared. "Ah, I think I know your problem. You're in need of a tom. Is that what you're trying to tell me?"

She blinked her golden eyes at him, meowed a second time, then moved up to sprawl next to him.

Scratching behind her ears, he said, "I should take you to meet Mac. He's a huge gray tom with quite a reputation among the lady cats of Galveston. He'd—" Travis stilled his hand and jerked upright in bed. He couldn't recall ever calling McTavish Mac before. Yet the nickname came out of his mouth so easily, it was as if he'd used it a hundred times. And how the hell did he know about McTavish and the female cats on the island?

Blackberry rolled over, batting her paws at him for more attention. Travis lifted the cat onto his lap, then scooted up to sit with his back against the wall.

He closed his eyes and drew a deep breath, then exhaled slowly. He forced himself to relax, to clear all thoughts from his head. For the first time since recovering from his illness and experiencing inexplicable urges to go to a place he'd never been and find a woman he didn't know, he tried to prepare himself to face the truth. Taking another deep breath, he opened his mind and let it wander at will, allowing it to gain entry through a door he'd previously kept tightly sealed.

At first there was only darkness behind his closed eyelids, and the loud rumble of Blackberry's purring. Then the black curtain lifted, revealing images of his childhood on his island home, of the first ship he'd sailed on with his father, of the last voyage he made on the *Empress* before taking ill.

Those images were followed by vignettes of Meghan. In the first her face glowed with happiness as she stood before a church altar wearing a dress of cream-colored lace, a bouquet of oleander in her hands. In the next she stood at the wharf, her face etched with fatigue and pain as she waved at a ship moving away from the dock, the skirt of her pale lavender dress whipping in the wind.

Meghan's image faded away, replaced by a scene straight from hell. The air was filled with the deafening roar of cannons and the acrid scent of gunpowder as two armies engaged in battle. All around him men fell, crying out in surprise and anguish, their faces and limbs locked in the agony of death. Travis winced with the recalled pain of a bullet ripping through his side, felt the stickiness of blood soaking his gray uniform and the ground beneath him. And just before the oblivion of unconsciousness claimed him, he remembered the last word he'd spoken: Meghan.

Travis pulled his brows together, the corners of his mouth turning down. Everything had been so real, so vivid, and yet he knew he'd experienced only part of the memories his mind had dredged up. He hadn't seen Meghan on her wedding day, or watched her from a ship as he sailed away. And he hadn't fought in the recent war. Those were memories of—

His heart thudding against his eardrums, he opened his eyes with a start. *No! It can't be.*

Meghan stared at the bolts of fabric she was supposed to be straightening, the bright colors blurring before her eyes. She couldn't concentrate on even the simplest of chores since the morning Travis left her sitting in the restaurant down by the wharf. Every time a customer came into the mercantile she looked up, hoping to see him standing in the doorway. Since his rude departure a week earlier, she had continued to keep her hope alive, praying he would come back. Then, after Grady heard the *Empress* was taking on cargo, she feared her prayers were not going to be answered, that Travis would sail away from Galveston and never return.

Forcing herself to concentrate on her work, she tried not to think about Christmas, now only a week away. What had promised to be the happiest holiday she'd had in two years

now had the potential of becoming the saddest. Even the time
she spent helping with the Christmas program, hearing the
laughter of the children, listening to them sing carols, hadn'
lifted her sagging spirits. She swallowed the lump lodged in
her throat and resigned herself to accepting whatever the fates
dealt her.

By midmorning Meghan had finished straightening the
fabric table when she heard the door open, then the low murmur of voices on the other side of the store. Not bothering
to turn around, she moved to the notions counter.

"Meghan."

Her hands froze in their task of sorting spools of thread.
Afraid she was imagining the identity of the person standing
behind her, she didn't turn around but continued working.
Her movements stiff and awkward, she managed to say, "Is
there something I can do for you?"

Travis chuckled, then said, "Yes, you can give me a swift
kick in the behind."

Meghan gasped, then swung around, one hand pressed over
her pounding heart. "Why . . . why would I want to kick
you?"

"My behavior the other day was rude and insensitive, and
kicking me is the least I deserve." When she didn't respond
he said, "Meghan, I shouldn't have left you the way I did.
But what you told me was just too much for me to accept."
He gave her a weak smile. "I mean, it isn't every day someone says your body has become the haven to more than one
soul. Can you understand even a little how shocked I was by
what you told me? How difficult it was for me to even consider your suggestion?"

Meghan tipped her head to one side as she studied him.
He looked drawn; lines bracketed his mouth and his eyes
looked bloodshot. "It was hard for me to accept, too. So I
do understand, as much as I can, though it must be a lot
harder on you." She paused, then added, "You look tired.
Haven't you been sleeping well?"

He gave her another smile, this one a little broader than his previous attempt. "No, have you?"

She shook her head. "I was so afraid I would never see you again."

"To be honest, for awhile I considered leaving Galveston and not returning. But I realized I couldn't do that to you. The woman both of us love."

Her eyebrows rose. "Both?"

"You were right, Meggy. I know that now. I don't know how or why, but when my life was spared Drew's spirit was given the chance to live on through me. It's rather unsettling, knowing my soul is not entirely my own—that part of it belongs to another man. But I've done a lot of thinking these past few days and I finally realized everything you said was true. Now all that remains is to fulfill not only Drew's wishes, but my own as well." He reached down and grasped her hands with his. "Meggy, ever since I awoke from the coma part of my soul has belonged to you; now my heart belongs to you as well."

"Oh, Travis," she said in a shaky voice, her eyes filling with tears. "I love you, too."

"Do you?" He stared down at her with solemn eyes. "Do you love me, or is it Drew you love?"

"I'll always love Drew—nothing will ever change that. I can't deny what I feel for you will be forever linked with my feelings for Drew, but it's you, Travis Garner, I now love more than anything on this earth."

When he didn't respond she drew a deep breath. "Do you . . . do you believe me?"

His voice was thick when he replied, "Yes."

He bent to brush a quick kiss across her mouth, then whispered, "I want you to be my wife, Meggy. What do you say? Will you marry me?"

Meghan blinked away the fresh spurt of tears, then smiled up at him, love and laughter now glowing in her eyes. "Yes, of course I will."

Travis released her hands, then pulled her into his embrace for a long, thorough kiss. When he finally pulled his mouth from hers, he said, "I do see a problem facing us. How are we supposed to explain to our children that they have two fathers?"

"There's nothing to explain. On the inside you may be the blending of two men, but outside there's only one." She flashed him a saucy grin. "It's a good thing, too. If there were more than one of you physically, I'm not sure I could keep both of you satisfied."

"Is that so?" he replied with a chuckle. "Well, I know you can satisfy me, right down to my toes. But just to be certain, how about going to your house and you can show me again?" He ran the back of his hand down the side of her face, his eyes flaring with both mischief and desire.

Meghan laughed, then rose up on her tiptoes to brush a quick kiss on his mouth. "Should I ask Grady and Moira if I can take my dinner break early?"

"I already took care of that. You have the rest of the day off. Now, come on . . ." He reached for her hand. ". . . we can make our wedding plans while we walk; then I'm yours to command. . . ." He dropped his voice to a husky whisper. ". . . in the bedroom."

Another gale of laughter spilled from her lips. "You're incorrigible."

He turned her toward the door. "Yes, but you're not complaining, are you?"

"No, never."

Epilogue

Meghan folded one of her dresses and laid it on top of the others in the trunk Travis had brought from his ship for her personal belongings. She hummed *O Come, All Ye Faithful* as she worked, still finding her marriage to Travis hard to believe.

They'd spoken their vows in a Christmas Eve ceremony with only Moira and Grady in attendance, the church resplendent with holiday decorations. Now, two days later, she was packing the last of her things in preparation for their setting sail for St. Croix on the evening tide.

Leaving Galveston would be hard, but her life was with Travis now, and since he, too, lived on an island, she looked forward to setting up a home with him. And since she loved the sea, he'd promised she could accompany him on the *Empress* whenever she chose.

She turned back to her dresser. The only drawer left to empty was the bottom one. She opened the drawer, then reached inside and withdrew the contents, piece by piece. Finally only one item remained. She stopped humming, the Christmas carol forgotten as she stared at the tissue-covered package. Her fingers wrapping around the tissue, she lifted it from its hiding place and sat down on the bed with a sigh.

McTavish meowed and jumped up onto the bed beside her. "I forgot all about this, McTavish," she said, unfolding a layer of tissue paper. "I should throw it out, but I think I'll keep the frame. It's really quite lovely."

McTavish meowed again, then rubbed the top of his head against her arm. Meghan chuckled, turning to look at the cat. "You're a nuisance," she said as she removed the last of the paper. Shifting her gaze back to the picture frame, her mouth dropped open. Unable to believe what she saw, she closed her eyes for a second. Certain her imagination was playing tricks, she slowly lifted her eyelids, then sucked in a sharp breath.

"Oh, my God. McTavish, look!" The cat moved closer, peering over her arm to see what she held clutched in her hands. No longer was only the photographer's backdrop visible beneath the glass; no longer was the image the picture once contained faded from view.

Her hand shaking, Meghan ran her fingers over the photograph of the man she would love forever, tears of joy blurring her vision. The Christmas portrait she had treasured for so long had somehow been restored—with one major difference.

The man smiling back at her was Travis.

If You Believe

Elizabeth Ann Michaels

One

"I love Alex Chandler."

From the gallery overlooking the entryway of her family's country estate, Bellemore, Lady Jenna Stanton made her declaration to her cousin, Beth, with a smile gracing her lips and absolute certainty shining in her pansy blue eyes.

Beth pulled her startled gaze from the laughing group assembled below and studied her cousin in genuine wonder. "You're in love with Alex Chandler?"

"Surprising, isn't it?" Jenna sighed.

"I had no idea your feelings ran in that direction."

"Is it so hard to believe?"

"Yes. I mean, you are so light-hearted, while he can be such a serious man at times."

"I cannot argue with that. Alex is certainly prone to deep thought."

Beth gave into a doubtful grimace, her round face creasing with a series of soft lines. "Profound is more apt. Thank goodness he is capable of laughter; otherwise I would feel intimidated to stand in his presence." She lowered her voice to a giggling, conspiratorial whisper. "But his being as handsome as he is doesn't hurt. That alone is enough to make a woman fall head over heels."

"This is more than a matter of facial appearances, Beth. He's our closest neighbor. I've known him all my life." And for the last six of those nineteen years she had loved Alex Chandler with all her heart.

"Still, I am simply amazed," Beth breathed, following Jenna's line of vision downward to the man in question. Alex Chandler, Earl of Carswell, stood among the guests, his dark head bowed to catch the voice of the gentleman beside him. "You never made any mention or even hinted at how you felt."

"I wouldn't be mentioning it now except that I'm going to marry the man."

Beth's gaze shot back to her cousin. "What?"

"I'm going to marry Alex. You're my very best friend, Beth, and if I didn't tell you, I was going to burst from happiness."

"This is wonderful," Beth exclaimed joyously. "When did his lordship declare himself?"

"He hasn't yet."

"I beg your pardon?"

The guests moved off into the front drawing room, freeing Jenna at last from her enchanted study of the man she loved. "He hasn't declared himself."

Blinking in patent amazement, Beth asked, "Then how do you know you're going to marry him?"

"Oh, I just know," Jenna murmured, turning for the head of the stairway.

Beth trailed alongside her, her expression one of doubtful misgivings. "Jenna, you've got that look on your face again."

"What look?"

"The one you get when you're about to plunge headlong into one of your fanciful reveries. The one you get that makes me very nervous."

Jenna laughed, the sweet sound echoing in her wake. "There's nothing to be nervous about. It is the Christmas season, and you know wonderful things happen during Christmas time." Charity abounded, the air was filled with anticipation and goodwill. People were more loving and kind. Each in its own way was a miracle—a Christmas miracle.

Jenna believed in Christmas miracles as much as she believed in her love for Alex. How could she not? Past experience had proven to her time and again that special things happened if you trusted in the magic of Christmas.

There had been that time five years ago in 1815 when her younger brother, Andrew, had taken ill the first day of December. The surgeons had predicted his death, declaring the boy wouldn't see Christmas Day.

Jenna had refused to believe a word of it. Instead, she had placed her faith in the conviction that Christmas was a blessed time of goodness and joy, of miracles large and small. That year her miracle had been Andrew's recovery on Christmas Eve.

And she couldn't forget about the local orphanage the year before last. Faced with the threat of closure, the institution had been forced to literally beg for donations. Jenna herself had headed up the campaign to raise money, calling on local merchants and landed gentry with equal fervor.

It hadn't fazed her in the least that by the end of the second week of December donations had been woefully inadequate. She had never once doubted that the spirit of Christmas would prevail, that she would be granted her Christmas miracle.

On Boxing Day her faith had been fulfilled. An anonymous donation had secured the orphanage's future for years to come.

Through her childhood, similar instances had been more usual than not, to the point that now her confidence in Christmas could not be swayed, not by the rationalizations of doubters or by the worries of well-intentioned cousins. For that conviction she had been labeled by her family as naively optimistic—a silly, hopeless romantic. It was no more than what friends and acquaintances had to say about her, and she supposed that was to be expected. After all, to most people's bewilderment, amusement, or disdain, she chose to see the brighter side of life.

Which was why Jenna knew in her heart and soul her

Christmas miracle this year would come true. Alex would realize that he loved her as much as she loved him.

It would be a miracle of major proportions. At the best of times Alex had the tendency to look right through her. Such hard reality didn't discourage her, though. This year, with the spirit of Christmas abounding, he would realize that they were meant to be together forever.

The sheer joy of that flushed her cheeks and glistened her eyes. Entering the drawing room to the sounds of laughter, she couldn't contain her smile, nor her runaway thoughts. Before the night was through Alex would know how she felt— that was, if she could manage some time alone with him. Her parents had invited scores of people for the Christmas season. Privacy was a rare treasure with lifelong friends and numerous relatives filling the house.

At that moment it seemed as if all forty guests stood between her and Alex. She had to squelch the unladylike urge to elbow her way through the clusters of people, dash up to his side, and throw her arms about his neck. That would set every gossiping tongue to wagging for the next six months.

Nonetheless, the image did strike her as humorous, and it showed. Those with whom she stopped to chat as she discreetly tried to make her way toward Alex were treated to the full force of her delightfully capricious charm and a disarming dose of her infectious laughter. In a flatteringly short amount of time she was surrounded by friends and family, eager to enjoy her company.

She honestly couldn't say she was disappointed. She genuinely liked most people and truly believed that good existed in everyone. There was a measure of joy to be found in that.

"I am so glad to see you," she told the dowager duchess of Wilberford, meaning exactly what she said. The duchess was a frail woman, as sweet as she was elderly, and so horribly lonely, it broke Jenna's heart. Jenna always went out of her way to spend some time with the woman.

"And I am positively green with envy over your dress,"

she told Lady Charlotte Faye moments later. It was a wee stretching of the truth. With its overabundance of lace, Lady Charlotte's gown was far too fastidious for Jenna's taste, but Jenna knew that wasn't what Lady Charlotte needed to hear. As shy and timid as Jenna knew Charlotte to be, the compliment supplied a much-needed bit of reassurance.

"And you are looking wickedly handsome tonight, Freddie," she made a point of whispering to her second cousin.

From beneath his cravat a pleased blush stole up Freddie Hendrickson's smiling face. "You are a wicked little chit," he whispered back.

She feigned an expression of wounded bewilderment. "How can you say that when I am only repeating what I heard Lydia Afferton say?" Her pout softened into an affectionate smile. "She is definitely smitten with you."

There was no disguising his eagerness. "Truly?"

"Truly."

"I had been hoping."

"Then what are you doing standing here talking to me, when only minutes ago I saw her casting you the most longing glances?"

It took Jenna a full half hour before she could, in good conscience, wend her way to the far side of the room, and Alex. One look at him and she told herself the wait had been well worth it, for he was quite possibly the most wonderful man on earth. And nothing she saw of him contradicted that sentiment.

Taller than most men, at two inches over six feet, he was the epitome of the perfect man. Broad shouldered, narrow waisted, he had a long-legged stride that lent him a remarkable masculine grace ideally suited to a man of thirty-five. His deep brown hair set off the gold of his eyes, and the hard edge to his jaw framed high cheekbones and a bold slash of a mouth.

As physical attributes went, he was quite perfect, as excellent and unequalled as the character contained within all that virile beauty. Kind and honest, he was also possessed of a masculine strength she found exhilarating. Even as a child she'd recognized his air of command for what it was, and she'd responded to it in the manner of a child.

As the woman she was now, she reacted in a different manner entirely.

"My lord." She greeted him breathlessly, lifting her hand out of habit alone. Her insides were whirling with anticipation, making it difficult for her to remember that for the moment decorum was required.

Alex Chandler took Jenna's hand in his own, smiling into her upturned face. "My lady," he intoned, lifting her hand for a brief kiss. "As always, it is a pleasure to see you."

"As it is you, my lord. I hope you have been enjoying yourself."

"How could I not with such delightful company?"

To his amusement, Alex watched Jenna pinken at the comment, and he had to resist the urge to give into a chuckle. It was a rare thing to see Lady Jenna Stanton succumb to what was, after all, nothing but a social compliment. Such flattery was standard fare in such a situation, and even more standard for the lady herself.

There was no denying that Jenna could be very entertaining. She had a convivial air which, together with her quick wit, made her one of the darlings of the *ton*. People flocked to her easy nature and ready smiles, all too eager to lavish upon her their attentions and their adulation.

To some extent, Alex could appreciate their regard. It was easy to get caught up by her loveliness, most specifically her deep blue eyes. Like twin orbs of dark blue velvet, they dominated her face, nearly eclipsing the beauty to be found in her lusciously curved mouth and the delicate turn of her jaw.

Oh, yes, his little neighbor had most definitely grown up into a beautiful young woman. Sinfully, deliciously round where it piqued a man's interest for a woman to be round, she was nonetheless slender of waist and thigh. A combina-

ion as tantalizing as the contrast between the ebony of her
hair and the ivory of her skin.

"You are looking as lovely as always," he told her. "It is
difficult to believe you are the same child who used to insist
on scaring the geese from my pond." His eyes took on a
teasing glint. "Something about pillows, I believe."

Jenna rolled her eyes. "You are an absolute wretch to remember that, my lord. I was only nine at the time and had
just realized why my pillows were so soft."

"Were you determined to save every goose in the world,
or just mine?"

"Oh, all of them, a notion with which my parents quickly
lost patience."

"Why so?"

In wide-eyed innocence, she explained, "Because they
couldn't tolerate the goose-droppings my nanny found in the
nursery."

Alex roared with laughter, imagining the scene as it must
have looked.

"Father was incensed," Jenna expounded around her own
mirth. "Mother called for her salts, and my nanny threatened
to go into an early retirement. It was all extremely dramatic,
with people yelling and geese honking."

"And what of you?"

Jenna sniffed in a show of annoyance worthy of the royal.
"I was banished to the chapel to reflect on the ways of an
unruly, disobedient child, and then to the classroom, where I
had to write one letter of apology to my nanny and one to
my mother for frightening them as I did."

Shaking his head, he regarded Jenna with smiling eyes.
"And did you learn anything from your lessons?"

"Yes." She tucked in her chin and gave him an audacious,
unrepentant look from beneath her lashes. "The next time I
try to bring geese into the house I'll put them in the attic
where no one ever goes."

Laughter seized Alex again. He didn't give a damn that

people turned to stare and smile his way. "I pity your parents," he said at length. "And it will be your just desserts to someday have a daughter as impudent and reckless as you."

For a long moment silence fell between them. Still caught up in the remnants of his good humor, Alex didn't notice the teasing radiance fade from Jenna's eyes.

"There is something I wish to discuss with you, my lord."

"And what could that possibly be? How best to muzzle a goose?"

"Nothing so frivolous, I assure you."

"Oh?"

In a gesture he found completely out of character for the young lady, Jenna cast a nervous glance in either direction, then leaned close to impart, "It is of a private nature, my lord."

His brows rose in question. "Private?"

Nodding, she whispered, "Would it be possible for you to meet me tonight?"

It was certainly possible, but not bloody likely! He didn't go around meeting young innocents in the middle of the night for *private* discussions. And he had no idea why Jenna, who certainly knew better, would even suggest such a thing. Then again, he had no idea why her mind worked as it did. The crime of the century was that she was breathtakingly beautiful and entertaining to boot, but he'd never known her to have a serious, worthwhile thought in her head.

He frowned down at her, trying to recall an instance when her conversations hadn't been limited to the virtues of a pretty ribbon, the lighter side of gossip . . . or her foibles as a child. Having a limited tolerance for such inanities, he had made certain never to spend much time engaged in conversation with her.

Quite simply, she was not to be taken seriously. Her reputation as a gay little butterfly, flitting from one place to next, cajoling all around her made for a certain pleasantness, but he preferred to mingle and associate with people of substance.

eople who thought to see past the obvious, people who were
intent enough to be discerning and mindful. As far as he could
ell, Jenna was none of those.

A good deal of his humor dissipated, leaving behind only
shell of his earlier pleasure. "Your suggestion is highly un-
onventional, my lady."

Her brow creased with a frown. "I know, my lord, but it
s terribly important that I speak to you."

"Important," he repeated blandly.

"A matter of life and death, actually."

He blinked at that, wondering what she could possibly con-
ider in such an extreme light. No doubt something as *mean-
ngful* as a discourse on the latest mode in which gentlemen
ed their cravats.

"Please, my lord."

It was the slight catch in her voice that snared him, prick-
ng his interest even though it went against his better judg-
ent. She was in deadly earnest, gazing up at him with a
rave expression he had never seen on her face before.

"Is there something wrong? Are you in trouble?"

"No, my lord," she averred quickly. "All is well." A smile
roke across her lips. "And soon to get better."

"Yet there is a matter of life and death somehow involved."

"Yes, my lord."

She was completely illogical, claiming dire circumstances
n the one hand while predicting improvement of some mys-
erious, private predicament on the other. Solemn and secre-
ve one second, she was beaming in anticipation the next.
s usual, he found her to be completely lacking in design
r worth, and part of him was thoroughly annoyed with her.

However, he found himself relenting to her plea. He could
ot turn his back on her, not when she continued to peer at
im so fervently. "Very well, my lady."

Her eyes filled with pure delight; joy suffused her face.
At midnight," she murmured for his ears alone. "In the north
alon. It is rarely used."

"I will probably regret this," he muttered on a sour note

"Oh, no, my lord. After tonight you will have no regret at all."

After months of deliberation Jenna had decided that the best way to handle this matter with Alex was to come right to the point. She could find no reason for dissembling, no cause for reticence. However, the moment was at hand, the clock on the mantel was striking the midnight hour, and what had seemed perfectly wonderful in theory was now causing her stomach and her heart to work without any normalcy whatsoever.

Standing before the cheerful flames in the grate of the north salon, she toyed with a curling ebony ribbon of hair that trailed down her neck. She was, she realized with a small start, nervous.

She turned at the sound of the door opening. Her eyes rounded and a gentle smile came to her lips when Alex entered. In the shadowy depths of the room, he appeared dark and mysterious.

"My lord," she breathed softly, enthralled as he came to stand in the fire's light. She gazed at him in open admiration not caring a whit that her feelings had to have been shining clearly for him to see. That was why they were there; why she had asked him to meet her. She wanted him to know how she felt. "Thank you for agreeing to meet me."

"What is this about, Jenna?" he asked, his voice edged with impatience and displeasure.

He rarely called her by her given name. That he did so now overshadowed the fact that he stood scowling at her, his annoyance barely held in check.

"Would you like to sit down, Alex?" It was even more rare that she used his name. A trill of excitement skipped over her skin.

"No, I would not like to sit. I would like to get on with

whatever it is you seem to think is a matter of life and death. Neither one of us should be here like this, and you know it."

"You're right, of course." She clasped her hands together, lacing her fingers together so tightly, her knuckles hurt. "But I think that after you hear what I have to say you will see the necessity for such privacy."

"If you're going to be enigmatic, Jenna, I shall leave at once." He matched actions to words and pivoted sharply.

"Oh, no, you mustn't," she exclaimed, reaching out frantically to stay his progress. "The Christmas miracle will never happen if you leave now."

He turned to face her again. "What the devil are you talking about?"

"Christmas miracles." She waved her fingers about, as if to better define the wondrous occurrences. "They happen every year. Extraordinary incidents that change people's lives."

"As usual, you are making no sense, my lady."

She liked it better when he called her Jenna. "I suppose not." She sighed. "But only because I am a touch nervous. I'm not exactly certain how best to proceed. I thought I did, but now that we are face-to-face, I am not so sure."

Alex planted his fists at his waist. "Jenna." His voice was as dark as the warning in his eyes. "Say what you have to say."

Brightening instantly, she gave in to a huge smile. "That was my very first instinct, to just come right out and tell you all. How clever of you, Alex, but that is one of the things I like best about you. You are so clever. And discerning. Very well." She took a step closer and lifted her chin, love bursting in her heart, happiness erupting in her veins. "I love you, Alex. I have for many, many years."

Of all the things Alex had expected her to say, that was the absolute last. "I beg your pardon?" He'd heard her; there was no mistaking her words. He simply could not believe—

no, he did not *want* to believe what she had confessed to him.

"I love you." Her face creased with anxious lines. "Oh, I know this is sudden, that you must be startled, but I couldn't wait another day, Alex; truly, I could not."

He exhaled slowly, staring at her as if seeing her for the first time. "Jenna, you don't know what you're saying."

"Yes, I do. I've known for six long years." In her excitement she stepped closer. "You must think I'm extremely un-ladylike, most likely without a pinch of refinement, or brains, for that matter, but there really was no other way, Alex, really there wasn't. Even a Christmas miracle needs a little help."

"Mira . . . what in the hell are you going on about?"

"This." Rising up on her toes, she wrapped her arms about his neck, lifted her mouth to his, and kissed him.

For the space of three heartbeats Alex was well and truly stunned into immobility while his mind tried to register what was happening. Jenna Stanton was kissing him. Impetuous, feather-brained, silly little Jenna Stanton was kissing him, slanting her lips over his with a stunning passion.

The reality of that set in with a vengeance, taking both his brain and his body by storm. His shock gave way before the onslaught of a scorching surge of desire.

Mentally, he yanked back from the sensation. Physically, he thrust her to arm's length. "What the devil do you think you're doing?"

Jenna stared at him through a misty veil of happiness, oblivious to his refusal. She had waited too long for this very moment to let his shock interfere. "I was kissing you. Did I not do it right?"

He nearly choked on a muttered curse.

She continued breathlessly. "I don't have a great deal of experience kissing men, but I do know that both parties involved are supposed to enjoy it. Did you, Alex? Did you like the way I kissed you?"

He felt as if he had just stepped off a cliff and fallen into a realm of complete and total absurdity. Fingers gripping her upper arms, he bent low and drilled his gaze into hers. "Listen to me, Jenna. I don't know what game you're playing, but it is dangerous."

"This isn't a game. I told you, I love you."

"You don't love me."

"But I do." Her smile took on a dreamy quality. "That's what my miracle is all about."

He clenched his eyes shut for a second. *"What miracle?"*

"My Christmas miracle. I explained earlier. They happen every year, if you believe in them, only most people don't stop to consider that. I do, and this year you are my miracle, Alex. You're going to realize that you love me. And that you want me for your wife."

Two

Her words echoed through his mind. The memory of her breasts cushioned against his chest suffused his body. Even a day later Alex could not rid himself of the aftereffects of the scene with Jenna. They ripped his concentration to shreds, a precarious situation considering he was presently astride his favorite mount. The restive stallion required all his attention.

Collecting his wits, he set his mind to the present. An adventurous group of fifteen had decided to take their festivities outdoors. They rode over the rolling grounds of Bellemore, some wont to leisure, others preferring a more grueling pace. Alex kept himself at a distance, liking the distraction the group provided and yet, oddly enough, disturbed by their laughter and camaraderie.

Disgusted with his reaction, he turned his mount toward the trees, deciding the solitude to be found in the cool, quiet hush of the forest suited him better. With jeering disdain, he realized he was not going to be able to ignore his memories of Jenna.

The question of what he was going to do about her weighed on him heavily. There was no doubt that she actually believed herself in love with him, although how she could have come to such a conclusion was beyond him. For as long as he could remember he had treated her with a casual friendliness and no more. He was polite, respectful; he laughed at her quips and took a socially obligatory interest in her comments. But at no time had he ever said or done anything to spur her emotions to love.

Damn, what a bloody mess. He had no wish to hurt her; she was a likable little thing, but she had to be disabused of her infatuation. And that was all this was: a girlish infatuation.

His mind scoffed in contradiction. There had been nothing girlish about the touch of her lips or the way her body had molded itself to his. He could still feel the imprint of her tender curves, her breasts against his chest, her thighs pressed to his. His reaction had been as instantaneous as it had been unexpected.

Damn it all, he wasn't used to thinking of Jenna in terms of sensuality. She was his neighbor's daughter, the childish hoyden who had grown up into a flirtatious little baggage. Yet a single kiss was all it had taken to make him view her in an entirely different light. Against his will, he thought about that kiss.

It hadn't been prolonged or even practiced, but it had speared straight into him with astounding force, making his blood pound wildly. If he hadn't recognized her relative inexperience for what it was, he could easily have thought her a teasing jade. But women of that ilk knew how to use mouths and bodies when they kissed. They did not offer up closemouthed sweetness and lush naïveté. They did not stare up at men in a starry-eyed kind of insecurity and ask for a critique of their kisses.

Bloody hell; Jenna had actually stood there and asked him if he liked the way she had kissed him. He had never known a woman to make such an inquiry. He had never known a woman to proclaim her love. Or to propose marriage!

He drew his mount to a halt and sat fuming. Not for the first time he thought Jenna Stanton the most absurd female he had ever encountered. It was ridiculous enough that she fully expected him to realize he loved her, but to insist that he would want to take her for a wife pushed the bounds of all that was rational.

Didn't she have any sense at all? And what was all this rubbish about Christmas miracles? The only miracle he could foresee would be the insurance of his sanity. If he made it through the holiday without becoming crazed, it would indeed be a miracle.

Fortunately, he was of a more sensible bent. He could not have Jenna traipsing about thinking they were going to wed. Practicality demanded that he set things straight with her as quickly as possible.

He would have done so last night if the very drunken Baron Welton hadn't entered the salon. The giddy old sot had stumbled and mumbled his way to the divan, chuckling at some private joke, singing for all the world to hear. Alex had wanted to throttle the man.

Now, in retrospect, he thought it best that he and Jenna had parted at that point, as they had. As astonished and amazed as he had been, he doubted he could have been as considerate as he would have liked. Telling a young woman that her affections were not returned required a certain amount of tact and patience. He had been lacking both last night.

Morning had restored his composure and his sense of diplomacy. Given that, he was now ready to get on with the business of dealing with Jenna.

Urging his horse deeper into the forest, he felt better for his conclusions. With a clear understanding of how best to proceed, his mind was released from the misgivings and problems the lady presented. Now he had only to rid his body of its dilemma, for as much as it disturbed him to admit it, the answer to Jenna's artless question was, yes, he most definitely did like her kisses—more than it was safe or proper for either one of them.

He swore at great length, taking the Lord's name in vain. A rather telling bit of irony, considering he had just come upon the ruins of a twelfth-century abbey. Studying the crumbling stone structure, Alex had half a mind to cast a quick, wary glance heavenward. Common sense and the delightful sound of feminine laughter kept his gaze firmly fixed on the old priory.

The two muffled voices came again, more clearly this time as the ladies obviously drew nearer. One called to the other about the abundance of ivy, holly, and mistletoe to be found there, then fretted in worried tones.

"I don't think this will work. It will be terribly inconvenient, don't you think?"

It was impossible for Alex to hear the second lady's comment. In mere moments it didn't matter. The pair emerged through what had once been a doorway, and Alex's opinion of irony was intensified tenfold.

He had determined to settle things with Jenna as soon as possible, and there she stood beside her cousin Beth, her face lit with a smile, her blue, blue eyes shining brightly. In her ruby red cloak she was a splash of color amid winter's pewters and grays.

"My lord," she exclaimed, doing nothing to curtail her apparent joy in seeing him.

Inwardly, Alex groaned. He felt like a heel about to crush a brilliantly beautiful flower. "Jenna, Beth." Informality came readily, he supposed, in an unconscious effort to soften the severity of the scene to come.

"What a wonderful surprise seeing you here," Jenna said. Looking to the basket linked over her arm, she explained, "We were gathering greens."

"There are ever so many," Beth added.

"Apparently," Alex commented, not giving a damn about mistletoe. He had just been presented with the ideal time and place in which to have the necessary discussion. Privacy was as abundant as the surrounding holly. Only Beth stood as an obstacle.

Dismounting, he tethered the stallion to a low-hanging

branch and approached the pair with serious eyes. It was no more proper for him to be alone with Jenna here than it had been last night in the north salon, but formidable circumstances demanded formidable measures.

He gave Beth his most persuasive smile. "Would it be possible if you could spare your cousin and me a few moments alone?"

Beth blinked as a raging blush stained her cheeks. "Oh, my." She looked to Jenna in a patent appeal for guidance before dissolving into giggles. "Oh, Jenna, this is so wonderfully wicked."

"I assure you," Alex was quick to tell her, "the last thing I have in mind is something scandalous."

"I know how to be discreet, my lord," Beth teased, clearly coming to her own conclusions. To Jenna, she laughed. "We'll work on your plan at another time." She was on her way without another word.

"What plan is that?" Alex asked, annoyed with Beth's assumptions and with his own curiosity. Whether he liked it or not, he felt compelled to know what Jenna was plotting.

"It's a secret," she informed him, her dainty chin elevated. "Something I've been thinking about for quite a while."

"That sounds ominous."

"Quite the contrary. I've hit upon a rather unique idea."

"You seem to be full of unique ideas."

"Thank you, my lord."

He hadn't meant it as a compliment, but in her usual, audacious style, Jenna chose to interpret things as she saw fit. Trying to remember every one of his good intentions, he shoved one hand deep into the pocket of his trousers and leveled his gaze on the woman who fancied herself his future wife.

"We need to talk, Jenna."

"Splendid." She lowered herself to a low stone wall and peered up into his face. "We were interrupted last night before I had the chance to tell you half of what I had intended."

Breathing in deeply, she set her basket aside and gazed about the setting. "This is so much nicer, don't you think? No one about to bother us."

"Which was why I asked your cousin to leave us. You need to understand several things, Jenna."

"And what are they?" Eyes wide, lips curved, she appeared as unaffected as a newborn babe.

Keeping his tone as gentle and polite as possible, he said, "I am flattered that you think you love me, but you have misjudged your feelings. What you feel for me cannot possibly be love."

Jenna remained silent for a moment and then burst into laughter. She couldn't help herself. She had expected this of Alex. It was absolutely wonderful to know she had pegged him so accurately.

"I'm glad you can find humor in this matter," he contended.

"I beg your pardon, Alex, but you can be so amusing, even when you are wrong. I do love you."

He heaved an impatient sigh. "No, Jenna, I do not think so."

"Yes, actually, I do." Reaching out, she took his hand between her own. "I realize this is awkward for you, but you mustn't let that affect your better judgment. If you are honest with yourself, you will admit that you can't possibly know what I am feeling."

"I do know," he challenged, yanking his hand to his side, "because you have no sound basis for this love you supposedly feel."

"There is no supposing about it. And I have a great deal upon which to base my feelings. After all, Alex, I have known you all my life."

"As a casual acquaintance. We are not close, we have never been confidants. You don't know the first thing about me."

"Is that what you think?" Tilting her head to one side, she studied him through eyes filled with love. She came to her feet and wandered to a nearby bush to pluck at a collection of berries. "Let me see; where should I begin?"

After a moment's pause she started with the obvious. "You're thirty-five years old, the eldest of five children, possessor of four titles and six estates. You spend the season in London, are a favorite with the ladies, are extremely lucky at the faro table and dislike Mozart operas immensely." She lifted one dark brow in a pert gesture. "You have never been married, although rumor did have you linked with a certain marchioness last year. Russian caviar, Indian curry, and French brandy are among your favorites, while you rarely touch figs, sausages, and ratafia." She gave him a jaunty smile, tickled to find that she had rendered him momentarily speechless.

"How do you know all of this?" he finally bit out. "Have you taken to spying?"

"Of course not, and I could be highly insulted that you would even think that." She tossed the last of her berries aside and faced him squarely. "I am not blind, Alex. Our paths have crossed frequently for nineteen years. And besides, I hear what others say about you."

"Gossip?" he grated out, displeasure saturating his voice.

She shrugged his pique aside. "There is no cause for you to be angry with me. I am merely pointing out that I know you better than you'd like to think. For instance, I happen to know that you have a formidable temper when the situation warrants."

"Now could be one of those times, Jenna."

"Oh, I hope not." The blue of her eyes filled with appeal. "I would hope that you would rely on your patience and your sense of decency."

"Both are waning rather quickly."

She surrendered to a delicate frown. "Are you trying to warn me?" The lines of her worry quickly changed into an exuberant smile. "But that is so like you. You truly are kind and considerate. I would expect nothing less from a man of such rare intellect. You deal equitably with everyone, regardless of rank or station. You are as fair as you are generous." She finished with a wistful expression, her emotions surging to the fore. "It is no wonder that I love you as I do."

He spun to pace a short, irate path, only to turn and pin her with a steely gaze. "Very well; perhaps in your own mind you have reason to believe you love me."

"Thank you."

"But that does not mean that we are going to be married. That doesn't mean—" He clenched his jaw and checked his temper, clearly striving to collect the finer points of all the compassion and generosity she claimed he possessed.

He returned to stand before her once more. "Jenna, I am flattered to be the recipient of your affections. You are beautiful and spirited. I like you. But that does not mean we will suit as husband and wife."

If Jenna hadn't already considered his every objection, she might have been discouraged by his declaration. As it was, she had thought the matter out in its entirety. "We do suit, Alex, only you don't know that yet. Which is where my miracle comes into play."

He muttered a curse beneath his breath. "Do not start with that again, Jenna."

"Very well. What would you have me talk about instead?"

"This foolishness about our marrying. You must put it out of your mind. I will not have you telling people that we are betrothed."

Her spine straightened on a surge of indignation. "I would never do such a thing."

"Thank you," he breathed in relief.

"It is the prospective groom's place to make that sort of announcement."

His exhalation was nothing short of a furious eruption that pricked Jenna's concern. She laid a tender hand along his hardened jaw.

"You shouldn't get so angry, Alex. It can't be good for

your digestion or your heart." Her fingers trailed down to the vein beating violently in his neck. "All will be fine, my love. I promise it will." Driven by the purest of emotions, she lifted her head and pressed her lips to his.

If there was ever a Heaven on earth, Jenna knew this was it. The feel of Alex's mouth against hers sent currents of heat throughout the whole of her body. Her heart beat wildly in her breast, while her limbs began to tremble.

Guided by feminine instinct, she deepened the kiss. Any thought that she was behaving like a wanton was slain by the utter rightness of what she was doing. She loved Alex. It was only natural that she would want to express that love with more than mere words. Without thinking, she pressed her body close to his and slipped her hands over his shoulders.

The instant she did, Alex grabbed hold of her arms with every intention of shoving her away. Scowling fiercely, he yanked his head back only to be caught by the sight of Jenna's face. Lips parted, eyes glazed with desire, cheeks suffused with high color, she was more beautiful than he'd ever seen her before.

"Oh, Alex," she whispered, her lips grazing his. "I love you so."

She kissed him again, startling him anew. This wasn't the Jenna he knew. And then that thought and most others dissolved. Without warning, the artlessness of her actions captured him until all his mind and body could register was the sweetness of her mouth and the feel of her curves.

Desire erupted within him, taking him by surprise. For a man well versed in the art of lovemaking, his reaction stunned him. Conscience and good intentions fell before the craving she evoked and he took command of the kiss. His arms circled her, molding her tightly to him as his mouth claimed hers with heated expertise. Along the length of him, he could feel the delicate shivers that assailed her—and he was doing nothing more than kissing her.

For the first time he was given a hint of the passion lying

undiscovered within Jenna, and he was amazed. And aroused. That he was the sole target for all that passion was heady stuff. Just how deep did her desires run? He could not shake the impression that once he found the answer he would discover an entirely new Jenna, one completely unlike the flighty miss he had come to know.

The vibrant woman in his arms bore no resemblance to that Jenna. The woman who was kissing him with such tender ardor was at the moment, neither silly nor frivolous. She was as earnest, as considerable, as undeniable as the hunger that ate at him.

"Open your mouth, Jenna," he ordered, needing this further intimacy like a man desperate for his next breath of air. Impatient to have more of her, he didn't wait for her to comply. He traced the curve of her lips with his tongue until she did as he had asked, and then thrust into the warm recesses of her mouth.

He felt her reaction, a small reflexive start of her body, and he tightened his arms about her. Where only seconds ago he had been loath to hold her, he was now half afraid that she would bolt. He cupped the back of her head to hold her still for this small invasion, but his fleeting worry had been for nothing. Her trepidation gave way to a gentle yielding.

Never in her wildest imaginings had Jenna ever thought that Alex would kiss her in this manner. The familiarity of it was bold, disconcerting, hinting at forbidden pleasures. She drew back in shock, only to find new delights in the searching of his tongue.

Giving herself up to the kiss, she gloried in this newest facet of her love. In her mind it was all connected; loving Alex, kissing him, wanting to share every part of her being with him, wanting him to share of himself.

She twined her tongue with his and was instantly rewarded by the guttural groan that vibrated up from his chest. A little dazedly, she realized that in her sharing she had inadvertently increased his pleasure. Her heart soared. More than anything she wanted to give Alex all the wonder and enchantment he was giving her—surely paltry terms to describe what she was feeling.

Wave after wave of longing swept through her, washing over her lungs and stomach to collect in a spot centered in the secret flesh between her legs. Helplessly, she clung to Alex's shoulders, a low whimper of innocent longing sounding in her throat.

Alex absorbed the sound, reveling in the tiny, feminine sigh. She was like fire in his arms, responding with unguarded eagerness and a drugging ardor that pulled relentlessly at everything that was male within him. Her response was so genuine, so utterly feminine that she touched him on a very primal level. In ways he had never experienced before, she defined him as a man.

That man needed her, ached unbearably to take her down to the mossy ground and bury himself in the soft heat of her. He parted the front of her cloak and found the round perfection of her breasts. His other hand roamed to the round curves of her hips and lifted her into his thighs.

"Alex," Jenna choked out, unprepared for the dual assaults of sensation. Frisson after frisson of pleasure shot out as Alex stroked her breasts. Low and inside, all that pleasure collected with frightening pressure. "Oh, Alex, something is happening." She gasped as his lips and teeth scored her neck. "I . . . I don't know what to do. I don't know what is happening to me."

Alex knew . . . and it sobered him with jarring cruelty. Through eyes smoldering with need, he glared down at her flushed face and saw reality. Cold, mocking, insulting reality. It jabbed him in the gut and made him ask what in the living hell he was doing.

Hands fierce and strong, he shoved her to arm's length. "Enough," he grated, hating her for putting him in this predicament, hating himself for succumbing.

"Alex?" She gazed at him in wonder, trying to adjust to
the sudden shift in her world. "What's wrong?"

"What's wrong?" Outrage permeated him entirely. "You
have to ask that?" Goaded past reason, he gave her a small
shake. "You little fool. Don't you know how dangerous it is
to tempt a man this way? Or don't you care that I could have
ruined you right here, right now?"

"I didn't think—"

"You never think. That's your biggest problem. You have
a brain that doesn't function past the immediate or the trivial."
He released her abruptly and stepped back. "Well, I am neither. I am a man, not some imbecilic fop with whom you
can toy."

"I . . . I know that."

"Do you?" He spun around and strode off, turned and
faced her from a safe distance. "Do you? I don't think so;
otherwise you wouldn't be playing with fire as you are."

She pressed shaking fingertips to her bruised lips, feeling
as if a steely band were wrapping itself about her heart. She
thought he had liked her kissing him. She had believed that
in some small way she had touched him with her love. "Is
it necessary that you insult me this way?"

"Apparently, since I cannot make you see reason."

Her lips parted, her eyes rounded. All the signs of her
dismay were there for Alexa to see, and he felt his stomach
grip in near painful remorse.

Heaving a sigh, he searched the treetops, tamping down
his frustration as well as his displeasure. "Ah, Jenna, I don't
wish to hurt you this way, but you must cease with these
foolish notions you have of us."

"It isn't foolishness, Alex."

He held up a hand before she could continue. "I know,
you think you love me."

"No, I *know* I love you. And there is nothing foolish about
that." Tears of genuine distress threatened, but she refused to

let them fall. She refused to give into the hurt, or to allow Alex's skepticism to sway her.

Picking up her basket, she sent him a quelling look for ruining her day, for hurting her feelings, and most of all, for doubting her love. Without a backward glance at him she headed for home, more determined than ever that he would come to the realization that a love did exist between them.

He would see, she vowed, that the magic of Christmas was real.

Three

He could not shake the memory of her. That more than anything chafed at Alex's disposition. It was damnable that in the past two days he had found that if he wasn't thinking about the taste of Jenna's mouth, he was contemplating the hint of tears he had seen briefly in her eyes before she had left him standing in the forest. Both vexed him sorely, and that in itself grated on his nerves.

Seated across from her in the formal dining room, he listened to her converse with the dowager duchess of Wilberford, and his annoyance was elevated another notch. The duchess was prattling on in her usual ridiculous manner. And Jenna seemed to be hanging on every asinine word as if each was a pearl of wisdom.

"And then she had the audacity to snicker at my new pink bonnet," the duchess vouched, looking as if her entire world were about to end.

"I shouldn't be too upset," Jenna consoled. "I'm sure your maid is lacking in good taste as well as manners."

"Do you think so?"

"Oh, yes."

Alex could barely contain his scoff. Who cared about the color of a hat, or that some maid obviously had a sense of humor?

"I happen to like my new bonnet," the duchess went on. "It took weeks for the milliner to arrange the netting to my exact instructions, but I wouldn't be satisfied until she got it right."

"It is so very important that you be satisfied," Jenna assured her.

It was all Alex could do not to roll his eyes. Was the woman daft as well as inane? Did she honestly believe that the dowager duchess of Wilberford's satisfaction with a blasted hat qualified as important?

And Jenna thought she would suit as his wife? he mentally jeered. The notion was as laughable as her conversation. He knew without hesitation what qualities he wanted in a wife, and those attributes did not include foolishness or absurdity. The woman he would wish to marry would be someone capable of far more than gossip.

In the solitude of his room that night he sat before the fire and contemplated that woman.

He had no clear image of her face, although he could imagine her pretty. He had never placed much store in breathtaking loveliness, other than that it was easy on one's eyes. In the final analysis, though, physical perfection didn't matter. Character did.

Slouching into a comfortable sprawl in his chair, the glow of the fire dancing on the white of his shirt, he studied that character in detail. Honest, devoted, loving, kind, generous, and unselfish: He knew the list by heart. This future wife would be all of those and more. She would be someone with whom he could share his hopes and dreams, someone to bear his children, someone with whom he would grow old.

He would roll over in the middle of the night and take pleasure from her spirit as well as her body. Her smiles as well as her tears would be his, and in return she would have his devotion and his heart for all eternity. They would share a timeless, enduring love.

The necessity of love in a marriage was nearly unheard of for a man of his position. In his social realm it was convenience and fortune that governed matrimony. His amber eyes grew flinty when he thought of such cold avarice. Marriage was a holy institution that bound one man and one woman for a lifetime. For him it could never be reduced to a dowry, the combining of estates or the need for social advancement. Marriage should be based on love.

His conscience pricked him sorely at the thought of Jenna's claims of love. He hadn't taken them seriously, but how was he supposed to have known that she carried a tender affection for him? Such devotion on her part had taken him completely by surprise. It had also created a tension between them that made for social awkwardness.

Thankfully, there had been no repetition of the scene by the abbey or the one in the north salon. For the past two days she had not sought him out for any further "private" discussions. For Jenna's sake as well as his own he hoped she had come to an understanding of how things stood between them. If not, he would have to take stronger measures.

The immediate alternative would be for him to return home, but he had no desire to do so. It wasn't in his nature to run from anything, or anyone. And besides, the holiday atmosphere as well as the company were enjoyable. The best thing for him to do would be to avoid being alone with her whenever possible.

He managed to do that with remarkable skill for the following week. Through outings and formal dinners, dances and recitals, they saw each other, but they were never alone. And in the presence of others there was little Jenna could do in the way of pursuing him.

Unfortunately, after a full nine days of near constant company he was in desperate need of a respite from the celebrations. A private man at heart, he wanted nothing more this Christmas Eve than a few moments of solitude. To that end he set his sights on Bellemore's library. Not only was the room as far removed from where most of the guests were gathered, it also provided an intellectual gratification. He required the kind of mental stimulation found in a good book.

The fire in the grate was as soothing as it was beckoning. The quiet was to be treasured. With a sense of contentment, he drew near the chairs placed in a cozy setting before the hearth. Too late, he discovered his mistake.

"My lord," Jenna said. Curled up in one of the wing backs, she gazed up at him in startled pleasure.

He swallowed his grunt of exasperation. "My lady."

"I would have thought you would be playing cards with the others."

"I chose not to."

"I can understand why." She shifted to a more dignified position with her feet on the floor, the folds of her emerald green gown falling in a circumspect drape. "There is only so much revelry one can tolerate."

"Precisely." Already he was mentally taking his leave, without the book he had come for. "If you'll excuse me . . ." He turned for the door.

"You don't have to leave on my account," she said. "I promise to behave myself."

Her words checked his progress. Her expression gave him pause. Indigo eyes filled with an irreverent humor, she smiled at him like a naughty little pixie.

"You have been avoiding me," she chided.

"You have made that necessary."

Sighing heavily, she confessed, "I suppose you are right." She pursed her lips as her brow aligned with the beginnings of a frown. "Are you terribly angry with me?"

"I was." Caution made him wary. He could not justify her past behavior for her present.

"Are you still?"

"That remains to be seen."

"There isn't any reason, Alex. I realize I shouldn't have thrown myself at you the way I did." Tipping her head to one side, she coaxed, "If I promise not to impose on you again, will you stay?"

He shouldn't; he knew that for a certainty.

She came to her feet. "Very well, *I'll* leave. That way you may have this spot all to yourself."

"That isn't necessary, Jenna."

"I think it is. You obviously require a kind of privacy other than that which is to be found in your rooms. I won't deprive you of that."

Not for the first time Jenna made him feel off balance. She had a way of doing that to him, reacting and behaving in ways he could never anticipate. After her advances last week he would have expected her to be chasing after him or insisting that they both remain. Instead, she was willing to walk away and relinquish her privacy so that he could have his.

The only conclusion he could come to was that her infatuation was over. And if not, then she had taken him at his word and was coping as best she could.

For some reason that didn't sit well with him.

Not liking the twinge of disappointment curling inside him, he gestured Jenna back to her seat as he took his own. This might not be the wisest thing for him to do, but in good conscience he could not turn her away. And she had hit upon a truth: He did need the solitude to be found here.

"This is splendid," she declared. And it was. It had been too long since she and Alex had been alone. She had missed him until her heart ached.

Necessity and Alex's shrewd maneuvering had forced her to observe all the proprieties. It had also given her time to rethink the logistics of her miracle. It did not need her help; that was the whole premise of a miracle. The Christmas spirit would prevail without assistance from anyone.

Of course, she didn't regret having declared her feelings. She was glad that Alex finally knew that she loved him. And she was enthralled by his kisses. Every night, beneath her covers, she hugged her memories close to her heart, treasuring the remembered feel of his hands and his mouth.

Unable to help herself, she eyed him now, studying the

length of his fingers. Just thinking of the way he had touched her so intimately brought the glow of love to her cheeks.

"Were you seeking any book in particular, my lord?" She forced out the query, knowing she could not sit there and ogle the man. Although she dearly wanted to. It was Christmas Eve. It wouldn't be long before her Christmas wish was granted and she would be able to ogle—and kiss—him to her heart's content.

"No." Stretching out his long legs before him, he relaxed further into the chair.

"I know how you feel. There are times when I cannot make up my mind, when I simply wish to be distracted."

He turned his head slightly against the cushion to give her a dubious glance. "What makes you think that's what I was seeking?"

Shrugging one shoulder, she reasoned, "Because you're here, and because you are now content to talk. If a book had been all that important, you would be standing before the shelves."

In answer, he growled out a sound that could have meant anything. She did her best to hide her smile. "You don't like it that I know you so well, do you?"

His head snapped about. "What the devil do you mean?"

"Just what I said. You would prefer to be a closed book." At her choice of words she chuckled merrily. "Rather apropos, given where we sit. I think that was rather clever of me; perhaps as clever as something you might have said."

Alex's exasperation was back in full force and it plainly showed. "Do you ever have an unspoken thought?"

"Of course. I can't go about saying everything that comes to mind. What would people think?"

"I was under the impression," he drawled, "that you said and did as you pleased and to hell with people's opinions."

She shrugged before propping her elbow on the chair and her chin in her palm. "Some people's opinions matter, but not all. I can't please everyone; I don't even try. What's im-

rtant is that I am true to myself." She paused for a weighty
gh. "But the truth can be most trying at times."

"Why do you say that?"

"Because it is the truth." She laughed. "And because so-
ety doesn't allow for a great deal of honesty."

Alex stared at her in an annoyance so apparent, that Jenna
ughed again. "Explain that," he demanded.

"If you wish."

"I do."

"Very well, but I suspect you are well acquainted with this
ain of thought. You know how false life among the *ton* can
. Every gesture, every glance, every word is calculated,
eighed, and judged. One's clothing, appearance, and rank
nd to count for far more than one's actions or thoughts.
adies are expected to behave one way, gentlemen another.
truly is sad, because none of that matters."

For a long moment Alex continued to stare. Finally he
rrowed his eyes. "You surprise me with these opinions."

"Do I really? I'm glad. Some surprises are nice, aren't
ey?"

"Some are. Some are mystifying."

"Which am I?"

"The latter."

Pouting prettily, she said ruefully, "Most people would
gree with you. People think that I'm pretty enough but frivo-
us, that I am amusing but not always sensible. Even my
arents find me a lost cause when it comes to certain mat-
rs."

"Such as?"

"Faith, hope, and charity."

At her rapid fire response Alex gave a shout of reluctant
ughter, shaking his head slowly. "Damn, but you are an
npertinent little thing. You always were."

It pleased her to no end to see that he had put aside his
isgivings and was enjoying himself. Until last week she had

always been able to make him laugh. She had worried tha the ease of spirit between them might have been ruined.

"What do you know of faith, hope, and charity?" he asked

"Only what I have learned from life." A little self consciously she tucked her chin. It was rare that someon asked her opinion on matters so close to her heart. Alex' asking was in some ways far more personal than any touc of his hand or kiss from his lips.

"Faith is what makes us human," she said, her gaze di rected at the flames in the grate. For all of the beauty of th fire's glow she saw only the strength of her inner convictions "The faith we place in others, in our ideals, and in Go makes up the basis for all the good in life. We trust, we live we love because of faith."

She chanced a peek at Alex, prepared to see ridicule an skepticism. Instead, his mouth was a sober line and the gol of his eyes was filled with an intense wonder. From that sh drew the courage to continue.

"Hope takes up where faith leaves off. It is a baby's firs step and a dying man's final breath. Hope is the promise o tomorrow, the impetus for life."

"And charity?" came his strangled query.

Gazing directly into his eyes, she whispered, "Charity i the best mankind has to offer. Like love, it is a gift from th heart."

His gaze held hers, mesmerizing in its intensity, powerfu in its ability to strip her down to her deepest secrets. Sh could only peer deeply into those eyes and surrender to th feeling of utter contentment.

The clock chimed the hour of ten. With a start she realize the time and came to her feet, forcing herself to cast off th intimacy of the moment. "I'm late."

But Alex was not ready to let her go. "Where are you of to?" he demanded to know.

"That," she teased in true form, "is a secret."

"Another of your plans and schemes concocted with your
cousin Beth?"

"Perhaps."

"Which you won't confide to me."

"No. Tell me you're jealous."

"Should I be?"

Her smile faded to a sad parody of its full glory. "I would
like it very much if you would be." Reaching out, she touched
her fingers to his cheek. "Could I make you jealous, Alex?
Should I take up with another man in order to spur you to
a jealous rage? Would that make you realize you love me?"

"Jenna—"

She silenced him with her fingertips, the cobalt of her eyes
softening to sapphire velvet. "It's Christmas Eve, Alex. A
time for miracles." Her smile returned a fraction of a second
before she brushed her lips over his. And then she fled the
room, anticipation a riot in her veins.

She had done it again, tilted him off center. He didn't like
the feeling one damn bit, and he didn't know what in the
bloody hell to do about it.

Pacing the length of the library, Alex thrust a hand back
through his hair. Irritation sizzled through him, taking his
patience and his good humor as unwilling victims.

"Damn it all." At the sound of his own voice he drew
himself up short and took stock of his actions. Where clear
thinking was needed, he was on the verge of surrendering to
pure emotion. He crossed to stand before one of the windows
and there forced himself to face several brutal questions.

Had he been wrong about Jenna all along? Was she more
than the gregarious minx who breezed her way through life?
Her confessions to him hours ago would lead him to believe
that there was more to Jenna than she let on, more than he
had taken the time to realize. That spoke poorly of him.

He prided himself on certain things in life, not the least

of which was his ability to define a person's character. It was galling to think he might have misjudged a person so badly. How could he have overlooked this finer, more noble side of her? More to the point, why had he?

The answer, when it came, filled him with shame and regret. For all his high-flown ideals he had been guilty of an arrogance that had blinded him. Like the very people he condemned for their shallow thinking, he had accepted and believed the popular opinion of Jenna Stanton. He had never once bothered to see the woman beneath the charm and smiles.

That woman was one of remarkable depth and emotion. She had spoken of tenets and beliefs close to his heart. With an honesty and candor he had never encountered in anyone, she had touched him on an intimate level he kept reserved for very few people in his life.

The question came again; had he misjudged Jenna? The answer was yes. That in turn gave rise to another question. What was he going to do about it? He could walk away, as if nothing had happened, content to perceive her in a different light in the future. But there was no contentment to be found in that course. He had held her in his arms, felt her passion. That combined with his new discoveries of her compelled him to learn all there was to learn about her, and so doing, himself.

He let his thoughts stray to love and a wife. All too easily he pictured Jenna in relation to both. The promise to be found in that was as exhilarating as it was astonishing. She loved him, and the more he considered that, the more the notion settled into his mind and seized hold of his heart.

For the first time in over a week he felt like his old self. Better, in fact. Rejuvenated; eager. Was it possible? he asked himself. Had he spent years looking for that special woman and all along she'd been right in front of him? A distant voice in his mind replied yes. Smiling, he strode from the library and down the hall, impatient for morning, impatient to see Jenna again.

It was the sound of her voice that arrested his stride. Into the still quiet of the house, her laughter followed, coming to him from behind the closed door to his left. At two in the morning, with all others asleep, he couldn't imagine what she was about.

The door yielded to his touch, swinging open on silent hinges. The room lay in moonlit darkness, revealing shadows and silhouettes in equal measure . . . revealing the cloaked shape and form of Jenna with her arms wrapped about a man.

Bitterness stunned him; betrayal swept through him. Damn that he might not be entitled to feel such. He did. Pain lashed at his insides, deepening when Jenna drew back and locked the door behind the man's departure, intensifying when she made her way toward him, oblivious to his presence.

Shrouded by near darkness, he reached out and grabbed hold of her arms.

Jenna cried out, alarmed to the marrow of her bones. In the next instant her fright gave way to relief and then pleasure when she realized exactly who held her.

"Alex, you gave me a scare."

"Did I?"

"Well, of course. I didn't know you were there. I wasn't expecting you."

His fingers tightened their grip. "That much was obvious."

Standing as they were, she had to squint hard to see the details of his face. What she saw was not encouraging. A lethal shine glittered in his eyes; his lips were a thin cruel slash, his jaw clenched.

"Alex, what's wrong?" She imagined any number of horrid problems. Instinctively wanting to help in any way she could, she laid her hand on his chest.

"You have a perverse sense of humor, madam."

She flinched at the grating condemnation icing his every word. "Excuse me?"

"You rushed from my side hours ago, claiming to be late, teasing of taking up with another man, of trying to make me jealous. Only it wasn't a joke, was it, Jenna?"

"I don't understand what you're saying."

"That doesn't surprise me. You're more accustomed to gaily phrased untruths and deceiving witticisms."

"No," she breathed in growing dismay. "That isn't true."

"What would you know about the truth? You profess your love for me one minute and in the very next stand with your arms about another man."

Understanding came to Jenna, and she didn't know whether to laugh or cry. "Do you mean Tom? Oh, Alex, you have it wrong."

"Shut up," he snarled, dragging her up against him with brutal force.

She gasped for an even breath and found it impossible. His arm across her back held her with enough power to crack her ribs. "Please, Alex, you're hurting me."

"It is the least that you deserve."

"Please," she cried, pushing against his shoulders to no avail. "You've made a terrible mistake."

"The only mistake I've made was in believing that you were capable of decent, honest emotion." He caught hold of her chin in his other hand and jerked her face up to his. "You made a fool of me, carrying on about faith, hope, and charity. You almost had me believing that beneath this beautiful face is a loving, caring woman."

"I am. I didn't lie to you."

"You're nothing but a shallow, cunning slut, anxious to play your warped little games."

His words struck her with agonizing impact, piercing her heart, making her want to crawl into herself and die. "You're wrong, Alex." Tears gathered in her eyes.

"Appearances would prove otherwise."

"Forget appearances," she choked out. "I did nothing wrong tonight."

"Tell me you haven't been gone for hours; tell me you didn't meet that man for clandestine purposes; tell me I didn't see you in his arms."

All of what he said was true, but not entirely. Desperate to make him understand, she could barely gather her reeling senses. "It wasn't like that. . . . I mean, I did leave, I . . . I was gone, but—"

"Spare me more of your lies."

With that, he thrust her away. She landed in a forlorn heap, bruised from the inside out. Confusion mixed with her sorrow as all her dreams and hopes crashed down about her, leaving her open and vulnerable. She loved Alex. Why couldn't he believe that? Why couldn't he see that she would never deceive him, never hurt him as he was hurting her?

She knew the answer and it brought a cry to her lips. Still, like some naive skeptic who needed sound, visible proof, she forced herself past the pain. Through tears and a numbing grief, she peered up at him. "Why are you so ready to believe the worst of me?"

Straightening his shoulders, Alex flexed his chin, his hands knotted into fists at his sides. "Why? To paraphrase your own words, my dear, because you are the *worst* mankind has to offer." He turned then and left her sitting in the dark.

She cried out in agony, her body cringing in misery, her mind in a whirl of anguish. Everything had happened so quickly, she could hardly make sense of what had transpired. Only the most hideous truths stood out: Alex hated her, despised her, believed her to be a lascivious slut. He had refused to listen to her, to give her a chance to correct his misconceptions.

Doubling over, she sobbed into her knees, her despair so deep, she knew she would never be whole again. She couldn't be. Alex had stripped her of her spirit. He had taken all the love she had to give and trampled it into the ground. He had taken her innate faith and hope and destroyed it.

Nothing would ever be the same again, not her trust in others and never, *never* again her belief in Christmas miracles.

Four

"Merry Christmas, my lord," Beth exclaimed from the bottom of the grand stairway, her round face a study of impish delight.

Ten steps up, Alex was forced to spare the young woman the semblance of a smile. The effort needed for even that minimal greeting stretched his forbearance to a dangerous degree.

"It is a glorious day," she pressed on, oblivious to his mood. "Have you seen Jenna about yet?"

The mention of Jenna sent a shaft of anger straight through him. If he never had to set eyes on her again, it would be too soon.

"No," he growled, descending the remaining stairs to stand beside Beth. "I have not seen her today."

Beth's smile faded and her brow creased with apparent worry. "Oh, dear. Have I said something amiss? Have I upset you in some way?"

It would be an easy task to verbally annihilate this young woman, to rip her to shreds with a few well-chosen words. His temperament was primed for such, but Beth wasn't to blame for the scorching fury that claimed him. Jenna was.

Damn her soul. Damn his own. He had been ten kinds of a fool to have let Jenna sway him with her pretty-sounding words. She had spouted eloquently about faith, hope, and charity, and he had lapped it all up like a green lad. Damnably, in all of her assertions she had said nothing about hon-

esty or virtue. He could well imagine the sordid state of th
last fine quality.

The memory of seeing her in the arms of another ma
gripped his insides viciously. That one image butchered a
honest intent she might have had about loving him. For th
hundredth time he told himself he shouldn't care one way
another. However, the inescapable truth was that he did car
more than he would have liked, more than he would hav
thought possible. And the fact that he was so angry prove
that he was not impervious to her. She had managed to tou
him deeply. For some reason he had allowed her to do s
Without realizing it he had come to prize her declarations
love.

"I apologize if I seem out of sorts this morning." Into h
voice he injected a studied politeness. It was the best he cou
summon. For several priceless moments in the dark hours
that morning he had yielded to his heart, to the certainty th
he had found the woman to love for a lifetime, only to di
cover he had been cruelly deceived. More than one sleeple
night would be needed for him to recover from that. "Perha
the holiday excitement has taken a slight toll."

"I can fully sympathize, my lord, especially with Jenn
going in ten directions at once. She tends to do that at th
time of the year. I've never known anyone to take Christm
to heart the way she does." Leaning close to impart what sh
obviously considered a matter of grave importance, she fre
ted, "I do hope all went well last night. I admit, I was
excited as she with the entire plan, but I am a coward of th
first water."

Hearing her refer to last night was like taking a fist to h
stomach. First he felt the pain and then the shock of disbelie
In stunned silence he scrutinized Beth's face, wondering ho
she had been involved with Jenna's late-night rendezvous
and why in the hell she would mention it to him!

"What plan are you referring to?" He posed the que
without conscious thought. The second the words were o

he wished to recall them. He didn't want to know the details. He'd seen enough to last him a lifetime.

"Didn't Jenna tell you?"

"No."

She pressed her index finger to her lower lip. "Oh, dear, that is so like her to act from the heart and keep it all to herself. Not only is she brave, but humble as well."

"Humble?"

"Oh, yes, beneath her cajolery she is remarkably modest. That's what makes her so special. She's forever going out of her way for others and expecting nothing in return. Take last night, for instance. She never gave a single thought to her own welfare, or even safety, for that matter. She simply ran off to the village in the middle of the night to ensure that a local family had its Christmas wishes fulfilled. As I said, I am much too cowardly for that."

With each word of explanation Alex's irritation and confusion grew. "What are you talking about?"

Beth cocked her head to one side. "She really didn't tell you, did she? After coming upon us at the abbey that day I thought you would have been let in on her plan. I thought she would have embroiled you along with the rest of us." Sighing, she shook her head in exasperation, but the effect was ruined by her smile. "Mr. Benson, the cobbler in the village, has fallen on hard times. His wife has been laid up in bed recovering from an illness. Between tending to her and to his four little ones, poor Mr. Benson's business has begun to suffer.

"Jenna found out about his plight and decided to help. Unfortunately, Mr. Benson is a proud man and wouldn't accept a bit of charity. That made Jenna's task a little more complicated, but she didn't let that stay her. She simply did what she does best. She beguiled everyone in the village to assist her, and last night they delivered foodstuffs and clothes for the children to Mr. Benson's door."

The memory of the muted conversation he'd overheard at

the abbey came back to Alex. Beth had wondered if the abbey was the most suitable place, if it wasn't going to prove to be an inconvenience of some kind.

"What did the abbey have to do with any of this?"

"To spare Mr. Benson's pride, Jenna thought the abbey might be a likely place to gather the presents. With all the greenery, it has a whimsical air she thought might make the entire situation more acceptable to Mr. Benson. In the end she decided to simply leave the packages at his door with a card that read, 'From the Spirit of Christmas.' " Beth laughed. "I ask you, how can a man argue with that?"

Alex had no answer. In fact, in the wake of Beth's disclosures, he was left with a host of unsettling questions, the first of which was why he should give a damn about what Jenna did. So she left his side for supposedly honorable purposes; what did that signify? Her return had been marked by more disreputable designs.

At the reminder, scorching contempt blazed a path from his brain to his stomach. "Why would she bother to go to such lengths?"

"Why does Jenna do anything?" Beth replied with a shrug. "Why does she make a point to offer compliments to people who don't warrant them; why does she bother with the dowager duchess of Wilberford?"

"I'll be damned if I know."

"You do have a point, my lord. The duchess can be annoyingly silly. But the truth of the matter is that Jenna cares, about everyone and everything."

"That is highly debatable."

"Oh, she does, my lord, I assure you. She sees the frailties in others and it touches her heart."

By sheer will alone he refrained from telling her that Jenna Stanton didn't have a heart. Instead, he jeered, "Don't try to tell me that old harridan of a dowager duchess is frail."

"I didn't think so either until Jenna made me see that the old woman is simply lonely and in need of a kind ear."

"Lonely?"

"It is sad but true. I wouldn't have ever guessed if Jenna hadn't made me look past the obvious to the reasons for the duchess carrying on as she does."

That caught him up short. He had never examined the reasons for the duchess's behavior. It had served his purposes to take her at face value. But now he admitted that Beth, and therefore Jenna, was correct about the old woman. She had to be eighty if she was a day, a widow who had outlived her children and had few friends her own age. It made sense that she was lonely, and in that loneliness craved attention from any source.

As admissions went this one made him squirm mentally; so much so, he damned himself for standing there. "You make it sound as if the *ton* is a walking army of the emotionally wounded."

Again Beth shrugged. "To an extent they are; at least Jenna believes so. That's why she makes the effort to befriend the most unlikely people." Smiling in sweet resignation, Beth sighed. "She simply cannot stand the thought of someone being hurt."

That one statement was enough to push Alex past his bounds. Silently, he condemned Beth to the realm of idiocy for her sugarcoated impression of her cousin. What Jenna knew about hurting someone could fill volumes.

"Unfortunately," Beth continued, "such compassion has gotten her into a score of scrapes."

He would be damned if he would remain a minute longer, listening to such delusions.

But Beth went on like a woman with a mission. "If I'm not watching out for her best interests, then her brother is, and if Andrew isn't, then one of her cousins is. Freddie usually comes to her rescue—"

He did not want to hear this. He started to turn away.

". . . and if not, then Tom does."

The name pierced him, freezing his muscles, rooting him to the spot. "Tom?" he choked out, gold eyes glittering.

"Yes, Tom Clarke; Reverend Clarke from the village."

"He's a cousin of Jenna's?"

"Third or fourth, I believe, on her mother's side." Tilting her head to one side, she asked, "Why?"

In the pit of Alex's stomach, a knot of unease began to form. "Would this Tom have been with Jenna last night?"

Beth laughed. "Most likely. As I said, he keeps an eye on Jenna when she's about her more philanthropic endeavors. And besides, it was Tom who helped Jenna gather the gifts for the Bensons."

The knot in Alex's stomach expanded to encase his entire chest. "Are they close?"

Lifting her brow, Beth professed, "I should think so. Jenna was Tom's wife's maid of honor and is godmother to their eldest daughter."

And it was Tom whom Jenna had hugged at two that morning.

Realization tore into Alex's mind with all the impact of a burning spear. He ground his eyes shut, cursing himself to hell and back.

"My lord, what is it?" Beth cried.

He had been wrong. Dear God, he had been wrong! He hadn't caught Jenna in a sordid tryst. He had come upon her thanking a cousin for helping her, for watching over her.

Swinging away, he was incapable of speech, uncaring that he had shocked Beth. He was consumed with images of Jenna as he had last seen her, her beautiful blue eyes filled with tears, her face a mask of misery. She had pleaded with him to listen. Instead he had called her a slut and thrown her aside like a worthless piece of refuse.

He considered now those times he had asked her about this plan of hers. She had dismissed his questions with a smile, a laugh, or a jaunty quip. All along she had been striving for the most humane of purposes, and in return he had hurt her, both physically and emotionally, and then left her to sob out her sorrow.

"My lord," Beth persisted, going so far as to touch his arm. "Are you ill? Is there anything I can do?"

Without a word he bounded up the stairs, his face drawn tight in self-loathing. He was a hundred times worse than the fool he had called himself. He was a bastard, a blind, heartless, arrogant bastard who had taken the rarest gift a man had ever been given and brutally crushed it.

Her heart was broken, shattered beyond hope, ravaged beyond repair. Where love and laughter had once filled her, Jenna knew she now had nothing. The hope and optimism on which she'd always relied were gone. She was empty, a void without even despair to fill the nothingness. The prospect of a lifetime of the same stretched out in dismal horror.

She wrapped her arms about her waist in an effort to stave off the chill that claimed her. Despite the healthy fire in the grate she shivered and curled more tightly into the window seat of her bedroom. Still wearing the same green gown she'd worn the night before, she drew her knees to her chest, rested her head against the windowpane, and shut her eyes.

Fatigue threatened and yet sleep eluded her. As it had through the night, her mind was still racing unchecked. It refused to relinquish its hold on all that had transpired with Alex. Again and again she heard him call her a slut, heard him accuse her of being a liar . . . and worse.

Tears flooded her eyes and slowly trickled down her cheeks. She let them fall, oblivious to their descent as pain overwhelmed her once more. If she could block out the agony she would. If she could escape the torment by some means she would. She didn't want to have to live with the kind of heartache that devastated her being, leaving her feeling worn out and useless and hollow.

In silent self-defense she opened her eyes and gazed about

her room. Everything looked the same, and yet all was changed, ruined; this room, herself, and certainly Christmas.

She scoffed in a rare and new cynicism when she thought of her Christmas miracle. *Idiotic* was only the first of the words she could use to describe herself. Foolish, naive, childish . . . the list was endless, and well deserved. She had been the epitome of conceited and vain to have thought that she could force Alex to love her.

He didn't. After last night there were no doubts remaining. He had made his sentiments brutally clear as to how he felt about her. She'd go to her grave remembering the contempt and hatred she'd seen in his eyes. And, pitifully, she couldn't muster the hope to imagine that someday her heart would be able to withstand the memory.

The sound of muted voices slowly drew her attention out the window. Guests were out and about for a Christmas stroll, reminding her that she would have to send word to her parents that she wouldn't be in attendance today. The explanation of illness would suffice, for it was the truth. Her head pounded and her stomach rolled with nausea.

The act of rising to summon her maid required every ounce of her energy. Perhaps tomorrow crossing the room would be easier; perhaps not. For the moment she had to concentrate on putting one foot in front of the other. She managed to reach the fireplace when her door opened.

Belatedly, she thought to turn. Belatedly, she realized it was Alex who had entered.

She grew completely still, her benumbed mind struggling to make sense of his presence. When her thoughts solidified they did so as separate, disjointed pieces of a whole. Alex. The man she loved. The man who hated her. The man who couldn't even stand to touch her.

It was her body that finally responded. Instinctively, she took a step back as the memories rushed forward more clearly, more cruelly than ever before.

Inside she cringed, her muscles twisting, her heart colliding with her lungs. Reaching for a nearby chair, she held on with one hand in a futile effort to still the quaking of her limbs. Her other hand crept up to her stomach in an attempt to knead the sick feeling into oblivion. All the while she frantically tried to deny reality.

"Go away," she whispered, the words torn from the depths of her. He didn't love her. He never would. In dismay, she watched him take a step closer. "Go away," she insisted, wanting to be as far from the hurt as possible.

"Jenna, I'd like to talk to you."

She shook her head in adamant refusal, unwilling to hear the ragged tenderness in his voice, incapable of seeing the regret and remorse lining his face. Desperate to be left alone, she demanded, "Leave here at once. I do not want you here." If he stayed, she'd crumble into a million pieces of despair.

"Please, Jenna, we need to talk."

"Everything has been said."

"I thought so last night, but I was wrong. Please, let me explain." He lifted a hand in appeal as he stepped closer.

In a panic she sidled toward the window, frantic at the thought of his coming closer, of his touching her. She didn't think she could bear that, not after the things he had said to her, the things he had implied. Her words a tumbling rush, she queried, "Why should you want to explain anything to me? I'm not capable of decent, honest emotion. You said so yourself."

"Jenna, don't—"

"Why should you bother with a shallow, cunning slut, anxious to play warped little games?" Just as they had last night, his words had the power to pierce her heart. Tears rose up swiftly, eroding what little she had of composure. Trembling, frightened, she inched her way backward, not even aware she did so. Her mind craved surcease from the hideousness of it all; her body acted accordingly. "Why should you care?"

"I do care, Jenna." He dropped his hand to his side, but he wouldn't let her retreat from him. For every step she took away, he advanced another. "After the way I treated you, I have no right to ask, but please, let me explain."

"I tried . . . to explain to you," she muttered, her voice as broken as her thoughts. "I . . . tried to tell you that you'd made a mistake." Her gaze darted about the room, seeking some kind of relief, anything to distract her from the pain tearing her apart. "I tried, and you threw insults at me."

"I'm sorry, Jenna."

"Then you threw me away," she whispered, gathering the last of her reserves, knowing what was next but unable to stop herself. "You said . . ." Misery of the soul suffused her in a single great wave. The last of her control unraveled, frayed, and then snapped. Sobbing, she choked out, "You said I was the worst mankind has to offer."

Alex closed the distance between them before she could finish. He swept her into his embrace and held her close.

"Stop," he grated, absorbing the wild shuddering that wracked her. "Please, Jenna . . ."

"Why?" she cried, struggling to free herself. With hands planted against his chest, she twisted and turned, dying inside, withering like a flower helpless before the brutal elements. "How could you have said . . . have thought . . . Let me go."

"Jenna, stop."

"Let me go." But her demand was for nothing. She didn't possess the strength to gain her release.

Exhausted from the inside out, she suddenly sagged in his arms, uncaring that she was exactly where her heart had once longed for her to be. "You've ruined everything," she cried into his chest. "You've ruined . . . everything."

Her words lashed at his heart; her tears tortured his soul. "Forgive me," he murmured into her hair. "Forgive me." If she heard, he didn't know. She cried as if her life was ending.

And he was to blame.

Cursing himself again, he swept her into his arms, stepped to the chair before the fireplace, and sat with his precious

urden held securely. Arms wrapped about her, he tried to
bsorb the quivering that shook her slender body.

"Don't cry so, love." This was his punishment, he thought,
) hear her sorrow, to see her anguish, to feel her grief—and
ot be able to help. For his mistrust, for his unmitigated ef-
rontery, this was his sentence. And he deserved it. "I'm
orry."

The stifled words barely penetrated the shroud of Jenna's
eartache. Dimly, she heard the apology, but she was no more
ble to comprehend its meaning than she was able to control
er misery. Not until the last of her tears had dwindled to
agged sighs was she capable of true awareness and under-
tanding. Then she took stock of the present and instantly
ried to lever herself away.

"No," Alex implored, his face ravaged by regret. "Stay.
lease."

Oh, how she wanted to, even knowing how foolhardy that
vould be. Comfort and warmth were here in his embrace,
uring her tired mind and assuaging her weary spirit with old
lreams. Those intimate reveries rushed back in reckless aban-
lon, and for one unthinkable moment she ignored her mind's
varnings about self-delusion and gave herself up to the fan-
asy.

Resting her head on his shoulder once more, she relished
he muscled feel of him, his permeating heat, the faint, spicy,
nasculine scent of his cologne. Beneath her, against her, sur-
ounding her, he was there, holding her with what she could
magine was tender reverence and pure possessiveness.

To be wanted and cherished and loved like that was heady.
)n a long sigh she closed her eyes and created a memory
o have for the future, something to sustain her through the
vears of loneliness. She didn't let herself think that this was
iow it could have been. In silence she doggedly acknow-
edged only the minute details of the immediate; the pulse
n his neck beating against her forehead, her fingers resting
n his shoulder, his hand curved about her waist.

Into that bliss came the low sound of his voice. "I'm sorry, Jenna."

The apology was abhorrent. It shattered the illusion and opened the mental gates for reality to come flooding back. Her reprieve was over.

Collecting the frayed ends of her being was one of the most difficult things she had ever had to do. Emotions surged and ebbed from every direction. A bit frantically, she shoved all but one or two aside, dug deep for pride, and sat straight. Her attempt to rise, however, met with the same results it had before.

Alex's hands held her firmly in place. "No."

Where only seconds ago she had treasured his closeness, it now made her extremely uncomfortable. "Let me up, Alex. Nothing can be gained by this."

"We need to talk."

Her gaze resolutely fixed on her lap, she shook her head. "I don't have anything to say."

"Nothing?" he prodded, the gold of his eyes gilded to a brilliant topaz sheen.

"What would you have me say? That I made a fool of myself?" In a pitiful attempt at her old gaiety, she quipped, "Very well, I made a royal cake of myself. Stupid me."

"No," he vowed, hating the sound of her self-derision, hating himself because he was responsible for its existence. "No, love, I am the stupid one. I am the blind fool for not believing you, for not letting you explain about last night. Look at me." She shook her head, so he cupped her chin in one hand and lifted her face to his. "Beth told me all."

The gentle persuasion in his voice was evidenced in his eyes. She'd never seen the gold orbs burnished with such intensity, or so utterly bleak. It was as if all her anguish and pain had coalesced to gather in his eyes. Against her will she felt her heart give a squeeze of remorse.

"What . . . what did she tell you?"

"What I wouldn't let you explain."

"Then you know who Tom is . . . that I wasn't . . ."

"Yes." His fingers trailed over the line of her jaw. "And can only ask your forgiveness."

She was stunned and disconcerted. "I don't know what to say." It was obvious that he was genuinely sorry for hurting her.

"Say you will give me another chance."

Her eyes widened. "For what?"

"For your love."

Fright and hope and expectation surged through her and she jerked away, unable to control the melange of vulnerable emotions that charged to the fore.

"No," Alex ordered gently, his arms unbreakable bands round her.

"Please, Alex." She was afraid to feel and desire and trust again. All three had led to a miserable folly when she'd dared to love. In return she'd received a pain unlike any she had ever felt before. "Don't do this," she breathed.

"Don't do what?" The hand at her chin slid through her hair to cup the back of her head; the other swept low to ride along her hips. "Don't hold you?" His arms pressed her indecently close. "Don't kiss you?" Ever so slowly he brushed his lips over hers, stroking fires she had thought dead. "Don't want you until I'm half crazed with longing?"

His mouth covered hers in sweet mastery, filling her with longing that made her ache. The urge to resist played over the ends of her consciousness, taunting her with memories of his cruelty, but the moment his lips parted hers, she was lost. His tongue swept into her mouth and with it came heat, desire, and all the love she harbored within her.

Her mind chided her for relenting. Her heart rejoiced. Torn, she hung suspended between the two, wanting and yet unwilling.

"Kiss me," Alex breathed, needing her love as he had never needed anything in his life.

"I . . . I can't. I'm . . . afraid."

His eyes sought hers and only then did he see her fear
All the anger he felt toward himself grew apace with his
shame. Jenna was if nothing else audaciously courageous, and
he had ruthlessly stripped her of that most endearing quality

"How can I ever make this up to you?" He didn't wait
for an answer; he wasn't sure he wanted one. "You are so
special, so rare. I didn't know last night just how special you
really are." Cupping her face in his hands, he whispered
"Last night I didn't know what jealousy was, or that it could
drag me to such depths."

Mesmerized, Jenna searched his eyes, feeling his anguish
in her very heart. "You were jealous?"

"So much so that I lashed out at you. I saw deception
where there was only goodness; I saw lies where there was
only honest feeling; I saw lechery where there was only generosity."

"But why, Alex? I never did anything to make you react
that way."

"Yes, you did." His expression softened; his voice lowered.
"For years you've smiled your smiles and cast your glances
and made me shake my head at your impudence. You made
me laugh and swear and curse at us both." He lowered his
head until his mouth grazed hers. "You spoke of miracles
and made me fall in love with you."

He sealed the words with his mouth, taking her startled
gasp into his possession just as he wanted to take her heart
into his keeping and make it his. From this moment on. If
she would have him.

"Tell me all isn't ruined, that there's still a chance," he
urged, trailing his mouth down the column of her throat. "Tell
me you love me as much as I love you."

He loved her! Jenna felt her eyes fill with tears, too
stunned and happy to even think of answering him. Instead
she turned her head slightly and kissed him in joyous abandon, feeling whole again, feeling alive and truly loved.

"Does this mean yes?" he managed to ask.

Through her tears she smiled and laughed and then unable
to help herself, hugged him fiercely. "Yes, yes yes yes yes
yes! I love you."

The most wondrous sense of satisfaction swirled in his
mind and heart. Jenna loved him. And he loved her, this dar-
ing, lighthearted, presumptuous minx, this generous, compas-
sionate, loving woman.

"Tell me again," she implored, her heart greedy.

"I love you."

They were the sweetest words she had ever heard and she
would cherish them forever. "I had given up hope," she
breathed, drinking in the sight of his beloved face. "I've loved
you for so long, but after last night I gave up hope."

"Will you ever be able to forgive me?"

She laid a tender hand along his steely jaw. "I already
have."

"And will you marry me as soon as possible?" His hands
stole to her waist, his eyes filling with bold intent. "I don't
want to have to wait, Jenna."

Fresh tears rose, glistening in harmony with her smile.
Alex loved her and wanted to marry her. Her Christmas miracle was complete.

Her heart turned over. For a few terrible hours she had
lost her faith, but it was restored now and she would never
doubt again, not for herself or Alex or their children. Through
the years she would assure them all of the Christmas spirit,
and tell them that if you believe in miracles, they come true.

"Jenna?"

Filled with that spirit and with an endless, abiding love,
she lifted her mouth to Alex's. "I love you. And, yes, I'll
marry you."

The Christmas Carousel

Penelope Neri

One

Katherine tipped her head back and laughed out loud in sheer delight.

Her unruly brown hair had escaped its pins. It streamed behind her like pennants now. The grinning jester shields, the beveled mirrors, the misty oil paintings, and the prancing ponies moved around her in a never-ending blur of gilt and pastels. The band organ was bellowing a rousing German country dance, one that set your feet to tapping and filled your head with images of buxom farm *fraus* and tall steins slopping foamy beer.

Up and down she rode, seated sideways on the wooden saddle, for all the world as if her painted Arabian pony was galloping on air. Its creamy Baroque mane flowed, its mouth was agape, its eyes so full, so gentle and expressive in the finely sculpted head, it was hard to believe the horse was not real. Clinging to the brass pole before her, she felt like an eastern princess riding to a romantic oasis rendezvous.

Faster and faster she spun, for three glorious minutes giving herself up to the fantasy created by the carousel's jeweled lights, its thrilling colors, sights, and sounds. Her quarrel with her fiancé, Stone Armitage, and her flight from his carriage to Fairmount Park dwindled into obscurity. She would have to face Stone and her father soon enough over a hellish Sunday luncheon, during which her character would be found wanting in every respect, but . . . not yet, please, God! *Not yet!*

"Well, now, and is it the brass ring ye'd be trying to catch, mavourneen?"

The lilting male voice cut through her giddy euphoria. It even managed to penetrate the Wurlitzer organ's brassy oom-pah-pah melody.

Startled, Katherine glanced back, over her shoulder, to find herself drowning in a pair of the bluest eyes she'd ever seen. "I . . . beg your pardon?"

"I said, are ye after the brass ring?" the man repeated, loud enough to make himself heard over the band organ. He was smiling as he swung nimbly around a pinto Indian pony, then sidestepped between an armored medieval charger and a cavalry flag-horse, to stand at her Arabian's delicate head. His long legs were braced apart, his booted feet firmly planted on the running board as her horse rose effortlessly up and down, up and down alongside him, lifted by the over-head mechanism in the canopy.

Aware that he was staring at her with a deal more interest than was proper, she looked him up and down, too, and was surprised to find that she liked what she saw very much. He was very attractive, although he wore no jacket over his white shirt, which was collarless. Moreover, there was no sign of a stud or a cravat or a waistcoat anywhere, even though it was the Sabbath. Still, with Philadelphia smoldering in the eighties, perhaps such casual attire was understandable, she allowed, thinking what a blessed relief it would be to dispense with some of her own underpinnings. The temperature would also explain why his sleeves were rolled up like a common bricklayer's, baring muscular forearms. A flat brown cap was jammed down on a head of unruly black curls that no man had any right to. His looks, coupled with his bold manner and that wicked, irrepressible grin suited the rebelliousness of her mood.

Accordingly, she favored the handsome stranger with a dazzling smile—one that completely transformed her grave, sweet face and made it even lovelier.

"But of course!" she came back, belatedly answering his question. "Isn't everyone after the brass ring—or something very much like it?" She met his amazing blue eyes without so much as a modest flicker of her own gray ones and added, "The brass ring of Fame, say? Or Fortune? Or even something as simple as plain old happiness?" *Simple, yet enormously hard to come by,* she added silently, biting her lower lip.

The stranger's grin deepened. His merry eyes twinkled. Shoving his cap back on his head, he tucked his thumbs in his belt. "Well, now, and isn't that a deep thought for a slip of a girl t' be having? Perhaps ye'd allow me t' introduce meself before we continue our conversation? Logan Teague, Esquire, at your service, ma'am," he shouted above the giddy organ music. "And you'd be—?"

"Katherine," she shouted back, laughing. "Miss Katherine W—" She stopped short.

"Aye, go on, then," he urged. "Miss Katherine—what?"

She started to tell him, but she thought better of it. "Just . . . just Katherine."

"Ah. 'Just Katherine,' is it? But, are ye just, Katherine? Or are ye only fair? Well, now, that's a fool thing t' say, when any man can see that ye're fair as a summer's day! But . . . could it be that you're fairer than ye are just—or only just as fair?"

He winked, and a giggle escaped her. "You're mad! What nonsense you speak! I do believe you're teasing me, Mister—?"

"Teague. It's Logan Teague, remember? And, aye," he admitted cheekily, "guilty as charged, yer Honor—but I don't repent my sins. See, I like it fine, teasing you, Miss Katherine! Teasing turns your cheeks to roses an' brings out the dimples."

Her hand flew to her face. "Nonsense. I don't have any dimples!"

"You do, too," he insisted with another wicked wink that made her blush deepen. "Right there!"

"Really, Mr. Teague, you're being much more forward than is proper. Oh! And the music's stopped! I really should be running along. Good day—!"

"Wait! Won't ye let me help ye down before ye tear yer frock, my lady?" he offered, doffing his cap.

Reluctant to refuse his offer—he looked so gallant standing there, with his cap rolled up in his hands—she gave him a quick nod of assent.

Both hands on her waist, he swung her down from her wooden steed's back, his fingertips resting lightly upon the rose silk of her gown long after the revolving platform had slowed. And even when it had he did not release her, but stood there, looking down into her upturned face.

The carousel came to a complete stop. The band organ's wild music faded into silence once again. Still they gazed at each other.

The moment was peculiarly unsettling—intimate, somehow, Katherine thought. It was suddenly difficult to draw a deep breath, as if her stays were too tightly laced. This close to the stranger, he radiated heat, like a young healthy animal, but unlike the men of her father's acquaintance who smelled of cigar smoke, pomade, and liquor, *he* smelled wonderful; an elusive mixture of carbolic, of sunshine and starched linens, and—curiously—of pine trees. The combination made her feel light-headed.

" 'Tis a fine dress ye're after wearing this mornin', too, Miss Katherine," he observed huskily, eyeing her in a way that made her feel beautiful, although she knew she was plain. "I'd say ye've been t'church, aye? St. Joseph's?" he guessed, naming his own.

"Church, yes," she admitted, unsettled by his forwardness. Imagine! He had his hands upon her waist! "But it was Christ's Church, not St. Joe's," she explained, naming the city's oldest Anglican church.

He whistled. "Old Church? But that's clear across town!"

She grimaced. "I know. I had—words—with my—with my

father on the way home, after the service," she explained, wondering why she'd lied. For whatever reason, she'd been quite unable to say *fiancé* to Logan Teague, and so had opted to say *father* instead. No matter. He had no need to know that something inside her had finally snapped this morning, after months of swallowing her anger about her father arranging her marriage to a man she detested. Nor did he need to know that she'd leaped out of Stone's elegant carriage at a busy intersection filled with carriages and horse-drawn trolleys. Or that she'd run west down Market Street like a hoyden, not caring when her Sunday hat sailed off to parts unknown, or if her hair had escaped its pins. Her rose silk was terribly wrinkled; her drawstring purse and her parasol had been left far behind. What a mess she must look, she thought, reaching up to neaten her hair.

"Do ye always come t' Fairmount when yer father's riled with ye?" he asked.

She wrinkled her nose like a rabbit. "Quite often, yes. I find a walk in the park and a ride on the carousel clears my head. It's been a habit since Mama brought me here when I was little." She sighed. "Papa disapproves, of course." She rolled her eyes heavenward.

Logan smiled. "Of course!" Her expressive face gave him a fair idea of what her father must be like. Strict, sober, Anglican, and overbearing—he'd bet money on it!

"He says carousals and amusement parks are no place for proper ladies—but I do so love to ride the flying horses! They're . . . they're magical," she shyly confessed.

Eyes still shining, she turned her face away to hide her blush. *Wretched man!* He had no right to be so devilishly handsome—nor to ask questions she felt compelled to answer.

With a chuckle, Logan sprang down to the grass and lifted her after him, holding her as if she were light as a feather.

"You may put me down now, Mr. Teague," she hissed, only too aware of the disapproving looks they were drawing.

"And if I won't?" he challenged.

"Then, sir, I shall scream bloody murder," she threatened, trying to keep a serious face. "And tell anyone who'll listen that you're a lunatic and should be locked up!"

Laughing, he held her a moment longer, then set her safely down on the grass. "A madman, am I? Perhaps I am, at that!"

Retrieving a brown jacket draped over a bush, he slung it over his shoulder. Then, raising his flat cap to the carousel attendant, he offered Katherine his arm. "My lady?"

To her surprise, she smiled and took it.

"So, ye like to ride my carousel, do ye, pretty Kate?" he asked teasingly as they strolled, arm in arm, along the path between the trees and bushes lining the river.

"Your carousel?" She looked up into his face, deciding she liked his crooked grin. Liked, too, the contrast of wind-browned skin against a dazzling white—if collarless—shirt. Liked most of all his sparkling, cornflower eyes. . . .

"As good as mine, aye. Ye see, I carved most of the new figures for the bicentennial with me own fair hands!" He held up those hands for her approval, the fingers splayed.

They were large hands, she noted, staring at them. An artist's hands, just as he'd claimed, the fingers long and square-tipped, the palms hard with callus, the nails surprisingly clean and neatly clipped for a working man. Powerful hands, yet gentle, too, she sensed, wondering what they would feel like, stroking her hair, her throat, her shoulder. . . .

It was a dangerous train of thought—one she'd never entertained where her fiancé was concerned. Her pulse raced. She felt faint, as insubstantial as a dandelion clock as she nervously cleared her throat. "So, you're a wood-carver, are you, Mr. Teague?"

"Aye, I am. As was my own dear father before me, God bless him."

She bit her lip and muttered, "Oh, I'm sorry. I do hope I didn't open an old wound?"

His dark brows winged skyward in confusion. "Sorry, mavourneen? About what?"

"Why, that your father's dead."

To her dismay, he laughed heartily. "Why, bless ye, me
ather's not dead, mavourneen. He lives in Brooklyn, New
ork—though some say it's as good as being dead! I'd beg
differ, meself, having been born and raised there. 'Tis a fine,
vely place!"

"Oh! I'm sorry."

"Sorry again, are ye?" For the first time since she'd met
im, he looked at her as if she puzzled him, shaking his
ead. "Whist, you've done nothing to be sorry about! Blessed
Mary, today's a hot one! Will ye have some lemonade with
e?"

"I couldn't, really. I—I don't think it would be proper to
et a stranger buy me refreshments, thank you just the same,
Mr. . . . Teague."

His engaging grin returned. "Call me Logan," he urged.
And you're right. In the usual way of things I'd agree that
'm too forward for me own good, Miss Katherine. How-
ver—since ye know my name and my business, where I hail
rom and that me father's still living—why, I could hardly be
onsidered a stranger anymore, could I? So—let's have some
emonade, aye?"

"Aye!" she echoed recklessly, amused by his persistence
nd his logic. A smile tugged at her lips. Mr. Logan Teague,
squire, could charm the birds from the very trees, if he had
mind to. His brogue was as thick as an Irish peat bog, as
mooth as Irish whiskey—and its effect just as devastating.
What girl could resist him?

Pleased, he grinned. "Two lemonades, if ye please, Geor-
ie."

They had come to a lemonade and pretzel stand, tended
y a stooped old man. Above, numerous cherry trees stirred
lightly in a sultry breeze, while beyond them, the broad
chuylkill River gleamed as it flowed between its banks.
here were long, narrow rowboats slicing through the water,
rewed by noisy university students. The rowers were being

cheered on by still other fresh-faced young men, jumping up
and down on the banks.

"Two lemonades, coming right up, Logan, you young devil
But first, who's this pretty miss on your arm?"

"This lovely colleen is Katherine, Georgie. *Just* Katherine
Say 'Hello' to Old George, Just Katherine. He makes the bes
lemonade in the city of Philadelphia. I have a suspicion he
stole the recipe from Ben Franklin!"

When George snorted Katherine laughed. "Don't bother
defending yourself, George. I haven't believed a word Mr
Teague has said since we met—all of fifteen minutes ago!"

"Fifteen minutes—or fifteen *thousand* minutes—what's in
a number, Katie, darlin'? People get married after shorter en-
gagements!" he joked, winking at her.

She felt that glance clear down to her toes.

"A good-afternoon to you, miss. And you see here, Teague
that's enough of your Irish blarney! You'll have to pay for
these lemonades. Ten cents. Hand it over, lad."

"Ten cents it is. Here ye go, my unkind friend," Logan
promised with a grin, fishing the coins from his pocket and
flipping them to the old man, who caught them on the fly
"Come along, Just Kate. We'll sit over here."

Katherine followed him to the banks of the river, where
he spread his jacket on the grass for her to sit upon.

There were daisies and buttercups everywhere, with hon-
eybees bumbling around them. A cloudless blue sky showed
between a leafy fretwork of foliage in every shade of green
imaginable.

It was an idyllic day, she decided with a blissful sigh—
idyllic in every way.

On the far side of the river rose the ivy-covered brick walls
of the university. She could see young men in their shirt-
sleeves there, playing a rowdy game of baseball. Their play
was punctuated by solid *cracks* as bat hit ball, followed by
cheers. Other students lolled upon the grass, studying, with

tacks of books at their sides, oblivious to the fierce game
1 progress.

*Whoever would have thought it? The Philly Hat King's
nly daughter—hatless, gloveless, unchaperoned—drinking
:monade on the riverbank with an Irish wood carver. She
:lt like one of her papa's factory girls, courting with her
weetheart—and loving every minute of it!*

Logan dropped down beside her, propping himself on one
lbow. "Now, then. Where was I?" he began. His musical
rogue rising and falling, he wove daisies and buttercups into
 chain while he told her about himself. He began with his
)ving, boisterous, working-class family, and growing up in
3rooklyn. His parents, Michael Teague, Senior, and his hard-
orking mother, Mary. His brothers and sisters—Michael,
unior, Sean, Patrick, Shannon, and Deirdre.

". . . I wanted something different from carving furniture
ke my father, see? Then Da heard that Charles Looff was
1 Brooklyn, looking for apprentice carvers to work on the
igures for his Rhode Island and Coney Island carousel ma-
hines," he explained. "Da knew I loved t'carve. He showed
Ir. Looff some of the work I'd done for the church—statues
f saints and angels, mostly. Looff liked them fine. He asked
1e to come and carve for his studio in Rhode Island that
vinter. Jobs were scarce, so for a year or two I did just that."

"Why did you leave?"

"It wasn't right for me, Katie. I didn't like roughing the
arousel horses' bodies. It was the fancy carving I enjoyed—
1e heads, the fancy saddle trimmings. Breathing life into
olid wood with me own bare hands!" he explained, his gen-
an eyes shining. "But o'course those were the parts Looff
nd his master carvers—'head' men, as they're known in the
ade—did themselves. Looff told me to be patient. In time,
e'd let me carve heads, but . . ."

"But you couldn't bear to wait?"

"I'm afraid patience is not one o' me many virtues," he
dmitted with an engaging, cocky grin. "One day a man

named Auchy came by. He owned several amusement machines and wanted to commission Looff to carve new figures for the Fairmount Park carousel machine here, in Philadelphia. But—since Looff already had several orders for that winter—he had to refuse. He was kind enough t'put in a good word for me, though. And so here I am, carving merry-go-round figures in Mr. Gustaf Dentzel's shop! Now, then. Fair's fair. It's your turn, Kate. Where do you work?"

"Work?" The question took her aback. What could she tell the Irishman that would not be a lie, since she'd already decided she couldn't tell him the truth—that Papa had been furious when she'd told him she was doing volunteer work at a nearby hospital and wouldn't hear of her working at a real job. No, sir. She'd been raised a lady. He'd seen to that, "no thanks to your worthless mother," who'd run off with one of his cutters when Katherine was only a baby, "and good riddance to her, too!" It was enough, Father believed, that Katherine embroidered and read, or made occasional calls on those rare Society Hill matrons who—since her engagement to one of the Philadelphia Armitages—would permit Katherine Weston, a common factory owner's daughter, to pay calls on them. She grimaced. Hardly what Logan would call "work"!

"Let me guess," he offered, noting her hesitation.

Her heart skipped a beat as those striking blue eyes thoughtfully looked her up and down.

"Ye're a—a seamstress. No? A milliner's assistant, then? No, no, not with those nails, bitten to the quick!" he observed, trying to look disapproving. "Do ye work in a shop or a factory? Ah, a factory," he decided, misreading the subtle change in her expression for a lucky strike. "My guess is you work at Turner's—no, *Weston's*. That's it! Weston's Hat Factory! 'The Very Best Hats are Weston Hats'!"

Katherine grew very still. He'd quoted the catchphrase Papa's slick young advisers had coined to keep abreast of a new business trend called advertising. It was pasted on bill-

oards, on trolley cars, everywhere. Surely her face would
ive something away?

But to her relief Logan seemed very pleased with himself
s he declared, "You're a felt blocker, aye? Or maybe a
Veston brim cutter!"

His scorn for her father's company needled Katherine's
ride. "That's right," she lied stiffly. "How clever of you to
uess."

"Clever? Hmph! My poor wee Kate—I only wish t' God
'd been wrong! Tell me, how does it feel to be one of 'Work-
orse Willy' Weston's slaves?" he commiserated, looping the
aisy chain he'd made about her fragile little wrist. Stroking
ie back of her slender hand with his fingertip, he murmured,
T'be sure, it must be like wearin' shackles!"

At his electric touch she withdrew her hand as if he'd
tubbed a hot match against her delicate skin. Her gray eyes
uge, she nursed her tingling hand to her bosom. "Of course
's not, silly!" she protested. "P—Mr. Weston is a very en-
rprising, hard-working man. Did you know he was orphaned
t the age of ten? Or that he built his business from absolutely
othing but a few rabbit and beaver skins? Today he owns
vo successful factories, one here and the other in Chicago,
hich produce men and women's felt, fur, and straw hats for
American cities as far distant as San Francisco?"

Logan grinned. "Why, now, you sound like one of the old
ivil's agents—! Katie, I do admire your loyalty—but every-
ne in the City of Brotherly Love knows Weston grew rich
n the broken backs of those worse off than himself!"

"That's not true!" she protested, clenching her fists within
er skirts. "He's worked hard for every cent he's earned!"

"All right, lass. Ye've no need to get riled!" He shook his
ead. "Tsk. You're a loyal one, aren't ye? But that's just fine
nd dandy. I expect loyalty in my colleens, I do."

"Well, but I'm *not* one of your 'colleens,' Mr. Teague!"
he protested smartly, shooting that—that Irish potato-head
n indignant look.

He suddenly ducked his dark, curly head and planted a smacking kiss on her cheek, crowing, "Ye are now . . . ! So, finish your lemonade, lass; then I must see ye home. Me landlady, the formidable Missus Maureen Flannigan, will have me Sunday dinner on the table, prompt at two. God help me if I'm late!" His blue eyes twinkled, noting the uncertainty in her own. "Cheer up, Kate! Your da will have forgotten ye riled him by now, sure. Ye won't be getting a smack."

"Da? A smack?" She stared at him blankly. "Oh! You mean my *father?* No, I don't expect I will be getting a sma— one," she agreed hastily.

Still astonished by his kiss, she took the hand he extended to help her up, looking anywhere but at him as she shook out her grass-stained skirts.

Did his kiss show? Had it left some indelible mark on her cheek, like a scarlet letter? She had no basis for comparison, for as sure as God made little green apples, Stone Armitage's dry-lipped pecks had never made her feel this giddy, *wonderful* way!

Tucking her hand through his arm, Logan waved to George, then walked her back to the carousel.

"You don't have to take me home, Mr. Teague. I'll be quite all right from here," she murmured, suddenly panicky that he'd insist on escorting her all the way home.

"All right. May I see you again, Kate?" he asked her when they reached the carousel, facing her squarely and gazing deep into her eyes. His voice was husky as he added, "I'd like to. Very much."

His handsome face was a little apprehensive, she noted surprised. Why, despite his devil-may-care manner, he was afraid she'd refuse! She gnawed her lower lip. "I really don' think I should."

"Please, Kate?" he implored, "Say you'll reach for tha' brass ring. Take a chance on—me!"

Despite her misgivings she smiled, feeling her reservations melt like ice cream in the hot sun. What harm could there

e in meeting him just once more, in broad daylight? she
:ked herself. "All right. I'll meet you. When and where?"

"Whenever and wherever you say, darlin'!" he came back,
nable to mask the pleasure in his voice.

She did a rapid appraisal of the coming week and settled
n Wednesday. On Wednesdays Papa was gone from luncheon
ntil late in the evening. He claimed he met with colleagues
> discuss business, but since he came home very late, a little
runk, and reeking of perfume and cigar smoke, Katherine
1spected he visited Etta, the plump mistress he kept in Ger-
1antown.

"I could meet you on Wednesday?" she suggested, secretly
mazed. What in the world was she thinking of, to be stand-
1g here, her lips sticky with lemonade, her cheek burning
om the touch of a man's lips, making an assignation with
blue-eyed Irish stranger she'd known for an hour, at most.
stranger who surely had no respectable designs upon
er . . .

Nevertheless, she was weak-kneed with relief, almost giddy
·ith excitement, when he nodded. "Wednesday it is then,
1avourneen. How does three o'clock sound? I'll meet you
ght here."

She nodded shyly. "Three will be perfect, Mr. Teague."

"Logan, Katie. Logan."

Logan. I'll be here."

"I'm awful glad t'hear it, Kate." Serious now, he leaned
own and planted a much firmer, far longer kiss upon the
imple at the corner of her mouth. A kiss that left her breath-
·ss. "Till Wednesday, then," he murmured huskily.

And before she could turn to see which way he'd gone he
ad vanished, swallowed up by the Sunday park-goers swarm-
1g over the grass.

Little boys in navy-blue sailor suits bowled hoops along
1e paths with sticks. Little girls wearing ribbons and starched
inafores headed straight for the pretty carousel, their long-
1ffering parents either in tow or pushing baby brothers or

sisters in perambulators ahead of them. Indeed, whole families were out to enjoy the sunshine and fresh air, strolling along the riverbanks. The mothers were dressed in bustled gowns and saucy straw hats, while the fathers sported panamas or straw boaters.

Katherine saw and heard none of them. A small smile playing about her lips, she left the park and headed briskly for the corner where she'd abandoned Stone and the Armitage carriage and pair.

She wasn't really surprised to see that the vehicle was standing exactly where she'd left it, the horses stamping impatiently, the sour-faced driver, Hennessy, scowling at the pedestrians. Nor was she surprised to find her fiancé still hunched inside the vehicle, his hatchet face as long and drear as any wet weekend. *Oh, dear me, no!* She would have been more surprised had Stone actually stirred his bones to come in search of her, the unloved, unwanted fiancée he considered far beneath him—but whose father's money he coveted.

"So there you are, Katherine," he greeted her return. "What must people have thought, with you screeching at me like a southwark hoyden, then tearing off down the street! *shudder* to imagine what Mama will say when she hears."

"Do you?" Katherine inquired coolly, nodding her thanks as Hennessy handed her up into the carriage. She arranged her skirts about her, then unfurled her silk parasol, angling it over her head. "Then why don't you refrain from mentioning our little—altercation—to her?" she suggested pertly. "After all, what you and I discuss is really none of your mama's business—is it, Stone, dear?"

She was rewarded by a shocked look from her fiancé, who flinched as if a fluffy lapdog had suddenly cocked its leg and made a puddle over his shoe.

Muffling a giggle, Katherine lowered her sunshade to hide her face. *What in the world had happened to her? She only had to remember the way Logan had looked at her and she felt capable of anything!*

"I shall ignore that remark, Katherine," Stone ground out, looking down his long nose at her. He consulted his gold pocket watch. "Furthermore, I think since—thanks to your tantrums!—we're going to be twenty-two minutes late for luncheon with your father, you should offer our excuses and apologies." While he might not respect William Weston for the man he was, he definitely respected his future father-in-law's healthy bank accounts—of which the Armitage family had all too few. He had no intention of jeopardizing the marriage settlement Weston had agreed upon by irritating the old lod.

"You had no right to insult my father. I will not stand for ., Mr. Armitage—nor will I apologize for my 'tantrums.' Now, having said that, would you still like me to tell Father exactly why we're late, and what you said to make me run ff?" There! She'd done it! She'd called his bluff!

Stone seethed. His fair complexion turned a mottled, purlish shade, a sure sign that he was having difficulty keeping is temper. "Are you challenging me?"

"I rather think I am, yes."

"Hrrmph! Well, rest assured, you will mend your ways vhen we are wed, Katherine. Neither Mother nor I will permit uch vulgar behavior then."

"No? That's strange. You see, I had a feeling you'd permit ny number of liberties, so long as my father paid off your ambling debts."

Though her tone was innocent, her implication was obvius. Stone's flush deepened, though his eyes remained cold nd hard as pebbles. "Hrrrmph. It's clear you don't understand the workings of a gentleman's agreement, Katherine. Iowever, since you feel so strongly about it, I'll make our xcuses to your father. Hennessy!"

"Yes, Mr. Armitage, sir?"

"Drive on!"

On the contrary, Katherine thought with a bitter ache in er heart as the driver clicked to the matched pair and the

open carriage drew away from the park, *I understand you.*
"gentleman's agreement" very well. My father is seeking you.
old and distinguished family name for the grandchildren I'm
to bear him. The Armitage name and its associations will be
bought with much-needed Weston money, tit for tat! In effect
Papa has sold me to the highest bidder, as if I were a—
slave on the auction block, with no regard for my future hap
piness!

Happiness. That elusive brass ring—

The hour she'd spent with Logan had been deliriously
happy. In fact, she could hardly wait to be with him again
To have him smile at her as he'd done this afternoon, and
make her feel beautiful, special, all over again! For a little
while she'd pretend she was truly Logan's special colleen who
worked amid the steam, shellac, and chemicals as a felt
blocker for Weston's, and that she didn't have to marry Stone
Armitage next Valentine's Day, as her father and Stone's hor
rid mother, Adelaide, had arranged.

Two

"It's snowing," Logan observed, four months almost to the hour later, as he cocked an eye at the murky panes of the woodshop's small window.

"Hmmm," Katherine murmured drowsily, rolling over and snuggling up against him. She rested her cheek upon his lightly furred chest, one arm thrown across his belly. "Snow—I knew it! You see? We'll have a white Christmas after all. How perfect!"

He chuckled, stroking her hair, which spilled across the cot's ticking mattress. "You're what's perfect, darlin'. From your fine golden-brown head to your little pink toes, and all the lovely rest o' ye between!" He tilted her chin up with his finger "I love ye, Katie—you know that?"

"Yes," she whispered. There were tears in her eyes as she nodded, for it was the truth. "I know."

"Then why haven't ye taken me home t' meet your family? Why all o' this secrecy? We've been courtin' for almost four months, Katie—and lovers for two!—but I don't even know your last name, nor where ye live! " He framed her glowing face between his hands. "Darlin' girl, don't ye trust me?"

"There's nothing to tell, really," she lied, hating herself for being such a coward, hating the double life she'd been living. "Father's a staunch Episcopalian. He doesn't like Catholics— or the Irish, either, come to that." That much, at least was no lie! Her father never had a good word to say about anyone. "He would never let me see you again if I told him about

us, I know he wouldn't. I won't take that chance. It's as sim
ple as that. I'm sorry."

His mouth grew hard. Blue eyes flashed angrily. "Simple
hell! I've told ye, I'm not afraid to meet the old divil, even
if you are, so what's holding ye back, lass? Are you ashamed
of me—of us?"

"No!" she protested. "Surely you know better than that
darling? I could never be ashamed of you. You're a fine, decent man—and besides, I love you far too much!"

"Do you, Kate? Really?"

She touched his cheek. "Yes!"

"Then prove it, darlin'. Tell your da that Logan Teague
loves you—and that he wants ye for his bride."

She swallowed, nodding, "I will. I—I promise."

"Aye, but when?" he pressed.

"Very soon."

"A month? Six weeks?"

"Before New Year's Day, I swear," she promised rashly
"Cross my heart and hope to die!" In that moment, holding
him close, loving him as deeply as she did, she truly mean
to keep that promise.

He grinned, placated for the while. "All right, then. A week
from now it is. And trust me, Kate, ye'll not lose me or what
we have together by telling him, darlin' girl. Whatever happens, I'll always be here for you."

"I know you will, darling." She kissed his smooth brow
the corner of his mouth, gasping as he caught her roughly
against him. "Oh, Logan, I know!"

He responded to her feverish kisses with a powerful hunger
born of desire. His manhood grew hard against her flank, as
if possessed of its own fierce, independent life.

Desire, raw and hot, stirred within her for the second time
that afternoon as Logan's tongue stabbed between her parted
lips. He cupped the fullness of her breast so that the velvety
bud of her nipple grew pebbled against his hand. "I—
know."

The latter came out as a groan as Logan turned her beneath him. Poised on his elbows, he lavished kisses over the rich, creamy splendor of her body, leaving no inch of her untouched, from the downy nape of her neck to her toes.

Her loveliness made the breath catch in his throat. He couldn't help thinking about Kate's father, hating the man with a passion although he'd never met him, because he knew he'd convinced Kate she was plain.

Plain? he asked in silent wonder, burying his face in the fragrant mass of her hair, stroking her flawless skin. Was the spalpeen blind, that he did not see his daughter's loveliness?

"Aaah, Kate, beautiful Kate," he murmured, beginning the slow, lingering caresses he knew she loved. Skillfully, he played her body like a Celtic bard playing a golden harp, drawing the sweetest notes from her strings. He caressed her with his lips, his tongue, his hands, caresses that kindled her fire and brought her to a fever of desire all over again.

She was quivering like an aspen, arching her body like a kitten's to meet his sensual touch, when Logan lifted himself onto her. He moved his mouth against her own, tasting the inner velvet of her lips, savoring their sweetness, while his knee pressed between her thighs, parting her for his entry in the same moment that his tongue parted her lips for the joining of their mouths.

She gasped and clung fiercely to him. His lovemaking consumed her utterly. For that short, blessed while they were as one she could forget Stone and her father and the lie she was living. Forget everything but Logan. . . .

With a sob she surrendered, taking him into her body with a muted, incoherent cry of joy. Her arms slid around his neck. Her fingers burrowed deep into the thick, inky waves at his nape as she moved with him, whispering, " Oh, Logan, hold me. Please, please, hold me. Take me—aah, yes!"

Afterwards, both drowsy in the peaceful aftermath of their lovemaking, they lay together on Logan's narrow cot like spoons. His broad, lean chest was pressed against her back.

His arms were folded about her. With his face buried in her hair, they watched the patterns the fire cast over the workshop rafters, or the snow falling beyond the murky windowpanes, wrapping the city in its magical spell.

He had begun bringing her here, to the wood shop, when the end of summer had brought her beloved carousel to a standstill.

Fall had transformed the grassy hollows of their first trysts into damp, inhospitable places, she remembered. They'd continued their walks throughout the park in misty October, or wandered the Philadelphia Zoological Gardens amid drifts of rustling scarlet and gold-colored leaves.

Other Wednesday afternoons, weather permitting, Logan had taken her to the area known as Little Italy, in south Philly, where rows of identical trim houses boasted front steps of gleaming white marble.

Arm in arm, they'd strolled through the open-air market, their stomachs rumbling at the mouthwatering aromas of spicy sausages and cheeses, pasta and seafood, that rose from stalls tended by dark-eyed, handsome people speaking rolling Italian.

It was in Little Italy that Logan made Katherine shriek with laughter, then beg for mercy as he chased her with a live crab. And it was in Little Italy that she'd looked across at him over a stall heaped with zucchini and eggplants and realized she loved him.

Through Logan's eyes, Katherine had discovered another lively, exciting city outside the walls of her father's Society Hill house. And, having sampled that wonderful world, she feared she'd never be content with half a life again. Her father had been terribly, tragically wrong. It was not money that brought one happiness. It was sharing. It was belonging. It was love.

A cold snap had driven the sweethearts to seek a warmer place for their weekly rendezvous in early November. Since

Logan's landlady did not allow her lodgers to receive female callers he'd begun bringing her here to the carousel builders' shop, after the other carvers had gone home.

There was a cot in the back storeroom for use when a carver had to work far into the night. Before long Logan and Katherine had become lovers, and that cot became their world for a few precious hours each week.

Katherine loved the carvers' studio. It was so unlike any other place she'd ever been.

Sawdust and curly wood shavings were scattered all about the floor, as if shorn from a flock of creamy lambs, while the smell of seasoned pine lay heavy on the shadows—the same pleasing, fresh scent she associated with Logan.

In the half light of the wintry late afternoon, the carving studio was a strange place, she thought, sipping from the mug of cocoa she'd made on the brazier as she roamed around.

Half-finished carousel horses lay on benches, were strewn on the sawdusted floor, or hung from hooks on the wall—oh, they were everywhere! Some had already been sanded, painted, and gilded, and looked ready to gallop off to the band organ's wild music at the drop of a hat. Others were unfinished, nothing more than beautifully carved heads that had yet to be dowelled to their wooden bodies, their identities a fantasy still locked in the heart, head, and hands of their carver. Ah, yes, only a master carver's skill could breathe snorting, fiery life into inanimate wood.

Sometimes, like this Christmas Eve afternoon, Katherine enjoyed exploring the studio on her own while Logan slept in the afterglow of their passion.

Running her hands over the layers of seasoned basswood that had been glued together to form a hollow body, she wondered if the unfinished figure would become a delicate Arabian or a bucking bronco, or even a pretty "star-gazer" carousel steed, with its long neck straight, its nose lifted as it gazed heavenward.

More than anything, though, Katherine loved to watch

Logan work, roughing out the shape of a horse's head, then defining and refining that crude shape with his wide two-handled knife; or else working with mallet and chisel. She delighted in the intense, utterly absorbed expression on his handsome face as he worked, the ripple of sinew down wiry arms, the leashed strength in those powerful hands that could labor with such strength on solid wood, yet could also caress her in a hundred different, gentle ways, too. Ways that brought her passion to breathtaking life—

I'm like those blocks, Katherine had thought once, after she and Logan had made love. *Like the wooden horses, I come alive beneath his hands. A part of me lies dormant until his magical touch awakes it, sets it free! Only with him am I truly, completely alive.*

Fierce Irish wolfhounds or mischievous leprechauns would sometimes appear as a result of Logan's imagination, springing from his hands to grace the saddle backs or pommels of his creations. Spry little folk frolicked around them, clutching garlands of shamrocks entwined with snakes, carrying a harp, a pot of gold, or a long-stemmed pipe.

Once he'd even carved a leprechaun wearing a felt hat that he solemnly swore had been inspired by one of Work-horse Willy O'Weston's own creations. Another time he'd carved a graceful goddess wearing diaphanous robes that were positively indecent. The hussy had been posed seductively across the romance—most heavily carved—side of an elaborate carousel chariot. And, to Katherine's dismay, she'd noticed only hours before the chariot was ready to be shipped that the "goddess Diana" looked very much like herself, with carmine-tipped breasts that were barely concealed!

Naturally, her wicked Logan had staunchly denied any resemblance, and had sworn his carving was fashioned after a painting of the goddess Diana, but she knew better. The rogue!

Remembering how furious she'd been, she laughed softly

to herself. The sound awakened him. He stirred and rolled over.

"Restless, are ye, Kate? Did I not pleasure ye properly, darlin'?" he asked. God, but she was fair, his Kate, standing quietly in the shadows, her nude body as rosy as a marble statue in the brazier's ruddy light. Her head was bowed, golden-brown hair falling in a loose curtain about her face, her expression in shadow.

"Of course you pleased me," she insisted, too shy to meet his eyes. "You always do. I was just . . . ohh, thinking, I suppose."

"About us?" His repeated insistences that she tell her family about them weighed heavily on her mind, he knew. He suspected the promise she'd made him was the reason for her restlessness. But her father had to be told, sooner or later—and it was far better done sooner, to his thinking. 'Twas a dangerous game they were playing—especially for the woman—and he had no wish t'see her suffer on his account—perhaps finding herself disowned by her family. He loved her far too much for that.

She sighed and nodded. "About us, yes."

"Shall I come home with ye tonight, then, mavourneen?" he offered, rising from the cot to step into his trousers. Barechested, his torso as lean and finely sculpted as his carvings, he padded across the studio to her side with the grace of a panther, fastening his belt buckle as he came. Drawing her into his arms, he kissed the crown of her head, then dropped another kiss on the end of her nose. "We can give the old divil a Christmas present he'll never forget!" His blue eyes twinkled at the prospect as he held her at arm's length. "What do you say, my lass?"

"No, not yet. I—it's best I tell him myself," she insisted quickly. "That way he won't feel as if I—we're—trying to back him into a corner."

"All right. Whatever ye think best, darlin'," he agreed with a heavy sigh. "Now. Come back t'the cot. I've something for ye."

"Again?"

He grinned, laughter in his eyes. "Why, shame on ye, Kate, ye wanton woman! Even a stallion needs awhile t'recover its wind! Nay, sweet, 'tis a present I have for ye. Something I made meself."

"A present? Really?" Her face lit up. "For me?"

"Just for you," he repeated, enjoying her childlike delight. "Here ye go, mavourneen." Suddenly embarrassed, he thrust a parcel, carefully wrapped in brown paper and string, into her hands. "Well? Go ahead! Open it," he urged when she hesitated.

"I can't. It's not midnight yet," she insisted. "I know—I'll take it home with me; then at midnight I'll—"

"Ye wretched, dithering woman! 'T be sure, it's mad I'll be, by the time you're done with me! If ye won't open it, I'll do it for ye—!" he threatened, making a grab for the package.

"Oh, no, you don't, mister! I was only joking—get away!" she insisted, smartly whipping the parcel out of his reach.

In short order both string and paper lay among the wood shavings and sawdust at her feet, and her eyes were warm with pleasure over the exquisitely carved gift she held in her hands. "Oh, Logan—a unicorn!"

The prancing unicorn was a miniature carousel figure that stood about twelve inches tall. The wood had been sanded until it was as smooth as satin, then carefully stippled with paint to give the creamy coat a lifelike quality. The spiral horn was gilded, while about the unicorn's arched neck draped a garland of crimson roses, gold ribbons, mistletoe, and holly. A gold-painted dowel rose from the middle of its back, like the brass pole of a carousel pony, its top crowned with a pretty gilded finial. The deep oval base upon which the unicorn stood was lacquered a festive dark green

" 'Tis the old symbol of innocence and purity, the unicorn—just like the wee cameo brooch ye're always after wearin', aye? Your name—Katherine—means *pure,* too. Did ye know that?"

Overcome, Katherine nodded, blinking back tears. Bless him for his thoughtfulness, his caring ways. He had said nothing, but he had noticed how much she loved the brooch her mother had given her. Deeply touched, her hands began to shake so, she had to put down the unicorn.

"Ye hate it!" he muttered, scowling.

"No! It's just that . . . I've never been given anything so—so lovely, nor so special. No one has ever . . . cared . . . enough to make me a gift, you see? Thank you, my darling. Thank you with all my heart," she murmured. Leaning forward, she kissed him on the lips, then rested her tousled head against his chest. Eyes closed, she listened to the steady beating of his heart—and wished that the golden moment need never end. That she need never go back to her father's household and resume her life of lies and pretense. *She must tell her father, and soon. She had to. She couldn't marry Armitage, not when she loved Logan! Not when she believed she . . .*

"There's more." Logan cut into her thoughts. Looking smug now, he gently pushed her away. "It's a musical box, too, see? The key's tucked underneath. Go ahead. Try it."

She wound the key, then placed the music box upright on the work bench. By the brazier's flickering light, the magical little unicorn twirled in time to the tinkling melody of her favorite carol, its gilded hooves and spiral horn shining. As it turned, Logan sang the Latin words in a fine Irish tenor;

> *"Adeste fideles, laeti triumphantes:*
> *Venite, venite in Bethlehem.*
> *Natum videte, regem angelorum—"*

"O, Come let us adore Him, / O, come let us adore Him, O, come let us adore Him, Christ, the Lord—!" Katherine finished in English, joining her sweet soprano voice to his.

He grinned. "Why, Katie, darlin', ye know the words!" he exclaimed. "Ye're not quite a heathen after all, are ye—even if ye are a bloody Episcopalian."

"Oh, you!"

It was still snowing a little later when—arm in arm—he walked her back to the horse trolley stop where the areas of Southwark and Society Hill touched, but never, ever met.

He'd given up asking if he could take her home weeks ago, though he never failed to grumble about her refusal, either. The way he'd been raised, when a fellow was courting a decent girl, with marriage on his mind, he was supposed to escort her home. It was as simple as that. Truth was, that he was unable to do so made him feel less of a man.

Their boots made footprints in the soft blanket of virgin white as they tramped along. There were few people on the streets now, only those who had to be. Everyone had hurried home for their supper. They passed a hot-chestnut seller on one corner, a muffin man, and a teary-eyed, red-nosed drunkard weaving his crooked way home, on another. Soon the horse-drawn trolleys would cease running, and the streets would be deserted.

From every house they passed the tiny candles decorating the Christmas trees within those cozy parlors shone out into the gathering dusk, twinkling like fireflies. Brightly wrapped packages added their festive colors and shine to the scenes they glimpsed within. Off in the distance, they could hear carolers singing seasonal favorites as they went from door to door.

Katherine swallowed over the painful knot in her throat and looked away. It was as if she and Logan were peeping into a row of dollhouses. She couldn't help envying the happy lives those vignettes hinted at, the family love and the closeness she could only dream of. If only she could spend Christmas Day with Logan—just the two of them. Father always managed to escape Weston Hall each Christmas for Etta's plump arms and cheerful company, forcing Katherine to either accept the Armitages' grudging invitation or spend the holiday alone save for their housekeeper's cold company.

"Well, here we are again. A Merry Christmas to you, me darlin'," Logan said as he handed her up into the horse-drawn trolley. Drawing a spring of mistletoe from his overcoat pocket, he held it over her head and kissed her, releasing her cold hands only long enough to let her draw on her gloves. Foolish though it was, now that the time had come to say good-bye he could not rid himself of the fear that, if he let her leave him now, he would never see her again. He crossed himself. "Until next Wednesday, then?"

"Next Wednesday, yes," she echoed, clutching the music box to her bosom and forcing a smile.

He hesitated. "New Year's Eve, Kate. Your promise—remember?"

She bit her lip. "I remember."

"I love you so much, Kate. When ye tell him just remember that."

"I will. I love you, too, Logan. Oh, we're moving! Have a very happy holiday, my darling! I'll miss you. Until next week. Good-bye! 'Bye!"

As the horse trolley rumbled off down the street, he waved until the falling snowflakes had hidden her from his view before turning back the way he'd come.

Katherine shivered and drew her cloak more closely about her. It was silly, she knew, but she could not seem to shrug off a chill of foreboding as the trolley pulled away.

Her last image was of Logan with his threadbare collar turned up, his handsome face smiling, one hand lifted in farewell as the snow swirled around him.

Three

"Katherine! Is that you?" a deep voice called from the library a short while later, as Katherine let herself into Weston Hall, her father's palatial Society Hill mansion.

"Yes, Father," she called back, shaken that her father was home from Germantown earlier than usual. "You're home early."

"Indeed. Unlike yourself, I might add," William Weston said sternly, appearing in the doorway of his library.

A tall, heavily set man, he dwarfed his slender daughter by a good nine inches and close to a hundred pounds. "May I ask where you've been all afternoon, young lady?"

"I spent the afternoon at the hospital, as usual, rolling bandages and so on. The sick need special cheering at Christmas time," she lied, crossing her fingers within the folds of her cloak so that the falsehood would not count as a sin. Truth was, she had not volunteered her services at the hospital even once since she'd met Logan. "The first cold snap fills all the wards in a matter of hours," she observed, removing her damp bonnet with trembling hands. It went against her inherently honest character to lie, then embellish those lies with still more lies.

Shivering, she handed both hat and cloak to Mary Cooper the housekeeper, who'd appeared as silently as a wraith from the direction of her quarters. "Thank you, Mrs. Cooper," she said with an uncertain smile for the woman, noting that as usual it was not returned. She nervously tucked a stray cur ack into her neatly coiled chignon. Several hairpins had been ost in the sawdust of Logan's workshop.

"Sick—is that what you call them? Ha! If you ask me, hey're nothing but idle, good-for-nothing idlers!" her father nsisted forcefully. "A swift kick in the backside would do hem a world of good—show them that they have to work or a living, as I had to do, instead of laying around, belly-ching, expecting someone else to put food in their bellies nd clothes on their backs. I don't want you going to that lace again, Katherine, do you hear me?"

"But, Father—"

"Don't argue with me, girl. Decent women have no place n hospitals, where there are half-clothed men and *nurses*. Immph. We all know what kind of women nurses are, don't ve, girl?"

"So you say, Father. How lovely it is to have you home arly! Did you cancel your meetings because of Christmas?" he inquired, trying to change the subject as she led the way nto an expensively furnished yet unfriendly parlor, where a right fire was burning. Going to the marble mantelpiece, he held her hands out to warm them. She could never seem o get warm here.

Weston scowled. "My . . . er . . . my business associate vas unable to keep our appointment at the last minute," her ather explained sourly, sounding annoyed. Aware that the ousekeeper was hovering in the doorway, he snapped, "Yes, Mrs. Cooper? What is it?"

"Dinner is served, Mr. Weston, Miss Katherine," the house-eeper announced, yet Katherine's attention was riveted on he brown paper parcel the woman was carrying, rather than er words.

She swallowed. Cooper had the music box Logan had iven her! She'd stood it on the doorstep while she'd let herself nside and had quite forgotten it was there! "Oh! You have y music box! Thank you for bringing it inside, Mrs. Cooper. ne of the—one of the patients at the hospital made it for me. He's a . . . he's a very talented old fellow," she quickly explained, the words tripping over each other in her nervousness. Guilty color filled her cheeks. *Why, oh why, was she such a coward? She loved Logan; truly she did! That being so, why couldn't she find the courage to tell her father she would not marry Stone Armitage? That she wanted nothing so dearly as to break her engagement to him and marry Logan, instead?*

She drew a deep breath. "Father, I have something important to tell you."

"Later, Katherine. Go on in to dinner."

"Father, it can't wait. It's—it's very important. You see, I have—"

"Katherine, later, I said! I'd like a word with Mrs. Cooper before I join you." Her father dismissed her, already turning aside.

Hating herself, Katherine bit back yet another protest. Giving the package in Mrs. Cooper's hands a longing look, she went on in to dinner alone, her eyes lowered, her head meekly bowed, like a chastened child who has been sent to her room. Yet in her secret heart seethed resentment, rebellion. Soon that resentment would boil over, she knew it. She'd been feeling the same way that Sunday back in August, when she'd quarreled with Stone. It was just a matter of time now.

"You said my daughter is gone every Wednesday afternoon, Mrs. Cooper?" William Weston repeated with a frown when he and the housekeeper were alone. The contents of the parcel had puzzled him. *A cheap wooden geejaw!* Yet, he hadn't amassed his fortune by being anyone's fool. He'd seen the look Katherine had shot the package before she'd left the room. She'd valued the musical box—or the person who'd given it to her—very highly.

Swearing under his breath, he went to warm his coattail before the fire, his scowl deepening as all the pieces dropped

eatly into place. Was it an old and ailing hospital patient
whom Katherine visited so devotedly every Wednesday after-
oon—or a young and secret admirer?

"That's right, sir. Every blessed one."

Weston's knuckles were white where he gripped the mantel.
And how long has this been going on, pray?"

"Why, ever since the summer, Mr. Weston, sir. Since . . .
h, early August, I suppose."

"That long?" Teeth clenched, he rounded on the woman.
And has Miss Weston never mentioned where she spends
er Wednesday afternoons?"

"No, Mr. Weston. Never." She sniffed. "And if you'll ex-
use me for saying so, sir, it weren't my place to ask."

"Oh, quite," he said mockingly, knowing the wretched
woman for a nosy, interfering old busybody who read her
master's mail and listened at keyholes. "And does Miss Kath-
rine seem in any way . . . different . . . when she returns
rom these outings?"

"Oh, indeed, sir! She looks . . . well, I'd have to say the
oung lady appears quite *flushed,* Mr. Weston. Breathless, too.
And she's much . . . noisier . . . than usual."

His brows rose. *"Noisier?* What do you mean?" Was the
ld harridan implying Katherine had been drinking in his ab-
ence?

"Oh, you know, sir, like humming and—and singing to
erself?"

"I see. Well, thank you, Mrs. Cooper. That will be all. Oh,
nd before you go, there's one thing more. After you've dis-
osed of this trash in the kitchen stove," he said, handing her
he music box, "I'd like you to ask Jackaman to join me in
he library after dinner. I'll take my brandy in there, too. Oh,
nd Mrs. Cooper—?"

"Mr. Weston, sir?"

"We are not to be disturbed. Not on any account."

Mary Cooper's thin lips twitched with malice. She wasn't
eceived by her master's outward calm. No, sir! The young

miss was in for it now, unless she was mistaken! Hospital volunteering, indeed. She knew better! Well, it served little snooty Goody-Two-Shoes right! For all her high falluting airs and graces, Katherine Weston was no more than a common factory worker's daughter underneath her Paris silks and satins—no, no better than Mary Eileen Cooper herself!

Bobbing a curtsy, Mrs. Cooper crossed the room to retrieve the offending parcel. Carrying it by the unicorn's horn, as if it was contaminated, she murmured, "Very good, Mr. Weston, sir," and made her exit.

Four

"So . . . you've had two weeks. What have you found out?" Weston demanded on the first Wednesday evening of 1883. He leaned back in his chair with an expectant expression, his fingers steepled upon his belly.

"It's just what you reckoned, boss," Jackaman confirmed with ill-disguised relish. "She—Miss Weston, that is—has been meeting an Irish bloke at a builders in Southwark. His name is Logan Teague. He's a woodworker with Gustav Dentzel's amusement machine company."

"Denztel, the carousel maker?" Weston thundered incredulously, his face growing beet red with anger and disbelief.

"That's him. Our Mr. Logan Teague carves carousel horses, he do!" Jackaman sniggered, clearly amused by the idea. "I poked about a bit, asked a few questions here and there. He's what they call a 'head' man. The workshop is where he and his bit o' skirt—" He coughed. "Er, I meant to say, where 'im and Miss Weston have been—er—meeting, sir. *After* hours, that is, o'course."

Weston didn't miss the knowing smirk on Jack's face, nor did he need any explanation for the malicious, scornful gleam in the coachman's eyes. Jackaman knew his master's daughter had disgraced herself. Ah, yes, the little slut had sullied the Weston name—*his* good name—along with her own virtue and reputation, and for what? He snorted and shook his head in disgust. For an Irish Mick, that was what! She'd taken up with a nobody, a laborer with the dirt of the potato farms still lodged beneath his broken fingernails. A whiskey-drinking, Catholic lout from the bogs of Ireland! By God, he wouldn't be surprised to find that half of Philadelphia knew what Katherine and her lover had been up to, either—and were laughing at him!

You stupid little fool! How could you do this to me after everything I've done to put that life and those kind of people far behind me—behind us. All your life you've lived in a fine house in the best part of town. Your clothes and hats are designed in Paris. Your shoes and boots are of the best Italian leather. By God, even the food you put in your mouth is the very best that money can buy! Aye, and served to you on the finest china and silver platters, to boot!

Why, Katherine? Why would you risk it all for this . . . this carver—? It's not you he wants, girl, don't you see? He's been using you—he's just a bloody fortune hunter, after your father's money! Well, I won't let you ruin it all for me, not now, not when I'm so damned close. In a few weeks time, after you're married to Stone Armitage, people will look at Willy Weston in a new light, you'll see! They'll look up to me, then, they will! I'll be somebody, then, God dammit! I will—!

Pain squeezed Weston's skull, as if a band of hot iron had been wrapped around his head and was now tightening painfully as it cooled. Feeling as if his head would explode, William Weston stuck two fingers down his high wing collar to loosen his cravat and gestured irritably for Jackaman to hand him a tumbler of scotch and soda water.

He drank deeply. And, little by little, the squeezing pain lessened. "You know what to do, right, Jackaman?" he murmured in a hoarse, strained voice when he could speak again, reaching into the inside pocket of his coat and withdrawing a sheaf of bills. He tossed them to the coachman. "Did you have an . . . assistant . . . in mind? Someone you trust completely?"

"I'd hoped Mr. Armitage's coachman, Ernest Hennessy, might be up to it, sir . . . ?"

Weston nodded. "Very well. Hennessy it is. But not a word of this must reach Mr. Armitage, is that understood? If it does, both of you will be looking for new jobs. My daughter's wedding will proceed next month exactly as planned. I don't give a damn what you have to do to get rid of Teague, Jackaman—but do it, and be discreet. Keep my name—and Miss Weston's—out of it!"

Jackaman grinned. "Leave it t'me. Logan Teague's history, he is!"

Five

"Evening, gov'na. Would you be Teague? Logan Teague, Esquire?" Sandy beetle brows cocked in inquiry above a pair of deep-set, watery blue eyes.

"I am, aye. What can I do for you, lads?" Logan set aside his tools. Dusting the sawdust from his hands, he came to meet the fellows who'd let themselves in through the unlocked workshop door.

His alarm at the pair's entrance so long after working hours was eased by their respectable appearance. Their smiles were cordial. They'd both tipped their hats. A harmless pair, Logan decided, though the ruddy flush to their cheeks suggested they'd had more t' drink than they should have. That wasn't unusual, though; not with it being so cold outside. More than once tonight he'd wished he had a tot o' the hard stuff for himself. He was no drinker, but it would have kept his fingers from growing numb as he carved.

Well into the fall of the previous year, Mr. Dentzel had taken on a late order for a large carousel: four rows of horses, a half-dozen menagerie animals such as tigers, zebras, and lions, and a couple of chariots. The machine was scheduled to be shipped west in early spring. Consequently Logan—one of the few single carvers—had volunteered to work late all winter, completing the figures. That way, the other, married men could be home with their families in the evenings.

Why not work all night? he'd decided ruefully. The days between the blessed Wednesdays when he could be with his

Katie seemed endless. Fact was, he welcomed the extra work, not to mention the extra money. Carving helped to fill the empty hours, while exhaustion guaranteed he would tumble into his cot too tired even to dream about his darling girl when his head touched the pillow. As for the money—Well, it would come in handy when he and Kate were wed. . . .

"A mutual friend said we'd find you 'ere," the taller of the two men began.

Logan's black brows rose. "He did, did he now? And what would this friend's name be?"

"It ain't a 'he,' Teague," the man supplied, drawing a rolled cigarette from a small tobacco can tucked inside his coat pocket. As Logan's gut tightened with the first stirring of foreboding, the stocky man in the bowler tapped the smoke down, then lit the end with a match struck on the sole of his boot. He took a single deep drag; then he blew the smoke out through his nostrils. "The lady's name is Katherine. Miss Katherine *Weston*. Ring any bells, does it, Mr. Teague?" He chuckled nastily and elbowed his sidekick in the ribs. "Miss Weston and her dad asked us t' deliver a message for 'em, right, Hennessy?"

"Right, Joe."

"What message?" Logan echoed, his throat suddenly gone dry with fear for Katie. *Blessed Joseph and Mary, had his darlin' girl been hurt?* What the devil had happened that she couldn't come herself, but had sent this unlikely pair to him? Unless—could they be her older brothers . . . ? "Tell me! What did she say?" he demanded.

Too late he sensed the second man—Hennessy?—moving, but thought nothing of it until a hefty two-by-four plank came out of nowhere and smashed into his nose, shattering cartilage, rupturing tissue. The blow exploded a sickening flare of agony in Logan's skull.

"Je—sus Christ!" he groaned as ribbons of scarlet sprayed cross his field of vision, stinging his eyes. "What the devil did ye—*aaagh!"*

This time the length of timber veered up from the ground to meet him, clipping him solidly under the chin with a meaty thwack of wood on bone that sounded sharp as a gunshot.

Logan groaned once, the air escaping his lips in a soft, whooshing sigh. He lay on his back in the sawdust, felled like a tree. There was blood all over his face; more stained the front of his workshirt and apron.

Jackaman knelt over him. Lifting Logan's head by a fistful of black hair, he thrust his pug face full into his and rasped, "Miss Katherine don't want you sniffin' after her skirts anymore. Got it, Micko? Fact is, she reckons it's high time you left Philly altogether—found yerself a nice gel someplace farther west. *Much* farther west! California, say?"

"Not my Katie, no. . . ." Logan denied, shaking his head despite the thundering cannons in his brain. "She—she'd never say such a thing, not my wee Kate."

"She already has said it, you stupid chump! An' her dear old dad sent the money for your one-way ticket out of town—nice of the tight-fisted old bugger, weren't it? Aye, and there's lots more where this came from, too, old son. *Five hundred dollars more!* All you have t' do is promise to stay away from Weston's daughter. Ye see, her fiancé wouldn't like it if he heard she's been . . . seein' . . . you on the sly—oh, dear me, no! Fact is, the boss reckons it'd be better all around if you didn't even exist—if ye get my meanin', *boyo?*"

"Go to hell, damn ye!" Logan exploded. Summoning his waning strength, he swung a punch at the sheaf of banknotes.

The blow, though clumsy, dashed Jackaman's hand aside and sent the bills fluttering to the sawdust like a handful of autumn leaves. "Go to hell—aye, an' tell your bloody boss t' keep his damned money and join ye there!" he growled, struggling to sit up, then to stand.

By some herculean effort he finally managed to haul himself upright, vaguely amazed at the pain the task demanded of him. "My Kate—my Kate's a grown woman. She can de-

de on a husband for herself. The devil take her da—and
ou!"

"Tsk, tsk! Wrong answer, old son! But then, Work-horse
'illy reckoned you might get difficult—didn't he, Hen-
essy?"

"Work-horse Willy—?" Logan echoed. But his shock didn't
st long, for it was then that the Hat King's thugs began
orking him over in earnest.

They hammered at his head, his chest, his kidneys, until
e was reeling like a punch-drunk prizefighter who could no
nger toe the scratch. And then, when they'd tired of using
eir fists, they used their hobnailed boots on him instead.

Although Weston's goons had the element of surprise and
umbers on their side, Logan fought back with everything he
ad. He even managed to land a damned good punch or two
the start, while he still had the chance.

But despite his efforts, when the pair was done Logan hud-
ed unconscious on the bloodstained sawdust of the work-
op floor. He was so bruised, so bloody and coated with
wdust, he looked as if he'd been tarred and feathered. Grin-
ng, Hennessy grasped him by his collar and hauled him
pright for another punch.

"Enough, Ernie, you bloody ape! Lay orf, do! Hit him
gain, you'll kill him, for Christ's sake! Go an' bring the cart
ound," Jackaman hissed. "And hurry it up before somebody
omes!"

Hennessy hesitated. "What about the money?"

"You'll get your share," Jackaman growled, tossing down
e smoldering butt of his smoke. Squatting, he picked up
e fallen bills among the curly wood shavings. "A fifty-fifty
lit, like wot I said."

"Fair enough, then, Jack."

Within the half hour the pair were hauling Logan's body
ut of a wooden cart and dragging it into the open boxcar
f a freight train.

"What if he makes it back?" Hennessy wondered aloud "He could mean trouble."

Jackaman snorted. "Him? He'll be a goner come morning or my name's not Joe Jackaman. Christ, let's go! It's bloody freezing!"

The pair left the station without so much as a backward glance, headed for the bright lights and loud piano music o the nearest billiards hall, where they intended getting wel and truly drunk.

Moments later the boxcar gave a great shudder. Its wheels screamed in protest as it was shunted out of the freight yard siding and onto the Philadelphia main line, where it was cou pled to several other cars.

Within the hour, the freight train had left the City of Broth erly Love far behind and was riding the rails west. The lo comotive's lonesome whistle was the last sound Logan heard before a crimson tunnel swallowed him up.

Six

"My, oh, my! You've surely met with an accident, have thee not, my friend?"

Groaning, Logan forced a swollen eye to open. Through the slit he could see a white-haired old man standing over him, framed by the gray light of dawn. *Sweet Jesus!* Surely he was dead? The man standing over him must be blessed St. Peter himself. "Help me . . ." he murmured thickly. "Must. Tell. Kate."

"Brother George!" The man beckoned to someone nearby. Snow had drifted into the freight container overnight, building up in the boxcar's corners as the locomotive rode the rails from Philadelphia to Pittsburgh on the first leg of its long journey west. More snowflakes were caught in the folds of the man's torn clothes, the angles of his broken body, or had collected around him. It was doubtful he'd survived the bitterly cold night, as well as his injuries. "Over here! This man's been beaten. Help me with him, would thee?"

Seven

"No! I don't believe you. You're lying," Katherine whispered, shaking her head in denial.

She and her father had been breakfasting together in the dining room of Weston Hall, just like every other morning, when her father suddenly flung aside his newspaper, unhooked his reading spectacles, and bluntly announced that he knew all about her four-month affair with Logan.

Stunned, the silverware had slipped from Katherine's fingers, clattering noisily to her bone china plate. The bloom had drained from her face. Yet, after the first numbing shock had passed relief had quickly followed.

It's over, at last! she thought, though she was still trembling. *After all these weeks—months!—of lies and deceptions we don't have to be afraid that Father will find out about us. He knows! I can tell him I won't marry Stone. That it's Logan I love; Logan I intend to marry!*

Her relief was short-lived, however, for in almost the same breath her father had gone on to say that Logan had left Philadelphia—and her—forever.

She gave a brittle, disbelieving laugh. "Try another tactic, Father. I don't believe you!"

"No? Then believe what you will, you wretched, foolish girl!" He'd added, "And don't bother trying to see your dirty little potato farmer again, my girl, if that's what that stubborn expression of yours means. He won't be coming back. Not next week, not next month—not ever!"

Not be back? She shook her head slowly from side to side. e must be lying. Logan couldn't be gone. "How do you ow that? What have you done, that you can be so sure?"

"The details need not concern you," he muttered, shifting s gaze. "I did what any father would do."

"They 'need not concern me'? I *love* Logan, Father! Of urse his whereabouts are my concern."

He looked up then, and she caught the flicker in his eyes; s smug, secretive expression. A knot of apprehension tight-ed in her belly. "What is it you're not telling me, Father? hat is it you know?"

"Very well. If you insist. Your noble Mr. Teague accepted payment of five hundred dollars. In return, he promised to ave you—and this city—and never come back."

She felt sickened, stunned, as if the bottom had dropped t of her world, leaving her with no support. Indeed, if some-e had punched her in the belly the blow could have done greater damage than her father's words. Icy with appre-nsion, sick with hurt, she yet insisted, "You're lying. You ust be because . . . because I know Logan would never do at." Overcome, she swallowed. "Scoff if you will, but . . . he loves me." Her lower lip quivered. "I *know* he es! He'd never let you buy him off, not in a hundred years! nd do you know why not? Because he's a fine, decent an—a man of honor and principles—and because I mean ore to him than any amount of money ever could. Far more an I've ever meant to you, Father," she added pointedly.

Weston snorted and flung aside his napkin. "Stop it, Kath-ine. Pull yourself together and don't be a fool. The clod's ne. The sooner you accept that he used you, the better it ill be." He shook his head, a sneer curling his thin lips. nd as for you, you deceitful, immoral little tramp—! You're rdly the lady I thought I'd raised! But then, 'like mother, ke daughter,' isn't that what they say, Katherine?" he asked intedly.

His words raised a hectic flush in Katherine's cheeks.

"Well, your nasty little affair is in the past now, thanks me. Water under the bridge. I'm prepared to overlook yo disgraceful behavior if you'll do the right thing now."

"By that I presume you mean marry Stone Armitage o Valentine's Day, as planned." She set her jaw. "No, Father, won't. Not now, not next month—not ever! You see, I can believe Logan would ever leave me—at least, not willingly.

"Then you'd be wrong."

"Would I, Father? I think not. You've done something him—something terrible—haven't you? Dear God, I can se it in your face! Well, I intend to find out what that somethin is!"

Flinging about, she picked up her skirts and fled the parlo

"Katherine!" Her father jumped to his own feet so force fully, the dining chair tipped over behind him. "Katherine Don't be a fool! By God, you'd best come back here imme diately, if you know what's good for you! Have you take leave of your senses, girl—? You'll destroy everything I'v worked for with your foolishness! He's not worth it! *Kathe ine—!*"

Ignoring her father's shouts, Katherine rushed headlor down the hallway, then out into the street.

"Katherine! Come back here at once! Katherine—!"

She could hear him calling for her to come back as sh ran down the icy pavements, but it was as if he was alread a great distance away; a part of her past she was eager forget.

Logan's name spilled from her lips like a litany as she ra blindly down street after empty street: *Logan! Logan, I' coming to you, darling! It's all over now. I've left Weston Ha forever! We can be together now.*

She wouldn't stop running until she'd reached the worl shop and had spoken to Logan herself. She'd tell him abou her father's efforts to separate them, his plans to force h into marrying Stone Armitage, and they'd laugh about the together. Very soon she and Logan would leave Philadelphi

ney'd start a new life together, somewhere else. Somewhere
ive and noisy, somewhere colorful and exciting! Somewhere
al people lived and loved and fought and made up and
ised their families—like Brooklyn, perhaps? And they'd be
ippy, too—oh, so very happy!

"So there!" she muttered, not caring that she was drawing
irious eyes, running down the busy street wearing neither a
iat nor a hat on such a bitterly cold January morning.

At the next corner she sprang aboard a crowded horse trol-
y, and pushed her way toward a space. So what if her hair
as disheveled, her eyes wild, her face so deathly pale she
oked a little mad? Devil take the damned lot of them! It
dn't matter what any of them thought, not anymore. She
d Logan were free, thanks to Father's dirty little spies. And
eedom was truly exhilarating!

Besides, it really *was* all for the best that it had happened
w, rather than later, she reminded herself, pressing the flat
 her palms to her belly to steady herself when the trolley
rched to a standstill. Time had been running out anyway.
ie would have had to tell her Father within a day or two.

She smiled dreamily. Oh, yes! Very soon she and Logan
ould be laughing at this crazy mix-up together. *Wouldn't
ey?*

Katherine pulled up short on the threshold of the carousel
iilder's workshop, wide-eyed at the activity all about her.

In the cold, clear light of the wintry morning the wood
iop she'd grown to love seemed an alien place.

There were men in bill caps and bibbed white aprons eve-
where. One worked at a band saw. Others wielded chisels
 planes, standing ankle-deep in wood shavings and sawdust.
n every side carvers were bent over work benches on which
y unfinished carousel horses, menagerie beasts, or ornately
rved chariots. In the pale winter light that streamed through
e murky windows, sawdust swirled like dust motes.

Too overwrought to knock, Katherine tottered a step o
two through the open door. She looked wildly about her. O
Lord! There was so much noise! Furthermore, the stron
smells of linseed oil, paint, turpentine, and seasoned woo
were almost overwhelming at this hour of the morning. Sh
swayed, feeling suddenly dizzy and sick. Where was he
There was no sign of Logan among the workers. Where coul
he be?

Maybe Father was right, after all? whispered a treache
ous, insinuating little voice inside her head. *Maybe Loga
took the money and ran, exactly as he claimed. . . .*

"No! Don't say that!"

"Fraulein? Miss? Can I help you?" asked a doubtful voic
Belatedly, she realized she must have spoken the word
out loud, for an old man was peering down at her through
pair of gold-framed spectacles. He had a thick white mus
tache and white hair and, unlike the other men, wore a broad
brimmed, brown felt hat that had seen better days—one o
her father's hats, she noticed absently. "Um, yes, if you'd b
so kind. I . . ." Her voice trailed away. What was it she
intended to say?

She stared blankly at the old man, who frowned. It wa
not every day that such a pretty girl appeared in his work
shop, looking for all the world like a damsel in distress. H
pursed his lips and tugged on his mustache. It was freezin
this morning, yet she wore no coat or cloak over her gree
velvet gown. Furthermore, flimsy house slippers encased he
feet, rather than stout walking boots. "Please, sit here, m
dear. You are unwell, *ja?*" Taking her elbow, he attempted t
steer her toward a low stool beside a brazier.

"No! No, I'm not ill. I'm just—I'm just . . ." *What? Whe
had he asked her? Oh, Logan. Where are you? I'm so frigh
ened!* She laughed shakily and shrugged. "Oh, dear! I ran s
far and so fast, I—I've become a little confused, I'm afraid.

The pretty little thing seemed so overwrought, he nodde
gently to reassure her. "Of course. But come, sit here on th

stool for a moment, *fraulein*. You'll be yourself again once you catch your breath, I think, *ja?*"

"I'm afraid I really don't have time for that. I'm looking for someone, you see. Perhaps you could point him out for me? He's a carver here. His name is Logan Teague."

The benevolent expression on the old man's face vanished like chalk wiped from a slate. "Teague, you say? Pah! That worthless good-for-nothing! He's long gone, young lady—*ja*, and good riddance to him, too!"

"Gone?" she echoed faintly. A strange roaring sound was gathering volume in her head, as if a hive of bees had settled inside her skull. "Gone where? Where has Logan gone?" She knew she sounded shrill but couldn't seem to help herself.

"West—or so his pals claimed when they stopped by for his tools. He just left one night last week—Thursday night, I think it was—*ja*, and with the petty cash in his pockets, too, and not so much as a by-your-leave for Herr Dentzel or anyone else! As if that vas not enough, he left a smoke burning back there." He jerked his head toward the rear of the storeroom, where a cot—their cot!—was propped against a wall, its ticking mattress charred and black on one side. Above it hung a red sign with glaring foot-high red letters that warned NO SMOKING. "If der police constable patroling his beat hadn't smelled smoke, all of our work would be ashes now, *ja?*" He shook his hoary head. "I vould not like to be in Logan Teague's shoes if Gustav Dentzel ever catches up with him!"

"He can't be gone—you're lying! I—I don't know why, but you *must* be!" Katherine cried. Her voice sounded panicky. She shook her head from side to side, her fingers tightening convulsively around the old man's lower arm. "Oh, please, sir, please tell me you're lying. . . ."

"I only wish it were so, *fraulein*," the old man said sadly. "But Teague's landlady hasn't seen him for over a week, either—and his rent's long past due. What else are we to think?" The hard expression on the old man's face faded to

one of sympathy and understanding when he saw the anguish
that filled her eyes. He patted her shoulder. "Aaah, so that's
the way of it, eh, *fraulein?* The young rogue's left you, too,
has he, my poor child?" He sighed and shook his head. "He
seemed such a fine young fellow, too—and what a carver he
was!—but—" He shrugged. "Well, it appears he had every
one fooled, *ja?*"

"I have to go," she whispered without answering him.

Turning away, she left the workshop and went out into the
blustery cold streets of Philadelphia once again. The gutters
were rutted with dirty slush, yet she stumbled in and out of
them as if she were a puppet made of wood. A puppet whose
strings had been severed.

". . . left you, too! . . . left you, too . . ."

The old man's words echoed over and over in her mind as
she stumbled down street after street, weaving like a sleep-
walker through tradesmen and shoppers, delivery carts, drays
wagons, and horse trolleys.

Somehow she managed to find her way to Logan's boardinghouse in Southwark, though she had never been there before. But she was forced to leave in a hurry by his irate
landlady, Mrs. Flannigan, when she told her who she was
trying to find. Her hair still in curling rags from the night
before, the woman ran down the sidewalk after her, brandishing her mop at Katherine's retreating back and screeching
". . . and if ye ever find the spalpeen, ye bold-faced hussy
tell him Mother Flannigan will be keepin' his things for the
rent he's after owin' me, sure!"

Snow was falling from an almost white sky when Katherine found herself wandering Fairmount Park. Puzzled, she
looked about her but could not have said by what route she
had come there, nor what hour it was.

The pretty carousel where she and Logan had first met
was gone now, put into storage for the winter. The circle
where it had once stood was bare but for a light mantling of
snow on the hard ground. There was no band organ playing

ively German music or rollicking Polish polkas; no misty water-colors with scenes of children at play. No grinning ester faces, reflected over and over again in the shining mirrors that adorned the canopy crown.

Gone, too, were the laughing children—the boys in their navy sailor suits, the girls in their ruffled pinafores and ribbons—who had come here in spring and summer to ride the painted ponies and the flying horses. The few children who were out and about were bundled up in scarves and mittens as they rode their toboggans down the hills, waged furious snowball fights, or skated on the frozen pond.

Katherine saw none of them.

Skeletal trees, bushes, and rolling parklands lay before her now, stark and leafless. The grass was blanketed in white, too—yet nothing before her was as cold, as empty, or as bleak as her broken heart.

"I was never meant to catch that brass ring, was I, Lord?" she whispered thickly, her voice cracking, her breath congealing like smoke on the frosty air. "Oh, God, Logan, why? I loved you so! *Why?*"

Dropping down onto her knees, she pressed her fists to her belly and sobbed.

Eight

In the wake of the man's words, Katherine swallowed and fingered the cameo at her throat. *So much hope, and it had all been for nothing.*

Rising from her seat behind the cherrywood desk, she turned and went to the window. "You're quite certain it was the same man, Mr. Baker?"

"Even if I wasn't, the landlady was, ma'am." The man she'd hired—a clerk who worked for her lawyers but did investigations in his free time—flipped through the pages of a small notebook and licked his pencil point. "Ah ha. Let's see now—ah, yes, here it is. Maureen Flannigan, her name was, ma'am. Mother Flannigan, her boarders call her. She's a widow lady who runs a boardinghouse down on Linden Street. She said she'd have known Teague anywhere. Claims you could have knocked her down with a feather when she opened the door and saw him standing there, bold as brass, after him being gone all those weeks without a word."

"Did he say anything at all? Give her any explanations for having left Philadelphia so suddenly?" she asked, her throat aching, her eyes smarting with unshed tears.

He shrugged. "No, ma'am, I'm afraid not. He paid her the rent that had been owing when he left, plus a little something extra for her trouble, then collected his things and went. He left no forwarding address," he added, tucking his notebook back into his pocket.

"And the carousel company told the same story?"

"More or less, yes. They did say he seemed fit t' kill when he heard about the fire at the workshop, though. One of the carvers—a Mr. Muller—said he wouldn't like to be those two fellers when Teague catches us with them, no, ma'am! If you'll pardon me mentioning it, Muller said his language turned the air blue, it did—whereas Teague was a quiet enough fellow before, one not much given to profanity."

"I see. And there have been no answers to the newspaper advertisements you placed?"

He shook his head. "I contacted the dailies in all the major towns in Ohio, West Virginia, Maryland, and New York. Not a single response, I'm afraid."

"Then that's that, I suppose. There's nothing more to be done." She released the breath she'd been holding as a heavy sigh. Returning to her desk, she sat, dipped her pen nib in the inkwell, then quickly signed and blotted the check before her. "Thank you, Mr. Baker. I know you've done your best with this. I trust you will find this sum sufficient?"

Baker glanced at the check. "Yes, indeed. Very generous. Thank you, ma'am." He tipped his hat, then slipped the banker's draft into the inner pocket of his coat. "I only wish I could have found your missing cousin for you," he observed with honest regret.

So do I, Mr. Baker. You have no idea how dearly! Katherine added silently as the investigator left the study.

She told herself that the search for Teague had been necessary, however expensive and fruitless, for she'd needed to know that he was alive and unharmed for her own peace of mine. Now, surely, she'd be able to accept that he was gone, and get on with her life, after a fashion? Be able to enter a room, cross a street, scan the faces of a theater audience, dine in a restaurant, live without forever hoping—wishing— praying—she'd find his face among the crowd. Wouldn't she . . . ?

Nine

Christmas Eve again. How quickly the months, then the years flew by! Just one more week and yet another year would be ending, and a brand-new one—1887—would be beginning.

Five new years had come and gone since Logan had gone away. What would this New Year bring, Katherine wondered, gazing into the hearth where a huge log burned, its heat reddening her cheeks. And what resolutions would she make this time around? Would she find peace of mind and acceptance, finally? Or would she endure yet another twelve months of the same vague, unanswered longings; the same sense of emptiness, the same depth of loss that had marred the last sixty months? Perhaps she—

What was that?

She cocked her head to one side and frowned. Firelight played over her burnished chignon; reflected sparkling light off garnet-and-pearl teardrop earrings as she pursed her lips. She had heard music in the park, but it wasn't one of the groups of carolers that were going from door to door or singing for the holiday shoppers on street corners. It was the faint strains of a . . . a band organ, of all things!

Setting down a dainty china teacup and saucer, Katherine rose from her armchair, swept back her bustled skirts, and hurried to the window, wondering if her ears could have deceived her.

Drawing aside heavy draperies of burgundy velvet, she

scratched a hole in the thin layer of frost that coated the windowpanes and peered out.

Fairmount Park stretched away from the wrought-iron palings that enclosed her gardens, neatly dividing the elegant red-brick walls and white marble steps of the Georgian colonial house that overlooked the park from the park proper. Warmth filled her. It was a view she had never tired of, winter or summer, spring or fall, in the years since she'd purchased Cherry Tree House for herself, following her father's stroke.

Her nose pressed to the icy panes like a child gazing into a sweetshop, she peered through the glass at the gathering dusk. At first she could see only the twinkling lights of other houses fronting Fairmount Park, and the universities across the river. And then, finding what she'd sought so eagerly, she laughed out loud in delight. She was right! It was really there!

For all that it was Christmas Eve and the middle of winter, someone had assembled the old carousel in the park. She could see its bright lights twinkling through the wintry dusk and—*oh, yes!* there it was again!—she could hear the faint strains of the Wurlitzer playing a stirring waltz. The sound made her feel young and foolish again—and oh, it had been so very long since she'd felt either young or foolish.

Deciding quickly, she pulled the tasseled bell rope to summon her maid. Maria came almost immediately.

"My hat and coat, if you please, Maria. Oh, and my boots, too! I'm going out," she added almost defiantly.

"You are going out, *Signora* Armitage? This late?" The maid's jet-black eyes grew round. She looked at the crackling fire in the fireplace, then at the shimmering Christmas tree in the corner by the huge bay windows.

The huge tree rose almost to the ceiling. Dark green and smelling gloriously of pine, it was decorated with tinsel garlands, colored glass birds, satin-covered balls, and other glittering ornaments, as well as tiny lighted candles in miniature brass holders. Around its base, heaped upon the elaborate velvet tree skirt she had embroidered herself with cherubs, trumpets, and Christmas garlands, were several mysteriously shaped, gilt-wrapped parcels that begged to be poked and prodded and giggled over.

Maria's expression clearly said that anyone who would willingly leave such a cozy place on Christmas Eve must surely be mad, but she only observed, "But . . . it is snowing, *signora!*"

"I promise you I shan't melt in a little snow, Maria," Katherine assured the girl solemnly. "Now, hurry, do! And when I come back you may go home," she added.

Maria blinked. "Home, *signora?*"

Katherine smiled. "Yes, Maria—home! I'm sure you'd like to go to midnight Mass with your family, wouldn't you? Billy can escort you home. Oh, and Maria—?"

"Signora?" Maria whispered, convinced now that her mistress had taken leave of her senses.

"You may spend Christmas with your family, too. I shan't be needing you again until the day after Boxing Day."

"But, *signora, signor* Weston, they will be bringing him here for the holiday tomorrow. Who will help you to lift him? Please let me come, *signora.* Mama, she needs the money, yes?"

"This won't affect your wages, I promise," she reassured the girl. "And I'm more than capable of seeing to my father's needs for one day, as well as cooking Christmas dinner for the three of us."

Now Maria beamed. Her plump little body quivered with pleasure. "Truly, *signora?* Oh, then—thank you, *signora!*"

"You are very welcome, Maria. Now—what are you waiting for?" Katherine demanded, smiling.

"Signora?" Puzzled, the maid frowned.

"My things, remember? Run along and get my things, Maria!" her mistress urged her, laughing as her red-faced maid suddenly gasped, turned tail, and bolted from the sitting room like a frightened rabbit.

Within the quarter hour, Katherine was dressed warmly in

a long, fitted woolen coat and knee-high boots. The expensive burgundy wool garment was trimmed at collar, wrists, and hem with creamy fur, and flared out at the back to camouflage a small bustle. A saucy fur cossack hat hid her golden-brown chignon, while her gloved hands were tucked warmly into a white fur muff as she tramped through the park, her warm breath billowing on the frosty air, an inch or two of powdery new snow crunching beneath her boots.

"Evenin', ma'am! Merry Christmas!" called a cheerful voice.

"Merry Christmas, Mr. Davies. Is that fat goose for your Christmas dinner?"

"Indeed it is, ma'am," the man agreed, beaming as he held the goose up by its neck. Under his other arm was tucked a bottle of wine and a gaily wrapped parcel. "Haven't had a nice goose in many a year, me and the missus haven't. Makes a nice change from turkey."

"Then I hope you'll enjoy it, Mr. Davies. Oh, by the way, there's a large parcel of land for sale down on Delaware Avenue. It's priced cheaply, and the location could be perfect for Weston's to expand. Call a board meeting for Monday morning, would you?"

"Splendid, ma'am. I'll see to it first thing."

"Thank you. Merry Christmas. My regards to Mrs. Davies and the little ones," she called over her shoulder.

"Thank you, ma'am," Davies called back.

The path was almost hidden under a layer of white. By instinct rather than by sight, Katherine made her way between leafless shrubbery and trees to the spot where the carousel was erected each spring.

When still several yards from the place she halted and simply stood there, snowflakes drifting down about her as she stared at the carousel, quite unable to take another step. Elegant pastels—rose pink, gray, powder blue, creamy yellow—set off by rich gilding and touches of black. Thousands of tiny white lights twinkled through the darkness, reflected in the snow, multiplied by the mirrors. She swallowed as memories bombarded her, filling her mind like moths hurling themselves against the chimney of a lighted lamp.

"Well, now, and is it the brass ring ye'd be trying to catch, mavourneen?"

"Isn't everyone after the brass ring—or something very like it?" she heard herself respond.

Five years! Five *long* years had come and gone since 1882, the year that the bicentennial of Philadelphia's founding had been celebrated with lavish exhibitions and entertainments.

Five years had flown since the hot August afternoon when she'd first heard Logan Teague utter those teasing words. Yet it might have been only yesterday, the pain of his desertion was still so keen. She swallowed, and the creams, the soft dappled grays, the pale chocolates, the bay, the gilts, the bright lights, and the flashing mirrors of the carousel blurred and ran together like rain down a windowpane as tears filled her eyes.

When would it end, this aching? When would she be able to think of him without that choking lump in her throat? When would she be able to pass the G. A. Dentzel, Steam and Horsepower Carousel Builder's shop, without this awful longing in her breast?

She didn't need a man to make her whole. That much she had proved when a stroke had left her father paralyzed down his right side, for ever since she'd been running Weston's Hat Factory single-handedly—and running it at even greater profit than her father'd done.

Oh, yes. She'd discovered when her back was to the wall that she could be stronger—more her father's daughter—than he would ever have dreamed. So why did it still hurt that Logan had abandoned her?

Because you still love him, little fool! came the answer, unbidden, unwanted. *Because you've never stopped loving him; never gotten over him, not really. And chances are you never will.*

She blocked her ears to the spiteful little voice inside her head. However true, those answers were not what she wanted to hear.

Lord! Her feet had grown quite numb, standing here this way, staring off into space. She stamped briskly a time or two, then pulled up her fur collar and began circling the carousel, which was unmoving, despite the wild hurdy-gurdy of the organ music that soared from it to fill the night.

Running her fingers over the wooden horses of the outside row, it was as if she'd been reunited with old and valued friends.

Her eyes grew dreamy as she stroked furled wooden manes; petted dainty wooden noses, smiled at the mischievous little creatures peeping out from beneath the carved saddle blankets; the pheasants, the monkeys, the chubby cherubs, the perky pups.

Here was the pale chocolate stander with the white blaze that she'd so admired, despite its Roman nose. And over there, a fiercely patriotic black flag horse prancing alongside a dainty, dappled-gray mare, and over there, an Arab stalli—

Oh, dear God!

She pulled up short, emotion flooding through her, for on the inside row, hidden between the other gallopers and flyers, was a prancing, creamy unicorn; a new figure in a brand-new coat of factory paint.

The unicorn wore a garland of prickly green holly, festive with scarlet berries and crimson ribbons about its arched neck—a life-size replica of the music box Logan had given her all those Christmases ago—the one her father had flung into the fire to become ashes, just like her dreams!

An uncanny coincidence—or a well-planned design? Either way, she had to ride it, just this once.

As if in a trance, she caught her skirts up in one gloved hand and climbed up, onto the revolving platform. A moment more, and she was perched sidesaddle upon the unicorn's back, the gilded pole gripped between her hands.

She was trembling, and there was a curious, feathery flutter in the very pit of her stomach, for there was no doubt in her mind that Logan had carved the carousel figure beneath her; that his own two hands had lovingly shaped the raw wood beneath her, even as they'd once caressed and stroked her body.

Oh, God, oh, God!

She pressed her flaming cheek to the hard, cold wood of the brass pole, emotion flooding through her along with the memories—oh, such memories! She swallowed, tears smarting behind her eyes. Her breasts tightened beneath her heavy layers of clothing as she recalled his touch, his kiss, the wonderful sensation of his lips upon her own; of his hard, lean body pressed to hers.

Where and when had he carved this figure? she wondered. Before creating her miniature unicorn—or at some time after? And—even more importantly—*why* had he done so?

Katherine sighed. It was a question she might never receive an answer to, for none of her efforts to trace him had been successful. In the months following Stone Armitage's death—just a year after their marriage—an unlamented passing that had left her not only rich and widowed but completely free—she had hired the law clerk, Baker, to make inquiries, but to no avail.

She'd eventually abandoned her search and purchased Cherry Tree House for them to live in—a darling little red brick house with white columns and white marble front steps that overlooked this very park and . . . *oh!*

At some point during her musings the carousel had begun to turn, she realized suddenly.

At first it spun very slowly; then the machine gathered momentum and turned faster, the music growing wilder, louder, as it spun.

Frigid air streamed past her cheeks, stealing her breath away. The lights in the houses fringing the parklands blurred and ran together in a frieze of amber. Laughing, Katherine plucked off her fur hat and flung it away, not caring when

landed. She shook the pins from her hair and closed her
eyes, letting the magical unicorn carry her back into the past
with the carousel's every revolution.

It was that August afternoon in '82 all over again. Tipping
her head back, she laughed out loud in sheer delight, just as
she'd done back then. Her golden-brown hair, freed of both
hat and pins, streamed behind her. The grinning jester-head
shields, the beveled mirrors, the oil paintings and the prancing
ponies beneath the carousel's crown streamed around her in
never-ending pageant of gilt and pastels, while the band
organ bellowed a rousing German Christmas carol that set
her feet to tapping.

Up and down, up and down she rode, as if her painted
unicorn were the winged horse Pegasus, galloping on air. She
clung to the twisted brass pole before her as if it were a
lifeline to all she'd once held dear—as, perhaps, it was.

Faster and faster she spun, for three glorious minutes giving herself up to the magical world created by the carousel's
jeweled lights, its thrilling colors, its exciting sights and
sounds.

And, wonder of wonders, when the music slowed and she
opened her eyes, he was standing there.

Just like the first time.

Ten

Unable to believe what she was seeing—half afraid she was imagining him—she blinked and whispered, *"Logan?"*

He looked taller, harder, older than she remembered him as he stepped between the rows of carousel horses to stand beside her, one hand gripping the unicorn's brass pole. His eyes met hers and seemed to go on plumbing the very depth of her as he murmured, "Merry Christmas, Kate."

"But I—How?—-Where—?" The words strangled in her throat. Tongue-tied, she fell silent, not knowing where to begin. All the hurt and loneliness came crashing down around her like an avalanche in that moment, numbing her, turning pain to anger. Whatever she might have said under other circumstances was lost forever as she finally blurted out, "Why the devil aren't you dead, Logan Teague?"

He frowned. A nerve ticked at his temple. His lips tightened. "Is that what you'd hoped, then, Kate? That I was dead?"

"Yes!" she lied, feeling as if her heart had been torn in two within her breast. "Yes, I did!"

"Ah. And might I ask why?"

"Because believing you were dead hurt less than the alternative, damn you!" she cried. Huge tears suddenly spilled down her cheeks like liquid crystal beneath the carousel's bright lights, but she didn't care. What she'd said was no less than the truth. Her father had been right all along. Logan had

ed her, then left her without a second thought for the price
a few hundred dollars and a ticket to parts west.

Dashing the tears away with the back of her hand, she
ipped from the unicorn's back, then jumped down from the
rousel's revolving platform. Another moment and she had
cked up her skirts and was hurrying across the park, bolting
r the sanctuary of her little house.

"Katie—wait!" he called after her.

"Go back where you came from and leave me be, Logan
ague," she flung over her shoulder, her voice thick with
ars. "It shouldn't be too difficult, not for you. You did it
ice, after all."

"Damn it, wait up and listen to me!" he rasped, catching
r elbow, spinning her about to face him. "It wasn't like
at, and you bloody well know it!"

They stood less than a foot apart, yet the Grand Canyon
uld have been between them for all the difference it made.
heir warm breaths commingling on the cold night air, they
ood glaring at each other, two dark, rigid figures etched
gainst the snowy park like shadow dancers. Above them
ched a sky of black ice, strewn with a billion pinpoints of
osty starlight.

How handsome he looked, that faithless Lothario. He had
right to look so damnably handsome after what he'd
ne—yet he did.

An expensive tweed overcoat with the collar turned up had
placed the threadbare overcoat he'd once worn. A soft black
ool muffler was knotted at his throat, instead of the scarlet
e she'd knitted him with such love. A stylish black felt hat
d replaced the flat brown cap she'd once loved to tease
m about. He looked wealthy, successful, dashing—every
others' dream. But how many fathers had contributed to
m looking this way? she wondered nastily. How many in-
cent young daughters had given him their heart, along with
eir virtue?

Despite her disparaging thoughts her senses devoured him.

A charming youth had left her five years ago; a tall, le[a]
striking man had returned. Indeed, she could not seem [to]
draw her eyes from him. Her nostrils flared in recognition [of]
his scent—a once beloved scent that was uniquely his ow[n]
yet underscored with the expensive, masculine spices of b[ay]
rum and lime. In truth, her skin prickled in response to [his]
closeness, craving his touch, courting the kisses and cares[s]
it remembered so very well. *Dear God, nothing had change[d]*
Five years—and she was still the gullible nitwit she had [al]
ways been!

"We have nothing to say to each other," she snapped, [her]
bosom heaving as she glowered up at him, willing herself [to]
meet his eyes without a flicker. Her chin came up. "The ti[me]
for explanations is long past, Mr. Teague."

"The devil it is, Katie!" he exploded, his voice like t[he]
crack of a whip on the wintry hush.

"Don't call me Katie," she hissed.

"I must! I can't help it, don't ye see, colleen? 'Tis t[he]
way I've always thought of ye, here, in my heart. As r[y]
Katie, not Katherine. I'll go to my blessed grave thinkin'[of]
ye that way, woman." His voice sounded thick, choked wi[th]
anger—or was it emotion?

"That's quite enough. It's late, it's cold, and I don't wa[nt]
to hear any more of your lies," she cried, covering her ea[rs.]

"No? Then what were you doing out here?"

"I live over there." She nodded toward Cherry Tree Hous[e.]
"I thought it might be fun to ride the carousel in the sno[w.]
That's all."

"Is that all, Kate? Really?" His voice was husky. It reach[ed]
down inside her and tugged at her heart. Played havoc wi[th]
her composure. His eyes searched her face, his gaze touchi[ng]
her like fire.

"Yes!" Furious at her response, she made to thrust pa[st]
him, afraid that if she stayed for even another moment, s[he]
might relent, might give her true feelings away.

"Ye weren't lookin' for me?"

"You! Of course not. Don't be ridiculous. Let me go!"

But he gripped her by the upper arms so fiercely, she could
el the bite of his fingers even through the thickness of her
at as he jerked her to face him and rasped, "No. I'm not
tting you go so easily this time."

His dark head was angled downward. It was so close to
rs, she could feel his warm breath on her cheek, sweet and
iced with spirits. Panic filled her. Did he mean to kiss her?
ould he dare? She was very much afraid this new, danger-
s, harder Logan would do much as he damned well pleased.
nd her? What would she do? Just another word, a gentle
uch, and she'd succumb to his lies all over again—and with
hat reward? None—none but heartache, surely? "Let me
!" she demanded again.

"Not a chance."

"Please!" she begged

"Not until ye've heard my side of it."

"Ha! I already know your side, Teague. My father paid
s thugs to buy you off. They beat you, then dumped you
oard a locomotive headed west. They told my father you'd
ken his money and left town—oh, yes, I know all about
at, thanks to my father! But it still doesn't answer my ques-
on, does it?"

"Which question is that?"

"If Hennessy and Jackaman didn't kill you that night,
here have you been all these years? Why did you never try
contact me, or come back to Philly, once you'd . . . re-
vered?" The latter word made her cringe, for it forced her
acknowledge the terrible role her father had played in part-
g them. William Weston's ruthless ambitions had almost
st Logan his life. It had taken her over four years to forgive
er father for that, and to permit him—now a defeated old
an in a bathchair, all dignity lost, dependent on his atten-
nts for his every need—to have a small part in their lives
gain. Could she blame Logan if he'd chosen not to return
cause of that awful experience? She had yet to forgive her-

self for her cowardice, which had proven no less damaging
to him. Perhaps none of this need ever have happened if she'd
told her father about Logan sooner, as he'd asked her to do—
Perhaps it had taken him this long to forgive *her.*

"I did come back to Philly," Logan confirmed in a bitter
tone. "Just as soon as the Quakers who found me and nursed
me back to health would let me stand on me own two feet.
February fourteen it was. I never forgot the date—Valentine's
Day. The day the newspapers carried your wedding announcement in the society column. I ran clear across town
to the Old Church, and there you were. Lovely as an angel
in your satin and pearls."

"You saw me? You were there? Ohh, nooo!" Her voice
sounded strangled. For him to have been so near, and she
had never known it, never felt him there . . . It did not bear
contemplating!

"Oh, aye, I saw ye, Katie. Like a damned fool, I stood
among the gravestones and wept like a babe as I watched ye
leave the church on the arm of your husband. *Your husband.*
Forgive me, Jesus, but I could have killed Armitage in that
moment! 'Look, ye damned fool!' I told myself. 'Your Katie's
gone and married herself an Armitage, no less. Work-horse
Willy's money has wed old Stone-heart Armitage's name! It's
over, boyo! Ye've lost her, sure. Forget her!' "

"But it wasn't like that! Father had thrown me out! I was
desperate and had nowhere else to turn, don't you see? And
I was— Oh, what does it matter? Yes, I married Armitage,
but I won't apologize for it. I did what I had to do. If you
knew that, why have you come back now?" she whispered,
moved to challenge him despite her tears.

"Why?" He smiled without mirth. "Because in five years
I couldn't make my bloody, obstinate heart forget ye, Kate,"
he said simply, cupping her chin and tilting her face up to
his. "In every crowd I looked for your face. In every lovely
woman I saw the woman you had been. Every damned horse
I carved, I thought of the day I'd seen ye riding your painted

pony, with your bonnie brown hair blowing in the wind." His sapphire-blue eyes were dark with desire, fierce with love as they searched her face. "I told myself you belonged to the past, and I threw myself into my work, because only by working could I ever begin to forget you. Aye, and I made something of meself, too, in the forgetting," he added with quiet pride, "for all the bloody good it did me. I bought a damaged carousel machine in Kansas and repaired it meself, then turned around and sold it at a profit. I have master carvers who work for me now. I own my own company. Teague's Carousel Manufacturing Company."

She blinked back tears, pleased by his success. "Oh, my! It sounds very grand. I'm happy for you."

"Business is booming, sure enough. But Katie—darlin' girl!—none of my success has meant a plugged nickel without you to share it. I've caught the brass ring—but when you're alone you discover it's not brass, Kate," he whispered huskily. "It's only rusted tin."

"And the unicorn?"

A sheepish grin creased his face and carved sun furrows at the outer corners of his eyes. He shrugged, looking boyish and devilishly handsome. "I made a wee bargain with myself and Lady Luck. If ye came t' ride my Christmas carousel in this weather, it meant ye still cared for me, married or nay. If ye didn't—I planned t' leave Philadelphia for good, and never come back. Was I right, Kate? Do you still care?"

"Of—of course not," she came back quickly but could not meet his eyes.

"The truth, now, Katie," he warned sternly. "There have been enough lies between us, lass. Do you love me still?"

A crystal silence hung between them for moments that were endless.

At length Katherine drew a ragged breath. "Yes." She uttered the word so softly, it was a miracle he heard it at all. But he did.

"My sweet, darlin' girl!" he murmured, and then his hands

were framing her face, enfolding her, drawing her to his chest. Another moment, and his warm lips were on hers and he was kissing her, his ardent mouth betraying a hunger that fueled her own desire.

A shudder moved through him when he released her at long last. His eyes had darkened to indigo in his passion, she saw. His grip was fierce upon her. "Sweet Christ, I need ye, Kate."

"Shh, I know," she murmured, brushing a wave of springy black hair off his brow, cupping his jaw with her gloved fingers. "Come. My house is nearby. I've given the servants the night off. We can be alone there." The thought of being alone with him made the breath catch in her throat.

"No! God knows I'm no saint, but I won't lay wi' you in your husband's bed, no matter how much I want ye."

She laughed. It was a husky little sound that was all sensual woman, owing nothing to the naive girl he'd known and loved a little lifetime ago. "Never fear, Mr. Teague. You see I have no husband. I've been a widow these past four years."

Eleven

When he had finished undressing her she stood shyly before him, snowy eyelet and silk undergarments pooling about her feet. Her skin felt flushed beneath his fingertips, her breasts taut with her need of him. In a word she was everything Logan had dreamed she would be.

Drawing her down to the bed beside him, he leaned over her and inhaled the fragrance of her hair, spread across the pillow; a rich, heady wine of honeysuckle and roses. "Ah, Katie, ye smell like a garden in midsummer, for all that the snow's falling outside. Come here t'me, mavourneen."

He drew her against him, sliding his hands down over her lush body to cup her breasts. God, but she was lovely by firelight, his Kate! Her skin felt like warmed silk beneath his fingertips. Dipping his dark head, he suckled her breasts, feeling the velvety pink buds harden into tiny peaks beneath his tongue.

"Ah, but you're a fair one, mavourneen," he murmured. "My wee rose of Kildare." He leaned over her and took her mouth with his own. Parting her lips, he kissed her deeply, groaning against her mouth as her fingers closed convulsively over his shoulders. A small, helpless sob broke against his lips.

She kneaded the muscular flesh there, lifting her hips against him, uttering little gasps and moans as their kiss deepened, mounting in intensity and raw heat. When she could bear it no longer her hands slid higher, framing his fine head, digging deep into his midnight hair. She drew his head down to hers and held it fast, her tongue darting to war with hi in the mating of their mouths.

The breath caught in her throat as his hand slid down he body to cup the cluster of curls that concealed her secret fire Delicately, a single, questing finger parted her velvety folds He stroked her there, delved deeper, gently easing his wa between each silky layer, fully aware that she was stirring responding wildly, growing moister, more abandoned, with hi deepening caress.

Clinging fiercely to him, she whimpered and arche against him, bringing her hips fully against his flanks "Now!" she urged. "Oh, now!" Burying her face against hi chest, she clung to him, her nails digging deep into his uppe arms as she uttered the single plea: "Please—!"

"Aye, darlin'. Aye, my sweet Kate," he crooned as he lifte himself onto her. Sliding his hands down her body, he cap tured her wrists, then pinned her arms above her head.

Looking down at her, he could see the desire that smol dered in her gray eyes, darkened to pewter in her passion In the firelit shadows of her bedroom, her lips seemed swol len, coral pink and delectable, inviting more of his kisses.

Ducking his head, he planted a kiss between her breasts then brushed another across each hardened nipple, "You're beautiful, desirable woman, Kate. And I want ye. But it'll b on *my* terms this time around. Aye?"

"Aye!" she promised. "Aye!" Dear God, she'd sell her sou to Old Nick himself if it would bring a speedy end to he torment!

"You're sure, mavourneen? There'll be no lies, no hal truths between us this time. Agreed?"

She nodded. "Agreed."

"And you'll marry me, aye?"

"I will. Oh, aye, I will! Oh, please!"

"Fair enough, then." He grinned, delight in his twinklin

sapphire eyes and in the smile that lit his hard, handsome features.

Flexing lean, powerful flanks, he drew back and slowly filled her with himself, going deeper and deeper until she feared she'd faint with the pleasure of it all.

She responded with a muted cry that was half groan, half sob, burying her face in the soft angle between his throat and shoulder as he began the slow, measured strokes, the escalating, sensual tempo that would carry them to the very heights.

Together at last.

Twelve

She awoke much later to find the fire in the grate had burned down, leaving only glowing orange embers.

Rolling over, she saw Logan propped up on his elbow. He had obviously been watching her as she slept.

"Good evenin'. Did ye sleep well, ma'am?" he asked with a lazy grin. His rumpled hair look inky dark, his well-muscled, tanned body overtly masculine against the feminine frills and lace edging of her bedlinens.

"Why, thank you, yes, Mr. Teague, sir. I did indeed," she answered him gravely, her own eyes glinting merrily—the younger Kate he'd once chased through the markets of Little Italy with a live crab. "But now it's time to get up."

"Get up, woman? At this ungodly hour?"

"Yes! Come along, Mr. Teague. In the interests of total honesty between us I have a surprise for you."

"Ah. A Christmas surprise, is it, Kate? And will I like it?'

She slipped her arms into a flannel dressing gown and fastened the sash, smiling as he drew on his trousers. "I fancy ye'll like it just foine, Mr. Teague," she teased, copying his brogue. She offered him her arm. "This way, if you please."

She led the way from her bedroom and down the landing to another smaller bedroom next door, where a tiny porcelain chimney lamp still burned, spilling soft golden light every where.

Katherine's surprise lay on her back in a gleaming brass bed draped with hangings fit for a princess. Her tiny thumb

ık from sucking, was tucked into her rosebud mouth. She
ıs dressed in a ruffled flannel nightgown, surrounded by
ımrose yellow sheets and a dainty primrose-sprigged cov-
et that was edged in several inches of white eyelet and
eaded with yellow ribbon. Her tangled ringlets gleamed
e coils of jet against the snowy pillow beneath her head.
From the foot of the bed dangled a large red-white-and-
een knitted stocking with a name embroidered upon it:
MANDA. Porcelain dolls, all dressed in their Sunday best,
t demurely in a white wicker perambulator nearby, awaiting
ir next outing, while a dappled-gray rocking horse with a
ıck string mane and tail had been stabled by the fireplace.
ı the cushioned seat of a bay window draped in old-gold
lvet sat a dollhouse, complete with gazebo.

"Well, well, now. This Sleeping Beauty is the young Miss
mitage, I presume? She's a wee beauty, Kate, just like her
ım," Logan observed, smiling. More slyly, he added, "And
t a drop of Armitage blood in her that I can see, thank
od!" Laughing softly, he drew Katherine against him and
ssed her cheek, leaving his arm loosely about her waist
ıen their kiss had ended.

"I'm glad you think so." She rested her head upon his
oulder. "Because she's—"

At that moment the little girl stirred, wakened by their
ices. Long, curling black lashes fluttered against flushed
eeks as her eyes opened. Blue eyes, like a lake beneath
e summer sky. "Mama?"

"It's all right, Amanda. I'm here, darling."

"Oh! And who are you?" Amanda asked Logan, gazing
at him in wide-eyed awe. Sitting up, she rubbed sleepy
es with her knuckles and asked with disarming forthright-
ss, "Are you Santa Claus?"

Teague chuckled and was about to answer the child in the
gative when Katherine squeezed his hand and answered for
m.

"Mr. Teague is much better than Santa Claus, darling. He's

your papa." Her voice had broken with the latter. Tears fille
her eyes as she looked up and saw the stunned disbelief i
Logan's expression.

"Mine? My daughter?" His expression was incredulous.

"She's yours, all right! The one and only reason I marrie
Stone, when it became apparent you weren't coming back—a
least, not in time! I made him a proposition. If he would giv
my child his protection and his name, I would go ahead wit
the marriage as planned. The money was all he'd ever wante
from our marriage, anyway. Besides, the Armitages wer
broke. He had no choice but to agree."

The grandfather clock in the hallway below chose that ver
moment to begin chiming the hour. *Bong! Bong! Bong!* Onc
twice, twelve times in all.

When the last chime rang out it would be Christmas da
Logan thought, still stunned with delight. They'd spend it to
gether—he, his darling Kate, and the lovely wee collee
they'd created together. It would be the miracle Christma
they'd both been dreaming of for so very, very long. "Merr
Christmas, Kate. I love you."

"Merry Christmas, my love. I love you, too. I always will.

He'd been wrong, Logan decided as he lifted Amanda u
into his arms, kissed her, then hugged her mother to him. H
had caught the brass ring after all—the only one worth striv
ing for on life's wonderful carousel.

The brass ring of happiness